For Darwin,
Enjoy your time

On Zion's Hill

A Novel

Anna J. Small Roseboro

Anna J. Small Roseboro

Illustrations by
Susan J. Osborn

COPYRIGHTS

DEDICATIONS

For my grandparents
Reverends Jammie E. and John C. Williams, Sr.

My husband
William Gerald Roseboro

My children
Rosalyn Renee Roseboro, William Gerald Roseboro, II
Robert Alan Roseboro

TABLE OF CONTENTS

Copyrights ii

Dedications iii

Table of Contents v

Acknowledgments vii

What Readers Say… ix

FIRST SUNDAY 11

MONDAY 75

TUESDAY 97

WEDNESDAY 117

THURSDAY 135

FRIDAY 155

SATURDAY 253

SECOND SUNDAY 285

Sweethearts of Zion's Hill 317

About the Author 319

ACKNOWLEDGMENTS

THANKS to God for the experiences that inspired this novel. Heartfelt thanks to my husband William Gerald Roseboro, the love of my life. Warm appreciation to my grandparents whose life of Christian service encouraged me to follow them as they followed Christ. I am grateful to my siblings for supporting me as I fictionalized family stories in this historical novel.

So many people had a role in my becoming an author. The professors in the San Diego Area Writing Project taught me to write along with my students on assignments I designed for them. Some of those drafts are the nuggets for episodes in this novel. After discussions on the historical fiction written by others, the members of my Heart to Heart Christian Book Group pressed me to try my hand at writing a novel myself.

When on the faculty of Calvin College, participating in their bi-annual Festival of Faith and Writing, I gained insight from Christian fiction writers and editors who talked about what makes an engaging historical novel. They shared ways to compress time, consolidate stories, to create composite characters, and to be intentional about anachronisms. I've chosen some songs and that may have come out later than 1963, just because they resonate with me and fit specific situations.

A cadre of critical readers helped shape this final manuscript. Warm regards and grateful appreciation to Stella Calloway, Nancy Genevieve, Marilyn Gross, Allison Bodenstab Miller, Verneal Y. Mitchell, Kate Murray, Roz Roseboro, Brooke Suiter, Veronica Vickers, and Joan Williams for your useful feedback. I thank you all.

I acknowledge with special thanks Susan Osborn for creating the playful, light and lyrical art for this book. She has been a generous colleague and friend since we taught together at The Bishop's School in California.

Thanks go to the men and women who have shared oral and written records about the Zion's Hill Campground that I have drawn on for this story. Some specifics have come from the National Association of the Church of God.

Most importantly, I acknowledge the current generation of Christians who are devoting their time and talents to preserving and sustaining the legacy inherited from the Brothers and Sisters of Love who began this national gathering of the Saints nearly one hundred years ago.

WHAT READERS SAY...

"For many of us Zion's Hill was not just a place in West Middlesex, Pennsylvania; it was an addictive summer experience. The novel *On Zion's Hill* is a nostalgic journey to a magic moment so real you almost cough from the dust raised by loaded cars and you can hear "the Saints" singing as the author leads you up the winding hill. It is well written, sufficiently accurate and successfully captures a unique and wonderful history of a romantic and glorious time many of us still try to re-live for a precious few days in August every year. If you have never had the experience - read *On Zion's Hill*."

Dr. M. Tyrone Cushman, Pastor

"As a white teen in the American South in the 1960s, I knew only church camps for youth where the counselors were the only adult mentors and role models. As I read *On Zion's Hill*, I was envious of this vibrant, multi-generational religious experience. No wonder the African-American churches have enjoyed such a long, vigorous and continuing role in the lives of members who were exposed to and who experienced living faith in action in their elders.

"Fortunately, the real camp of Zion's Hill continues its vital ministry today, a century later, adapting to changing times while maintaining the age-old wisdom of Biblical teachings. Long may it flourish!"

Brooke J. Suiter, Yale, MAT and NC Court-appointed Child Advocate

"...such a nice job of writing about .... how the magic of Zion's Hill keeps drawing people back. The way Roseboro writes about the experiences of the participants in their relationships with God is powerful ... without proselytizing. Instead, the challenges of Ken and Angie and the others in the story help to tell the struggle of finding and keeping one's faith."

Joan Williams, Educator

"*On Zion's Hill* is a great lighthearted novel of a young couple who met at the West Middlesex Camp Ground. The inclusion of realistic youth testimonies and thought processes for coming to grips with faith through the eyes of teens and young adults makes it a usable guide for camp counselors, youth leaders, young converts and those who want to share their Christian experience. The vivid description of the campground, camp members and activities, brings back heartwarming memories for those who'd been there and 'I wish I had' for many others."

Verneal Y. Mitchell, NP, Former Camp Nurse

"...it is Anna's setting that makes the story distinctive. Zion's Hill is an oasis from the outside turmoil of troubled race relations in a tumultuous time in American history. The injustice of segregated lunch counters and perils of driving while black fade from focus as we witness followers of Christ living in community. At Zion's Hill, the sacred and everyday intersect: preaching and worship are no less important than fashion, food, and gossip. Women parade the latest styles and men "strut their stuff" while singing to the Lord on Zion's Hill's holy grounds. Campers soak in the sermons and then gossip about the attendees. Residents share life and death stories, contrast dysfunctional with ideal family dynamics, struggle with the Christian standards of purity and sanctification in their outside lives, and put all aside to sing, pray, and worship God together.

"Warning: Anna's vivid descriptions of food will make you crave meatloaf and potatoes, fried fish served in paper cones and 50-cent double scoop ice cream cones!"

Kate Murray, Editor

First Sunday

1 - The Ice Cream Stand

"MY ARM FEELS LIKE TACKY FLYPAPER! I'm already a sticky mess up to my elbow," she grumps, arching onto her toes and leaning over the waist-high freezer to scrape a final scoop of maricopa ice cream from the cardboard tub.

"Three scoops on a sugar cone. That'll be seventy-five cents," Angie states.

"Seventy-five cents? It was only twenty cents a scoop last year."

"I know, but this is the price this year. Twenty-five cents a scoop on a cone or in a cup. You got three scoops, so that's seventy-five cents."

Frustrated, the customer turns to the others in the line, "Can you believe that? Gone up a whole nickel a scoop! You'd think Christians wouldn't be trying to make a profit off the Brothers and Sisters coming to camp meeting. They know we can't hardly afford the cost of gas and rooms and food for the week, plus offerings at every service. It just ain't right!"

By this time the caramel-swirled vanilla ice cream is melting down the cone, dripping onto the back of Angie's chocolate-colored hand. She's tempted to slurp a circle around the lip of the cone to stem the flow of what the customer apparently sees as liquid gold.

Instead, Angie stands patiently holding her outstretched hand and peeking around the woman to see how long the line still is. Miss Fuss Budget reluctantly hands over a crumpled dollar she's been clutching and steps aside and puts away her quarter change while tipping her head to catch a creamy butterscotch ribbon of caramel oozing from the vanilla in the maricopa ice cream before it slithers off the cone.

Too bad she's not the last. It's time to close the ice cream stand now, but the line curls around to the side with at least a dozen more people wanting a last minute something to eat before the evening service begins. Well, to be honest, it's a good thing that woman is not the last. If there were no customers, Angie'd have no job.

Anyway, Angie likes working here and has been trying to develop more patience. Customers may complain about prices, but they do return when they've been treated courteously. Stella, the woman who has this Conley Family ice cream concession, says "courtesy" is Angie's middle name; she seldom loses her temper, and she can make accurate change, too.

Her gaze pans the hill, watching the heavily-loaded cars creep up the last incline of the road leading into the campground. These older Fords and Chevys will be cast in the shade on the weekend when the Buick Deuce and a Quarters and Oldsmobile Ninety-eights show up. She dips a scoop of vanilla and one of black cherry into a paper cup for the next customer. Apparently, this one doesn't want to risk a single drip of the twenty-five cents a scoop ice cream! Multitasking, Angie scoops and scopes simultaneously.

Dust mutes the colors of cars trudging up the unpaved road between the Pennsylvania state highway and the rural church camp site, but the smiles on the faces of their passengers glow with delight to be back up on Zion's Hill. Cars roll in, rear ends nearly scraping the gravel road, so loaded with clothes and food for the upcoming week of meetings.

ANGIE HAS BEEN COMING TO CAMP MEETING every summer since she was a child. Though nearly twenty years old, she still bunks with her grandparents in their tiny room on the second floor of Richardson Hall. Her space is set off by a quilt hanging over a clothesline to give her privacy from the thinly mattressed double bed on their side. Their annual residence is the same tiny mid-corridor room they've rented from the time the mattresses were stuffed with hay till now when some rooms boast standard hotel quality mattresses that the campground board of directors bought at auction when a nearby discount motel chain went out of business.

The pungent smell of mothballs permeates the halls, reminding everyone that the building is again open for lodging after being shut up tight for nearly ten months. Grit recently displaced by the Lysol scrubbing, striped tick mattresses not quite fresh despite having lain out in the sun, and the clatter and scrabble of tired travelers bumping their loaded suitcases up the narrow exterior stairs greet the returning campers – year after year.

Few are put off by the last minute scrambling of the maintenance men there to see that all works as it should. The conscientious crew ensures that the single light bulbs on cords dangling from the center of each dorm room can be turned on and off by the switches that still turn to the left or right rather than flip up and down, that toilets in the shared bathrooms all flush, and that the dampness-swollen window sashes are unstuck and will open to let in the fresh morning air and close to keep out the evening mosquitoes.

Each year, the parade of cars snakes its way up the hill and splits off onto the narrow dirt roads that spread hydra-like from the main entry gate. A few cars slow to unpack in front of the dormitory; another car stops next to a single room cabin; two park next to an egg-shaped aluminum trailer; two more pull into the driveway of a freshly painted cottage. Others groan on up the hill to the various abodes to hundreds for the next seven days of the church's annual gathering. A few hardy campers still rough it in tents.

The Richardson Hall dormitory is named for one of the families in the Brothers and Sisters of Love, the fellowship of Christians who started the summer camp meetings nearly fifty years ago. The Richardsons helped to negotiate the sale of the property in the verdant hills above Western Pennsylvania's Shenango Valley near one of a row of steel mill towns dotting the banks of the sludgy Shenango River.

Her grandparents had told her about the Brothers and Sisters of Love who were members of the local congregation looking for a place for Negroes from across the nation to gather annually to rekindle their faith and renew their friendships. It was to be a place where families could spend a week with other Christians, singing, praying, and hearing sound preaching, and sharing fellowship in a beautiful natural setting. These worshippers called themselves the Saints with a capital "S" whether written or spoken.

WHEN THE BROTHERS AND SISTERS OF LOVE found this site up on the hill not far from their small town, some of the members mortgaged their homes to come up with a down payment for the property. Trudging up the hill each year reminded these men and women of the Old Testament Israelites' yearly trek to Jerusalem to worship in the tabernacle there. So thankful for the spacious grounds set atop a mini-mountain, the Saints called their camp Zion's Hill. Former southerners like Angie's grandparents had been coming every year since they moved north from Alabama in the late 1930's.

Angie notes the bulging suitcases and overstuffed garment bags the new arrivals drag from the grimy cars that hold more than the necessary clothes to adorn the women and deck out the men. Although this is a camp meeting, most folks arrive ready to parade the latest fashions from their area of the country. Nimbly tipping along in shoes too high for the terrain, trying to avoid the pebble or stone in the road that could twist the ankle or scrape their spiked shoe heels, the women from across the nation will strut their stuff.

The last time she'd seen so many different styles in one place was a few weeks ago in her hometown. Just this past June, the Reverend Martin Luther King, Jr. had led the Walk for Freedom down the streets of Detroit, Michigan.

===

IT WAS HOT AND HUMID THAT SUNSHINY SUMMER DAY. Angie's church youth group joined hundreds of other teens high-stepping to music blared by local high school and college bands and to songs blasted over the loudspeakers. Over 100,000 people marched to the music of Motown, dancing in the streets to the sounds of Martha and the Vandellas. What a rush to see colored and white men and women, members and leaders of local labor unions from the auto plants, state legislators, and even Michigan's governor, George Romney, marching together for freedom.

Her most vivid memory is the melodious rhythms of the Reverend Martin Luther King, Jr. delivering a speech in Cobo Hall. She still can hear him fervently repeating the refrain, "I have a dream!" The young preacher espoused so passionately the hopes of the men and women of all ages and races who had come together that day as a precursor for the bigger march in Washington. D.C. scheduled for the end of August. Going to that march is out of the question for Angie; she has to be back to work and her second year of college classes would be starting a week or so later.

===

THAT WAS THEN; THIS IS NOW. Women in the parade there in Detroit wore some of every fashion style. And just as big a spectacle will be on display here, this August, 1963 in Western Pennsylvania. Women will flaunt flouncy hats chosen to match the shoes, purse and gloves that complement the colors of their toned-down tailored suits and flamboyant designer dresses, but not pants. No pants or slacks allowed for women on these holy grounds.

Over the years that Angie has been coming to camp meeting, she's seen men swagger in brightly-colored leisure suits with flared legs or bop along in dark sharkskin straight-leg slacks, shod in stacked heels or Stacy Adams wingtips that dare the dust to settle on their toes. Depending on the fashion trending that season, the males may don stylish hats with stingy brims or pull on wide brim ones bent just so, shading their left eyebrows. Women and men strut and swagger, showing evidence of God's bounty and, adorned in their perfectly coordinated outfits, parading with righteous thanksgiving balanced with humility and flair.

Angie loves coming with her grandparents and looks forward to seeing forever friends who had promised to write every week, but hadn't. She'll hear roof-raising music and heart-thrilling preaching. And this year, she might even meet Mr. Right. Every year there is some guy with whom she sits in services and later eats crispy fish sandwiches bought at the concession stands. Maybe she would even hold hands with him during a clandestine walk around the grounds after evening service.

Though tempted more than once by the Lotharios who come each year, she's maintained her grandparents' trust and has not compromised her virtue. All who come to these hallowed grounds are not Christians.

She values Grammama's opinion, so Angie always returns to their tiny dormitory room not long after her shift ends, tiptoeing in to avoid awakening her grandparents. Even though on vacation, they go to bed early so they will be rested enough to get up on time for early morning prayer meetings. Her grandparents are among the regulars, the Faithfuls, who believe it is this sunrise meeting that establishes the foundation for successful services throughout the day. The seasoned Christians pray that the music, the teaching, and the preaching will draw sinners to Christ and Saints closer to the oneness of the Scriptures.

AT LAST, IT'S SIX THIRTY. Stella, the boss, signals it's time to close the stand, straighten it up, and then rush back to the dorm to get dressed for the evening service. This only gives Angie ten minutes to do twenty minutes of prep. This means she will arrive late and have to stand in the back of the rustic wooden tabernacle until the opening prayers conclude. She hates being late, but this evening she doesn't hurry.

Better to spend a little extra time getting dressed than standing restlessly at the back of the tabernacle, that barn of a building that is nothing like the one described in the Old Testament. No gold covered acacia wood or lamp stands carved with almond buds and pomegranates; no linen tapestry in blue, purple and scarlet.

No. Here on Zion's Hill, there is a massive bare bones structure with exposed beamed ceilings and whitewashed walls. One only sees such vibrant colors in flowers on the pulpit and in the clothes of the congregants. But, just as in the tabernacle of old, one senses the Spirit of God indwelling the hearts of the Saints, making His presence felt even in this unadorned building. Just as He is no respecter of persons, He is no respecter of places, either. Where two or three gather together in His name, He is in their midst.

2 - The Service

TONIGHT, ANGIE WEARS A NEW OUTFIT, purchased just for this week of meetings. Sure, she can't compete with the fashion kings and queens, but she just couldn't resist buying the suit and shoes. Anyway, she hadn't paid full price. She'd been watching the price go down each day she passed the dress shop on her way to work. This creamy yellow one really was a good buy and is a good color for her deep brown complexion.

She'll look good in this two-piece ensemble with a soft yellow and white striped top and solid yellow pleated skirt – not too long and definitely not too short, or her grandmother wouldn't let her out of the room wearing it. Angie chooses a pair of low-heeled white shoes already worn down some on the heels. She's particular about bringing her nice dresses, but Angie utterly refuses to bring her best shoes only to have them scraped and scratched on the uneven gravel pathways. These grounds take a toll on any kind of shoes, especially the slender spiked heels that are the current fashion.

Checking her stockings for runs, she finds none; glancing once more in the mirror at her hair, her flip hasn't flopped. Adding just a hint of lip color and one pass of the red sponge with clove-brown powder over her face, she's set to meet the night or knight of her dreams.

Angie leaves, careful to close the dorm room door, wiggles the door handle, checks the lock and then strides down the hall and descends the exterior stairs that face the blank front wall of the tabernacle where the evening service has already begun. "No surprise," Angie murmurs as she makes her way around to the back entrance where she will stand with other late arrivals.

The voices of the choir and congregation nearly raise the open beamed building as they sing with equal gusto and devotion an old hymn of the church,

19

Once again we come to the house of God
To unite in songs of praise;
To extol with joy our Redeemer's name,
And to tell His works and ways.

To thy House oh Lord, with rejoicing we come,
For we know that we are thine;
We will worship thee in the Bible way,
As the evening light doth shine.

Everyone knows the words! That's what's remarkable about coming to camp meeting. Folks from all over the country – California, Texas, Alabama, Florida, New York, Virginia, Massachusetts – join the folks from the Midwest states for this annual summer event held in this little town of West Middlesex. No one needs songbooks – even though the choir members all hold them.

These are the familiar songs sung each week in country, town and city churches, those congregations meeting in store fronts, clapboard buildings, and in brick and stained glass multiplexes. The words declare the mighty works of God, and the music challenges each to praise Him for His faithfulness as in the second song for the evening.

What a mighty God we serve!
What a mighty God we serve!
Reigning now above on His throne of love,
What a mighty God we serve!

The tabernacle throbs with the songs of the Saints. The organist nearly slides off the stool, his shoeless feet stretching to reach the foot pedals; the pianist tilts her head in jubilation, both musicians worshiping the Lord with toes and fingers; the choir sways in rhythm, and the hands of the congregation rise in praise. Angie beams at the doorway, watching it all. Ah, camp meeting has begun!

On her front, Angie feels the heat from the building; on her back, she shivers in the evening air gusting through the crowd bunched up behind her. She should have brought her sweater. The little boy behind her wiggles, trying

20

to see around her waist and the teenager holding his hand jostles her, trying to see across Angie's shoulder. Everyone is eager to get inside and join the singing Saints.

Female ushers dressed in fresh white uniforms with navy trimmed handkerchiefs cascading just so from left breast pockets stand erect with one white-gloved hand held loosely at waist level behind their backs. Those latecomers congregating at the back entrance know they will not be allowed in or led to a seat until after the opening prayer that follows one or two congregational songs. So the group, impatient to enter, but knowing the rules, is willing to wait.

Angie stands near the front of the growing throng and uses the time to peruse the audience, looking for empty seats. There are a few, and since she's in the front, she figures she'll have a choice. Which will it be? Near the back so she can slip out and get to the ice cream stand and prepare for the after service onslaught? In the middle where she'll be in the thick of things? Or way down in front where everyone can see her new outfit as she steps in to that empty seat third from the center aisle? During the instrumental interlude of the second congregational hymn, Angie scans the hundreds of heads, searching for just the right place to sit, somewhat ashamed that she is considering that seat up front.

Oh! Her eyes stop. There's a cute head about ten rows from the back. Nice haircut. Curly with a hint of kink. Neatly trimmed. Nice. Seems a little reddish brown from here. Nice. Gingery skin tone. Broad shoulders, but not too bulky. Real nice!

There's a seat right next to him and another right in front of him. Angie contemplates the advantages of choosing each seat and doesn't pay much attention to the minister walking to the podium to lead the prayer for the evening service.

His voice rumbles across the bowed heads of the congregants, "O Mighty God, Beloved Heavenly Father, we come to You this evening with humble hearts...."

But Angie is distracted by her impending choice, and thinks, *If I sit next to him, he probably won't be able to see me. On the other hand, maybe he brought a Bible and will offer to share it with me. I forgot to bring my own. Then again, maybe he didn't or he wouldn't. If I sit in front of him, he'll have to look at me all through the service. Then when I leave early, I can get a good look at him as I tiptoe out to get ready to work. Hmmm. That may be better...*

"...and our Blessed Holy Spirit, we invite You to come and make Your Presence felt among us as we sing Your songs and hear Your Words from the man of God chosen to bring it to us tonight. We ask all this in the name of Your Precious Son, Our Lord Jesus Christ. Amen. Amen and amen. You may be seated." The minister raises his head and returns to the seat flanking the preacher for the evening. The musicians play softly as latecomers are ushered in.

Folks behind Angie press in before the congregation is all seated. One of the national officers climbs the steps to the rostrum, takes a mike from the stand to officially welcome everyone to this forty-seventh annual week of evangelical services and to give a few announcements before the offering and special music from the choir. He intones the opening announcement given every year she's come. She can almost say it by heart....

"Remember, Saints, this is holy ground. For nearly fifty years, since 1916, we've met here on Zion's Hill. We expect the Spirit of God to rule over this camp meeting. We want God to be glorified, the Kingdom to be multiplied, and Satan to be horrified. We come to worship and to fellowship in a place chosen, set aside, and kept for us by the sacrifices of the many Saints who've gone on before. We expect each one here to dress and behave as becoming the Saints of the Most High God. Follow the Golden Rule and follow the signal of the evening bell to be quiet at night. ..."

"Yadda yadda yadda." Angie follows the uniformed usher down the aisle where Cute Head sits.

Next to or in front? Next to or in front? She nearly bumps into the usher whose gloved hand directs her to the seat next to Cute Head. But Angie's decided on the seat in front of him. With the anxious crowd waiting to be seated in just a

22

couple of minutes, the usher acquiesces, steps aside, and beckons to another latecomer to take that seat next to the guy.

She plops into the end seat, hoping Cute Head doesn't think she's clumsy. *Lord, let this plan work without me looking silly.*

The choir rises at the direction of the national choir director. It's the first night of camp meeting for this volunteer choir of folks who sing in their home churches. They've had just one rehearsal that afternoon and are not yet in sync, so their rising straggles a bit tonight. By next Sunday, after a week together, it will be executed with military precision.

Angie recognizes members she has seen up there every year and can identify which of the ancient sopranos will be unable to hit the high notes on the anthems the choir surely will sing later in the week. There never are enough men to balance the six to one ratio of females to males, so the choir director puts the men in the middle in hopes that they will be heard a little better in that central location. They'd be closer to the three microphones standing at the sturdy wooden podium ready for the minister of the hour. Though simple in structure, the tabernacle's acoustics really aren't too bad.

This is not a choir of trained voices. Few read music; fewer have ever studied it formally. All, however, love to lift their voices in song and exemplify the Biblical imperative, "Make a joyful noise unto the Lord." Thankfully, the noise usually is melodic – at least by the end of the week.

The experienced director is talented and insightful and usually chooses songs most of the congregation already knows. She invites guest ensembles or soloists to sing the specials for the services early in the week. This gives her time to get the choir shaped up – noting those who are still in voice, which new singers have a voice, and what anthems they all can manage.

Each year the camp meeting director includes at least one anthem from the traditional repertoire and will have sent a letter to the churches from which the regular choir members come, asking them to look over the planned songs before arriving on the grounds. The choir director at Angie's home church reads the letter to them in May, just after the Easter cantata.

Most of the choir members – old and new – sing by ear. So they wait till they arrive on-site for choir rehearsal in hopes that the person next to them will have learned the songs and they will be able to catch on. Returning choir directors know this, and just in case the old-timers haven't learned the more difficult songs, they save the really demanding repertoire for the weekend when the trained singers will be there to help carry the sections.

Yes, there'll be a little screeching in the soprano sections because the choir directors never make the older ladies stop singing just because they have difficulty reaching or holding the notes.

In fact, this is one of the things Angie likes about camp meeting. Everyone is welcome to participate wherever he or she thinks is a good place to serve. She can't keep from smiling when things do not always go as smoothly as they could have if only those who were perfect were on stage or in the choir. Oh well. Let them "Make a joyful noise…" By the end of the week, the sounds will be more harmonious and in sync. But this is the first night, and the singing is certain to be somewhat ragged, but authentically passionate, nonetheless.

FOR THIS OPENING SERVICE, the pianist and organist are together and play an upbeat introduction to a campground favorite. "Be Strong and Valiant for the Truth." For some reason, this song always gets a bunch of Saints up on their feet and walking the aisles, hands raised and heads thrown back in praise or on parade. When younger, Angie always wondered how spirit-filled the people were because so many regulars seemed to "get the Spirit" at the same time and when they had on really sharp outfits.

Tonight, seeing them out there testifying and giving God the glory with their gestures, she recalls her first year working for Stella and bursting into the ice cream stand to start her after-service shift.

===

Angie chucks her purse under the shelf and grabs an apron, her back to Stella.

"Did you see them?"

"Who?"

"The folks dancing in the aisles during that song. They always seem to get the Spirit at the same time."

"And?"

"And they seem to only do it when they have on their glad rags."

"Most people dress well for services on Zion's Hill."

"I know, but…"

"But what?"

"But, they always look like they're more parading than praising."

"Who are you to judge?"

"I'm not. I'm just saying. Some of them look more like they're styling for the Saints than shouting to the Lord."

Angie, oblivious, doesn't even notice that Stella has not joined her gossip fest as others on the grounds usually do when the subject of the old folks and their worship styles is raised. "I mean. Don't you think they look rather ridiculous? Women flopping all around and everything, clothes hanging funny."

Once her apron is tied, she washes her hands and turns toward Stella. Angie, obviously amused by her detailed descriptions, continues "Sweating men, running around. Bellies bobbling over their belt buckles. Some of them just look so funny!"

Stella stops Angie with a stare.

"Are you the fashion police?"

"Well…no."

"One of the Holy Trinity in a position to judge?"

"No…"

"Do you know what their lives have been like or why these Saints may be shouting or walking the aisles?"

"Um...no. Do you?"

"Yes, as a matter of fact, I do," Stella reprimands, looking Angie directly in the eyes. "They come to Zion's Hill for fellowship and revival. And more genuine Christians will be hard to find."

Angie throws back, "So....how do you know this?"

"Well, I've known many of them most of my life. One of them out there this evening is my cousin." Chagrined, Angie looks away in shame.

Stella explains, "My cousin's had a tough year with family and finances. She's just grateful she could even travel this year. I imagine the same can be said for several of the others."

Angie, silenced by guilt and by fear, then mutters. "I'm sorry".

"You know, Angie, tittle-tattle is unbecoming of you as a Christian. I know you've taught to love, not judge."

"Yes, ma'am," she murmurs. Guilt-ridden for being judgmental and fearful that Stella may fire her for talking bad about her relatives, Angie stands with bowed head, but says a little louder, "I'm sorry."

She looks up when Stella says, graciously "Apology accepted. Now, let's get to work. The Saints are coming and they expect their ice cream served with a smile."

"Yes, ma'am!" Angie smiles with relief.

===

ANGIE'S STILL WORKING ON IT, but she has become somewhat less judgmental since that conversation, and less inclined to join in gossip about the Saints. Who knows their stories and why certain songs get them up and walking the aisles? Only God can discern whether they're really shouting or showing off in service. And anyway, who is she to judge?

This First Sunday, the volume of the old song swells, and members of the congregation sway and clap to the beat. And though she doesn't yet understand why this song evokes such an emotional response from the older folks, she sings as though she does. She's learning,

> He is our Rock, our Tower high,
> And to the meek He giveth grace;
> A shield He is to them that trust,
> The joy of those who seek His face.

For now, Angie is just relishing being on Zion's Hill and hearing the Saints sing with fervent joy. *What's that?* She hears a rich tenor coming from behind her. *Ah... he can sing. Good. Another point for him. He can sing and he knows the words of the old songs. Maybe he's a Christian or at least been brought up in the church. He must be since he's here on the first night.*

Most of those who come on the last weekend seem to come for show. Or at least that's what Angie believes based on her experience coming so many years. It's on the Friday and Saturday that the sharp dressers – male and female – arrive in their later model cars that look as though they've been run through the car wash just before heading up to Zion's Hill. The people who come this early, Angie rationalizes, usually are more serious about the religious aspects of the meeting and less concerned about outward appearances. Or so she thinks, based on her experience coming so many years. But, who is she to judge?

Maybe Cute Head will be okay. Maybe this will be the guy she'll spend time with this year. But of course, she has to meet him first. She'd really like to see his face too. He certainly looked good from where she stood in the doorway and the quick glance at him just before she decided to sit in front of him. What if he was already dating someone else? That would certainly put a damper on the week. There are slim pickings this early in the week. Or so she thinks, based on her experience of coming to Zion's Hill for so many years.

===

WORKING IN THE CENTRALLY-LOCATED ICE CREAM STAND, Angie has had a good view of the campgrounds. From that vantage point, she can study the crowds as they gather, looking for the young people her age, and spy out which girls might be her competition and which guys they'd be competing for. There always have been more girls than guys.

Angie comes for the full week because her grandparents always do, and they invite her to come along. She's in college now and has a job working for the father of one of her classmates, but he's granted her time off with pay. That's a blessing, but since she's stashing away money to pay tuition this fall, Angie really doesn't have extra for a vacation that costs much, so why not come one here more year? She gets along well with her grandparents, and they seem to like having her around. So here she is a sophomore in college, during her only time off for the summer, at camp meeting on Zion's Hill.

Few males in their late teens and early twenties choose to attend the whole week of services. Most arrive in time for the Friday evening through Sunday morning services; the attendance on the grounds nearly trebles. But the ice cream stand also is busiest then. If Angie hasn't connected with someone by Friday morning, it will be too late. So, Cute Head may be her chance to get a jump on this girl/guy thing before too many other young adults arrive.

Angie isn't looking for anything permanent in a relationship. She fully intends to get her BA before getting her MRS. So, not looking for anything serious, it still would be fun to have a handsome young man to spend time with during this week of vacation, and maybe even to correspond with during the school year. She's a good pen pal and has been exchanging letters with lots of people she's met at regional youth meetings and state conferences.

She even maintains a written relationship with an Air Force guy as a favor to her uncle, the airman's pastor. She's been writing for nearly a year now. But, she doesn't expect anything to come of that. Anyway, she's only seen the guy once. He is nice enough looking, but she hadn't felt any chemistry when she met him. Sure, it's been fun hearing about his adventures up in Greenland where he is stationed, and he expresses interest in her adventures at college. But Angie doesn't sense a future with that guy. Cute Head might be different. *Back to the service, Angie. Back to the service.*

ANOTHER MINISTER STRIDES to the wide wooden stand in the center of the platform and makes the call for the offering. This is the first night, so he'll just ask people to "give as the Lord has given to you", reminding everyone that "The Lord loveth a cheerful giver."

It's not until the second weekend when the grounds are full and the tabernacle overflowing that the person taking the offering will plead for people to "dig deep and give sacrificially" and ask those who have "purposed in your heart" to give $100 or more to lead the way in a march for the Lord.

Sometimes the financial officers will count the offering during the service, and if enough hasn't been raised to meet the expenses for the week, one of the more charismatic ministers will make an entreaty for more money. But this is the first night, and the offering time runs pretty smoothly and efficiently.

The ushers, men militarily erect in navy suits and white gloves and ladies similarly gloved, proceed down the aisles. They pass shiny white paper pails that look like Kentucky Fried Chicken buckets without the red and white logo of the colonel. Perhaps the size is to indicate how much they hope to collect in this first evening offering.

A dapper saxophonist stands to play an offertory song. The organist and pianist soon join him in a worshipful, soulful rendition of "How Great Thou Art". Angie sways as the talented horn player mimics the human voice teasing out emotional responses and sensory memories. She stiffens when she notices some of the older folks pursing their lips and shaking their heads in disapproval when the horn player plays some bluesy notes and jazzy progressions. These folks frown on crossing the line between worldly and Christian music.

But Angie is moved by his interpretation of the lyrics:

> When through the woods and forest glades I wander
> I hear the birds sing sweetly in the trees,
> When I look down from lofty mountain grandeur,
> And hear the brook and feel the gentle breeze:

She's taken on wings of his emotive playing to early mornings on Zion's Hill when the sun is just cresting the mount. The music evokes the scent of trampled grass glistening in the morning dew and the whiffs of breakfast bacon from the first floor kitchen.

Musical notes educe the misty morning, still and quiet. She hears the chirp and chitter of little brown and white wrens scrounging around the plants edging the narrow path up through the copse overlooking the dormitory section of the grounds.

Viewing a movie screen inside her eyelids, Angie sees the faithful senior citizens sleepily walking from their cabins, cottages, and trailers or emerging from the second floor dormitory rooms, tightly grasping the stainless steel tube railing that guides them down the steps.

The Faithfuls gather at the tabernacle for early morning prayer services. The Saints are praying on the way, sensing God in the silence of the morning.

===

DRAWN BACK TO THE SERVICE in the sanctuary, Angie finds herself singing with the saxophone, proclaiming the greatness of God, the creator of it all. "Then sings my soul, my Savior God to Thee, How great Thou art..."

Bluesy or jazzy, this saxophonist is speaking to Angie's heart. Musically, he convinces her to put more in the offering plate than she's planned. She usually decides ahead of time how much she'll give for the whole week of meetings and doles her money out a little each night so she can give something every time, but not exceed her preplanned limit. Oh well. She can hold back a little tomorrow and get herself back on track. Tonight, it seems right to give what she has in her hand. This guy really is good.

The usher reaches for the offering bucket from the lady in the opposite row at the same time the bucket on Angie's side gets to her, so she just turns around and hands hers to the person behind her. It's Cute Head! She gulps and nearly drops the half-filled bucket. He's as good-looking from the front as he is from the back! She swerves back to the front, clasping the handle of her purse, breathing more rapidly.

He looked at her. Does he think she's as good-looking from the front as from the back? Will he want to meet her? Will he come up to the grounds during the week, walk her up to the concession stands and buy her a fish sandwich? Will he sit next to her in church and share his Bible? Oh she hopes so. She really hopes so. Maybe this will turn out to be a good week. Maybe it will. Why wouldn't it? *Back to the service, Angie. Back to the service.*

It's time for the special music. She'd seen the Jenkins sisters earlier today. They're her age and have been singing duets at camp meeting since elementary school. They sing with poignant expression and their voices blend in unison and in harmony. Will it be them tonight?

Angie likes the sisters, but often is a little jealous because no one asks her to do solos like they do at home. Last summer, she rationalized to her friend, Lily, "Well, I don't really have time, anyway. I have to work while I'm up here." From working together on grounds for years, Lily has been friends with Angie, and just nodded her head. She's felt the same time crunch.

Like Angie, Lily's family doesn't ask her to help with gas for the car trip or contribute to the rent of the dorm room they share. But she is responsible for her own meals and other personal expenses. This means she has to bring cash with her or work when she arrives on Zion's Hill. Thankfully, she and Angie have been able to get a job on the grounds for the past five years or so.

Working leaves no time for rehearsing anyway. To be honest, the current music staff here really doesn't even know Angie. Anyway, she'd probably be too nervous and either would start off on the wrong key or forget the words halfway through – even with the music in front of her, she sometimes loses her place. "Truthfully, Lily, I do like listening to good music during services and working between them suits me just fine. Most of the time." Lily would just nod, knowing Angie prefers friends to agree with her.

===

FOR SEVERAL SUMMERS, she and Lily worked in the dining room. That was fun, most of the time. The same girls usually came back each year and they got along pretty well. And though they didn't earn a salary, or even tips, they did get all their meals for free.

Brother Willie Patmington was in charge of all the dining services. A martinet, he took no mess off of anyone. "You are working for the Lord," he'd expound and insist that everything be done just right. "Waiters," he'd admonish, "you show you are Christians by your love. So," he demanded, "come ready to serve love with each meal." That included arriving on time, every time, all fired up and ready to go with neat aprons, clean hands, and hair entirely stuffed into those hairnets. Who can look cute in a hairnet?

Thankfully, waitresses got to eat before the dining room opened to the public, so they didn't have to worry about the kitchen running out of food before they got theirs. That was a good thing. The not-so-good thing was being assigned to work downstairs in the kitchen. Working there, they came to understand the expression, "hot as Hades"!

The most unpleasant job down there was not scrubbing the pots and pans. It was cutting the butter. Every summer, the newest girls got that job. Angie remembered how each was given a five pound block of butter to cut into neat one-half teaspoon square pats, place them on those tiny crinkle-paper circles, arrange on cooled cookie trays and store in the refrigerator until needed. It was one of those impossible tasks that had to be done. And, despite the slippery knives and buttery slick hands, the girls were expected to cut even slices into consistent size pats and complete the task before the block melted in a gloppy smear across the cutting board.

Working downstairs brought alive that despicable story about 'Lil Black Sambo. Many a day, she felt as though she were running around in circles getting hotter and hotter and would very well melt into a puddle of grease.

Later, promoted to working upstairs in the dining room, however, Angie enjoyed her job much more, especially interacting with the diners. During the early part of the week, before the grounds got crowded with the weekend campers, the diners were pretty patient. Folks who stayed in the cabins, trailers and cottages sometimes cooked their own meals. But those who rented in the dorms frequented the dining room, and by the end of the week were good friends among themselves and with the waitresses.

Angie's grandparents, though, would eat only one meal a day there. They'd bring food from home for breakfast and supplement it with purchases at the little grocery in town. Sometimes they'd get a snack from one of the food concession stands lined up across the way from the tabernacle on the dirt road behind the ice cream stand. But for dinner, they'd come and sit at a table near her station. She glowed each time she served the older folks in the spirit of loving service that Brother Patmington instilled in them, whether or not the customers expressed words of appreciation in return. Thankfully, her grandparents always did. They were proud of her.

Few people complained about the taste or the size of the servings. Sister Mattie Callon, the head cook, and her longtime colleague, Sister Sarah Mae Dillard, knew how to order for, prepare, and serve tasty meals to the masses. Consequently, the same people returned year after year, confident the meatloaf would be tasty, the potatoes fluffy, and the collard greens, English peas or string beans nicely seasoned and not too salty.

Everyone looked forward to Wednesdays when the ladies served fried chicken. Frying chicken for hundreds can be taxing in the basic facilities of the campground kitchen, even for a veteran staff. So Sister Mattie didn't even try to do that on Sunday when there could be even more diners expecting a hearty meal after morning service. For that day, Sister Mattie and her crew served roast turkey and dressing with the trimmings. Angie figured they planned a meal like that for Sundays because the staff could prepare so much more with less last minute work. They were an experienced team, but they worked together only once a year.

The girls who served in the dining room were expected to arrive early to set the tables with salt and pepper shakers, napkins and silverware, get the cold drinks poured – usually red Kool-Aid – and to set out the cups for hot tea and coffee. They had to position the chairs just so around the tables and, when there were fresh flowers in the fields near the campgrounds, to cut and arrange them in the bud vases so the hall would look special without an extra expense.

About half an hour before the dining room opened for business, the helpers went through the line and got their own meal, ate it quickly, tidied up and were ready when the doors opened. A grown-up usually collected the money so the teenagers would be free to rove around the room, helping the diners as they arrived, carrying plates for those who needed it, and being alert to spills and calls for extra napkins. This had been Angie's summer job for several years.

Two years ago, though, Stella approached her to work for her in the ice cream booth. Stella offered a nice salary, so Angie eagerly took the job. She now earns enough to buy some of her meals from the concession stands and still comes out with money left each summer.

She also gets a good view of what is going on all over the grounds without appearing to be nosey. She had liked serving in the dining room, but now that she is older and in college, she likes even better having cash left at the end of the meeting, rather than going home well fed, but broke.

So she has returned again this year to work with Stella. Too bad, though. Working in the stand cuts down on the time she has to stroll the grounds and to sit and talk with friends. Still, a college student needs cash, and the central location of the ice cream stand has turned out to be a good place to scope out the guys. Still, Angie wonders if she will ever be able to make it to the service on time. When she hears the preludes, her hearts starts pumping. She's eager to join in and always tries to guess who's been asked to do the specials.

===

NO, THE JENKINS SISTERS aren't singing tonight. Ah, it's the Boisman Sisters, a young ladies' quartet from the minister's congregation. Once the sisters are arranged behind the microphones, the soprano steps up to the center mike, singing *a cappella*, the first clause of "Come Thou Fount of Every Blessing." The alto comes in on the next; the second soprano joins in a rich sweet tenor, and the final singer comes in on the fourth clause in a surprisingly deep, rich alto singing the baritone line.

> Come, Thou Fount of every blessing,
> Tune my heart to sing Thy grace;
> Streams of mercy, never ceasing,
> Call for songs of loudest praise....

The final lines they sing in four-part harmony.

> Praise the mount! I'm fixed upon it,
> Mount of Thy redeeming love.

On the second stanza the tempo slows dramatically as the alto leads, singing melody. Her sisters join in, adjusting the rhythm dramatically to reflect the images in the lyrics.

> ...Jesus sought me when a stranger,
> Wand'ring from the fold of God;
> He, to rescue me from danger,
> Interposed His precious blood.

The sisters sing the third stanza in typical hymn meter. And then the organist plays an interlude, raising the key one half step, escalating the tempo until all four voices erupt in unison the "Hallelujah!" All stop.

Gasps ripple across the congregation. Then hands and hallelujahs rise throughout the tabernacle and congregants sing in affirmation "I have found it!" and then sit back, listening as this talented quartet of young ladies finishes the song, softly and reflectively, preparing the listeners to receive the Word that is to come.

> Hallelujah! I have found it,
> The full cleansing I had craved,
> And to all the world I'll sound it:
> They too may be wholly saved....

An old hymn sung a new way affirms gratitude toward God the Father, Christ the Savior, and the sweet Holy Spirit.

The singers return to their seats as another minister on the rostrum rises and walks forward to introduce the speaker for the evening. He's unfamiliar. But Angie's not surprised; the popular, well-known preachers usually don't speak until the weekend when the crowds are bigger.

===

FOR OPENING NIGHT, the program committee schedules the older, more sedate preachers who appeal to the old timers who come early and stay for the whole week. Or, the young untried preachers given an opportunity to see how they do before an eclectic national audience. The old guys are good, though. They typically deliver traditional sermons – scripturally sound, spiritually nutritious, but seldom delivered with the energetic physicality of the weekend preachers. Those ministers are as sought after as famous entertainers and are as charismatic as motivational speakers. Their messages are just as good - just delivered more theatrically.

Those weekend speakers woo the crowds in ways that the weekday ministers didn't, couldn't or wouldn't. That's okay. Though still a teenager, Angie has come to appreciate thoughtful exegesis. Hearing exploration and interpretation of religious texts presented during the week gives her more to chew on after the service than some of the excitement and drama on the weekend. Though still in her teens, Angie looks forward to gaining new insights about her Christian walk.

The weekday speakers – even the real old ones – provide the meat and vegetables of the Word needed to sustain one in the day to day challenges of living a Godly life. Of course, dessert on the weekend has nutrition as well and sends listeners home with a sweet taste in their mouths. Doesn't the Psalmist say the Word is like honey?

She smiles recalling the antics of one particular preacher who jumps around a lot to show how the Spirit of God keeps one fully alive in the Lord. As expected, he's preaching Friday evening. For now, though, she focuses her eyes to what's going on the rostrum.

The preacher for the evening leans over to pick up his well-worn leather Bible from the table next to his high-back chair – the one in the center reserved each evening for the person preaching for that service. Sometimes, like tonight, the chair dwarfs the speaker; but there is at least one speaker, Reverend Reeves, who dwarfs the chair.

Reverend Reeves is one of those weekend speakers who preaches with such vivacity that folks vocalize in the call and response style often caricatured in movies with Negro churches. He really stirs up the crowd and challenges folks to live a holy life joyfully and vibrantly.

His wife has a great voice and plays the organ as well. She probably will sing too when he preaches Sunday morning. It's good to see a couple who complement each other that way. Maybe Angie and her husband will become a team working for the Lord. Who knows, her life's partner may be sitting right behind her tonight.

AGAIN, ANGIE REMINDS HERSELF to pay attention to the minister who by now stands leaning forward, gripping the edges of the podium, raising his palm-up hands, inviting the congregation to stand. They do and he prays.

"Most gracious Heavenly Father, we know You are here in our midst, and we invite You to remain among us as I attempt to break the Bread of Life for these who have come to hear Your Word. Open my mouth to speak what You've laid on my heart to bring to these folks tonight and open their hearts to hear what thus saith the Lord. We ask this in the name of Your Son, Jesus Christ. Amen. Please be seated and open your Bibles to…"

Just as she is seated, Angie feels a tap on her left shoulder. She turns and sees Cute Head pointing his index finger up at an angle. His hand barely rises above the back of her seat; he wants her to look up. Something with a long tail skitters along one of the open beams crisscrossing the top of the tabernacle. "A mouse!" Cute Head whispers and smiles.

She shivers, tamping down a squeal. Torn between fear that the mouse will drop on her head and the thrill that Cute Head has spoken to her, she tenses with anxiety and anticipation and whispers, "Oh, don't fall on me. Please, please, please! And don't let Cute Head think I'm too weird to look for me after service."

The mouse skitters along the rafter and she no longer can see it, but she does spot what looks like a nest in the window ledge up near the roof. She shudders and watches the mouse flit through one of the rafter openings that helps ventilate the tabernacle.

She soon loses interest in both the mouse and the young man behind her. The minister is getting into his sermon, and she disciplines herself to listen. That really is the reason for coming to camp meeting. Right? To learn more about living for the Lord, to meet with the Saints from across the nation, and perhaps, to meet her partner for life. But first things first.

ANGIE HAS TO TIPTOE OUT just before the altar call because the ice cream stand opens immediately after evening service, Tonight, she must scurry back to her dorm room, change into her work clothes, and be in the stand ready for the after service customers. Timing her departure always is a challenge: how to tell when the speaker is winding down the sermon but has not yet begun the invitation for prayer. It would be rude to leave during that reverent moment when listeners are making crucial decisions about what they've heard.

From years of attending such services, she recognizes the clues and cues for when to leave. Sometimes it's a change in the vocal rhythm, the volume, or even the pace of the speaker. It may be when the minister closes his Bible or begins stacking his notes, evening up the corners just so. She has become quite adept now that she's been working for Stella a couple years. Angie has missed her timing enough to have been scolded by her boss who always sits in the back row and seldom disturbs anyone when she leaves.

Tonight, though, caught up in the sermon, she nearly misses the signal. The minister has just reminded the congregants of God's love and the fact that He will always be with them as they mature and through the indwelling of His Spirit become more like Him That's something to chew on. That relationship, the minister promises, will help her to face the challenges at work and at college, and that she can just relax and be.

She gathers her things to leave and reflects. *That's good news. There is no need for a Christian to appear to be more than God has made one to be, or to despair when one fails in some way.* "God," the minister says, "is Sovereign. He, a God of Love, knows all and controls all that Christians will let Him control and whatever occurs in our lives is for our good and His glory."

This causes her to wonder if she should trust God to help her meet the guy sitting behind her. He looks good, sings well, seems to have a sense of humor and wants to share it, and he is at camp meeting – the first Sunday.

She glances at him and tiptoes out, scrunching her shoulders to appear smaller. She quietly heads for the rear door, around the tabernacle, and back up to the dormitory room to change out of her new yellow outfit.

Why, she wonders, would a handsome guy in his early twenties be here on the first Sunday? Most guys this age either are in the military or at home working. Few will have been on their jobs long enough to take more than a week's paid vacation, and very few young men who are up and coming come to services the first day. She is having second thoughts about this guy. Maybe he isn't someone she wants to meet, marry and spend her life with.

Yes, Angie has leaped into the future in her thoughts about the attractive man who was seated behind her. When her eyes first spotted him, she'd noticed his broad shoulders, his firm, but not stiff stance. He leaned forward listening attentively and stood to sing with apparent enthusiasm. He neither slumped in his seat nor swayed when standing. He didn't seem to be a clapper, yet appeared comfortable when those around him rocked, raised their hands or clapped to the rousing opening songs.

But what is a handsome, respectful young man his age doing at camp meeting this early in the week? Is he a slacker? Or is he well-off, can afford the time, and has the interest to come to this place at this time? Hmmm. Is this his first year on Zion's Hill? Is he related to one of the big, influential families? She'd been coming for years and has met most of the guys who come regularly. No time for such cogitation, though. She must hurry along and get back down to the stand.

From her second floor dorm room, she can hear sounds from the service – just faintly – through the speakers mounted on the outside corners of the tabernacle roof. The choir has already sung, "Just As I Am," the standard altar call song, and she now hears the opening bars of the closing song, "God Be With You Till We Meet Again." Scurrying, she's back in the stand by the final chorus.

3 - The Meeting

ANGIE ONLY HAS A FEW MINUTES to get the apron on, her scoops in the water, and ready for the coming customers. She's got to adjust her attitude, too. It's a shame how many folks leaving a church service leave their manners on the seat with their cardboard fans. Thankfully, there are enough polite ones to make working in the stand more a pleasure than a pain for her. Not much time for talking though. Business is business.

Stella is experienced and orders the Conley flavors her customers like and opens the stand at just the right times to be available for them. She and her husband have negotiated a rare contract to sell the renowned gourmet ice cream on Zion's Hill during this annual meeting. With attention to detail, they've qualified for renewal three straight years. Stella assures Angie that it's the combination of premium ice cream and courteous service that brings the customers back year after year. When the stand is open, they usually are busy.

It takes a few days to regain the rhythm of pulling the cone from the tube hanging from the wall, grabbing the right sized dipper, locating the requested flavor, and scooping a solid, round scoop of ice cream. It takes skill to position the creamy confection firmly on the cone so the balls don't tip over when handing the cone to the customer or topple off on that first lick as the customer strolls away from the counter.

Angie prides herself on being fast and organized. It never takes her long to memorize the pattern in which the eight kinds of ice cream are arranged. She usually remembers the favorite flavors of the regular customers and amazes them when she offers them what they plan to order. It takes a couple of days, though, to build up the arm muscles needed to scoop quickly and efficiently.

She really does relish interacting with the customers, even though, when bending over to dip the cream, she mostly sees waistlines, belts and bulging midsections, and the customers mainly see the top her head and the back of

40

her collar. Angie's boss must be satisfied, though. The stand stays busy, and Angie has been invited back for the third year.

It's nearly two hours before the lines trickle down and Angie is pooped. Stella says Angie can go and lets her know the time to arrive on Monday.

NOW, SHE'S OFF FOR THE EVENING and has a half hour or so to spend on the grounds before going back to the dorm room for the night. She respects her grandparents' curfew, even though it seems a little strict for a woman her age. She's a college sophomore, but in their eyes, she's still "little Angela Jeanette".

She hangs up her apron, takes a moment to straighten her skirt, tug down her knit shirt, and pat her hair into place. Who knows, she may meet someone interesting this evening. She lifts the latch on the slatted door and steps down, careful not to land on the rut just to the right of the exit and twist her ankle the first night of camp meeting.

Rounding the corner, she spots a group of young people chatting near a post lamp puddling light in the grassy green common area between the tabernacle and road in front of the concession stands. She spots her friend, Lily, and ambles over. Although they had exchanged addresses again last summer and promised to keep in touch, their correspondence dwindled off before Thanksgiving. Nothing new about that. Happens every year.

Earnest though they are, few of the teens who meet during camp meeting remain in touch for more than a few months after it ends. The impetus to write fades, entropy takes over as each gets involved in school, local youth groups, and jobs. Now with college, who knows whether this year the writing will last even until October?

Angie sidles up to the group and stands at the edge, listening to the banter, feeling welcome but reluctant to join in until she can follow the flow of the conversation. What? There's Cute Head on the other side of the group. He has put on a blue windbreaker, which billows slightly in the gentle night wind, and he stands comfortably with his hands in his pockets.

He remains outside the circle, and like her, is listening attentively, but saying nothing. When he looks up, he acknowledges her presence, but makes no move to get any closer or to ask anyone to introduce them. Doesn't he

41

recognize her? She was sitting in front him in the service that just got out. Her chest tightens with disappointment. Maybe she's not as memorable as she thought. Just then, Lily turns her way, sees her, greets her, and puts her arm around Angie's shoulder, drawing her into their circle.

"Hey, guys. This is Isaac's sister. You remember Isaac from youth camp? He was camp king a couple of years ago. Well, this is his sister, Angie."

"Hi. Were you at camp that year, too?" asks Charles, the guy standing possessively next to Lily.

"No, she hasn't been to youth camp, but I know her from the years we worked in the dining room together." The others in the group extend their hands as Lily introduces them. Each greets her verbally and continues talking to one another or asking something of her. Questions and comments tumbling over each other.

"Yeah, I remember, Isaac."

"Quite a guy. What's he doing now, Angie?"

"Is he coming this year? I know he's in college now and probably working this summer, huh?"

"All of us here worked at youth camp this year. Earned a little dough that way, but I'm still going to have to get back home in a couple of days so I can help my uncle with his lawn care business. He pays pretty good, and I need all I can earn for tuition this fall."

"You too? My aunt's helping me out this year. Says if I'll stay here all week watching my cousins so she and my uncle can enjoy their vacation, she'll pay me enough for books this fall. The prices are out of sight!"

"Yeah. Those professors certainly don't mind assigning expensive texts, do they? They always pick the latest book their friends just published."

"So right! It's a racket I think. 'You write a book and I'll make my students buy yours. When mine comes out I expect you to make it a required text for your class.' I can just hear 'em talking by the mimeograph machine."

"Some racket and we gotta pay to play. Anyway, I'm glad I'm staying and still earning rather than spending. What about you, Kenneth?" Lily says, turning to the guy in the blue windbreaker.

So. His name is Kenneth. Kenneth what? And why is he here for the first Sunday? Has he been a counselor, too? Will he have to leave for a job? Will someone introduce us? Is he even interested?

Angie looks up to find him looking at her. He gives a half smile, and she shifts her eyes to glance over his shoulder, afraid that her look will give away her eagerness to meet him. Just then, Lily helps out.

"Hey, Ange, this is Kenneth Robertson. He was a counselor with us at camp this year." She rattles on, revealing more. "Ken lives in town and is home for the summer. Ken plays ball for Penn State. You know Brother Ralph who heads the camp? He knows Ken from church. Well, Ken came to help out with the sports this year," she says, thumping him on the shoulder and smiling up at him.

Oh no! Maybe Lily and Ken already are an item.

Lily commends, "We had a pretty big camp this year--more teens than ever, and Ken did a great job with them. Of course it helped that he's a local hero from his days playing high school basketball. Ken's team beat Shenango Valley's three time regional champs! Plus, he's a solid Christian and did a great job with the Bible study with his guys." Why is Charles looking like that? Is he jealous of this jock?

Grabbing Ken's hand, Lily pulls him across the circle and resumes the introduction. "Ken, this is Angie. You know, the one I told you I wanted you to meet? Well, here she is. She's finished her first year in college too. Right, Ange?"

Angie nods, feeling surprisingly shy. She looks at Lily, who continues, "I thought you guys would have lots to talk about being that you're both serious collegians and committed Christians too. Yeah, Ange, I think you'll get along well. And Ken, she's good people. We go way back. We used to work together in the dining room. I've moved up to cashier. Angie's moved up to the ice cream stand."

By this time, Ken is standing right next to Angie, looking down at her quizzically. *Will Lily's promise prove true? Will they really hit it off?* Angie takes a deep breath, extends her hand and looks up at Ken. His eyes warm to hers in recognition. "Ah, yes. You were sitting in front of me in service, weren't you?"

"Yes," she smiles. "That was me." She should have said, "That was I." After all, she is an English major and should set a good example. But she doesn't want to sound all proper and superior. She'd been teased about that a lot in middle school.

Instead, shivering in retrospect, she goes on, "And you pointed out that mouse. You don't know how scared I am of mice. It was hard to squelch the scream. It was crawling up my throat!"

"You didn't look scared to me. In fact, you appeared remarkably calm and collected."

He seemed remarkably calm and collected himself. Good thing he hadn't seen her knuckles popping when she clinched her the edge of her seat, trying to hold herself in place and not run out in the middle of service. She looks back up at Ken, who's still talking.

"Oh, the mouse just ran along the beam and out the opening. I didn't see it anymore. By that time, though, I was drawn to what the minister was saying. He was good wasn't he?"

"Yeah," she replies thoughtfully – thinking about Ken and how mellow his voice is and also about the sermon. It's good to meet someone who appreciates a well-delivered message. Especially a well-spoken man who also is handsome – in Angie's opinion anyway.

It's hard to tell for sure in the shadow of the overhead lamp, but she likes what she sees of this man. He's a little taller than her five feet eight inches. Her dream man is about six feet two. Ken seems about that height.

He stands erect, proud, but not haughty, even though Lily and her friends rattle on and on about Ken's athletic prowess and his success with the rowdy teens at youth camp. Good. He can take a compliment and not get all blown up. Maybe there is something worth considering about this guy. And maybe he feels the same about her. But what does he know about her, really?

Ken continues to make eye contact with Angie as though he is interested in extending their conversation. He steps a little to the side and asks her, "Well, how long have you been coming to camp meeting?"

"Oh, I've been coming since I was a kid."

"Really? I only came a couple times before I graduated from high school and went into the Air Force. I haven't been home during the summer in years."

"Oh!" Angie utters. That's why she hasn't seen him before. He lives nearby. That may explain why a guy like Ken is up here this first Sunday. Not that it's really all that important.

But her experience has been that the really eligible guys come up for Second Sunday. Now, wouldn't it be nice if Ken could come up afternoons this week before evening services. That would give them a few days to get to know each other before the weekend when the grounds get crowded and the ice cream stand is opened longer after services. Before other competition from more popular women, is what Angie really thinks, as the conversation continues among the rest of the group.

She isn't all that bad looking, but she seldom stands out in a crowd. Her clothes are nice, but rarely are the height of fashion and never the expensive brand names. Her figure is all right, but she has rather skinny ankles and generous hips. Her complexion is dark brown, and her skin is clear. She keeps in pretty good shape running some track in college, walking to and from the bus stops going to work, and hoofing it back and forth across campus between classes. She's okay, but she can use all the lead time available to get to know Ken before he is distracted by other better-looking, better-dressed women. But maybe Ken has a job and can't come during the day.

"Lil mentioned you're in college, Angie. What are you studying?" Delighted that a man is interested in her and not going on and on about himself, she tells him about her goal of earning a bachelor's degree in English and then pursuing a career as an educator. She hopes to teach in high school.

45

He listens, avidly probing her to expand her reasons for wanting to teach and then commending her for her choices.

"What about you, Ken? You're going to school in State College. Why'd you pick Penn State? What are you studying?" And so the conversation goes. It's a while before she realizes that they have drifted away from the group and are walking companionably along a path toward her dorm. When Angie sees where they are, she also notices the time and reluctantly brings the conversation to an end.

"Ken, it's been great talking with you, but I promised my grandparents I'd come in soon after finishing my stint in the ice cream stand. They worry when I'm out much later. Yeah, I know, I'm a grown- up, but to them I'm still their little Angela Jeanette. Anyway, I am a little tired. This is my first day, and my shoulder aches a little from all that dipping and scooping."

"Yeah. Sure, I understand. Well, will I see you tomorrow?"

"I guess so. But not in the morning. I promised the couple who heads the children's ministry that I'd be there early tomorrow to help with check-in. It's sorta like Vacation Bible School."

Too bad they have to cut short their time together, but her grandparents won't sleep soundly until she comes in. And she really is pooped. She doesn't want to slip up and start talking gibberish and drive Ken away thinking she is a dithering idiot.

Ken seems to understand the situation. He courteously releases her from the conversation, says good night at the bottom of the dorm stairway, and walks down the hill toward the parking lot. She stands there for a moment, watching his upright stride, the left arm swinging a little more than the right, and his long legs, revealed to be just a little bowed as his heather grey slacks flutter in the wind. She notes the slight tilt of his head and his assertive gait. He's comfortable with himself and knowledgeable of the terrain. No stumbling along the gravel paths for Ken.

"Not bad," she exclaims aloud, "Not bad, at all." Deep in thought, Angie starts up the wooden steps, grabbing the handrail once she nearly trips on the third stair. Yes, she is tired, but she also is eager to get washed, in bed, asleep, and up on Monday to see whether or not he keeps his promise to seek her out when he returns to the campgrounds.

4 - Reflections

"NOT BAD," Ken decides as he walks down the hill to his car, his mind still on Angie, the handsome dark-skinned woman he's just met. As is often the case with Negroes, men and women describe each other in terms of skin color, complexion and hair texture. The women in his family run the gamut.

His grandmother, Leona, a feisty bittersweet chocolate, with springy grey hair she keeps crushed under soft brimmed hats; his older sister, Joann – mocha fudge round-faced. She wears her short wavy hair sometimes pulled severely back in a ponytail of sorts, more often covered with a full curly wig or extended with a hairpiece of one color or another. Thia, the baby of the family, caramel toffee face framed by such dark brown hair that one would call it black were it not for the reddish highlights. She styles hers in a neat pageboy or gently pulled back in a fancy barrette at the nape of her neck. His mother. She's the creamy tan of white chocolate and sports her wavy reddish brown hair cascading to her shoulders. Like his grandmother, she usually wears hats – a wide-brimmed one to protect her delicate skin from the sun or a colorful turban to corral her mane of hair. The myriad women in Ken's life are as different as the gourmet chocolates in Daffin's Chocolate Factory.

Semi-sweet chocolate Angie would fit right into this rainbow of browns. He noticed she straightens her ear length hair, but he isn't sure if it only grows that length or if she's had it cut that way. With her deep brown skin, her natural hair probably is coarse and kinky, the kind that would look great in a close-cropped Afro he's starting to see that Negro students on campus are sporting. Whatever style she chooses, she'd look fine; Angie seems to be the kind of lady who will always be well-coiffed.

KEN HAD PARKED his stepfather's Corvair in the lot closest to the entry gate. Didn't want to be caught in the maelstrom of after service traffic. Lots of locals come for the first Sunday night of camp meeting and would be anxious to get on the difficult-to-navigate two-lane dirt road back down to town. No streets light yet. He'd better be careful. There'd better be no dings

48

anywhere on the surface of that little car. His step-dad is particular about everything he owns.

"Hard to come by," he always says. "Gotta take care of your stuff, Ken. Not easy to replace it if you don't keep it up. I work hard and I like nice things. Work hard. Buy smart and take care," he'd repeat, wiping each of his tools with an oiled cloth before returning them to the racks in his storage shed. His stepfather is careful about everything. Especially this year-old Chevy he'd gotten at a good price. His very first brand new car. Good. There it is. By the time Ken gets down the hill, his is one of only three left in the lower lot.

No need to worry about traffic now. Didn't think he'd be hanging around that long after service. Could have parked anywhere. He pulls the key from his pocket, opens the door, and sits there a minute before starting the engine. "Not bad at all," he muses. Maybe coming to services each evening will work out after all. It certainly has been stimulating so far.

The service was pretty good. He's surprised. It's been years since he's heard those old hymns sung that way. Sounds different when there's a choir of one hundred singing with a full congregation joining them. There're more in this choir than in his whole church most Sundays.

He turns the key to start the engine, and then remembers to buckle the retro-fitted seat belts. If someone asks, he'd say the preacher's delivery was a little dry, but his message did speak to him. God just wants Christians 'to be' – to be His. Feast on His Word, let it become a part of them and they'll become more like His Son. Just be.

He twists around to look out the back window, checks his side mirrors, and then eases the car over the ruts in the once-a-year dirt parking lot.

THE MESSAGE TONIGHT SOUNDED DIFFERENT from what he thought about what it means to be a Christian. His pastor makes it sound like a list of rules to keep. Ken planned to consult his Bible for this idea of relationship instead of rules. He pulls onto the road and steers down the hill thinking about the sermon and thinking about Angie and what he'd heard the Lord say about Angie.

His fellow counselors during youth camp had all expressed differing opinions about hanging around another week for camp meeting. Most said nothing much happened until the second weekend. Things got interesting when more men and women their age arrived. He smiles as he recalls Joey, one of his campers, promising to introduce Ken to his older sister when she comes up next weekend.

===

"SHE'S REALLY GOOD LOOKING, Brother Ken," Joey brags. "Sorta tall, like you. You'll like her. She's got a great job as a legal secretary. She's ready to get married. You ready to get married, Brother Ken? Y'all'd make a great couple. She's a Christian, like you." Walking together from the camp cafeteria, Joey looks up at Ken to see how he's responding to the description of his sister.

"She don't waste her time dating guys she's not likely to marry. She's not seeing anyone right now. I know she'll like you too. I told her all about you when I wrote home last night. She's coming next Saturday."

Ken just nods, saying nothing. By this time they're near the playground, and Joey, seeing some of the guys shooting baskets, bolts off to join them, calling back, "Bye, Brother Ken".

Fourteen-year-old Joey has been a challenge all week. He's been raised in the church and coming to summer camp for years. He's a "know-it-all" who responded neither to Ken's attempts to keep his attention nor his efforts to spark interest in digging into God's Word.

The kid just likes being the center of attention and thinks being a clown will make him popular with his peers, especially with the girls. Ken never knew what monkey business would arise when the girls joined the guys at the evening meeting for singing and then a message from one of the camp directors.

THE FINAL EVENING OF CAMP, THOUGH, each of the counselors meets alone with his or her own group of eight or nine campers. Sitting around the flickering fire in the area, Ken's guys gather for final Bible study.

Joey and all the boys seem more contemplative, surprisingly reluctant for camp to end.

They've sung all their favorite rousing songs and settle down a bit. Though the guys say they're "hokey", one of them always requests "God is So Good" and "Kum Bah Yah". After a short prayer, he invites the boys to recount ways they've experienced God's goodness during the week. At first the boys wriggle and snicker.

Restless. Reticent about testifying to peers. They fidget and look around, but avoid making eye contact. No one wants to be the first to speak. Ken begins humming "Kum Bah Ya" and prays that the boys will sense the presence of the Spirit, and equally important, know they are safe sharing their experiences in this setting. He's spent the week creating a nurturing environment to earn their confidence in him, their counselor, and to develop it in one another. Each day, he noticed more and more of them listening attentively to the morning Bible lessons. Comfortable with silence, he awaits their responses.

Yes, Brother Ralph, the camp director provided the counselors printed materials they could use with the campers, but he encouraged the counselors to prayerfully consider what God wanted them to share with the specific boys and girls assigned to them. Brother Ralph urged them to adapt their lessons based on the counselors' growing understanding of the youngsters they had. Be honest. Be authentic. The campers would believe what they teach is true if the counselors reflect on their own walks with the Lord and freely weave in their own personal insights and experiences.

Ken has told lots of stories about his being an athlete and an airman in the United States Air Force. That always got their attention. He wants the boys with whom he has worked these two weeks of camp to understand that they can stand up for right, even in the midst of pressure to go along with the crowd doing things they all know in their hearts will be displeasing to God. Ken has experienced the strength of God's Spirit, has found living the Christian life to be preferable to what he'd tried, what he'd seen, and what he'd heard from his fellow airmen and basketball teammates.

Whenever it seemed right – during a lesson, on the playing fields, at meals, or just goofing off with the guys – he shared his stories. He told of those up days when he felt he was living according to his understanding of the Scriptures and the down days when he gave in to temptation. He also told them that he has sought and received God's forgiveness. He strove to engender an understanding of the breadth of God's mercy towards everyone, those committed to Christ and those who had not yet made that decision. Now, on this last evening of camp, he wants his guys to feel equally confident about sharing their own stories. Patiently, he waits.

JOEY WIGGLES AND GIGGLES. STOPS --- STILL --- and stares at the boy across the fire from him. Unexpectedly, Larry, the top athlete in the group, begins speaking, quietly, cautiously. His head is bowed. He's looking at dirty Converse shoes, talking a little hesitantly. Then, looking around at the curious questioning faces of his campmates, he confesses.

"God, He been good to me this week." Their puzzled expressions and eager eyes encourage him. He sits up straighter and raises his voice so more can hear.

"I know 'cause I feel safe here." This gets their attention. The campers lean in, curious about what this new boy will reveal. Spurred by their response, Larry goes on. "Even when Joey there teased me about missing that last shot in the game yesterday, I know he be kidding. He wasn't trying to hurt me."

"Ah, man. You fun to tease," Joey jibes.

"You also a bad ball player. All us wanted you on our team, didn't we guys?" chimes in Pete. "He real bad, ain't he?" They all nod.

"Yeah, Lare, you play pretty good!" Joey concedes.

"Thanks, man. Hearing y'all tell me that is real different for me. It ain't like that at home."

"What you mean, Larry? It ain't like what at home?"

"Y'all seem to like me. Y'all make me feel welcome. This is my first year at camp. I figured all y'all be knowing one another from way back." Retracting a bit, he admits, "I was scared to come. But I was even more scared to stay at home."

Of course, the guys perk up to hear more. Larry continues.

"My Moms got married last summer. To a guy with two boys older than me. We supposed to be a blended family, but we not. They won't let me in. Sam and Ricky, I mean. Most of the time they act like I don't even exist." Eyes leaking tears, Larry keeps talking, words tumbling out, thoughts he'd kept locked up for months.

"They daddy's house is bigger than ours so Moms and me moved in with them. They got three bedrooms. Sam and Ricky had they own room before Moms married they daddy. When me and Moms moved in, Moms, of course, moved in they daddy's bedroom. I coulda shared a room with Ricky, 'cause he's the youngest, just a year older than me.

"I was looking forward to having older brothers. But it ain't happening. Ricky moved in with Sam, and Sam hates that. He hates me like it's my fault he don't have his privacy no more." Larry swipes at tears, but feeling them pulling out his story, he goes on.

"It's miserable when they daddy and Moms ain't home. Sam and Ricky talk bad about my mother and how she couldn't take care of me and her when Pops died. Now, they blame us for messing up they lives. They say they had they dad to theyselves until my mother come along. It all changed even worse when I came into the picture."

"How come, Larry? How'd they think you make things worse for 'em?"

"They thought having a mother would be a good thing. She'd cook and clean for them and they'd have all the time they wanted to run around and hang out with they friends. Before that they had chores. They daddy had made them take turns doing the cooking and stuff. You know, cleaning up they rooms and washing they own dirty clothes. They thought that'd be over when they had a woman in the house."

"That wouldn't happen in my house," Pete laughs. "My mother don't do none of that stuff. She makes my sister do it." The other guys shut Pete up with their eyes.

Larry seems to have missed Pete's remarks; he continues, "But no. They still got to do chores. They say they daddy don't make me do enough. It was true. At first, he didn't make me do much."

"Musta been good for you. Having a nice house and no chores. Huh? Okay. What happened, man?"

"By the time they daddy put me on the work schedule, Sam and Ricky already hated me. They take turns picking on me. Most times they work together at it. Not just calling me names, but ganging up on me and stuff. You know, locking me out of the house. Not letting me get into they bathroom when they know I gotta go bad. Telling me I can't come in they room or use any of they stuff."

"Sounds like your house, eh, Joey!" Joey shushes Pete. The others, riveted, shush Pete as well.

"When the parents are around, Sam and Ricky treat me okay. But they daddy and my Moms both work. Sam and Ricky and me, we home alone a lot. I'm mostly alone by myself though. They don't take me with them no place."

"Are you surprised? They older than you. Anyway, ain't you got any friends at school?"

"Nah, man. I go to they school, now. They don't let me be friends with them at school neither. They act like they don't know me. The guys hunkering around the campfire fidget, trying to get comfortable on the uneven log seats. Still, they keep their eyes on Larry, listening intently as his story outpours, emitting unexpected empathy for their fellow camper. Encouraged, Larry keeps talking.

"I thought it would be better when school started, but it ain't. It's hard, guys. Real hard. I don't understand why nobody likes me at this new school. Goin' to they school is horrible. The kids there act like I got a disease or something. I think Sam musta told all the kids to not like me."

The campers don't seem to understand, and it shows on their faces.

"It wasn't like that at my old school. I was popular there. Moving to this new neighborhood and going to high school for the first time is just awful. I don't know nobody. Everybody there hates me," Larry concludes.

Balling his hands so tight his knuckles stand at attention listening to the pain, Larry keeps talking. Ignoring his trembling voice, the young man sounds relieved to be revealing his aching heart. "My new brothers ain't nice to me or nothin'. They take things out of my room when I ain't there and then act like they don't know what I'm talking about when I ast about it. And they lie and tease me when I tell on them. Moms and they daddy think I'm the one lying! They say I'm jealous and tell me to grow up. I ain't never had no brothers and sisters. I just don't understand it."

But his campmates around the fire do. They sit nodding their heads in sympathy. Several boys identify with being a younger sibling; some know about being unpopular; others know about being part of a blended or a dysfunctional family. They listen wholeheartedly. Larry unloads his burden, and he's telling their stories.

Ken remains silent and lets the Spirit do His work.

Tears trickle off Larry's cheeks, but he doesn't seem embarrassed about it. More details tumble out. Knowing he has their attention and sympathy, Larry sits up, gesticulating broadly, as though to release more tension. "At home Sam and Ricky act like I ain't even there. They won't let me in they room or nothing. We be sitting in the family room watching TV or something and they talk about me, never to me. It's awful! Naturally, they don't never do this when our parents is home. Just when we home alone. Ricky, he walk by me and sock me in the shoulder. If I say something, he turn his back and ast,

"'Sam, do you hear something? I don't see nobody. Do you see somebody, Sam? Must be my 'magination. Ain't nobody here but us two. Must be my 'magination.' Then they go back to watching TV or playing they silly games."

"Ah, man. That's awful. Can't you do something?" asks Pete.

"They both bigger than me. When they not ignoring me, they beating me up. They'd gang up on me, twist my arm, even hold me down and tickle me.

They think that's so funny. Any kind of stuff to make me miserable. If I start crying, they just laugh."

He looks around, wondering whether he's talking too much to guys he'd just met. But he feels them drawing him out, so he doesn't stop. "It hurts guys. Y'all know I ain't no wimp. I really ain't no crybaby. But it hurts being on the outside and invisible, but still getting beat up." By this time, Larry is standing and begins pacing.

"A lotta times I'd just go out in the backyard to get away from they teasing. Then they close the sliding glass door to shut me out that way. Lots of time they won't open the door till one of the parents come home. Then Sam and Ricky act all surprised that I'm out there. It's awful. Just awful." Larry stops. No one says anything.

Larry takes a deep breath and looks around, making eye contact with each of the guys. "But here at camp. Y'all let me in." He grins and chortles nervously. "Yeah, y'all tease me some, but y'all been nice to me. Around here, I can finally relax." Blowing out the deep breath, he exclaims, "For two whole weeks I ain't been scared somebody gonna come by and punch me and then pretend like it didn't happen."

Larry stops again, and tenses, stiffening into a bronze statue, exhales, relaxing into a Gumby, and then stands proud. "Y'all let me play ball with you, and my old skills are coming back. I'm having fun again. I got friends here." He squares his shoulders only for a moment. "I got friends here." Then he slumps over like a melting candle. "But I ain't got none at home. At home I'll go back into being left out and alone". He sits back down, relieved to have told his tale, but loath to return home.

Ken is tempted to interject with the, "You're never alone. God is with you wherever you are" spiel. But he doesn't have to. Without moving physically, the campers have encircled Larry. Confessions flow. They share their own stories about being alone or picked on. Some talk about ways their faith in God helps them to deal with going to a new school – four of them had been freshmen in high school this past year. Their stories unveil similar experiences with siblings or parents.

Soon, though, talk slows down, dries up. The boys withdraw – wondering if they've said too much, let down their masks, sloughed off their shields, revealed soft, vulnerable underbellies, and opened themselves to become targets of scoffing the next day. Patiently, Ken waits.

Then one of the boys, George, speaks up and asks, "Larry, do you want to pray?" Silence.

"Do you want to invite Christ into your life?" Silence.

"You can take His Spirit home with you." More silence.

Ken gingerly steps back, out of the firelight. He feels led by the Lord to let the boys handle this situation. Standing there in the shadows, he scolds himself a bit for the unwarranted pride – feeling he's been responsible for reaching these young men -- then sighs a prayer of thanksgiving that it has happened through him. He remains out of their way and lets them minister to their fellow camper.

One by one, these adolescent boys stand up next to or kneel around Larry. Each one inches close enough to put a hand either on Larry's shoulder or on the shoulder of a camper nearby.

They wait. Patiently. Silently. Sensitive to the moment. Letting the warmth of the Spirit move on Larry's heart. Some close their eyes. George watches. He sees the slight nod indicating that Larry is ready to pray. George glances toward Ken. He nods his head, signaling George to take the lead.

And with quiet confidence, George invites Larry to repeat what he says,

"Dear God, I understand that I am a sinner who needs you. I understand that Jesus died for my sins. I accept Him as my Savior and ask that you send your Spirit to live in me. Thank you, God. Amen."

Larry repeats the words in trembling voice – a little incredulous that speaking the words sincerely is all that it takes for this change to take place in his heart and mind. His tears flow for joy this time – instead of sorrow. He looks around at the boys encircling him, smiling shyly as the campers move closer to give him a quick one arm hug or pat on the shoulder; some surreptitiously wipe the tears from their own eyes. Larry doesn't shrink from this physical interaction; he welcomes their manly tenderness.

Pete, a little embarrassed by the damp emotions flowing around them, perhaps to relieve the tension, begins singing, softly at first, and then more lustily, "I've got the joy, joy, joy, joy, down in my heart." Other boys join in. Soon all stand with arms around shoulders like athletes in a locker room huddle, rocking to the rhythm of the song.

> I've got the peace that passeth understanding
> Down in my heart.
> Down in my heart.
> Down in my heart.
> I've got the peace that passeth understanding
> Down in my heart
> Down in my heart to stay!"

Ken decides to say nothing more that evening. He just gives the boys a gentle thump on the shoulder as each passes him towards the path leading back to the cabins. As a coach sending his team onto the playing field, Ken prays for a victory and that they each will continue to experience the presence of the Lord in their lives. As he covers the lingering embers of the campfire, Ken also prays a prayer of thanks that God has answered their prayer to Kum Bah Ya. Clearly, God did indeed "come by here" tonight.

THE NEXT DAY, Ken joins Larry after breakfast and they walk in the shade of the tree-lined path to the small clearing where the group would meet later for Bible study. "Larry, I appreciate your sharing your story with us last night. That took a lot of courage. It must have been tough to relive those hard times." Larry nods shyly and looks up. Ken turns and locks eyes with him.

"You know, Larry, we're all glad you came to camp this year. You've been a great inspiration to the guys on and off the court." Larry shrugs embarrassed shoulders and looks at his dusty gym shoes. Feeling somewhat exhausted from lack of sleep after the emotional evening, Larry finds it hard to believe that this morning his new friends aren't questioning his story and teasing him. He can hardly believe he dumped it all on these guys he'd just met.

"Really, Brother Ken?"

"Yeah, man. We're really glad you came. After hearing your story last night, though, I wondered what made you decide to come to this camp."

"Oh, that. Well. The guy next door goes to y'all's church. I guess he been seeing me sittin' around. I think he seen what Sam and Ricky been doin' to me. Well, one day, he musta seen I been down."

Sensing the embarrassment, Ken nods, reassuring Larry to go on.

"I ain't been crying in public or nothing. You believe me, don't' you, Brother Ken? I ain't no crybaby. But I do sit outside a lot – by myself, you know? He musta seen me. Anyway, about a week after school got out, he called me over to his yard. He ast me what I gonna be doing this summer."

The counselor and counselee walk companionably along the path. Larry explains, "I had no idea. I just knew I didn't wanna be hanging around with Sam and Ricky for no two whole months. No tellin' what they'd do all summer. I told Mr. Richmon – that's his name. I told him, I didn't have no plans. I wondered if he had a job for me at his company. He own his own business, you know. I believe he kinda rich. He said no, he didn't have no job there – at his office, I mean. He say if I water his lawn and cut his grass the two weeks when him and his wife go on vacation, he pay my way to camp here. I jumped at his offer. Of course, I had to ask Moms about it. But, she was OK with it, so here I am."

By this time the other boys have arrived, gathering in their regular spots for their final morning Bible study, and Larry, no longer embarrassed, just keeps right on talking, first to one, then another, bubbling over with gratitude for the friends he's made at camp and for all that he's learned. He looks around and sees they are eager to have him go on. With lively confidence, he admits,

"Man. I had no idea it would be this cool. I thought it would be all religious and stuff. You know, singing hymns, talking God stuff, and reading the Bible all the time. Shoot, I didn't even care if it was. Anything would be better than being around Sam and Ricky all summer."

The boys settle in knowing Larry will keep talking until his and their story is told.

"Now I has met you guys and hear Brother Ken talk about God and, you know, how He want us to come to Him when we having problems and all. I just can't believe He sent His Son to help us get back to God. I don't understand all that. It's weird. . . that we can be friends with God. But that do sound cool to me. That God gonna be fighting for me. Hey, Brother Ken, you think maybe God gonna do something to Sam and Larry so them boys stop messin' with me. That be really cool."

Ken smiles, but says nothing. Larry continues.

"But about Thursday, after hearing all y'all talking about Christ and God and all that, and listening to Brother Ken, I started to understand that God may not change Sam and Ricky, but He might could change me, if I repented and all that stuff." Larry is totally unaware that he is giving testimony to and affirming the value of a Christian camp.

"I started thinking about how I wanted to be strong and not feel like cryin' all the time 'cause of what them boys be doing to me. I ain't never been no crybaby and it made me mad that I been actin' like one. Like I told you, I been real popular and I thought I was a strong person. But these past few months was just awful...until I got to camp."

The boys' attentiveness draws out the story. They are thirsty to hear how the same old camp they've been coming to for years is different for a new guy.

"You guys didn't know me. But y'all treated me OK. Y'all let me in. Y'all pick me play on y'all teams and everything. My old good feelings come back. Nobody picked on me." The boys laugh, a little embarrassed to be complimented.

"Well," Larry brings them down a bit, "no more than y'all pick on everybody round here. I started reading my Bible during quiet time and, you know, I think I'm getting to know more about God." He turns to speak directly to Ken. "I really like those Proverbs and some of the Psalms you told us about, Brother Ken. I know Proverbs is your favorite. But I really like the Psalms. I gonna start memorizing the first chapter."

"Really, Larry? You're memorizing the Bible?" scoffs Ronnie – gently though. He can tell that Larry is really serious. To soften his teasing, he asks Larry to say as much of Psalms as he could. He thinks that may make Larry feel better.

"Sure, Ronnie. Yeah, I can say the first coupla verses of Psalms 1,

> Blessed is the man that walketh not in the counsel of the ungodly,
> nor standeth in the way of sinners,
> nor sitteth in the seat of the scornful.
>
> But his delight is in the law of the Lord;
> and in his law doth he meditate day and night.

"I don't know about that meditating day and night stuff, but I know I feel better after quiet time when I be thinking about what I be reading and learning here at camp. I think I can go home now and put up with what be going on there. I ain't sure I got enough nerve yet to stand up to Sam and Ricky, though."

Then, looking around at his new friends, Larry drops his head, then raises it, smiling shyly and says with growing sureness, "Maybe with God's help, I be able to just stand them." He laughs, and then looks up with new found confidence.

His fellow campers nod for him to continue. He does. "Now when I learn how to pray, I think I'll pray that they get saved, too. You know, will get to know God, and all. I gotta learn how to tell them what I learned here. But I sure don't believe I got enough nerve to talk about it yet. I just hope I can show them they can't get to me no more."

The guys nod reticently, knowing they'd be as reluctant to speak religious stuff to their peers as Larry admits he is.

"Yeah, Larry, you right. You gotta stand up for yourself and for God. You a Christian now." Ronnie challenges, "Remember what Brother Ken says about 'Greater is He that is in you than He that is in the world?' I learned about that in youth group and I've had to repeat it a lot now that I go to high school. It's hard to be a Christian in high school. I know what you mean, man. Do I sure know what you mean!"

Ken, remembering what happened the past evening around the campfire, let the boys talk among themselves about their ups and downs once they invited God to be the center of their lives. Sure, the boys listen to him all right, but he's a grown-up. They will be more convinced when their peers testify to their own experiences as Christians.

The conversation soon winds down. Ken stands, holds out his hand signaling his campers to join hands. He invites them first to give God thanks for what they've experienced and to pray for God's keeping power once they return to their homes. He asks each one in the circle to pray especially for the person standing on his right.

How gratifying to hear the heartfelt prayers, personalized by the young people in his group. It sounds like they've gotten to know the special needs of their fellow campers and are comfortable verbalizing them, asking God's help in meeting those needs.

His silent prayer is that they keep in touch after camp and support each other as best they can once they disperse to their homes around the country. He's heard several of them exchanging addresses. He just hopes they'll write. Writing back and forth and praying for each other will help them maintain their own resolve and resist the temptation to fall back into their old ways. But, to be honest, he knows from personal experience how the zeal of camp diminishes once the kids are back at home. They'll probably get busy and forget to write.

THAT AFTERNOON, AS THE CAMPERS WAIT in front of the cinder block dining hall, Joey steps closer to Ken and whispers, "Now, don't forget. Brother Ken. My sister'll be here Saturday. Our cottage is just up the hill from the tabernacle. You know, the cottage with the blue door. We're the only one with a blue door up on that road. I told Celeste we'd meet you in the back of the tabernacle about half an hour before service Saturday night. Okay? We'll meet by that big tree. Yeah, the one with the big knot in it... about five feet up. You know the one? Great. Brother Ken. I'm sure you'll like my sister. I know she'll like you."

Joey rattles on, bragging to the guys still waiting for their parents to come for them. "Hey, guys. I'm gonna introduce my sister to Brother Ken. Maybe they'll get married and he'll be my real brother. That'll be cool. My sister married to Brother Ken. What you saying, Pete? You got a sister, too. Well, I got dibs. I'm gonna get to him first. He already promised to meet my sister first! Right, Brother Ken?"

===

AND SO IT HAD GONE, ALL WEEK. Most of Ken's campers have older sisters or cousins or some woman they wanted him to meet. Personally, he is not interested. He's just finished his first year of college and has three more in one of the toughest programs at Penn State. Though he's not the first, few people from his town even go away to college; even fewer start a degree in chemical engineering, and fewer still complete academic work for any degree. Apparently that was typical at Penn State, too.

He grimaces, recalling that first meeting with the chair of the metallurgy department in the College of Engineering.

===

"All right you guys. Look to the left. Now, look to the right. This may be the last time you see these fellows. Half of you will have dropped out by the end of the first year. Half of those left will be gone by the third year. Only about twenty-five percent of you have what it takes to get a degree from this department!"

Some greeting to a freshmen engineering class! But, Ken picked up the gauntlet and committed himself to being one of the twenty-five percent who graduates. That means he doesn't have time for women in his life at this time. Especially since he's earned a basketball scholarship to help pay his expenses. He has to keep his grades up to stay on the team, and he has to stay on the team to stay in school. Even with the VA benefits, he doesn't have enough saved to finish his Bachelor of Science degree without this scholarship. So, no women!

STILL. THAT ANGELA JEANETTE SEEMS NICE. She speaks intelligently. Lily recommends her. She, too, is pursuing a college degree, is active in her church, carries herself well and her girls at camp certainly seemed fond of her. He is puzzled and not sure how his regard for Lily carries over to Angie. But he's sure it means something. Yes. It confirms his positive take on Angie.

What's the big deal in seeing more of her? It's only a week of camp meeting. It may even be diverting to spend a little time getting to know her while she's in town. He won't promise her anything, though. When he gets back to school, he's got to be able to refocus his attention on his game and on his coursework. No problem. It'll be okay to look her up tomorrow.

BY THIS TIME, KEN IS NEARLY HOME, having cruised mentally on autopilot the few miles from the campground and he soon will be turning onto the road leading to the gravel driveway and up to the place his parents are building their dream ranch home – a red brick one with snow white mortar.

They've come a long way since he lived here during high school. They've got the basement dug and capped, but they're still living in a small trailer. It's been nearly ten years since they bought this property just across the school district line of the town where he'd grown up. They plan to furnish the basement so they can move in this winter. They'll stay down there until they save enough to finish the rest of the house, exactly the way they want it.

Ken is not sure if he'll ever really forgive them for moving out here just when he was entering high school. He had grown up playing pickup ball with the guys on Coach's team and longed to join the lineup that surely would keep up their winning streak. But no! His parents decided to move less than half a mile from the district boundary for the high school where Coach Mac worked. It just wasn't fair!

Still, he did get to play ball at his new school. To tell the truth, even though at fourteen he had been quite skillful, he probably would not have made the first team at Coach's school. The guys in the old neighborhood were outstanding, many of them taller and stronger than Ken by the time he'd started high school.

At Hillside High, his new school, he'd made first string his first year and held a spot on varsity his whole four years. By the time he got to be a senior, their school had an enviable reputation and a strong enough record to earn a slot in the invitational tournament run by Coach Mac, a craggy faced Ernest Borgnine kind of guy from Pittsburgh whom everyone admired. Teams all across the state vied for a chance to play against Coach's championship team. His squad always made it to the finals and every year drew a sellout crowd to that last game of the tournament.

Each summer, even after the family moved, when Ken was not working on their new property, collecting junk with his uncle, or in the garden his mom had up on that uncle's farm, he would ride his bike back to the old neighborhood to play pickup games with the guys he'd known all his life. They kept him sharp.

The older guys didn't pick the young guys if they wouldn't be an asset to the team. They wouldn't even play one-on-one if the player couldn't be a challenge to them. For several years, Ken only got to play in the afternoon when the older guys still were at work. After dinner is when the best guys came out and the toughest games were played. By the time he was sixteen, Ken had picked up some weight and developed enough skill to hold his own against most of them. More and more often they picked him to be on their team. They played fast and physical ball, and he'd certainly honed his skills playing in the old neighborhood.

Sometimes Coach would come out and watch the pickup games. He even called Ken aside one time during the summer between his junior and senior year and asked him if he planned to go to college. Ken's playing impressed him, and Coach thought he could help if Ken needed introductions to college coaches. "Wow, the Coach thinks I'm good enough to play college ball!" Ken thought with a grin of pleasure.

He had ridden home from the game that evening, swiping his sweating forehead and peddling the old cycle. He'd put it together from spare parts picked up when he helped his uncle on his junk collection route. Industrious, Ken had worked at any kind of honest job just to earn spending cash.

His stepfather, a hardworking man, almost always had some kind of job, but often was laid off from those that paid well. There just seemed to be no steady employment at the local steel mill. With the on-going recession, the plants in the area were always having layoffs, so he seldom was able to give pre-teen Ken an allowance or any nonessential extras at all.

Sure, he always had a roof over his head, balanced meals, and satisfactory clothes. His parents, however, had been saving for years to buy that piece of property and now were well on their way to having enough to start building the main floor of the ranch home they'd been dreaming about most of his life.

So, young Ken, knowing he needed to accept whatever jobs came his way, gladly accepted the offer to work with his uncle in his junk-collecting business. That was years ago, but Ken still remembers the good times with that entrepreneurial uncle. Now, making the right turn off the main road onto the dirt road to his house, Ken recalls coasting along on his mutt of a bike. He smiles, reflecting on those days.

===

AT THE END OF THE DAYS of driving through the alleys of town, his uncle always stopped at the hot dog stand. He'd get Ken two chili dogs and a big drink – Nehi Grape or Nesbitt's Crush -- and then drop him off at home before heading back across town to his own farm. Neither Ken nor his parents had money to buy him a bike. Uncle Joe couldn't really afford to do so either.

That memorable day, while collecting in the alley in one of the better neighborhoods, they saw the frame of the red bicycle sitting next to the trash cans. Banged up, there really was nothing much wrong with it except that it needed a paint job. For an inordinate amount of time Ken looked longingly at the frame; Uncle Joe picked up the vibe, the message that to his nephew this was a special find.

"Why don't you put it on the truck, Ken? You can keep it if you want. You never can tell. You just might find other bike parts. You know you can buy used parts for little or nothing. Pretty soon you can have yourself a real nice bicycle."

"Really, Uncle? You don't mind?" Uncle Joe shook his head.

"But, this could bring you a pretty good penny. It's really okay if I keep it?"

Uncle nodded his head.

"I've never had a bike. I can get along all right without one."

Uncle shook his head.

"Sure, walking up the hill and 'cross town are good for your legs, but sometimes you want to get there faster. It's okay by me if you keep it."

Ken nodded his head.

"I only have a couple more years of school and then I'll be out of here. I can get along without a bike. Uncle, you can get a good price. It's a Schwinn!"

Uncle nodded, then shook his head.

"No, Son. It's for you. Go ahead and put it up in the truck. Yeah, right over there. Stand it straight and cushion it with this folded tarp, so it won't get bumped around too much by the rest of this junk. Yeah, that's right. Tie it to the side panel with that there rope." Ken tied it securely.

They climbed back into the cab of the truck and continued down the alley. "This is your special day, boy! You know a Schwinn's a real good riding machine. That frame'll fix up real nice and you'll be on your way."

And over the rest of that summer, slowly but surely, Ken collected bike parts and earned enough to fill in for what they didn't find. He's sure Uncle Joe paid him a little extra, but Ken did work hard to deserve it. By fall, with his step-father's help straightening the frame, spraying it with some of that new Rustoleum paint, and assembling the parts, he had himself a pretty good ride.

===

THEN, ONE EVENING, THREE YEARS LATER when Coach offered to help him get connected with college coaches, Ken was glad he was riding and not walking. He was eager to get home and tell his parents what the coach had told him.

Everyone in the family knew Ken's grades were good enough to get into a decent engineering program, and everyone also knew the family had nowhere near enough income to help pay for such a program. All, therefore, would be thrilled to learn that Coach Mac had noticed Ken and wanted to help him out – even though Ken hadn't gone to Coach's school. What a guy!

That long ago day, junior year, when he had come home from the gym he had set his bike against the shed just behind the trailer, then sat on the step to untie his shoes. His mom wouldn't let him inside with those dirty gym shoes no matter how much he claimed to have cleaned off every mud clod and shaken out every grain of sand. That was all fine and good, but no stinky gym shoes in her house.

In the summer, he would store his shoes in a wooden bin his step-father built just for outdoor footwear. In the winter they all put their boots in there. Whatever could be done outside gave them more room to navigate what was to have been their temporary living quarters for just a few months.

Unfortunately, with the layoffs, it had taken his parents longer than they'd expected to even get the basement finished so they could at least move down there and have more room. That also is a reason Ken knew he wouldn't ask them to help him with college. He still had another sister behind him who was just a seventh grader. He was nearly grown and had to pull his own weight to secure the luxury of a college education.

Proud of his achievements yes, but realistic about the likelihood of their being able to be of any financial assistance, his parents encouraged Ken to consider military service. His stepfather, a veteran, was using his VA benefits to help them finance their new house. He advised him to do his tour of duty, qualify for veteran's benefits, and afterwards go to college on the GI bill.

But he yearned to go to college right after graduation, so he'd been researching in the library to learn which colleges had the kind of engineering program he wanted. How shocked he was to learn how much it would cost to go to Penn State, his first choice college. Even with in-state residency discounts, he knew he'd never be able to earn enough in time to pay his way right after high school.

So, that summer afternoon, he did stop by and see Coach Mac about his offer. Maybe there could be another way of getting a college degree without being a burden to his family. Ken was willing to work, and maybe the combination of scholarship and campus job would be enough. Sitting there on the steps that day, Ken decided not to bring up the topic right away. He'd just wait until he had more solid information to go on. He didn't want to get his hopes up only to be dashed. Anyway, he had a whole year to go before graduating. Who knows what might turn up in that amount of time?

===

NOW, SIX YEARS LATER, here he is again, sitting on the steps of the mobile home, shaking dirt off his shoes. Getting up from the stoop, Ken unlocks the door and steps into the tiny trailer entryway that also is the kitchen, living room, and his bedroom. The dining area banquette converts into a single bed, and that's where he sleeps. He listens a moment to see if his sister or parents are moving around in their tiny spaces at the opposite end of their cramped quarters. No. Everything is quiet.

Everyone must be asleep. He hangs the blue windbreaker and his grey slacks over the same cardboard cylinder covered hanger and squeezes it into the tiny closet the family shares.

Tip-toeing, he slips into the bathroom to wash up before hitting the sack. Oh, if it were nearly as soft as a sack! He's in for another rough night. Even though he's been home all summer, he's not re-acclimated to this hard narrow bed. Four years in the service and a year at college have spoiled him. Oh well. Just another week and he'll be heading back to campus.

In the little lavatory, the shallow stainless steel sink is hardly deep enough to hold a water-filled washcloth, but Ken is careful. He quickly and quietly washes his face, brushes his teeth, rinses and wipes the sink dry, hangs up the cloth, and then tiptoes back into the kitchen, turns up the banquette top, pulls his bed covers from the storage bin below and makes up his skinny sleeping space. He'd forgotten how awfully tight it is in the trailer. Though a twenty-four footer, this is a vacation trailer, not designed for three adults to live in year round. With him home again, that makes four.

The whole family had expected to have the basement completed so they could move in before he returned from college this first year, but the money just didn't come in as quickly nor go as far as they'd expected.

Thia, his younger sister, just graduated from high school and wants to be an executive secretary. This means she'll be home another couple years doing course work. He feels sorry for Thia living so long this way.

She's always loved fashions – clothes and costume jewelry. She's longed for space and a place for her own things. But, her room at the end of the trailer is really just a single cushion on a shelf behind a curtain. All her personal things have to be stored in the drawers beneath her bunk. Ken is sharing the entry room closet for the summer. He can imagine how really frustrated she must be at how long it's taking for their new home. At the rate things are moving along, both she and he will be out of college before their folks finish building.

Their parents both are perfectionists, satisfied only with the best materials and the most skilled craftsmen. They'd rather wait than do something half-way. They don't mind looking for a bargain, which they view as a modest price for top quality merchandise and workmanship. His mother shops at fine stores, and they've contracted local Amish carpenters who are helping frame rooms in the basement and will return later to help with cabinetry upstairs. When asked why it's taking them so long, his parents just respond with confidence, "We're trusting God to help us get the house of our dreams."

So far, his mother has put fixtures into storage that she's bought at estate and year-end sales. Their shed is stacked to the roof. She's put things like the crystal chandelier for the dining room and the lamps for the living room into crush proof containers. She has even salvaged a white marble fireplace mantle from a house a builder was demolishing. That was quite a find. She will be ready to totally furnish it when they eventually finish the house.

Ken feels similarly about worth in terms of any woman he gets involved with. No, he doesn't think of women as things, but he does know he wants a quality woman for a wife. He won't settle for less than the best.

LYING ON HIS BACK, TALKING TO THE CEILING, Ken tries to convince himself, "But, I don't have the time to date now and I'm not about to rush into a relationship and take a chance on someone who won't last. When I marry, I'll be marrying for life." Even though his mother and stepfather have been married for nearly twenty years, they both had been divorced. "I don't want that to be my story."

He remembers what it was like when his mother and biological dad had split up. He doesn't want that for his kids, and he definitely plans to have a family of his own and be able to take care of them.

That's why he wants to get his college degree first. He doesn't want to be at the mercy of companies who lay off their unskilled workers every other year or so. His stepfather, fed up with that, spent over two years attending a trade school thirty miles away across the state line in Ohio.

Thank the Lord, his dad finally has a steadier income, and both parents are more optimistic now. His dad now has the potential to earn a better salary, but he still is low man on the totem pole and isn't bringing home that much more than before. The future looks brighter for them, but the future is not here yet, and they still are crammed into a vacation size trailer sitting next to a capped hole in the ground the size of their anticipated red brick ranch home with pure white mortar.

Ken wiggles on the dinette bench, aka bed, trying to get comfortable, and pulling his hands from behind his head, clasps them on his chest, and prays before going to sleep. There really isn't room to kneel down in the kitchen-living room-entry hall-bedroom where he sleeps. He knows God won't mind that he does his praying on his back.

God can see what things are like here – even in the dark. Ken smiles at that thought, thinking of his campers' humor. God can see in the dark. He loves them so much, He can't keep His eyes off of them. Ken had reminded them that God doesn't need light to see since He is a Spirit, not restricted to physical limitations. Not that it had kept them from pulling pranks and telling borderline jokes during lights out.

God also can see Ken's heart and that he is drawn to that Angela Jeanette he's met this evening. God also can read his mind and understands He's rationalizing that he is not ready for a relationship even with an attractive woman like her. He doesn't have time for this. Ken tries to push from his mind what he heard God say in the tabernacle when she sat down in front of him.

As distinctly as if He were sitting behind him and whispering in his ear, Ken clearly heard, "She's the one for you." After that, he could hardly concentrate on the service! Thankfully, he'd grown up with these songs and knew the lyrics by heart, so he could sing along without concentrating on the words. Instead, he was thinking what a good voice he had. Recalling the years he sang in a quartet and attracted the attention of screaming female fans. He hoped that good-looking lady there in the tabernacle could hear him. Shame, shame, shame.

Ken and some of his high school buddies used to croon and harmonize a cappella. "September Song" and "Blue Moon" had been their signature songs. They hadn't needed guitars and drums like a lot of the rock and roll groups out of Memphis or the rhythm and blues quartets out of Motown and Philly. Steve, their lead singer would just pitch a song, and the rest of them could hear their parts and come in right in tune. When they sang "Duke of Earl" the girls nearly fainted with delight.

It had been fun and economical singing at school dances when he was a teenager. He could go to them all without the bother or expense of a date. He'd always been somewhat shy. His older sister, Joann used to tease him about it and always tried to fix him up with girls in the neighborhood. Not anymore. She's married now and has a kid of her own. Still he does love her for thinking about him and wanting him to find a good woman.

He wonders if his Joann would like Angie. His sister's outgoing and a good judge of people. Maybe he can get them together before the camp meeting ends. "Wow," he tells the ceiling, "I'm getting ahead of myself! I haven't even asked Angie out on a date, and already I'm planning to introduce her to my sister.

"Hold it, buddy. Slow down. Remember, you don't want to get involved with anyone now. You've got three more years of college and no dough for dating anyway. Sure, God said this is the woman for you. Maybe even the one you will marry, but He didn't say next week. You've got time, old man. Take it easy. Time to get some sleep."

But he doesn't right away. Instead, he continues to share his thoughts with the kitchen ceiling light, "Anyway, I doubt Angie would be interested in anything more than the typical camp meeting fling. I've heard all about those from Lily and other youth camp counselors who've been coming to Zion's Hill since they were kids.

"Most of them just try to connect with someone for the week. Nothing serious--just somebody to be with, something to do, someone to walk around with on the grounds, have a snack at the food stands maybe sit next to in services, and share a Bible during the sermon. I can handle that. Nothing permanent. Just socializing for the week. Easy. No problem.

"Thank you, God, for being with me today, for the wonderful service and sermon, for the friends and fellowship…and for showing me the woman who is to be my wife. That's what you meant by 'She's the one for you.' Right? For me? Much, much later, right? Great… Amen." He rolls over on to his side, resettles his pillow, and tries again to find a comfortable position to sleep.

Monday

5 – An Early Start

"BONG, BONG, BONG, BONG, BONG!" the cool iron of the bell vibrates, sending deep tones rippling across the campground. Angie awakens to the bonging bell the campground manager rings every morning at 5 a.m. It's been the tradition from the early days when few folks had watches and fewer brought clocks with them to Zion's Hill. Back then, the old timers just pitched tents and cooked outdoors over fire pits. The first tabernacle was a simple tent, just like in the Old Testament. Of course, not as elaborate as that one, with its acacia wood, bronze, and gold.

Today, in the cabins, trailers, and cottages, and in the dormitory rooms, the Saints are slowly awakening to a new day. The Faithfuls soon will be heading towards the tabernacle for the early morning prayer service, as in the early days. The Brothers and Sisters of Love, as they were known when they first felt the call to establish an annual gathering of the colored Christians from the Midwest, always began the day together, praying for the place, the people, and the program.

Through fervent prayer, these faithful followers of Christ invited the Spirit of God to guard their tongues and guide their hands and feet. They wanted to be and to do all that God called them to be and to do, and to demonstrate through word and deed what they called The New Testament Church.

The founders of this denomination believed that God could infill the Saints with His Spirit and they, the blood washed ones, could be His witnesses at home, at school, as well as in the church buildings. The Faithfuls wanted these meetings on Zion Hill to be a fruitful time, a place for campers to respond to the urging of the Spirit and accept the call to be sons and daughters of God. For them, and for those who planned this 1963 gathering, the ultimate goal is the same: everyone will leave stronger, wiser, and more committed to living out the Word each day until they assemble the next year on these hallowed grounds.

HER GRANDPARENTS RISE QUIETLY. Angie can hear them through the blanket that hangs between her bed and theirs. They gather their soap, wash cloth and towels, shrug into their bathrobes and slip on their house shoes, gingerly open the door, and peek out the hall hoping not to see a line in front of the communal bathrooms at each end of the corridor – men to the left and women to the right. Apparently things look okay because they both tiptoe out of the room and close the door, thinking they are not awakening Angie. She lets them think so, and turns over on her narrow cot, hoping to catch a short nap before it's time for her to get up, do her own morning ablutions, and get ready to help with the children's ministry that meets in the building down the hill next to the playground.

Angie plans to become an educator and work in a secondary school but also finds working with the younger ones is fun. The children, aged five to twelve, meet with the children's ministry staff for two hours Monday through Friday for a vacation Bible school, with songs, lessons, crafts and snacks. For three years now, she has assisted in this program that presents practical applications from Biblical stories and corresponds with the annual camp meeting theme. Angie helps the littlest ones cut, paste, and glue pictures and to create mementos to remind them of the lessons and show their parents what they've learned.

She recalls the crafts she used to do. Macaroni collages, leather change purses, and those woven key chains that few kids ever got right – the skinny strips kept slipping loose! One year, they even tried making potholders with multicolored loops on those square metal frames. Today, as when she was their age, the kids either get a kick out of the artsy things or are frustrated to tears by them. Angie smiles as she gets up, prepares to get washed and dressed for the morning, and wonders what the stories and craft will be this year.

Today, Angie has breakfast in her room with her grandparents when they return from prayer meeting in the tabernacle. They have fresh fruit and pastry bought from the little store in town at the bottom of the hill, washed down by tea made in the little electric pot Grammama packed in her suitcase.

She cautions them to be extra careful to clean up the crumbs to discourage the critters likely to invade their sleeping quarters. Last year, Angie had dropped one of those packets of sugar. Apparently it popped opened, and a parade of ants met Angie one afternoon when she returned to get dressed for work. It had taken the rest of the week to rid the room of the raiders.

Now, having dressed and eaten, Angie gives her grandparents a hug and leaves. She walks down to the back stairway at the far end of the dormitory hall, and then the few yards to reach the playground where the eager early arrivals await. Inside the building, the leaders gather, confident the children can entertain themselves on the swings and slides for twenty minutes or so until the grownups finish getting set up for them.

Angie enters the small room that opens from the grassy knoll into the lower level of the three storied dormitory. The bottom floor is divided between this meeting room and the kitchen prep and store rooms under the second floor dining room. The third floor has sleeping rooms and communal bathrooms. Trapped closed-in-all year air greets her. Her nose twitches at the musty smell. Even though the director had already opened the windows that face the playground, there still is a dampness that makes Angie sneeze.

Arranged in rows are grey metal folding chairs facing a battered pulpit that has seen better days. Every year this furniture goes into storage and every year it comes out looking older and more warn, even though the maintenance crew lovingly try masking the scars on the wood with oily Lemon Pledge.

Colorful banners and Bible story posters brighten the space and Angie strolls around the room identifying each of them. Jesus feeding the five thousand. Jesus and the disciples on the Sea of Galilee. The widow preparing bread for Elijah. Moses in the bulrushes. Mary sitting at Jesus's feet and Martha glaring from the doorway of the work area. A lady cradling a stack of purple cloth talking to some bald old man. Hmmm. Oh, that must be Lydia, the woman from Philippi. Paul commended her for letting him stay at her house.

Angie stops and studies a poster of men pulling tiles from the roof of a flat topped building. Oh! Yes, that's always been one of her favorites. The one where the men lower their crippled friend down through the roof so he could be healed by Jesus. She has always wondered what made them think to remove the roof tiles, and couldn't imagine anyone going to that much trouble nowadays. In the rear of the room is set up for crafts; tables neatly stacked with art supplies, scissors and tape. On a side table are little tins of water colors, jars of water, and a Hills Brothers Coffee can bristling with fresh, supple paint brushes.

Footsteps of the other leaders draw her attention to the door. Fred, the director, beckons them all to join him at the front of the room for prayer and last minute instructions. Angie can see through the window that the children are gathering in clumps. Younger children and those coming for the first time stand anxiously with a parent or older sibling.

One pudgy little guy is wiping his eyes, and the woman with him pulls out a Kleenex and hands it to the boy. His shoulders tremble as he sniffles and sup-sups, unable to explain why he'd rather not be there. Then his mother stoops and whispers something in his ear, gives him a hug, and straightens up again. He wipes his eyes and nose with the tissue and looks up at her with a tearful smile. With a gentle hand on his shoulder, she directs him to the doorway.

Fred and his wife greet him there and, with smiles, invite the rest of the children to come in. If it were not for the adults blocking the way, the older kids would trample the younger ones. Children returnees seem as eager to be on Zion's Hill again as their parents.

The dress code for campground attire applies to children as well. Women are not allowed to wear slacks or shorts here; little girls aren't either. Girls arrive in lollipop tints and coordinated ice-cream colored skirts and blouses, some with print dresses that tie in the back. Most of the girls are crowned with ribboned plaits or ponytails held in place by matching barrettes clipped to the ends.

On this opening day, the boys still are neat in navy, tan, and dark green shorts topped with a range of solid or striped tee shirts. By the end of the week there will be little evidence of such careful dressing. But today, the girls and boys sit upright in their crisp, clean first day outfits.

Fred's wife Sharinda plays the piano and their teenage daughter Cherise will lead the singing. "Good morning, boys and girls. Welcome to Children's

Church!" she gushes with natural exuberance. "How many of you are here for the first time?" The little ones look around at each other and then, slowly about a dozen children raise their hands. "How many came last year for the first time?" Another nine or ten hands. "Oh, that's wonderful! We're so glad you've come back again. We think you'll all be glad you came!"

Angie looks to the left where the older rowdies sit slumped in their seats as though they'd really rather not be here, even though they nearly trampled the little ones through the door. Cherise continues her survey. "OK. What about the rest of you? Who's been here three years or more?" Not surprising, this is the largest group with nearly two dozen raised hands. "Well, you're the ones who probably know all the songs, and I'm depending on you to help us get started. How about, "I've Got the Joy, Joy, Joy Joy Down in My Heart?" They nod and grin, look around and stop. Can't look too enthusiastic about church; but they are.

Sharinda plays as joyfully as she can, doing her best to avoid the sticking keys in the lower register. Showing off, the older group sings with gusto, much louder than necessary, but they sing nonetheless. So begins another year of Children's Church on Zion's Hill.

After Fred leads them in the Lord's Prayer, one of the younger returning boys asks if they can do a motion song, "Deep and Wide". It's been a full year since some have sung and gestured to this perennial favorite, so they're a little rusty. Angie watches them bumble through the motions. One hand, palm down hand raised above the head, the other hand palm up held waist high. Then, hands waist high, perpendicular to the floor. And, as though playing arpeggios on the piano, fingers wiggling from left to right, they gesture the words,

> Deep and wide
> Deep and wide
> There's a fountain flowing
> Deep and wide.

What fond memories arise as Angie recalls her own times in Children's Church. She started coming when she was nine years old. Just as she and her peers put their whole bodies into singing songs with movements those ten years ago, so do the ones here this early Monday morning. They seem to be getting a charge out of seeing who remembers the most words and who flubs the fewest hand gestures. Not surprisingly, the older ones request the stand up, sit down song, "Hallelu, Hallelu, Hallelu, Hallelujah! Praise ye the Lord!"

Angie doubts the children have any more idea what they are singing about than she did at their age, but they do seem to enjoy singing just as much.

Inevitably the older boys become boisterous and one bumps over a chair while scrabbling to sing faster than Cherise directs. She gestures broadly, expecting them to mimic her movements so that alternating sides remain seated on the "Hallelu" when the other side stands up on "Praise ye the Lord!" It's a little raucous the first time through, but, thankfully no one gets hurt. There are no tears, and a great time is had by most. Next is a calmer song, "God is So Good" and then eager silence during the Bible story.

Devoted as she is to being a positive Christian witness for these youngsters, if someone could see inside her head, they'd know Angie's mind is not on the story being told by the youth pastor. Her mind is on Kenneth.

She hopes he'll come back to the grounds today and that they'll have time to continue their conversation. She'd like to know more about his plans for the future, and she'd love to know if what she feels for him is a passing emotion or something that will grow.

After clearing up the cups and crumbs from snack time, Angie tunes in to the announcements about the plans for Thursday, Children's Day. During that evening service, the Children's Choir usually sings two special songs that fit the theme of the year. It's amazing what the children's music leader can teach the youngsters to do in just four days.

Fred tells them that Sylvia Jenkins will be leading the Children's Choir. The regulars are excited. She'd worked with them last year. Sylvia is a talented musician and Marie, Sylvia's sister, probably will be playing the piano. Charles Smitherman, who accompanies both the adult and children's choirs works well these sisters. With the two skillful accompanists, Sylvia manages to keep the children's choir pretty much in tune and on beat. Few in the audience even notice that the musicians cover for the little singers botching a line, peeking around the director to wave at their parents, or skipping to the next verse when the director had gestured a circle to signal the kids to repeat the chorus. Angie remembers and smiles.

The children who'd been to previous camps will have reminded their parents to pack a white blouse or shirt to wear Thursday evening. The new ones somehow borrow the appropriate apparel from a friend, relative or they buy something from the dime store and will be ready on Thursday. While the director prefers that they all wear navy blue or black skirts or slacks, she will not keep a child out for wearing something different. Even the most devilish of the kids looks angelic up on the platform uniformly dressed in choir attire. Somehow, looking adorable in whatever they wear, songs they sing sound heavenly, too.

Before landing a job in the ice-cream stand, it had been a part of Angie's responsibility to meet with the children during rehearsal each afternoon and to help them line up for the service. Having sung their two songs, the children would march out and down to the lower auditorium where the leaders arranged to have popcorn and a film based on a Bible story. The kids remained there until their parents came by for them after the service.

This year, Angie learns, the new song is "Servant of All" based on Matthew 20:26. It clearly reinforces the camp meeting theme this year and the stories that teach the children how Jesus did useful, practical things to help people feel better – like providing food for the hungry masses, healing the sick, or calming the sea for the scared ones. He even cooked fish and served breakfast to his disciples. The overall goal each year is to teach the children to be like Jesus. This year, to be willing to serve.

Angie loves hearing Fred tell the Bible stories and watching the wide eyed children hesitant, but trying to comprehend the miracles of the Savior. The children probably believe the miracles are like bedtime fairy tales and television. If true, the incidents could have happened then and there, but not here and now. It would be years before some of these boys and girls recognize the myriad miracles manifested around them every day.

It certainly took Angie a long time. But about yesterday evening at church, she still wonders Who prompted her to sit in front of Ken and then arranged a meeting through a mutual friend? Who provided enough helpers so she would not be needed at Children's Church this year and therefore be free in the afternoons? Hmmm. Miracle? Maybe.

Anyway, she gives God thanks for them. She also is curious about what will happen as a result. Will Ken come back this evening? Will their friendship grow or just peter out like all the ones with guys met at previous camp meetings?

Once the children all have left, Angie heads back to her room to get ready to go work in the stand. She lays the outfit on her cot and grabs her toiletries. Morning service is in session now, so she probably will not have to wait to get to the shower, and she's delighted to discover that the water is almost hot again after the drain on the supply from the morning. Standing under the cleansing spray, Angie recalls an incident with one of her customers last night. She was an older lady who, from her comments, was a first timer attending with a friend who'd been coming to Zion's Hill for years.

===

ANGIE HEARS THEM CHATTING IN LINE about three customers back from the man waiting at the window. He comes all the time and always asks for two scoops of vanilla in a cup. She dips and serves him right away.

The new lady gushes, "This shore is nice. Y'all got a Conley ice cream stand and ever'thing. It's clean and neat. I don't buy nothing to eat from a place that ain't kept clean. Do they paint it ever' year?"

Her friend nods.

"I shore is glad it ain't too hot out here this evening. Them mosquitoes would be eatin' me alive. They ain't bothering you, is they?"

Her friend shakes her head.

By this time there is just one person ahead of them and when Angie is handing the lady a single dip of black cherry on a cone, Angie hears,

"You say they got the best ice cream around? I shore hope they got some of that Neopolee'tn ice cream. I shore love me some Neopolee'tn!"

Her friend gently replies, "Oh, Mother Milton, you can't get Neapolitan at an ice cream stand where they hand dip it for you. Neapolitan only comes in half-gallon boxes or in those little individually wrapped squares with strips of vanilla, chocolate and strawberry. Here you get scoops of a single flavor! It's absolutely delicious. I know you'll love it."

"They ain't got no Neopoleet'n! That's the only kinds I like. I thought you said they got any flavor I kin think of. I'm thinking Neopolee'tn!"

Mother Milton and her host now stand at the front of the line, both staring at Angie, both hoping they will get what has been promised. Angie looks at the younger lady and nods her head ever so slightly indicating, I'll take care of this for you.

"Good evening, ladies. Welcome to our ice cream stand. How can I serve you?"

Mother Milton looks at her friend and back at Angie, and moans. "Y'all ain't got none of that Neopolee'tn so I don't know what I'm gonna do. I was really wantin' some good cream tonight."

"Not a problem, Ma'am. I can put a little of each flavor in a cup and you'll be all set."

"Can you get'em in those little stripes like they got at the Winn-Dixie down home?

"I doubt I can make them even, but the taste will be so scrumptious you won't mind, I'm sure. Will that do?"

"Well. I don't know. I really like them stripes. I eat them one at time. That's the way I always does it. What you think, Mary Ella? You believe it gonna taste all right if they ain't in stripes?"

85

"Mother Milton, let's try it this evening. It'll be something special just to have some this famous Conley ice cream. You know I'm paying. It's my treat."

"Your treat? I was gonna treat you for bringin' me up here this year. I been hearin' 'bout Zion's Hill all my life. This is the first time one of y'all offered to bring me."

By this time, the two ladies next in line were showing signs of impatience, so Angie offers,

"Mother Milton. Since this is your first time up here, let me treat you with my special cup of three flavors of your choice. Am I correct that you like chocolate, vanilla and strawberry, in that order?"

"You'll do that for me?"

Angie nods her head.

"You shore is a sweetheart. Yes. I believe I'll try me some of that since you gonna give it to me. You gonna give a cup to Mary Ella, too. She brung me up here you know?"

"Yes, Ma'am. I'll give her a dip of her favorite maple walnut. She's a regular and I look forward to serving her every year." The ladies in back smile in concert when Angie quickly dips the flavors and hands them to Mother Milton and Mary Ella.

Before closing the stand, Angie leaves the quarters for the two complimentary servings in the cash drawer since it was her choice, not Stella's, to give away ice cream. It was worth it, though, to see the pleasure on Mother Milton's face as she relished the creamy smoothness and rich flavors of the premium ice. And also the pleasure of the next two customers whose patience had worn just about as thin as a butterfly wing.

===

ACROSS TOWN, KEN HAD HAD A PRETTY GOOD MONDAY. He'd ridden his old bike up to work in the vegetable garden and then stopped by Gram's to help her pull weeds from her flower garden. His widowed paternal grandmother prepared him a hearty lunch of fried bologna on Wonder Bread, one of his favorites as a teenager. She added Wise Potato Chips and Faygo Red Pop, too. He'd eliminated chips and soda pop from his pre-season diet, but he wouldn't dare hurt her feelings and refuse them. And, both still quite a tasty treat.

He'd not slept well Sunday night and had been weary when he got back home, but having spent the afternoon chilling in the chaise lounge and studying out in the side yard under the only tree big enough for shade, he felt ready for whatever happened when his dad returned from his errands today. Relaxed, Ken didn't get ticked off when, asking to use to car to go up to the campgrounds, his dad cautioned him for the six hundredth time,

"Now, you be careful up there in those gravel parking lots. Don't be driving fast and kicking up dust and flicking up stones. Yeah, I can wash off the dust, but I don't want no dings in the paint. You hear me?"

Thinking, I'm a grown man, raised in this house and I know how you take care of your things...aloud, he courteously agrees, "Yeah, sure Dad. I'll be careful".

=== ===

Ken jiggles the keys and heads for the car. When he opens the door, heat spews from the smoldering interior. By habit, his dad always rolls up the windows even if the car is parked in the yard. It's like a furnace in there! Ken decides to stand outside a couple minutes to let the trapped heat escape before he gets in and starts to sweat. He'd already freshened up and changed for the evening.

Ken admits to himself he is anxious to get back up Zion's Hill. That hadn't been the case when he was a teenager. He'd always known about the camp meeting because of the increased traffic in town. After all, the meetings have been held consistently for nearly half a century, but his family didn't belong to that denomination when he was young. Even later, they hadn't gone regularly even when they joined the congregation that helped host the annual gatherings.

That wasn't the case for many of the other camp staff he'd met this year. Lily, his co-camp counselor, said her family had been coming every year since her grandparents got married. In fact, they met on Zion's Hill. They both were related to the original Brothers and Sisters of Love who'd started the annual gathering of colored Midwestern Christians, many of whom had migrated to Michigan, Missouri, New York, Ohio and Pennsylvania during the Northern Migration in the twenties and thirties. Lily claims her grandparents were the original Sweethearts of Zion's Hill. Over the years, dozens of couples have qualified as Sweethearts of Zion's Hill, including Albert and Christine Taylor, the missionary couple who are to be the Women's Day special guests for this year.

===

A COUPLE OF WEEKS AGO, SITTING AROUND after one of their camp counselor's meetings, Lily had told them about how her widowed grandmother would hyperbolize, "I'll die if I don't get up to Zion's Hill this year!" Lily had told them...

"None of my aunts and uncles wanted Gramma to come last year, but she insisted. Her grown children didn't have the heart to say "No" when, despite her failing health, Gramma always begged them to take her just one more year." The team of counselors leaned in attentively. Pensive, many thought about the relations they had with their own grandparents as Lily shared her story.

"Somehow, just planning to come to Zion's Hill perked Gramma up. Osteoporosis had her nearly bent to the waist. She couldn't walk very far and struggled even to breathe. Like every year, my mom and her siblings threatened to make that year the last year they'd drive her to her cottage on the grounds. It was just too rustic and isolated for her to be there in her condition. But, somehow, just mentioning not going made Gramma stand taller. She'd get up and walk more purposefully and plead her case.

"Of course, during those entreaties, to hide how tired or out of breath she really was Gramma would sit down in her favorite leather chair by the window, not saying anything. She'd close her eyes to make it look like she was thinking about her and Grampa. We all knew it was to rest. We also knew she'd start reminiscing about the early years, try to sing some of the old songs, and inevitably would reach for camp meeting program booklets that she kept in the wicker basket next to her reclining chair. We listened as her words painted pictures of our favorite stories, some of which we'd shared with her and Grampa up here in their cottage."

"Really," Charles asked. Your family has your own cottage? Do you all stay there?"

"Yeah. Grampa bought it not long after they got married. It's that little one just across from the parking lot by the tabernacle. It's small. But we manage."

"Wow! That's convenient. You staying there this year, too?"

"Uh, huh. Gramma's been coming to Zion's Hill every year for nearly thirty years, including this past August. For the past five years, since Grampa died, one of our cousins has shared the cottage with her. Last year, even when Cousin Betty did promise to come again, none of us thought Gramma was strong enough for the trip. But she insisted. The family gave in. Last year, as they had in the past, my parents hired someone to open and clean the cottage. Gramma and Cousin Betty still liked to come up early to get groceries, to unpack their luggage, and be ready to sit on the porch to watch the rest of the campers arrive.

"Last year, though". Lily gulps and pulls tissue from her pocket. "Just three days after they got up here, our cousin called my parents. I answered the phone and heard the alarm in her voice. 'Yore Gramma. She don't look so good.'

"Mom and Dad didn't wait for more details. They had me call my aunt, Cecelia, in Kentucky. She's the one with medical training; she drove nearly non-stop to get there. Up at the cottage, Cousin Betty knew things looked bad, but was not sure what to do, so she just sat with Gramma, prayed for her, and waited for relief to come.

"When Aunt Cecilia arrived, Gramma sat crouched in her chair, struggling to breathe, so Auntie bundled her into the car and sped to the nearest hospital. Thankfully it's one of the best in the Valley, staffed with doctors from the university. Within an hour, though, Gramma suffered a mild stroke. Her vital organs started to fail. Before I'd hung up the phone, my parents were packed. They jumped in Dad's car and left right away.

"Auntie called the rest of the family to come as quickly as we could. My mom told me to drive across the town to bring my Aunt Vonita. Her husband took off work and drove us back over here. We joined Mama, Daddy, and Auntie in the hospital room. Cousin Betty was too upset to join us until later."

The young counselors held their breaths as Lily talked, gasping for air themselves as they followed the story of the family gathering at their matriarch's bedside. They thought, too, about their own aging grandparents.

"When we got to the hospital, Gramma's dark brown hands and toes were turning dark blue. I touched her foot. It was icy cold. We saw she was dying inch by inch." Lily looks around at her fellow counselors' shaking their heads. Seeing the doubt in their eyes, she nods that she's telling the truth. They concede and nod for her to continue.

"Mama had called her only brother, who was down in Fort Lauderdale on a business trip and told him to get back fast. That's a thousand mile trip! Sensing the urgency, he'd canceled his meeting and left at once. Thankfully, his wife was with him this trip and shared the nearly non-stop drive here. Unfortunately it started raining so hard, they couldn't see and had to stop until the rain let up. It was too dangerous to drive and they were too tired to be driving in the pouring rain, so they took a hotel room for a couple of hours for a short rest.

"While awaiting Uncle's arrival we tried to keep Gramma alert. The hospital staff's shaking heads and somber conversations, however, didn't give us much hope. Still we sang Gramma's favorite songs of the faith and prayed the prayers of the faithful. We just wanted her to stay alive until my uncle got there.

"Cousin Betty knowing the camp meeting was starting the next day, called the ministers who already had begun pre-camp prayer meetings. We knew the Saints would pray for Gramma and felt a little less anxious; even when Gramma kept drifting off into unconsciousness."

Suddenly, Lily perked up and smiled. She rushed on, watching the riveted eyes of her fellow counselors.

"Gramma rallied. She couldn't sit up, but she did speak up. 'I wanna go home,'" she said weakly.

"We jumped up and crowded around her bed wondering if we'd really heard her say something. Everybody looked at everybody else. Our eyes agreed. Gramma wasn't strong enough to survive the trip. So we just smiled and nodded and sat back down. I wondered who would tell her how really sick she was.

"Praise the Lord, everybody! Gramma in a spurt of energy, exclaimed, 'I want some hot tea. Can one of you get me a cup a orange pekoe tea? I want lots of honey and a slice of lemon? I don't want none a that store brand tea. Gimme some of that Twinings kind.'" Lily looked at their dubious shaking heads and nodded to their unasked question.

"Of course she got it. The nurses, who'd been so professional, were also solicitous. One of them found china cups and some colorful napkins and brought them in on one of the trolleys. She even added a flower in a bud vase. Yes, indeed! We had an impromptu tea party for Gramma with Twinings orange pekoe tea and lots of honey! She didn't notice the missing slice of lemon."

"You kidding us," Josie challenged with what all of the counselors were thinking. "Your grandmother had a stroke, was already turning blue and y'all had a tea party for her? That's hard to believe."

"Yes. It was a miracle to be sure. Just then, Uncle breathlessly burst into the room. His wife trotted behind him. He looked around with what can only be described as 'askance'. He clearly doubted our word. He and his wife had driven nearly non-stop till night fell, rain poured and was unsafe to continue only to arrive to see his mother sitting up drinking tea and talking like nothing was the matter. But, seeing her sitting up and chatting with us, he was both livid and relieved.

"You know, I'm not sure to this day that he believes that Gramma had one toe into Jordan's chilly river. In our mind's eye, those of us with her that first evening saw the death's door open for her and it was only the power of our songs and prayers that closed it."

Ken picked up on the mixed metaphor but said nothing. This was an oral narrative of a real story not a college essay. As he listened with the same incredulity, he also was thinking of Gram and Mom Bessie. His own grandparents who lived nearby. He'd been visiting them regularly during this summer at home. But could this happen to one of them while he was away at college? Would he be the one called home to their bedsides?

His fellow counselors with similar imaginings and anxieties just sat silently considering what they'd do in a similar situation. Eager to hear what happened next, their stillness quietly encouraged Lily to continue.

"I doubt the doctor was misled by Gramma's revival. But knowing she really wanted to go home, he told us they probably could use medication to balance her systems and get her numbers down to a safer level. He warned us, though, that her days were numbered. Thanks to the prayers of the Saints and the skill of the doctors, in two days Gramma did stabilize.

"My parents arranged with an ambulance company to transport her the three hundred miles back home. While being gurneyed from the ambulance, she reached out to my uncle, tugging his arm so he looked into her eyes. She just murmured, 'I'm tired. I'm ready to go home.' This time we all knew she meant her heavenly home. Our family caravanned behind the ambulance praying that Gramma would survive the trip.

"Did she?" asked Josie with her hand gently on Lily's shoulder.

"Yes. She did and that evening in the hospital room, once the nurses got her settled, we gathered again at her bedside. Cranked up in her hospital bed, as the nurse was leaving, Gramma asked her if we could use the phone to make long distance calls. The nurse advised us to just dial nine and then the number. She also cautioned that the long distance fees would be billed to the room. Dad nodded okay. Anything for his beloved mother-in-law.

"Gramma, the baby girl in her family, wanted to speak to her three brothers and older sister. They range in age from eighty-to ninety years old. She also asked us to call my cousins who were not there with us at the hospital. Next, she instructed us to find the numbers of a couple of her dear longtime friends. Thankfully, with the phone book in Gramma's handbag, among the six of us in the hospital room, we located numbers for most everyone Gramma wanted to talk to."

Josie interjected, "She was strong enough to talk to everybody? It's a wonder they all were at home at the same time."

"Yeah. That was amazing. Miracle number two. One of her younger brothers kept assuring her that he and his congregation were praying for her healing. Gramma begged him not to be angry with her, but to please stop praying. Eventually he wept and told her she could go if that's what she really wanted to do. Gramma nodded and smiled."

"I bet that was some phone bill!" Ken remarked.

"You'd win, Ken. But that expense was worth it. Gramma got to say her goodbyes."

"Wow. What happened next?" Charles queried.

"Well, after the phone calls, we relaxed. Auntie pulled out the letter Gramma had written ten years ago. Auntie's a nurse and she thinks of official stuff like this. It was the statement that Gramma didn't want any heroic medical intervention should her health decline.

"A little while later, Uncle asked Gramma if that still was her wish. Gramma nodded and replied firmly, 'Yes, I'm ready to go home'. Looking around at all of us there in the room, Aunt Vonita asked Gramma if she'd be willing to initial that letter so we could add the current date. Gramma said, 'Yes.' The nurse was still in the room, so she left to send in the doctor on duty to witness the signing.

"The doctor came in right away. He asked Gramma the same questions and she gave the same answers. She signed and they asked me, as the oldest granddaughter present to co-sign. Aunt Ceci handed the doctor the newly signed letter. He looked at it, nodded, then left and sent the nurse back in.

"She removed all the tubes and monitors, called in orderlies who efficiently transferred Gramma to a stretcher, wheeled her out, and led us all up to a quiet, private room on a higher floor of the hospital. What a parade we made. Little did we know we were marching Gramma off to Zion…for real this time."

Though it seemed a little out of place to those listening, Lily tittered a bit, then continued. "Gramma was always a little vain. So none of us was the least bit surprised when settled in the new room, she commanded, 'Comb my hair and let me go!' My mom looked at me, indicating this would be my honor. 'Be sure to comb it smooth. I want to look good for my Jesus.' Gramma, ever the boss, gave orders to the very last. And we obeyed.

"Once ready, Gramma lay there like a queen, giving us instructions for her funeral, making sure we knew what songs she wanted sung, the specific outfit she wanted to be wearing, and even what color casket she wanted to be laid out in! She wanted her yellow Easter hat on her head and her mother's rose-gold watch pinned to her suit. We did it all, of course."

Brother Ralph interjected. "Didn't anybody call her pastor? That's protocol at our church."

"Yes sir, we did. In fact, just as Gramma got to the part about who she wanted to read the Scripture, Reverend Stokeley got there. He read some of her favorite Bible verses, prayed with us, and then assured her that she wouldn't die that day. He waved goodbye. Gramma smiled at him and called after him to have the choir director ready to lead "We Have a Hope".

"She fluttered a wave and lay back quietly, eyes closed. All ready to meet her Maker. About midnight, Gramma opened her eyes, looked around and exclaimed with astonishment, 'I thought I'd be gone by now!' She wasn't."

The whole group of counselors released a laugh, but beckoned Lily to go on.

"Gramma humphed and decided she must not be ready. So she asked my mom and Aunt Ceci to help her sit up on the side of the bed. Gramma had begun to perspire enough to dampen her gown and bedclothes. She wanted clean everything. We found a fresh gown, my aunts gently washed Gramma and dressed her while my cousin and I changed the bedclothes. We got Gramma re-settled.

"Then, sitting silently, circled around her bed, we waited, satisfied that all that could be done had been done. No singing this time. We'd also given up praying to keep her against her will.

"Within an hour, Gramma made her transition and slipped over into eternity. With acceptance and joy, our family witnessing her peaceful passing, we just murmured almost in unison, 'Praise the Lord. She's gone home.'"

BY THIS TIME, THE COUNSELORS SAT with their heads bowed in reverent response to the testimony. They were torn between feeling sad for Lily at the loss of her beloved Gramma and rejoicing that God had taken her surrounded by her family, just the way she wanted to go. Miracle number three.

However, when they looked up and saw the beatific look on Lily's face, sitting in peaceful resignation, having just recounted the death bed experience, they instinctively reached out and held hands. No one said anything for a full minute, and then quietly Brother Ralph prayed a short prayer for Lily and her relatives who probably would be a little sad this first year back on Zion's Hill without the matron of their family.

===

Thinking of time spent that afternoon with Gram, his own widowed grandmother, gave Ken pause. He wishes he'd taken the time to ride by and see his mother's parents, Mom Bessie and Bubba. It could be the last time.

Tuesday

6 - Ken and Angie

KEN DIDN'T come up to the grounds until late Tuesday afternoon. He'd worked early in the garden, and then returned home to study because the library was closed. Thankfully, he had the place to himself because his mother was out with her Bible study group praying for the Wednesday Women's Day service.

While in the Air Force, Ken had enrolled in correspondence courses to keep his academic skills sharp. He didn't want to lose his edge from high school during his tour of military duty, and though the correspondence classes weren't hard, they reminded him how much there is out there to learn. Still, the first year at Penn State had been more challenging than he thought it would be even after those tech classes in the Air Force. So, he'd been using the summer to preview for organic chemistry.

Basketball at college takes so many hours a week – what with time in the gym, practicing, traveling and playing all over the Midwest and Southeast. He has made the varsity team for the coming year, and he hopes to be a starter. That means getting into shape both physically and academically.

He also knows how much mental time and emotional energy it takes for both. That's another reason he doesn't want to get involved with women at this time. They can wait. Well, will Angie wait? He likes what he's learned about her so far. Maybe he can learn something more about her family, too, this afternoon. She probably will hit it off with his sister, Thia, who is about the same age. Ken even considers inviting Angie to come along when the youth counselors and their guests, not dates - not on a date - go bowling Sunday night.

THAT AFTERNOON, KEN AND ANGIE FIND A BENCH TO SIT alone, but not far from the hullabaloo of children playing on the nearby swing set. They've already talked about the service Monday and his studying this morning, and who and what she saw from the ice cream stand.

"Ken, you got a middle name?"

"Yeah. It's Holley."

"Holly, like at Christmas?"

"No, H-o-l-l-E-y. I'm named for my great, great uncle. He was in the Ninth Calvary."

"Ninth Calvary? What's that?"

"The Ninth Calvary were Buffalo soldiers, an all Negro Army unit. My uncle was one of the first park rangers in the Sierra Nevada Mountains. You know, after the Civil War lots of former slaves continued to serve in the military. Uncle Holley never married. We're not really sure where he is buried. Anyway, there's a male child in each generation named Holley. I'm the oldest male cousin, so I am named after him. You know, to carry on his name since he died before he had a son of his own."

"Well. That's a nice tradition. To keep a name going in the family for that many years. Not many colored families can go that far back, can they?"

"Not many that I know about."

"We have a different tradition in our family. My father's mother, a Cherokee, was Angel Grace, but they named me Angela. I'm here with my mother's mother. Her name is Jeanette. That's my middle name. Jeanette. It's a tradition in the family to name the first grandchildren after the grandparents."

"So are you the first granddaughter on both sides of your family?"

"No, just on my father's side. That's the same with my brother. He's the third. You know, because my dad is named Isaac after his dad, so he's a junior, and my brother's Isaac, the Third! Huh? Sorry. I'm babbling. Not giving you time to talk, am I?"

"No. That's okay. You're really proud of your family, aren't you?"

"Yeah, I guess I am," she replies, rising when he does, and accompanies him up the gentle incline opposite the tabernacle and over to the food concession to get a snack. Carrying their cups of colas and a cone of French fries to share, they meander back down to a table near the playground. Though out in the open, it's really more private.

The playground swings are set up on a low sloped knoll, just across the dirt road leading from the parking lots near the bottom of the hill, up to the rows of cottages further on the hill, before the road curves around the tabernacle, and back around and down the hill. Other roads swivel even further up to the small one-room tin cabins perching on the scrubby hillsides.

Between a row of food stands and the tabernacle, is a grassy expanse with green slat-back benches. Folks congregate between services. In the day time scads of seniors sit with their grandchildren chasing each other around and behind their benches. It's quite a physical challenge for older people on Zion's Hill to climb the steep hills back to their cottages between the various meetings held in the tabernacle. Consequently, a goodly number come down for the morning service, attend Bible study classes, and then go have lunch in the dining room before returning to their various sleeping quarters for an afternoon nap. At night, this flat grassy space is where younger folks mingle to see and be seen.

The seasonal cottages, trailers, and dormitories surrounding the tabernacle often are Spartan... with only the basics, furnished with twin beds or cots, a toilet area with a face bowl for washing up, and often, protruding from the walls, round head nails or hooks to hang up clothes. Suitcases are just shoved under the beds. Some places may have a card table and a pair of folding chairs, but few of these temporary domiciles are large enough for comfortable seating, nor open enough for fresh breezes on those hot and humid August days.

Occasionally a family may fit out their kitchen with a two burner hot plate and something to keep food cold. It is seldom anything more than a picnic cooler with ice bought daily to store milk and juice, a pound of grapes, a few peaches or plums or to chill bologna for sandwiches.

Every once in a while, in the packed dirt yard or concrete pad porch, one will see a cast iron Hibachi or a small charcoal grill for hot dogs, hamburgers or chicken. However, that kind of cooking takes more time than most folks want to spend during the short week on the grounds. Thus, the booming business at the food concession stands where throngs line up for quick meals prepared by someone else. That's also why Angie usually has a line waiting outside the window of the nearby ice cream stand where customers mosey after eating their fill of fast food.

Cozy groups of benches invite small groups to sit and reminisce about years gone by, to discuss the music and sermon from a recent service or gossip about those who attended it. Adjacent to this grassy space and across the dirt road from the row of small fast food vendors is the square eight by eight feet ice cream stand where Angie will return to work later this afternoon.

FOR NOW, SHE ENJOYS SITTING DOWN THE HILL, away from the oily fumes from French fries and fish sandwiches, the pungent smoke of grilling hamburgers, and the cloying smell of nearly full trash cans. They're spaced strategically for folks to throw away greasy waxed paper from sandwiches, ketchuppy napkins, greasy conical cups from the fries, and other leftovers of soggy bread crusts from sandwiches, and the soft bottoms of ice cream cones.

She still is incredulous that Ken sought her out this afternoon. He'd come up yesterday and now he's back again. They've talked nearly non-stop since starting to share their light snack.

Angie has learned that his summer job in the steel mill lasted only for June and July and that's the reason he was free to work at youth camp the first part of August. Brother Ralph, the director, called when last minute sign-ups exceeded the camper to counselor ratio required by the state camp licensing bureau. And being camp counselor did help Ken fill the days before returning to college for his sophomore year. It added to his small cache of savings, too.

The athletes have to report back the last week in August, which means Ken has been free this interim week. She'd wondered, because he seems to be a conscientious man, physically fit, and smart enough to be doing something besides hanging out on the campgrounds. Not that Angie minds. He's really good company and handsome to be seen with, too.

KEN AND ANGIE SIT COMFORTABLY, basking in the gentle winds whispering through the tall grasses in the uncut fields just beyond the playground, and watching the frilly Queen Anne's lace bow gracefully to each passing breeze. What a delight to see this field adjacent to the camp grounds has not been shaved and trimmed, but left in its natural state. Angie pops another grape into her mouth, savoring the firmness and the sweetness.

"How thoughtful of you Ken. These make a lovely dessert. I've had enough ice cream to last for an eon, and it's only Tuesday."

"No problem. My neighbor sells them at a stand on the road in front of his house. I know they're fresh."

Between sampling the grapes himself, he tells her about the small mobile home in which his family lives. Without a job this week, the challenge is nearly more than he can abide. Once everyone gets up and moving around, the cramped space becomes a cauldron for short tempers.

"Just one more week", he says, "before heading back to State College. I usually go to the library in the afternoons, but today the library is closed. To get out of the trailer, this week, I've been going up to my uncle's farm to work in the family garden."

"It must be really hot out there this time a year. I'm a city girl, but know that's got to be a scorcher of a job"

"Yeah, it is. But, it's a relief to Mom. I go pull weeds, hoe the rows to keep the soil loose, and then pick whatever's ripe and bring it home. She's canning the green beans and tomatoes to supplement groceries over the winter. She makes pickles sometimes, too. You ever heard of chow-chow? She makes that, too."

"Chow-Chow? What's that?"

"I'm not sure what all's in it, but it tastes like relish with lots of chopped vegetables, sort of sweet and sour at the same time."

"Sounds yummy. Do you put the chow-chow on hamburgers?"

"Oh, no. We eat it with cooked greens – you know, mainly collards and kale. I prefer them to turnip and mustards. We have all four kinds up in the garden and the rest of the family eats all of them. Growing up we were

103

expected to eat whatever was set before us, but since I got out of the Air Force, my parents no longer insist. So...no turnip or mustard greens for me!" he exclaims.

"Does your mother can greens, too?"

"Yeah, sometimes. Does yours?"

"No. Mine doesn't do much with vegetables, but she does can jams and jellies. That's about it. Oh, if somebody brings by fresh fruit, she may can a few jars of say, peaches and applesauce...but not vegetables."

"No vegetables at all. Not even for soup?"

"No. My mother had bad luck with vegetables spoiling...you know, getting all black and gushy, oozing out of the lid. That put her off from trying vegetables anymore."

And so the conversation continues in casual chit-chat. Sitting so close to the playground, she finds herself casually monitoring some of the boys and girls from the children's program.

Sarah Anne, a rambunctious nine-year old can't resist pumping her swing so high the chains look about to snap. She digs her blue Keds into the crusty ruts under the swing, leans first forward, pushes hard, shoves off, then curls backward, throws her head back, stretches her skinny brown legs board-straight, and swoops up into the air, singing her heart out. "Yes, Jesus loves me. Yes, Jesus loves me. Yes, Jesus loves me for the Bible tells me so!" Her ebullience thrills the soul, but nearly stops the heart.

Not surprisingly, Ken's glance drifts to the nearby court where the young guys try shooting basketballs into the orange hoops. Both activities remind Angie and Ken of their time that age.

As they talk about those experiences, Ken disciplines himself, resisting the temptation to go give the guys a lesson on how to hold the ball and where to aim it so it sinks more often through the frayed nets. He's quite content, sitting and sharing grapes with Angie. All too soon, though, it's time for her to get back to work, and they prepare for the hike back up the hill to the ice cream stand.

"What're you going to be doing while I'm working? You heading back down to your place until time for service?"

"Not today. I'm meeting some of the guys from youth camp. We're going to shoot hoops over at the high school."

"Wish I could come. I'd love to see you play. Lily says you're pretty good."

"I do OK. I like it. It keeps me in shape during the summer and gives me something to do and keeps me out of that trailer. You can imagine what it's like with four adults living in that hot tin can."

"You all been living in the trailer since you were in high school? That's a long time."

"Yeah, but I've been away for almost five years – in the Air Force, you know, and now a year at college. It won't be much longer for them though. My folks got the basement poured earlier this summer. They capped it right away so they could start working on the plumbing and heating. My mom wants to have a kitchen, bathroom and a couple of bedrooms down there so they can move in and get out of that trailer. My stepdad even plans to put in a brick fireplace. Everyone's getting a little impatient, though, and our tempers ignite more quickly now."

Ken clams up, a little embarrassed. While what he's shared is true, he doesn't want to sound as if he doesn't appreciate having a place to stay during the summer, a place that doesn't require a financial outlay. He's a grown-up now, and at his age, his parents could be asking him to pay rent.

Angie and Ken gather up the cups, napkins and paper bag and walk over to put their trash in the nearby wire mesh receptacle. He presses the lid down tight. Here, at the edge of the campgrounds, critters come out at night. No use taking the time to throw away trash only to have raccoons scatters it all over the place. Angie leads the way back up the hill, resuming their conversation.

"I can't imagine living that tight with my family. There were six of us and we'd be at each other's throats on a regular basis."

"Yeah, I know. I know what you mean. But my folks've been planning this home for a long time. It's their dream house and they refuse to take short cuts or accept second best. That's one of the reasons I went to the service right out of high school. Since the steel mills have been closing around here, jobs are scarce and inconsistent. My step-dad kept getting laid off, so he decided to go back to school and learn a trade."

"Really? That's cool. What'd he study?"

"Oh, he's always liked working with his hands, you know, on motors and fixing things. He's a welder now and doing fine, but he's new there, not making top salary yet. In the meantime, they wait. They've got my younger sister starting her first year of business classes this fall, so I'm glad I got that basketball scholarship, even if it doesn't cover all my expenses. That's why I came back here and put up with the tight quarters. I've been working twelve hour shifts and trying to save it all for school. It's not all that bad at home. Just tight."

By this time, they've reached the ice cream stand. They say their *a tout a l'heures* knowing they'll see each other later.

BOTH WONDER WHERE THIS RELATIONSHIP IS GOING. They have similar family backgrounds and similar academic goals...both are committed to completing their college education before doing anything else, they both have to work to pay college expense, and they're both Christians. But, they also live in different states: Michigan and Pennsylvania.

===

"YES, MAY I HELP YOU?" Angie calls to the pair next in line who are so busy talking they don't realize the man ahead of them has paid and gone. "What would you ladies like this afternoon?"

"Ah, darlin', I'll take two scoops of that black cherry. I just love me some black cherry, don't you, Lucille?" the first lady says to her friend, without looking at the sign listing the flavors and prices. "We don't have this gourmet flavor at home in Harlem, and I get it every time I come up here to Zion's

Hill. What you want?" She flutters her hand and rushes on. "I'm buying today. My treat."

"You don't have to do that, Hattie," her friend replies reaching inside the scooped neckline of her loose flowing dress. "I got my money right here." Leaning on the wooden ledge of the pass through window, the portly lady huffs, exhausted from the effort of extracting that leather change purse from between her breasts. She leans towards Angie, "Do y'all have cups? I want mines in a cup."

"Yes, ma'am, we have cups. What flavor ice cream do you want?"

"Well, since Hattie is having black cherry, maybe I'll have me some of that, too. Just to taste, you know. But I really like plain vanilla. Hey, Hattie, you think that kind taste good with vanilla?" Turning to Angie, "What's your name, sweetie?"

"My name's Angie," she replies as patiently as she can with six eager customers in line behind this duo. "My name's Angie and I'd be happy to give you a scoop of each if that's what you want. That's one plain vanilla and one black cherry in a cup, right?'

"Hattie, what you think? Think I oughta just stick with the plain vanilla? I know I like that."

"Well," Angie says in hopes of moving things along, "while you're making up your mind, I'll get the ice cream for your friend, here. Miss Hattie, you want that in a cup or on a cone?"

"What kinda cones you got this year? Last year you had two kinds – that flat bottom cone and that pointy bottom cone. What kind you got this year?

"Both."

"They the same price? I'm on a budget and can't afford no extra for special cones if I'm gonna be buying for the two of us."

"Now Hattie, I told you. I'm buying my own. I got my money right here." Lucille holds up her bulging change purse.

"Ladies…." Angie calls out. The folks in line peer around looking at Angie, signaling her to get the line moving. "Ladies."

Even Christians run out of patience some time, she mumbles. Even Christians on Zion's Hill.

"OK," Lucille concedes, slipping her change purse back down inside her bra. "You buy today, but it's my treat next time." Turning to Angie, "All right, since she's buying, I'll have me one scoop a black cherry and one a plain vanilla in a cup."

"I'll have two scoops of black cherry on one of them pointy bottom cones since you say they don't cost no more. Give us a couple extra napkins, too. We gotta keep ourselves nice for service tonight. Right, Miss Hattie?"

Chattering and daintily slurping their specialty flavor and plain vanilla ice cream, the two leave as the nearly exasperated next customer steps up to the window.

And so begins the afternoon shift for Angie. For the next three hours, she dips the cream, collects the money, and daydreams about Ken, who's off playing ball with the guys.

KEN SELDOM WEARS A HAT, even in the bright noon sun, but he does put on a sweat band when he plays basketball. On the way back down the hill to his car, he checks his pocket for the blue and white Penn State band he thought he'd put there when he left the house this morning.

"Good, I got it," he says aloud, then ponders silently. He's got a couple hours to shoot hoops and then plans to return home to clean up and have a bite to eat before coming back up here to the campgrounds. "Thia has to work tonight, but she better not hog the bathroom and use up all the hot water."

Ken opens the car door and trapped heat smacks him in the face. He swings the door open wide and stands outside a couple of minutes before getting into the metal sauna on wheels. He leans with one hand on the top of the car, then jerks it away, checks for blisters, sees none, and ruminates about the afternoon with Angie.

She sure liked those grapes. Doesn't take much to please her, does it? That's a good thing. he doesn't need to be getting himself involved with some princess expecting to be treated royally right now. "Can't do it. Don't want to do it. I don't mind spending something on the ladies, but I don't want to have to lay out big bucks all the time just to have a good time with one of 'em." Checking the time, Ken realizes he'd better get a move on, then looks around and sighs, glad there's no one nearby listening to him talk to himself.

He slips into the seat and starts the engine, leaning forward to keep his back off the sizzling vinyl upholstery. He uses just his fingertips on the still hot steering wheel. In seconds, the wind whooshes through, cooling the inside enough to settle back. He now grips the wheel and maneuvers down the unpaved road of the campground and out onto the oiled one down the hill.

"Why am I even thinking about all this? From what I heard from the other counselors, nothing comes of these dalliances anyway. You meet someone, spend the week getting to know each other, exchange addresses, write a couple of times, things taper off, and you go on with your life.

"That's fine with me. I've got three to four more years before even thinking about getting married. Married???" He stomps on the brakes, nearly skidding off the road. "Where'd that come from?" He nearly careens into the mail truck stopped at a roadside mailbox. Ken regains control, steers around the truck, mouths an apology to the startled driver, and continues to the gym, trying to pay more attention to the winding road leading into town than to his thoughts of Angie.

"Yeah," Ken rationalizes aloud, "but I remember what I heard in my head Sunday night when Angie sat down in front of me. Something about 'She's the one for you.' Hah! Maybe God didn't mean she'd be my wife. I'm not even thinking about getting married. Still, if I were, Angie'd be on my short list.

Ken turns onto the main street and enters the flow of traffic, cruising slowly behind the eighteen wheeler signaling a turn at the only stop light on this end of town. Ken decides to go that way, too, and take that road over to the high school.

Once Ken makes the left and revs up to speed, his thoughts resume. She has plans for the future, too. She already told Ken she doesn't plan to even date seriously any time soon. Well, that's fine with him.

She seems comfortable with her relationship with God and doesn't mind talking about it. That's a good thing, too. When he does decide to get married, that's a quality he'll be looking for. A nice looking, confident woman, who's a Christian. Like Angie, but not now. No, not now. It's too soon. Way too soon.

In another three minutes or so, Ken reaches the high school and pulls into the parking lot nearest the side door. On really hot afternoons, Coach Mac opens the gym for college athletes in town for the summer to come practice. It's one of several places the variety of ethnic groups that settled the Shenango Valley meet and play as equals. He believes iron sharpens iron so he makes it possible for top players from the Valley to play against each other. Nice how he calls all of them his guys whether they're from his school or not. Ken gets out, grabs his gym bag and locks the car. Taking a deep breath, he strides through the door nearest the gym.

In the boys' bathroom, he changes from his slacks and loafers into shorts and sneakers and carries his folded clothes and lays on them on the bleachers. Coach opens the gym, but not the locker room.

"Hey, Ken. What's up, man? You ready to get blown out the gym?" challenges Scott, running the ball down the court, dribbling a couple of crossovers to show-off his skill. He slams the ball into Ken's chest, signaling that he's ready to get it on. Ken catches the ball, controls the bouncing down the court and swishes in his first attempt at a basket. He's ready to get his mind on to the game and off of Angie.

Back and forth, up and down, left and right, non-stop for nearly an hour, the ball players dribble and pass, shoot, block and stuff the ball, first at one end of the court, then the other. Seldom a miss and seldom a foul. There's no one to call fouls anyway. Sweat-drenched bodies raise the gym temperature nearly as high as the outdoor temperature. Still, they play on, each player keen to show his stuff, to prove he's playing a higher level of ball than those pickup games at the neighborhood parks.

These are the starters from top collegiate teams across the Midwest and as well as from Southern Negro colleges. They've honed their skills in the Valley of Champions here in Western Pennsylvania. It's all in fun, though. These guys have been playing against one another since their junior high days. Now playing in Coach's gym brings back the old days and brings out the new skills.

"This is great!" Ken calls out jubilantly. He remembers how torqued he'd been when his parents decided to buy their own property across the school district line. He'd grown up planning to play for Coach. Ken seldom spends much time thinking about the past, but occasionally, the thoughts creep up on him and he indulges himself in a moment of melancholy. But now the game is moving too fast for more than a nanosecond of negative thought.

"Hey, dude!" huffs Junior, lunging to snatch the ball from Ken. "What'cha trying to do? You forget you playing against the state finalists?"

"Yeah," Ken dredges a deep breath and slings back, "but that's because I've graduated. We beat you guys bad when I played for Hillside High!" Ken snags the ball, pounds down the court and hits it from midcourt. Smacking high fives with his teammate, Bob, the two sprint back down the court to guard their team's basket.

"Still got the legs. Still got the moves. Still can lay it on," Bob grins as they set up to defend their territory.

"You got it, man. And it sure feels good to be out here." Ken gets set in defense stance, knees bent, arms up, ready to pounce and protect, grabs the ball and runs back down for another attempt at scoring.

All too soon, however, he notices the time and signals the guys that he has to go. They nod and he leaves the court stating the obvious. "I'm really funky now and thirsty as all get out."

Since the guys didn't have access to the shower room, Ken grabs the shoes and folded clothes he'd left on the bench, and heads out to the drinking fountain out in the hall before going out to the car.

"Yuck!" The water is just wet; tepid and not at all refreshing. Still, Ken drinks deeply, knowing he has to rehydrate after all that sweating. He pauses a few seconds, takes a couple of deep breaths, and strolls out to the car, pleased with the game he'd just played. Then his thoughts project forward. Three years of college to go or not, he's going to see where this relationship with Angie is going to go…tonight.

===

KEN WILL BE TICKED IF THIA'S STILL IN THE LITTLE TOILET and there's no more hot water, so she aborts her showering and goes to dress in her parents' room. They have a bigger mirror in there anyway. That's important because Melvin's coming to drive her up to work, and she wants to look her best for him and for the job.

Yesterday, at dinner, Ken told her about Angie, and this raises Thia's curiosity. In high school, Ken had been so focused on his basketball and now the same in college that he's not dated much. Other than a couple times to the movies, he's mostly been working and studying all summer.

That engineering program at Penn State is particularly demanding, especially for someone playing varsity basketball. He'd explained when she'd complained about his non-existent social life. "Coach keeps up with our grades, and if any of us get into academic jeopardy, Coach'll red shirt us. If I get benched, I could lose my scholarship. No point in risking that if a little boning up during the summer can prevent it."

So, most evenings this summer, when he gets off early, Ken eats with the family and then heads off to the library riding his old bike. Dad is particular about anyone using his car every day. This week, without much hassle, though, he's letting Ken drive it for camp meeting. Dad's even been carpooling to work. Ken and Thia, however, had better make sure the gas tank is full Sunday night. You borrow something, you return it like you got it.

"Thia, you want me to drive you? Looks like Melvin's not coming. I can swing by and drop you off on the way back up the hill," Ken invites, reaching for the door handle, and looking down at the one step leading from the trailer into the yard where he's parked the car. It's a little cooler now, and Ken doesn't expect the car to be the sauna it was this afternoon. He's fresh now and wants to stay that way.

After years in the Air Force wearing uniforms most of the time, and not wasting money on civilian clothes, Ken has a limited wardrobe. Tonight he's wearing pressed navy slacks and a light grey golf shirt…just a plain one from Sears without one of those alligators or polo players. He's got a muscular physique and his clothes look good on him, but he's not really a clothes horse like the women in his family, all into name brands and the latest fashions. That's fine for them, but he's not willing to spend hard earned cash or hard to come by time to shop for bargains on clothes. The females, though, seem to love it. They like shopping and get a kick out of catching stuff on sale.

Thia bragged at dinner how much she'd saved on the outfit she's going to be wearing Sunday. That's one of the things that bothers Ken about camp meeting…so much emphasis on outward appearance. Few of the women wear gaudy earrings and necklaces, but they sure go in for flashy brooches, flamboyant hats, and fancy dresses.

The men are little better. He remembers the couple of times he'd gone in earlier years that Sunday seemed to be a fashion show with much more strutting and preening than one would expect on the Lord's Day. "But maybe I'm just jealous." He concedes that and vows to waste no more time on the sartorial splendor of the guys on the campgrounds.

"Thiaaaaa. Last call or I'm leaving!" Angie probably will be late for service, but he wants to be there at the back of the tabernacle when she arrives so they can sit together again. He's not sure why he's so eager to do that. Once the service begins, they both seemed to focus on the singing and the preaching.

It would feel good walking in with her, sitting next to her, hearing her joyful singing, and sensing her attention when the preacher speaks. It's just good being with someone who enjoys so many of the same things important to Ken.

Thia prances out the door, tipping carefully to avoid scraping her heels in the gravel walkway. "Well, aren't you going to open the car door for me? I know I'm just your sister, but this will give you good practice for when you go out with Angie," Thia teases playfully when she finally joins him next to the car.

"Sure," Ken says, opening the door and bowing to his sister. He chuckles, closes the door, and walks around to get in and get going. Thia's taking Melvin's absence in stride. That's unusual.

Ken backs in a Y turn and steers out of the yard onto the private drive in front of their family homestead. So far there is just one other house on the road. The Coopers, friends of his parents, bought their corner lot at the same time Ken's folks bought theirs. The Coopers, though, already have their basement in, the first floor framed and roofed. At this pace, they'll probably move in by Christmas. Ken wonders how Thia feels about living in a trailer for so long and maybe in a basement until she gets her secretarial certificate. No point asking. He can't do anything about it anyway.

He hangs a right up the half block to the main street and turns left onto the main road. They only have a short drive to the department store where she works, and being Tuesday, the traffic's not too bad.

"Thia, why in the world are you wearing those high heels? You could walk to work if you'd wear your Converse or flat shoes," he teases knowing she'd never wear either kind of shoes when she considers herself dressed up.

"Hey Ken," Thia probes, ignoring his questioning her fashion sense. "What's so special about this Angie? I thought you'd sworn off girls until you graduate. You haven't talked this much about one since high school when you dated Jackie for a couple of months."

For the remainder of the trip, Ken tries to articulate for himself and to his younger sister what's so special about Angie. "I'll introduce you when you and Melvin go up to Zion's Hill on Thursday."

That will be Thia's first time back on the grounds since she was a camper in junior high school. Once she got into high school, she no longer could stand the griminess of camp, and camp culottes and T-shirts just don't make the grade for Thia. With her weird work schedule last year, she hadn't come even on the weekend. Her sales job in Wilson's Better Dresses has turned out to be a thrill and a waste. Once in the car, their conversation continues.

"Oh, Thia. Better roll up that window."

"Sure. Gotta keep my hair nice until I get to the back room. I gotta get to work early to change. It's my evening to work in the stock room. Gotta unpack, label and hang up the new fall line of dresses for our sale this weekend."

"I thought you're a sales clerk in the Better Dresses department. Mom says your boss was pretty impressed when you interviewed and has already promoted you. You must a been looking pretty sharp."

"I am. She was. She did and I did. But we have a small staff. We all have to do everything."

"Isn't that dirty work back there?"

"Yeah, it is. But, working in the stock room is okay. I get to see the latest fashions as soon as they come in."

"Well, I know you love that! So how'd you get promoted so fast? She must have been keeping an eye on you."

"You're right. After a week or so she asked me why I spend my breaks wandering around in other departments."

"Well, why do you? You should be putting your feet up and sipping a cool drink"

"Oh no, Ken. I gotta keep up with the latest shoes, gloves and hats."

"So, your boss thought you were looking to get a job in another department?"

"Maybe at first. But, she doesn't mind any more. You see, lots more return customers are starting to ask for me. Especially when they're shopping for a special occasion. Once we find a dress they like, I walk them down right down to find shoes, hats, and gloves, suggesting the right colors and styles to round out their ensembles. I'm even getting to know what costume jewelry to recommend."

"Aw come on, Thia. You're just a teenager! Where'd you learn all that?"

"Trailing behind Mom and Joan. All those weekends we spent walking around the stores downtown and at the new shopping center. You know Joan skips lunch just to check out the sales. Then, when the markdowns hit bottom, Joan asks the clerk to hold the items till she gets paid on the weekend."

"That's too much work for me. I don't have that kind of time to waste. When I need something, I go to the store, see it, and buy it."

"Well. Of course! You're a man. And you have no fashion sense."

"Cut it out. I look pretty good in my clothes. Angie seems to like me."

"That's only because you're a tall athlete in good shape. Anything looks good on a jock."

"Thanks, Sis. That's make me feel better, for sure. So, you're doing pretty well there. Dad'll be glad."

"Well, I do earn commission on all I sell, but it's not really helping much! With the sales and my employee discount, the bargains are too good to pass up. I'm not saving enough for books this fall. Dad's gonna be mad."

Thia jabbers on about what she'll wear Thursday night, but Ken's mind jumps forward to the time he'll spend with Angie.

Wednesday

7 - Women's Day and Basketball

"A SERVANT OF ALL" IS THE THEME FOR CAMP MEETING 1963. That mission message blazons across the posters hanging all around the campground. Colorful posters display photos of missionaries the church has serving on six continents.

This year, over half the posters are of Albert and Christine Taylor, the special missionary guests for Women's Day. Albert is a dynamic speaker who plays piano and organ with equal virtuosity. He and his wife, Christine are home on furlough from their assignment in the Virgin Islands. And, the church ladies have been all aflutter ever since the letters went out that their very own Taylors would be at the campground this year.

In honor of Women's Day, most of the women wear white. It's a tradition. But for these church ladies, dressing in white does not mean wearing a utilitarian nurse's uniform. The saintly ladies will be adorned in shades of white, from the cool Chantilly of whipped cream to the warm creams of Pet milk fresh from the can.

AT BREAKFAST, KEN'S MOTHER WHEEDLES him into driving her and two ladies from her prayer group up to the campgrounds for the special afternoon service. She assures him he will have study time before he begins his shuttle run. In fact, she advised that on his way from the library he could swing by downtown to pick up the oldest of the three, Sister Geneva Grimsby.

He parks as near to her house as he can and emerges from the car with his politeness suit neatly in place, ready to escort her to the car. Sister Grimby's sitting on the porch fanning with one of those paper fans churches get from the funeral homes. She's probably been dressed for an hour and has set herself out here to catch a breeze and say a few prayers for the services as she awaits her ride.

119

"Praise the Lord, Ken," she puffs. "Aren't you just the gennelmen to come get me? Let me step into the house to get my handbag and Bible."

He nods. "How're you doing Sister Grimsby? Mother said you'd be ready and waiting."

She grabs the ample arms of the maple captain's chair she keeps on the porch, pulls herself up and grunts, "Yes, Praise the Lord, I tries my best to be ready when somebody's thoughtful enough to come drive me some place. You can wait right here a minute." Surreptitiously, seeing he's looking the other way, she tugs down her girdle. To distract him, she exclaims, "Isn't a beautiful day!"

Rocking from side to side on her arthritic knees, she walks across the porch and reaches for the handle on the screen door, stops, out of breath from that five foot trip, then opens the door and steps inside. "I sure hope there's gonna to be a little cooler up there on the grounds. It certainly been hot down here," she calls back to him. He nods.

"What a blessing to be able to be up and about this Lord's Day. You know the Bible says, 'This is the day that the Lord has made, Let us rejoice and be glad in it' and I'm certainly glad to be going up to Zion's Hill to praise the Lord with the Saints. I'm looking forward to seeing those precious Taylors. They're just the sweetest young couple. I just love that Albert and Christine and pray for them each and ev'ry day."

By now, she is backing out the door, holding the screen door open with her hip and pulling the wooden door closed to lock it. She looks over her shoulder at Ken, "I shore am glad you driving us today. My grandson is just so trifling. First he promise. Then he call and say he can't take time off to drive his grandmamma up to hear them Taylors from down in the islands. He knowed how much I wanted to go. Well, praise the Lord, you come to take me. Here, son," she asks, holding out her purse, "would you take this handbag a minute whilst I lock this here door?"

Ken reaches out, nearly missing the handle of the handbag heavy enough to be holding a week's worth of groceries. He lets the bag drop down the length of the leather strap when she hands him her worn leather Bible with the curling corners. Sister Grimsby wiggles the door handle, humphs to herself, satisfied the door locks, then adjusting the angle of her flop-brim white straw hat, turns to retrieve her belongings from Ken. "Bless your heart, Ken. You really is a gennelman," she acknowledges while pushing her purse handle up above her wrist and settling her Bible in the crook of her left arm.

Ken offers his right elbow so she can hold on with one hand and grasp the sturdy wooden banister with the other. Clumping in her sensible white tie up shoes, leaning heavily onto Ken, they walk down the short sidewalk and over to the back passenger side of the car. When Ken opens the door, and stands chauffeur-like, she coquettishly folds and holds tight to the full skirt of her button up white dress and pulls her thick legs into the car. Within seven minutes of his arrival, they are settled in the car and on the way to pick up Sister Pearlie Mae Green who lives just around the corner.

In contrast, Sister Grimsby, this second lady is a thin, skittery, woman. "Are you here already?" she questions when she opens her door and sees Ken standing there. "I'll be out directly. I gotta make sure I turn off the oven. You know, we won't be getting back here 'til close to suppertime, and I want to be sure my supper's ready for when Mister gets home from work," she explains before opening the door wide enough for Ken to walk in.

Once opened, she holds onto the knob with one hand and swings the other out towards the nearby stiff, square sofa. "Take a sit right there, Ken. I'll be right with you." She swirls around and scrambles down the dim corridor to the kitchen at the back of the tiny apartment. "It's so hot out there today I'll wager you could do with a glass of something cold to drink. I got some lemonade here in my new Kelvinator. I can get you some if you want a drink."

"No thank you, Sister Green. You know I got Sister Grimsby sweltering out there in the car. Do you think you'll be long? I have to stop back home to get my mother. She's on the program today reading the Scripture lesson. You know she hates to be late."

"Yessiree-bob. That shore is right. Sister Jackson always after me about holding her up and making her late. I'll be right there." Ken hears her opening and closing cabinet doors and rattling silverware drawers. "I'm just gonna set a place for my Mister in case we late getting back. You know how you men

121

folks is about your food. When y'all hungry, y'all want to eat right then and there. Just gimme a moment. Be right there, directly."

Ken resists the temptation to yell, "Then why don't you come on!" and stands tapping his foot and praying for patience. He hears her heels clacking down the hardwood hall but not returning to the living room. "What can she still be doing? She knows we're running behind."

"Say, Ken. You see my Bible out there on the table? I'm shore I left it there this morning when I was doing my morning Bible reading. God shore know how to speak through His Word when I'm doing my devotions." More shuffling and bumping from the back room. "I'm coming. I gotta hang up this housecoat I had on while I was cooking. Had ta to keep my dress nice."

"Yes, ma'am. Your Bible is right here." He picks it up ready to hand it to her when she comes out.

"O.K. Good." he hears from the bathroom opposite the bedroom. "Let me just rinch off my hands and put some lotion on. You know my hands get so dry from the soap I use washing them dishes. I'll be right there."

It's another five minutes before she hustles out the bedroom door and down the hall, adjusting her stiff-brimmed hat, pulling down the jacket to her suit, and banging her purse against the wall. She's dressed all in white, of course.

"Well?" she says standing at the open front door as though he's the one who's been keeping her waiting. "Let's go. Don't want Sister Grimsby to melt out there in that car."

"No, we can't have that, can we?" Ken mocks. But he does remember to offer her his arm as they approach the car and settles her in back next to Sister Grimsby. He slides into the front seat and turns down his mental hearing aid, not wanting to hear their chatter or lose his last inch of patience, either.

He drives as fast as he can without the older ladies noticing his speed. Yes, he's an adult now, but they still see him as a teenager, and neither will hesitate to tell him to slow down. It's only a five minute drive back across the town line and down the road to his home. He signals, turns carefully and drives slowly on the dirt driveway to the trailer. "Thank the Lord. Mother's at the door ready to go," he sighs.

"Honey Chile, that suit is really you," Sister Green gushes when Ken's mothers stops a few feet from the car, giving the others time to admire her white outfit with its modest neckline and fancy buttoned top. The slender skirt falls midway between her knees and ankles and flares with just a flounce, drawing attention to the spectator pumps she's chosen to ground this particular custard cream white. To top it off, she sports a cloche hat adorned with a trio of seven inch feathers fluttering in the breeze. Of course, she has cream-colored gloves, and a purse that matches the darker beige heels and toes shoes.

"You get that one on sale?" Sister Grimsby isn't really interested but knows Sister Jackson likes to share her shopping stories. Ken assists her into the front seat and walks back around to the driver's side. There's no point in turning on the radio because they'll just tell him to turn it down so they can hear themselves talk. Though it's only a few miles to drive, it will feel like an hour rather than fifteen minutes to make it there.

Well, it turns out to be more like twenty minutes before he can let them out just steps from the front entrance of the tabernacle. Arriving in droves are flocks of women, aquiver with expectation, clattering along, not paying attention to cars easing up the road, drivers scanning the grounds, looking for places to park.

Parading from all directions, the sisters walk, one at a time, in pairs, in triads, adorned in dresses, skirts and blouses and in suits all in shades of white, cream, and ivory. Most wear hats, many wear gloves. The elderly twin sisters, wearing matching short waist white boucle suits and Jacqueline Kennedy pill box hats, will be ushered to seats in the center of the sanctuary. All the ladies glide regally into the tabernacle to celebrate the servants of the Lord – a prince and princess – a royal pair of their own.

ALBERT AND CHRISTINE MET HERE ON ZION'S HILL when they were in their early teens. Most of the ladies who've been coming for years watched the relationship bud, blossom, and grow. They observed the two

123

youngsters timidly meeting, cautiously dating, then enthusiastically courting, and all were delighted when the pair announced their engagement right here on the campgrounds just ten years ago. Albert and Christine now have joined the number of the Sweethearts of Zion's Hill who met on the campgrounds and later married. The missionary ladies vicariously experienced the joy of their college graduations and glow with pride whenever Albert blesses their hearts with his music.

Naturally, when five years ago, the couple announced the call to serve the Lord as missionaries to African brothers and sisters on the Virgin Island of St. Thomas, the missionary societies from around the country lined up to support them. It is not often that colored preachers go across the waters as missionaries. And to have a couple the ladies all know and love to represent them in this way. Why, the saintly ladies had to pray to be delivered from pride.

Today is the first time the Taylors have been back in the States during camp meeting week and the first time many of the sisters have seen them in all that time. So, they're dressed extra special today, not just in the traditional white for Women's Day, but their best white, in thanksgiving for God's protection for these, their own missionaries come home.

LISTENING TO THE SISTERS CHATTER as Ken inches the car up to the drop off place, Ken feels the need to pray for deliverance from jealousy. The Taylors are great servants in God's kingdom, but aren't they doing what they all've been taught to do? Serve the Lord where He plants you. So what if they've been planted in the mission field? How is that so different from spending two weeks with high octane teens in the throes of hormonal adolescence? That's a mission, too.

Ken's mother keeps checking her watch and looking over at him. She intended to arrive early enough to join in prayer with the rest of the ladies who'll be seated on the rostrum this afternoon. She loves God's Word and counts it a privilege to read it so in this extraordinary service. "We're nearly there, Mother. I'm trying to get you as close as possible so you won't get your shoes all messed up walking across the gravel or grass."

"Thanks, Ken, I appreciate that. What about here? Turn here and drive around to the side door. That'll get me closer to the room where we're meeting."

"Sure. If that's what you want." Ken concedes as he pushes down the turn signal just a little too hard. He turns up one of the side roads that skirts around behind the dormitory and passes by the little cottages with the scrappy green yards. He takes a chance and pulls into the parking area set aside for the campground officers, and stops.

"Hold on, ladies. I'll open the doors for you." He shifts into park and hops out in chauffeur mode, scurries around to the other front door and assists his mother first. She heads right into the tabernacle, hurrying to the prayer room.

Sisters Grimsby and Green are in no such a rush, but are pleased as punch to be arriving early. It'll be a luxury to get a good seat near the front. They each exit the car grandly and accept the elbows Ken offers them. Both lift their chins, straighten their aging shoulders, adjust their handbags and smooth down their skirts before walking up to the door of the tabernacle. The usher on duty there signals that he will see them to their seats so Ken can move the car before the campground security sees him. Thank the Lord! Ken leaves. Released. Relieved.

He drives around the road that takes him between the food concession stands perched on the low ridge at the left and the ice cream stand on the right. He slows down in hopes of catching a glimpse of Angie, but there is a line of cars behind him and the one closest is near enough to tap his bumper. Ken accelerates to increase the distance between them knowing if anything happens to his Dad's car, he'll have no transportation the remainder of the week. He does want to see Angie again…today. It'll have to be Thursday, though.

Maybe not. Ken sees an open spot right near the gate in the parking lot and decides to take it. Maybe Stella will give Angie a short break while the Women's Day service is going on. He could pass the time with her until time to drive his mom and her friends back home.

===

WHAT AM I GONNA WEAR TONIGHT? Angie worries and watches the clock, eager for the signal from Stella that she can leave for a couple hours. She's running out of outfits she really wants to wear. This is not supposed to be an issue this year. A small scholarship hasn't been enough to pay her college expenses. Tuition, books, and lab fees eat up the money that other working women have to spend on clothes. Angie's only bought two new outfits this year and she'd already worn one of them, that yellow outfit Sunday, the night she met Ken. She certainly hadn't planned on spending this much time with one special guy or worrying about clothes.

She scrunches her stomach muscles, leaning over the edge of the cooler to scrape one last scoop of chocolate from the container in the back. They only carry eight flavors; the maricopa is already gone, and she's got just enough chocolate for one more scoop. Good thing they're closing up the stand in a couple of minutes. Angie carefully rounds the ice cream into a smooth ball and presses it firmly on the flat bottom waffle cone for the little boy wiggling next to his older brother. Their family is staying in that big cottage right up the road.

It's one of the more attractive ones on the grounds. Stella told her the siblings and their spouses pooled their resources and finished off their cottage with amenities as nice as one would find in a first class hotel. It now has a wraparound porch with six green lawn chairs that match the green shutters and the trim around the large fancy door on their white sprawling ranch style house. The stained glass in the door has their family initials.

Most of the cottages on the campgrounds sit on cinder blocks and have no porch at all and just have cement slab or a couple more of the cinder blocks sitting in the dirt outside the door. Few of the places have been painted in recent years and some having withstood buffeting winters for decades look too flimsy to stand up in another puff of wind. Those unkempt cottages, though, are further up the hill and less visible from the ice cream stand.

Those nearer to the tabernacle are better kept. On one little side lane parallel to the back side of the tabernacle, the owners have planted tiny lawns, put in a few shrubs, and one even set out pots of bright geraniums

Even though the small boy lives close enough to change if he spills ice cream, Angie still is careful to set the scoop of chocolate squarely on the cone.

Handing the boy an extra napkin, just in case, she looks up and sees Lily walking across the grounds. She must have finished her stint in the dining room.

"Hey, Ange! Looks like I'm your last customer for a while. Got a moment?

"Yeah, sure, Lil. Let me finish and I'll be right with you." She dries her arms and hands on the damp cloth used to wipe the freezer edges.

"I haven't seen much of you this week."

"Yeah, I know, Lil," she responds, wrinkling her nose at the bleach odor.

"How's it been going for you?"

"It's been real busy over here. I guess it's been pretty much the same for you over at the dining hall."

"You're right. This afternoon we were hustling trying to get the folks all served in time for them to get a good seat to hear the Taylors. I'd like to go, but I know it's crowded in there. Anyway, I need a break. Wanna get a cold drink and sit out here and catch up?" Lil says spotting a nearby bench.

"Stella. Okay if I leave now?"

"Sure, why not? But, let's tidy up a bit first."

Angie swipes a damp cloth across the ledge countertop, pulls down the wooden door to close the serving window, rinses the ice cream scoops in hot Clorox water, then drops them in plain water, twists the edges of the trash bag together, and heads out the back door.

"Will you take that round back?" Stella calls.

"Sure, I'll take it. See you about four thirty? Right?"

Stella nods, and remains to take care of refilling both the cone dispensers and bringing in extra ice cream from the big deep freezer she shares with the Liz, who runs the hamburger stand. The Conley Family ice cream is famous in the Valley, and people all over the country look forward to having some when they come to Zion's Hill, so Stella keeps well stocked.

Here on Zion's Hill, Stella is doing a brisk business for the Conley's. Apparently, the family is pleased not only with the volume of Stella's sales but also with the spillover clients who show up at the ice cream parlor in town. Instead of competing, the stand on Zion's Hill has helped spread the word about the quality products their family makes and sells. Still, Stella will retain the retail contract only as long as the Conleys are satisfied with the appearance and cleanliness of the premises.

On really hot afternoons, the stand always sells lots of the basic flavors – chocolate, strawberry and vanilla. But this year, they've been doing well with the new blue bubble gum, too. Things should be all right tonight; however this early afternoon's crowd sure has been bigger than the previous days. It's the Taylors today and tomorrow, folks will start arriving for the final weekend. It'll be teeming after Thursday service too, with grown-ups treating the singers in the kids' choir. Better bring over more napkins, too.

Making sure the lid on the trash can fits snugly, pounding once more with the flat of her hand, Angie signals Lily and they stroll across the road to get a cold drink. When they return to a bench beneath a mature shade tree on the lawn between the tabernacle and the ice cream stand, they can hear the service, drink their Cokes, and relax.

"Well," Lily begins. "I've seen you in evening service with Ken and sitting down by the basketball court with him, too. Didn't I tell you you'd like each other?"

"Yeah, you did. Ken's a good talker and listens well, too."

Lily smiles, but says nothing.

"I don't mean he brags about his accomplishments or anything like that."

"I didn't think so. He certainly wasn't like that at camp. It was the locals who kept telling him that it's a poor dog that don't wag his own tail. Ken didn't though. All that I told you Sunday came out over the two weeks from Brother Ralph and a couple of the campers who live around here."

"I can imagine. It seems he's quite a hero here in the Valley. What about you, Lily? I been seeing you around with that Charles guy you introduced me to Sunday night. You just meet him at camp this year?"

"Yeah. He's a first timer, too like Ken. We get along alright, but I don't think it's going anywhere. What about you and Ken?"

"I don't really know." Angie smiles shyly, thinking more carefully about Lily's query. "I can relax with him. You know. He gives me space."

"Space? What does that mean?"

"Um. I'm not really sure. I guess...it's because he doesn't crowd me."

"You mean, physically?"

"No. Not just that. It's true Ken doesn't push himself physically into my space. He talks, but not always about himself all the time like some guys. Maybe he doesn't like me enough to care if I think he's cool or not."

Lily sips her drink and nods. Angie keeps trying to explain.

"We talk, but I don't feel like I gotta be putting on airs for him," Angie acknowledges.

Lily's smile invites Angie to keep talking.

"I can be myself, whatever that means. Still, I do spend a lot of time thinking about what he thinks about me."

"Well, what you gonna wear tonight?" Lily asks knowing that Angie is sometimes self-conscious about her attire.

"Oh, I don't know? What about you?"

"I'll decide when I get back to the room. I'm heading up soon to take a short nap. I just wanted to see you a moment and get the skinny. What do you have in mind for this evening?'

"What about if I just wear a different top with that skirt I wore Sunday night? Ken doesn't seem like one of those guys who pay that much attention to what women are wearing, though. That's all me, I think. There's something comfortable about being with him, but I can't depend on that. Competition's coming this weekend!"

"You're right about that girl-friend. I wish I didn't worry so much about clothes either, but that's what it's like on Zion's Hill. And you know when the weekend folks get here, there'll be a fashion parade of all the latest styles!"

"Hmmm," Angie still on her wardrobe choices proposes. "I've got a really nice scarf I could use with that tan two-piece I wore last night."

"Don't think I saw that."

"Or, what about that suit jacket from Monday? It will look okay with the dress I wore Sunday morning before I even met Ken. Then I can save that other new outfit for the weekend. I hope that hat I made won't look too amateurish. Only two new outfits and a homemade hat. I'm lost!"

"You'll be okay, Ang. Now me, I wish I had time to do something with my hair. I didn't bring a straightening comb or hot curlers"

"Why? What you need them for?"

"Look at my hair! I thought it would be cooler being the cashier. But, I've been sweating like a pig in that dining room! See, my edges and kitchen are getting all nappy."

"Aw, Lily. You can wear a hat Sunday and no one will even notice!"

"I could, but I didn't bring one this year....Hey, Ang. Look who's coming?"

===

KEN HAS TAKEN THAT OPEN SPOT RIGHT NEAR THE GATE in the parking. He stopped to say "Hey" to guys playing basketball before heading up the hill. Now, as he rounds the corner of the dorm, he spots Angie sitting up on the bench with Lily. He's only a few feet away when Lily sees him and stands up to leave. No offense, Ken thinks, but I'm glad I'll have a little time alone with Angie this afternoon since I won't be back this evening.

"Hey, Ken. I was just leaving, but Angie will be here a little while" Lily informs Ken as she heads over to her folks' cottage.

"Hi, yourself. Well, Lily, since you're heading off, I'll just sit here if it's okay with Angie," he says to Lily, but looking at Angie for her approval to join her there.

"Yeah, it's fine with Angie. She's been waiting for you!" Lily says slyly as she departs, for real this time.

Angie swivels her head looking at each of them talking as if they think she can't hear. However, she is glad to see Ken and slides over a bit to give him space to sit with her.

Angie now speaks to him directly, "Hi, Ken."

"Hi Angie. Okay if I sit here while you finish your drink."

"Sure," she says, gesturing for him to sit.

"I drove my mom and some of her friends up for the service with the Taylors and thought I'd just hang around till time to drive them back home. How was Children's Church this morning? It will be nice to see a couple of my younger campers singing in the service tomorrow night."

And so it goes. They chat awhile, and then decide to head around back to see if a couple seats remain in the back of the tabernacle. There is a pair of seats. They enter quietly once Albert finishes his organ solo, slides off the organ stool and walks towards the small table where he'd left his speaking notes.

Reverend Albert Taylor basks in the adoration of the white dressed ladies filling nearly two-thirds of the tabernacle. Christine, who is seated on the rostrum with her husband, hands him a folder and gives him an encouraging pat on the arm before he walks to the podium. Sighing with satisfaction at this gesture of affectionate support, the ladies sit up straighter, eager to hear their darlings, the Missionaries Taylor.

ONCE AGAIN, ANGIE HAS TO TIP OUT EARLY to go get dressed in time to join Stella in the stand between the afternoon and evening services. Ken leaves with her to go get the car and drive up to pick up his mother and her friends at the side door where he'd dropped them off earlier. Angie cuts across the grass to get to the dorm while Ken heads straight down the road to the lot. She looks around at the folks just arriving, all changed for the evening and teens coming from all corners of the campground heading over to the concession stands.

Angie grabs the metal pipe that serves as the banister along the exterior steps up to her second floor dorm room. Once inside, when she reaches the bathroom, she cocks her head to listen, hoping not to hear water splashing, a signal that there may be a line and she'll have wait to get in to freshen up after a sweaty afternoon in the ice cream stand. She peaks in the door and hears from the shower, "Just a moment. I'll be finished in five minutes."

That's about the time she needs to gather up her wash cloth, towel, soap and deodorant. There won't be enough hot water for a shower, so she doesn't even plan to take one. Still she'll wait until she can have the bathroom to herself. This is supposed to be camp after all, and a thorough sponge bath will just have to suffice. That worked when she stayed on her other grandparents' farm.

As she waits, Angie allows her mind to wander back to one particularly vivid memory of a summer she spent with them. That memory first arose during a high school biology class lesson about salmonella poisoning. Now hoping for no longer than the promised five minutes before she can have some privacy in the dorm bathroom, the childhood love story again unfolds for her.

===

AFTERNOONS WHEN SHE WAS SEVEN OR EIGHT YEARS OLD, lying in wait, lurking at the edge of the gravel driveway, Angie would pounce on Granddaddy as soon as he got home from work! Though he worked with a construction crew and smelled like it, Angie didn't mind his musky odor.

She'd greet him with a full body hug, crunching dried mud on his overalls, smearing it with her sweaty cheek when she reached around his waist to grab the lunch box he hid behind his back. She could still hear the rumble of his rich baritone voice calling over her head to his wife, "Hello, Gracie-Girl. How was your day?" Angie did not learn until she returned as a teenager to visit them that Grandmommy always packed extra – more than he could eat – just so there'd be leftovers for her

Back then, little girl Angie'd grab the lunchbox, run back up the driveway and sit by herself on the concrete slab porch. With the black hump-topped lunch box perched on her knees, she'd flip up the metal latches and thrust back the top, rattling the silvery Thermos bottle clamped inside the lid. Ahhh…the welcome aroma of leftover bologna sandwich, the faint whiff of peanut butter cookies, and perhaps a limp sliver of carrot! She loved that Granddaddy saved a portion of his lunch for her – she'd been on his mind even when he was at work.

It was not until that high school Biology class when Angie learned about salmonella that she realized she could have died of love! But she hadn't.

===

SHE HADN'T THEN, and here she is now with her maternal grandparents, who also are sharing with her, not a leftover lunch this time, but generously given space in their campgrounds' dorm room.

How blessed she has been. How rushed she is now. She'd better get going, or she'd be later than usual getting cleaned up and dressed for duty this afternoon. She peeks out her dorm door to see if the bathroom door is opened. It isn't. She's got a few more minutes.

Angie has settled on the skirt and blouse and adds a lightweight woven sweater with colors of both the skirt and the blouse. That'll pull things together enough for this evening. She looks out the door and down the hall, noticing the bathroom door is open. The lady's probably finished showering, so Angie quickly scoots down there before someone else slips in ahead of her. She turns on the hot water tap. Good. There's still a little left. She's thankful that the previous lady, though late, has left the bowl clean and Angie won't have to use valuable minutes scrubbing out the sink before she begins her own wash-up.

While water fills the sink, Angie looks up into the mirror and yelps. "Ugh! My hair's a mess. I should have checked before leaving the stand this afternoon. Why didn't Lily say something? I don't have time to heat up the curlers and do anything with this head. What can I do with this hair in three minutes?" Shaking her head, Angie reaches for her washcloth and soap dish and does what she can do…freshen up.

Angie decides to brush her hair back and hold what curls are left in place with a couple of reddish combs. There are enough colors in the sweater that the combs will find a match there somewhere. Back in the room, she pulls on the stockings she always wears…even in the summer, and reaches for the dangling garters. Stockings make her feel more put together, and the lightweight girdle keeps her generous hips from being so noticeable. Probably not true, but she endures the girdle anyway. Black shoes and purse will have to do.

She finishes dressing and spritzes on a little Charisma cologne, her favorite Avon fragrance, and checks herself in the small mirror her grandparents have hung on the wall on their side of the room. "Good enough, I guess. This will just have to do for tonight."

She remembers her Bible just as she turns to lock the door, runs and grabs it from the chair near her cot, locks up, and scuttles down the steps just as she sees Stella hooking back the doors over the serving window and scanning the grounds for Angie. She'd better hurry up. She'll have no reason to rush to service tonight since Ken won't be there. Tonight's Thia's turn with the car.

Thursday

8 - That Lady in Navy

"LATE AGAIN! ON WELL. WHAT'S TO BE EXPECTED WHEN WE don't shut down the ice cream stand until half an hour before evening service begins!" Angie slows her hustling walk and reduces her gait to a more sedate pace. She just hums along with the hymn of praise, a little annoyed with the sputtering from the speakers that face the grassy expanse she crosses.

By tomorrow the sound man surely will have that adjusted to benefit the overflow crowds on the weekend. Lots of folks have to sit outside during the services, especially Saturday night when the youth choir sings and, of course, on Sunday mornings when some local congregations cancel services in their home churches and join the week long campers for worship that day.

Before she reaches the rear door to the tabernacle, the congregation is joyfully singing the chorus of another favorite old hymn of the Zion's Hill Saints,

> I am a child of God.
> I am a child of God.
> I have washed my robes in the cleansing fountain.
> I am a child of God!

"I AM a child of God," Angie sings with conviction. God knows she has to work and will be late for services. He's not worried about it, so why should she be?

Well, that's not what she's really worried about. It's meeting Ken. She still worries that he may decide to skip the meeting tonight because he's behind on his studying. He had told her that getting a jump on that organic chem class he's taking this fall is taking more time than he'd imagined. But he promised to be here, didn't he? Yeah, he'll be here.

Nearing the crowd waiting to go in, she slows down, trying to appear cool and collected, letting her eyes scan the group, looking for that handsome guy she'd met just four days ago. It can't be just four days. They've only spent a few hours together and yet she feels she's getting to know him quite well. Well? Where is he?

Someone touches her elbow. "Angie?"

Angie turns.

It's Ken.

Thank goodness.

But there's a woman with him. Oh, no! And she's stunning.

Long dark brown hair, glowing light brown skin with meticulous make-up and bright brown eyes. She's wearing an expensively tailored navy suit. Her blouse is the same light blue as the shirt Ken's wearing. She's about the same height as Angie, but with lovely long legs. She's shod in complementary navy blue sling-back heels and carrying a handsome leather purse. It's only Thursday and she's wearing a hat. A hat that matches her blouse and gloves. She's standing awfully close to Ken, too. This is just too much for Angie. She jerks her arm away and stiffens her shoulders.

"Hello Ken," she replies tersely.

"Hi, Angie. Glad you're still here. We thought we'd miss you." She purses her lips.

"It took me longer to find a parking place than I thought. I guess I didn't expect so many people on a Thursday evening. What?" Ken stops and turns when the usher gestures for them to follow her in.

There's no time to talk. The woman with Ken steps in front of him, behind the usher; and as Ken follows her into the sanctuary; he reaches back and gently tugs Angie to follow them. The usher has found three seats and directs them to hurry. The woman goes in first, then Ken, and then Angie.

Great. Just what she needed. Worry about competition when she says she's not interested in getting involved! Angie has just sat down when the song leader signals the congregation to join in singing the next song. "Sweet, Sweet Spirit". In fact they've sung it each evening since the choir introduced it on Sunday to remind them of the kind of service they're to give to one another. It's become the theme song for the week, and a challenge to Angie, especially this evening.

Angie can't concentrate. She has neither a sweet expression on her face nor a sweet spirit in her heart. But, why is she so upset? Sure, Ken has lived in this town all his life. He has friends here and is free to bring anyone to the campground he wants.

Christians are admonished to spread the Word, to invite others to worship, Yadda, yadda, yadda. Angie can't focus on the music. Instead she wonders why she should be concerned about who Ken brings. Just because Ken has a woman with him doesn't mean he's no longer interested in sitting with her. He did wait for her, didn't he? Or did he? He said it took him longer to find a parking place than he expected. Maybe he'd planned to get here early and be seated before Angie even arrived.

Angie looks up, hoping no one is paying attention to the frown on her face or sensing the spirit of jealousy. Her shoulders tense and clench. No, no one seems to be looking her way. Angie peeks around and sees people singing with their eyes closed.

The lady in the row in front of her is patting tears from her cheeks with a lacy handkerchief. The man to the left has raised his hand, as have several sitting around him. Angie notices, as the song continues, that others sing and gaze in front of them as though they see the Spirit answering their prayer to join them for services tonight.

Angie forces herself to sing along in hopes that the words or the music will calm her, or at least redirect her thoughts onto the reason she came this evening...or what should have been the reason she came come this evening. Not just to be with Ken, but to be in the congregation worshiping the God who sent His Spirit to dwell among the congregants.

She's got to let the Spirit refocus her attention and she's got to trust that her earlier estimation of Ken is not all wrong. Just because he's brought such an attractive lady doesn't mean anything negative about Angie. Unless he's brought her to show Angie the kind of woman he prefers. Someone well-dressed who looks so put together on a Thursday evening. Angie can't help it that she can't both pay for college and buy great clothes. Anyway, she's just met Ken, and this relationship probably isn't going anywhere anyway. She's got college first. Well, first she's got to get through this evening.

Angie tries, but can hardly keep her mind on the worship. All she thinks about is that woman sitting on the other side of Ken; that is, until the lights in the sanctuary are dimmed and the piano begins just the melody line of "This Little Light of Mine".

Right, Angie remembers, the children are singing tonight. It's Children's Day. Now that she thinks about it, she smiles. Then she thinks of Ken and his lady friend and frowns.

Ken feels Angie stiffen next to him and glances towards her. She's planted her feet evenly in front of her and is clinching her purse in a strange way. He can't imagine what's wrong with her. She's all uptight tonight, like something is bothering her. Must have had a tough day. Lots more people have arrived, and it has been awfully hot today. No problem. He's noticed that Angie usually gets into the music; maybe music will help her relax.

He'll take Thia by the ice cream stand and introduce them when Angie gets off tonight. They're about the same age. They'll have lots to talk about. Of course, Angie's finished a year of college, and Thia's just graduated from high school. But that should be no problem. Angie dresses nicely, and clothes may be a conversation starter. They should get along just fine. A flicker draws his attention when the lights break the darkness.

THE CHOIR IS ENTERING. Both Angie and Ken have been so sidetracked; neither even noticed there was no choir up there for the opening songs. Lines of children, dressed in black and white, holding small Eveready flashlights against their chests, enter simultaneously from the left and right side doors at the front of the tabernacle. The wee ones look serious and proud, clasping the lights in their tight little fists.

The older children – the eleven and twelve year olds – enter first, to set the pace. The younger children follow according to height so when all are in place, they really look nice with the tall ones in the middle and the little ones on each end. And to help keep order, adult leaders slip into the choir stand and seat themselves at the end of each row.

The Jenkins Sisters and the choir joyfully repeat the first verse until everyone is in place. When they get to the verse that goes, "Put it under a bushel, NO, I'm gonna let it shine," the kids, like statues of Liberty, hold their flashlights high above their heads.

"It looks real nice seeing all those lights shining down on all those innocent little faces," Ken whispers to Angie, but she turns her head away.

"This little light of mine, I'm gonna let it shine," the children sing. Angie's frown is enough to shade that light.

The director and pianist kick up the pace, and with a throbbing bass rhythm, the organist joins them. The pulsing beat inspires the audience to bob their heads and sway as the children sing with gusto. All but Angie, whose troubled mind drifts back a few years.

Angie remembers when she was their age and how odd it felt to be looking out at so many grownups looking up at the choir. Her current gloom dissipates a bit when she recalls her grandparents' beaming faces the year she had sung in a duet on Children's Night.

The children tonight finish their song to rousing applause. They turn off their flashlights, and overhead lights are turned on. As they're passed down the choir rows, only one or two flashlights drop on the way to the grown-up waiting to put them away. The organist plays softly, and the audience waits patiently.

Angie senses Ken turn to say something to the woman sitting on his left. Well, that's that, Angie concludes. He's here with that woman and is only sitting next to Angie because they were late, and she just happened to be standing there with the rest in the back of the tabernacle. It was nice while it lasted. Oh well. Angie sits up rigidly, looks straight ahead, and forces her attention to the children up front.

That's Sarah Anne! The little girl she'd seen singing on the swings Tuesday afternoon when Ken had brought her those luscious grapes. She and Ken had had a good time. Recalling that afternoon, Angie relaxes a bit.

Sarah Anne stands in from of her choir stand seat, smiles nervously, sends a shoulder high finger wave to someone in the audience, then bumps her way out of the second row of singers and over to the podium which looms up to her forehead. When she reaches up for the microphone, Sylvia, with a hand on Sarah Anne's shoulder, gently nudges the little girl from behind the podium and up close to the altar rail edging the platform so Sarah Anne can be seen a little better.

Sylvia nods to her sister to begin the introduction, but the soloist is still fidgeting. Marie waits. The little girl hikes the waist of her dark skirt with two fingers of the hand holding the microphone. She pulls down the sleeve on her white blouse. Then, cherub-like, she looks up at the director as if to say, "I'm ready now. You can begin."

Sylvia nods again to Marie, who plays the chorus of "Jesus Loves Me". Holding her arms out from her sides, Sylvia raises them shoulder high, forming a 'T,' and with her hands palms down, stands still and steady until she has the attention of all of the children. Then slowly turning her palms up, she raises her arms majestically forming a "V", signaling the choir to stand. Amazingly, they do so in relative order.

Sylvia must be smiling because they all break into full-toothed grins. She raises one hand, and then at the strong down-beat, the children burst into strong affirmation, "Yes, Jesus loves me. Yes, Jesus loves me. Yes, Jesus loves me, for the Bible tells me so."

Sarah Anne holds the mike down at her side until it's time for her to sing her verse. Angie holds her breath and sends up a prayer for the little soloist, feeling a little nervous for her, then relaxes, recalling how unabashedly Sarah had sung on the swings.

Up goes the mike, just like a professional, right in front of her mouth, and out comes that free and beautiful sound Angie had heard on the playground.

Jesus loves me this I know,
for the Bible tells me so.
Little ones to Him belong.
They are weak, but He is strong!

Then she sings a new verse about Jesus loving her when she's good and also when she's bad. A perennial kids' choir favorite with an extra twist. Still, a song and message that touches the hearts of all ages. What innocence; what trust; what a challenge for Angie to remember the truth of the song. She mutters, "Jesus loves me, even if Ken doesn't." Ken hears the mutter, but can't decipher the words.

It's offering time, but the ushers aren't collecting it tonight. The children exit the choir stand in as nearly an orderly recessional as an adult choir. No marching out and gathering in the lower auditorium in the basement of the dormitory where they'd have popcorn and a movie during the rest of the service, where their parents would meet them later afterwards.

Instead, tonight the children simply march around to put their offerings in the plates on the front table, and then return to their seats in the choir stand. The leaders probably planned that walk to help the children relieve some of their pent-up energy before the speaker brings the message for the evening.

For offertory, the organ is playing the song the children had been learning in Children's Church. "If you want to be great in God's kingdom, learn to be a servant of all." Each in the audience is challenged about their servanthood.

WELL, KEN HAS BEEN A SERVANT ALL WEEK. Working in the garden on Monday. Picking up those grapes Tuesday and sharing them with Angie during her break. Driving Mother and her friends to and from the Women's Day service and bringing Thia with him tonight. Didn't make him great then nor feel great now. He was impatient yesterday and is puzzled today. What's with Angie?

Rather than have the children sing a second song following the offering, Sylvia Jenkins approaches the microphone stand, then waits. The usher moves the second mike close to Marie still at the piano.

Ah, they are the special music for this evening. Chris, at the organ, begins playing a brand new Andre Crouch song. Marie, once the usher has adjusted her microphone, joins on the piano when he gets to the chorus.

Sylvia raises the mike, and the sisters sing,

> Take me back; take me back dear Lord
> To the place where I first believed you.

Sylvia solos on the verse,

> I feel that I'm so far from you Lord
> But still I hear you calling me.
> Those simple things that I once knew
> Their memories keep drawing me.

She invites the congregation to sing along,

> Take me back; take me back dear Lord
> To the place where I first believed you.

Ken bows his head in anticipation that his prayer and that of the song will be answered this evening. "Lord," Ken mouths, "please open my heart to the sermon this evening. And, I'm depending on Your Word to help me understand what's going on around here tonight."

Angie misses most of this duet. Her mind is still on the offertory song. Fat chance the kids will believe serving is a privilege, Angie argues in her head. Then the words of the Crouch song seep through. But, instead of letting them minister to her, she drifts again, fussing and fuming about how silly she feels for feeling...jealous.

Jealous! She can't be jealous of that Lady in Navy when Ken and Angie aren't even an item. They've just met and neither is serious about having the relationship continue.

He must not be, since he brought someone else with him this evening. Angie certainly is not serious! She may as well go ahead and leave now. Stella probably needs help getting set up for the after service rush. She has rationalized and now grumps, "They're going to be impatient and impolite even right after getting out of church. I'm out of here!"

With that, Angie grabs her purse and Bible and exits. She puts one finger over her lips and bends at the waist as though her stooping will help those seated behind her see the front any better. She hears his gasp and feels Ken's questioning eyes on her. She ignores both.

Oh! Where's Angie going? It's the middle of the service! Why is she looking so funny? She feeling okay? She's been a little tense all service. He decides to ask her about it when he treats Thia to ice cream. But he doesn't.

REVEREND BARROW, THE SPEAKER THIS EVENING, draws in the listeners with age appropriate stories and examples as she challenges the kids to trust in the Lord. She's small in stature, but big in heart. She's tailored the message for the youngsters with applications that resonate with the adults.

Like Ken, some of the young adults remember when they sang in the Children's Choir, not all that many years ago, but would be embarrassed to admit about how infrequently they remember to trust God in all things as they'd learned to do as children. Maybe that's why so many keep coming back to camp meeting year after year. Not to hear something new, but to be reminded of something old.

The children easily follow the outline the speaker is using because she's chosen a mnemonic, the acronym TRUST.

Think about what we know about God.
Remember that He loves us and wants to bless us.
Understand that we can be that blessing to others.
Serve God and serve others – family, friends, and even foes.
Thank God for the privilege of being a servant.

But, Ken's mind soon drifts away from the sermon and on to Angie who left in a huff. Maybe Angie's upset because yesterday after he'd driven his mother and friends home, he hadn't come back for evening services. He'd told her his sister might be using the car Wednesday evening. It turns out that she and her girlfriend had driven over to a sale in Youngstown and didn't get back until it was too late to come up to Zion's Hill.

Well, he used that time to study. True, much of his time had been studying his interest in Angie. He was trying to figure out the timing of what the Lord had said to him about Angie being the woman for him.

Did God mean to marry or just to spend time with this week? Surely nothing more than that right now. They both plan to graduate from college before marriage. Once she gets off work this evening, he can find out what's got her jaws all torqued. But he doesn't.

===

"HEY, ANGIE," STELLA CALLS OUT from under the counter, scrambling to pick up the plastic spoons she spilled. "What're you doing here so early? I haven't heard the altar call or anything," she huffs, scooting back into the center of the little booth.

Kneeling there, catching her breath, Stella rocks back onto her heels and looks up at Angie. "What's the matter?"

"Nothing."

"You certainly don't look like being in church has done anything for your attitude."

Stella stands up to get a better look at her helper standing there so stiffly. Her eyes stop at the "V" Angie's arms make and the tight fists clasping her purse handle. Her Bible sticks out of the side pocket, having been crammed there during the Angie-stomp from the tabernacle.

"You sure? You were in a dither all afternoon, hardly paying attention to the customers and leaving here as fast as you could to change for service."

"I just came early to help you get set up. It's still pretty warm and you know how those Saints are after church. They'll have fed on Spiritual food;

146

then they're gonna want some physical food for dessert. Ice cream to be exact," Angie sneers in a not-so-Christian way.

"Well, I'm glad you're here. You see I spilt this pack of spoons and now I'm gonna have to throw 'em out," she frets, flinging the handful into the trash can. "Yeah. Good thing you're here. I'm going over to the store room and get a couple more packages."

"Okay. What you want me to do?"

"You can start filling the jars with water so we can rinse those scoops between dips. Better push that bucket under the shelf there so we don't knock it over in the rush later." She heads out the door, calling back, "See ya. And try to get a smile up there on your face. Smiles help sell ice cream."

"Sure." Angie grouches. She chucks her Bible-stuffed purse in the cabinet, shuts the door and grabs one of those full length bib aprons Stella makes her wear. Good thing, because Angie can tell she'll probably be sloppy tonight.

By the time she has the jars of water filled and placed, she hears strains of the invitational hymn. This doesn't give Angie much time to do an attitude adjustment. She'd forgotten that on Thursdays they now keep the children for the whole service, but keep the service short.

"Whew," Stella gasps as she slams back into the stand. "They finished over there already?"

"I guess so. I doubt that the altar call will be very long tonight, Stella. The folks'll be over here soon."

AND SHE IS RIGHT! Before she'd done her mental inventory of the flavors, verified the location of each five gallon tub in the freezer, checked the wall-hung dispensers for the two kinds of cones, and eyed the stack of cups and container of spoons, the first customer is knocking on the wooden shutter. "Y'all open yet?"

Angie pastes on her smile, flings back the shutters, and shoves the hooks into the little U-rings fastened to the walls. "May I help you?" And so it begins…again.

147

TONIGHT IT LOOKS LIKE EVERY KID IN THE CHOIR is being treated to ice cream.

"Johnny, I told you just one scoop. Now, do you want chocolate or vanilla? No. No maple walnut. You know you're allergic to nuts."

"Aw, Mom!"

"No. I don't care if every child in the choir gets maple walnut; you're not getting any," she exclaims shaking her finger down at him. "I'm not staying up with you all night watching to see if you're going to swell up and burst wide open. I said, 'No' and I mean 'No!'"

The boy's eyes bulge at the thought of his body bursting. But he stands stubbornly, insisting, "But, Mom. You said I could choose if I didn't act up in the choir. I been good. You promised," Johnny whines and looks at the kids standing behind him hoping his mother will give in and avoid a scene.

"Johnny. You may choose chocolate or vanilla or nothing. Do you understand me?" He nods and whimpers.

"Mooomm."

"I'm counting Johnny."

"But Mom, you promised!"

"Johneeee! I'm gonna count to five. If you haven't told this nice young lady what flavor you want, we're leaving."

"One. ..Two…. Can't you see all those people waiting in line behind us?"

"But I want maple walnut."

"Three…Four…"

"OK. OK." He looks up at Angie, "I guess I'll have chocolate and vanilla mixed. Can you mix chocolate and vanilla on one scoop? That's all Mom'll let me have tonight. One scoop. Can you mix'em?"

"Do you want that on a cone or in a cup?"

148

"What kinda cones you got?" Angie holds up the flat waffle bottom and pointy bottom sugar cones. "Mom, which one should I get? Huh? The flat bottom or the pointy bottom? Which one, huh?"

"Get a cup, Johnny. That'll be neater and you won't drip all over your white shirt. If you keep it clean, you can wear it Sunday with that bow tie your Granny got you."

"But I want a cone. Mom; you said I can choose."

Angie taps her foot, grins her smile, and murmurs, "It's going to be a long evening."

"Will you fix Johnny a single scoop of vanilla and chocolate on…what kind of cone, Johnny?" He points to the pointy cone. "On one of those sugar cones. Thank you."

Angie has to take back her nasty thoughts about the impatience of Christians. Those standing in line this evening exhibit the patience of Job. Not even one snarly look and not one snide remark. She thanks the Lord and asks forgiveness. She truly senses His presence helping her calm down as she continues waiting on each kid customer as kindly as she knows is right.

She hardly notices an hour has passed before the line of youngsters and their parents thins and the tweens make up the bulk of her customers. It'll be a while before the older teens and singles notice the younger ones have left. They make up the next wave of trying customers.

On busy nights like this, Angie wishes they had two windows. Grownups without children have lined up in front of Stella. Stella's just as busy at her area of the window at Angie's right. Many look over indulgently at the little ones and with relief that they, too, have a choice… not to be in the line behind customers like Johnny. But building a larger, two window ice cream stand is a goal for the future. Tonight, one window and two dippers.

Once the lines peter out, Stella and Angie drop their scoops in the rinse water now nearly as thick as buttermilk. They've had no time to dump the jars in the bucket below the counter and refill them with fresh water. They do that now and then reach into the cooler and pull out Mason jars of cool water.

They drink deeply and then wipe their arms. Both are sticky from more than perspiration from the work.

"Hey, miss. Can we get some service, here? I want a double maricopa!" demands a teenager, her hand on her hip as though she's been waiting more than half a minute.

She can see Angie and Stella are busy, but Miss Priss wants to show off for her friends. Angie finds she's got to paste on a smile again. She'd been feeling pretty good about her change in attitude. Looks like it isn't really changed, just floating an inch below the surface. It's bobbing its head above the crest of her emotions, and Angie doesn't have time to deal with it now. So she fakes it.

"Sure, honey. What do you want? We're out of maricopa, though."

"No maricopa! I been waiting all day to get me some maricopa. I coulda got me some this afternoon, but noooo. I waited and look what happened?" she postures. "Well, I guess I'll have me summa that bubble gum. You haven't sold out of that too, have you? You got any of that left?"

"Yes, we have bubble gum. You want a cone or a cup? We have these two kinds of cones," Angie points. The girl decides on the waffle cone, and so begins the next wave of customers. Just as Angie hands her the two scoops and reaches out for the payment, she spots Ken and the woman with him.

That Lady in Navy, clinging to him like fungus on a tree trunk, leans in close, saying something in his ear. Angie can't hear, but can imagine. Well! They certainly look chummy. And she thought he wasn't interested in a serious relationship. They don't look all that casual from here.

KEN AND THIA STOP AT ONE OF THE BENCHES and sit down on the edge as though they'll only be there a couple of minutes.

Thia whines, "Ken, I thought he'd be here. He said he was coming tonight. That's why I got all dressed up. My heel was nearly raw from those shoes I wore all day at work today. I wouldn't have worn these new heels if he wasn't coming." Ken just nods.

150

"Ken," she implores and rationalizes, "Do you think something's the matter? He doesn't usually stand me up. He must have had to work late. He's been getting lots of overtime this summer."

Ken nods. He'd been through this with Thia before when, just to impress some guy, she's worn clothes that were not really comfortable.

"Maybe he tried to call and couldn't get through. Mom was on the phone all evening talking to Sister Grimsby about Women's Day. From what I could hear when I was brushing my teeth, Sister Grimsby served in the prayer room and lots of ladies came in for prayer."

Ken glared at Thia's implication that the Sisters are gossipers. She catches the silent question.

"Oh, no. I don't think they were betraying any confidences or anything, just talking about the general need for prayer. You know how they get when they feel the Lord is laying folks on their hearts to pray."

Ken nods, again. Thia won't stop talking until she talks through her angst.

"Melvin is such a sweetheart, Ken," she croons. "You know he brought me a rose the last time he came. A yellow one. Isn't that special? I know yellow flowers usually just mean friendship, but Melvin and I are even more than special friends. Most guys get red roses or something like that. But not Melvin. "

Ken shakes his head and sits back on the bench while Thia talks herself out of this funk.

"Most guys don't know that red flowers stand for passionate love. Melvin's too much of a gentleman to be that bold right now. He really does sweet things. Don't you think that's nice, Ken?"

"Sure. Melvin's real thoughtful."

"He'll probably stop and get me something this evening. He'll know I'm pretty upset that he didn't come. I know he's probably got a good reason. He's not the kind of guy to stand up a girl. He knew I could get a ride with you, anyway."

"You're right, Thia," Ken agrees. "Melvin's quite a guy. I don't believe he stood you up either."

Thia, pretty much over her snit, slides back on the bench, and using the toe of her left shoe, flicks off the strap of her right shoe. She leans back and pulls Ken closer. He slides over, puts his arm across the back of the bench and pats her on the shoulder.

"Melvin'll probably be at the trailer when we get back or will at least have called. It'll be OK." He leans down and kisses her forehead. After all, she is his little sister, and they've not had much time together this summer...what with their jobs and all.

ANGIE WATCHES ALL THIS across the shoulders of the customers she serves at the stand. Of course, she can't hear anything, so she makes assumptions. Not only does he bring another woman with him to the campground, but he flaunts her right in her face. He doesn't even have the decency to sneak off somewhere out of sight! Well, that's that! They're sharing so much personal space. And according to what Angie'd learned in her Psych class last year, they must be a couple.

===

ABOUT THIS TIME, KEN IS FED UP. Thia's started grousing again. "Thia, why don't I take you on home? You're tired anyway, and you have to help mom with the canning tomorrow. Let's get you a cup of ice cream, and we'll head on home," he offers, leaning forward to stand up. "I promised Mother that I'd go up to the garden and finish getting the rest of those green beans for her to put up for the winter. I think there's enough for one more batch before I leave for school. Anyway, there's someone I'd like you to meet."

"Ah, Ken. I just want to go home. I'm not in the mood for ice cream tonight. If I was, I'd want some maricopa. They're all out. I just heard one of those girls say so when the group walked by. If they don't have any maricopa, I'll take a pass." Thia grabs the bench seat and stands up, only to slip down onto his lap.

"OOOOOweeeee," she giggles when Ken catches her around her waist and tickles her like he used to do when they were kids. "Stop it, Ken! This is

152

embarrassing. She stands up again. "Ow!" She's bumped her sore heel and plops down again.

Angie sees them. She throws over to Stella, "Don't they have any respect for Zion's Hill? Can't they save such indecent behavior for a less public place! My goodness! And I thought he was so mature and all. Well, this is really too much!" Stella's busy and doesn't answer.

Ken and Thia finally get themselves up and begin walking to the car. Ken looks towards the stand and sees Angie. Their eyes meet. He heads that way. Thia drags on his arm. He turns, tells her to wait and looks back at Angie.

Her icy stare freezes him in his tracks. He stops. Stands. Stares back and questions with his shoulders and upturned palm. Angie clenches her jaw, scowls at him, and abruptly turns to her next customer.

"Come on, Ken. Let's go. Melvin's not gonna wait long. You can introduce me to Angie tomorrow or Saturday. I wanna go on home now."

Ken shrugs his shoulders, gives up, and grabs Thia's hand to assist her walking in those painful high heels. She stumbles, and Ken reaches around her shoulder to keep her from falling. Puzzled at Angie's freeze gun glare, Ken turns and props up his sister, and they gingerly walk back to the car for the drive back to their trailer. At least Thia has someone who will be glad to see her.

Angie flicks her shoulder as though to shake Ken out of her life. She goes back to scooping ice cream and wondering why she cares that Ken doesn't even come over and say hello.

We're almost friends aren't we? What pleasant afternoons they've had. Comfortable. Conversational. Congenial. Now look at him. She's convinced.

"We had had good times Tuesday and Wednesday." Comfortable. Conversational. Congenial. Why Angie's so cool this evening. He's confabulated.

Friday

9 - At the Trailer

KEN HAS SLEPT POORLY and feels grumpy. He cannot, for the life of him, figure out why that Angela Jeanette seemed so angry. She obviously is upset about something. But what? He shivers remembering the scowl she'd shot across to him. He was just going to introduce her to his sister, but Angie's icicle darts froze him in his tracks. Women! Who needs them?

Last night, Thia had been in a tiff, too, jaws all torqued when she learned that Melvin had neither stopped by nor called to explain why he hadn't come up to the campgrounds. The trailer throbbed with her moodiness the rest of the night. Thankfully, their parents, turning in for the night, hadn't stayed out in the kitchen area for long.

Neither did Thia. She stomped down the narrow hallway to her cupboard of a room and swished open her curtain of a door. Clattering shoes and banging drawers testified to her fury. However, one call of "Thiaaa!" from her dad curbed the thrashing around back there. But it didn't dissipate the disappointment eking from that end of the trailer.

THIA IS NOT USED TO BEING STOOD UP. She's always been popular with the guys at church and in high school. Most in her group have tried to date her at one time or the other. Some had even wagered on it. Not with money, but with words. Who'd get her to go out them more than once? She's always been picky. Rather high maintenance too.

Melvin doesn't seem to mind, though. They've grown up together. Been in the same Sunday School class since elementary school. He has always liked her, but kept his distance until this past year.

Though a soft-spoken teddy bear, Melvin has a spine of iron. The other guys don't much mess with him, now they see he's made his move. Like a magnet, Thia's gravitated toward Melvin, and the others guys have just given up. She's even stopped accepting their calls.

Now she's wondering if that had been a good move. Melvin didn't show up, didn't stop by, and didn't call. Ken feels sorrier for Melvin than for Thia. When Thia's upset, she sends out waves of mad in concentric circles, splashing all who come near her. Maybe Melvin knows this and is keeping his distance. From the tossing and turning he'd heard through the night, Thia's gotten about as much as sleep as he has.

HAVING SLEPT VERY LITTLE, Ken decides to get up anyway and go jogging. He rolls off the plank of a bed, returns his bedroom space to its kitchen format, and folds the bedclothes to store in the banquette next to the window. After his years in the Air Force, Ken's accustomed to living in cramped quarters, but he's never learned to like it. Here, he has to be up and out of the kitchen before anyone in the family needs the space to fix breakfast or pack a lunch.

Being home this summer means no privacy. No door he can close. The bathroom doesn't even work for that. It's just too small. He grumps, "Hardly enough space to rinse my face after a shave. Every time I bend down I bang my butt against the door."

Everyone else in the family at least has a corner to call his or her own. All Ken has is a foot of hanging space in the coat closet, a bin under kitchen banquette, and half a shelf in the bathroom medicine cabinet. True, he's never had all that many clothes, and he could store his school stuff in a bag on the floor of the closet. Still, there just has never been enough indoor space. No place to kick back and relax. So he's stayed away until mealtime or bedtime.

Before he'd left for the Air Force, he'd be playing ball, practicing with the vocal group he sang with, or doing homework at the library. Thank God for the gym and the library. On weekends, he'd spend Saturdays with his real dad's mother, Gram, and after church on Sundays, with his mother's mother, Mom Bessie.

They both had room for him at their places. They'd fix his favorite foods, let him eat as much as he wanted and then they left him alone. Mom Bessie's house was busier, but he had space where he could sit and watch the Westerns on TV with Bubba, his grandfather.

Sometimes he'd help Gram with chores around her house. Ken doesn't even remember her husband. It had always been Gram and Ken. She didn't even mind when he plinked on her piano. He never learned to play anything all the way through. But it certainly was nice to have a place to play in private.

His parents had divorced before Ken started kindergarten, and he seldom saw his real dad who lived just across the state line in Ohio. He'd gotten another family, too, and they didn't have much room in their place either. Ken used to visit in the summer, but never felt at home there. Never.

Ken's not sure why he feels alone so much of the time. He lives with his mother, sister, and step-father, but has always wondered if he really is a member of their family. Their family. Never really his family. Sure, his step-dad has always taken care of Ken's basic needs for food, clothing, and shelter, but Ken has always known that he is not his real dad.

Then, while Ken was in the Air Force, his real dad died. So this summer Ken can't even go spend time with him either. Sometimes he just feels bereft, adrift, fatherless. He's read about God, the Father. But he can't understand why Christians get so choked up about that relationship with God. It's not one of the characteristics of God that really resonates with Ken. Probably because he hasn't had that warm an experience with either earthly father.

"Thank you, God," Ken prays as he gets moving this morning, "for understanding and loving me even though I don't always understand You. When it's time, please teach me to be a good father. I want my children to have a good one. I know I'll love them. I want them to be able to feel it and welcome it."

Ken has folded his bedclothes into as neat and tight a bundle as he can, crams them into the left side of the storage bin, and from the right side, pulls out a set of clean underwear, his running shorts and a faded Air Force tee shirt. His good shirts and slacks hang military style in his twelve inches of the coat closet. His one pair of dress shoes sits on the floor where he used to store his school bag.

Ken hears his parents moving around in their cubby hole of a bedroom signaling they'll be out soon. They'll want to get into the bathroom and kitchen. They'll have a couple hours to themselves if he hurries up and gets out of there.

It's usually nine or ten o'clock before Thia stirs from her curtained space at the back of the trailer. She seldom is sleeping that long; she just doesn't emerge till she hears everyone's been in and out of the bathroom. It's her way of staying out of the way. But today she's got to work the early shift.

The three of them, mother, dad, and Thia, have all fallen into a pattern that works for them, and his being home for the summer has thrown a wrench in the works. But he's needed a place to stay while he worked this summer. There had been no problem at the beginning of the summer. For those first two months, he'd worked twelve shifts, and then evenings at the gym or the library. Things weren't so tense then. He usually was the first up and out every day.

Then, in August, during the two weeks as a youth counselor, he'd been living up on Zion's Hill in the cabin with his group of young rascals. Being back here this week is proving to be more of a challenge that he'd imagined. But he just has to finish off this week, and then he'll be back at school.

Ken completes his morning ritual, stores his toiletries on his half shelf of the medicine cabinet, and hangs his towel and wash cloth on the hooks his stepfather has mounted on the wall. Still the towel usually falls onto the floor two or three times a day as the family members bump around in this yard and a half square space.

"I can't imagine how I put up with it before I left for basic training," he tells the mirror, and then glances down to make certain the sink is clean. Most of his buddies found the barracks crowded and impersonal. Ken found them spacious – a welcome expanse after bunking four years in the kitchen of his family's trailer. His sneakers are outside. Finished inside, he heads out to get them; he's going to have to go run off his puzzlement. Maybe the fresh air will wake him up and clarify his thoughts. Yes, and a good run. That should do it.

Checking to make certain that everything in the kitchen is back in place in order to preclude cool looks from his parents and silent "I told you so's" from Thia, Ken grabs an apple from the fridge and slips out of the trailer just as he hears the bedroom door open. "Good morning, Ken."

"Morning, Mom. Bye, Dad" Greetings and farewells.

STEPPING DOWN INTO THE YARD, Ken inhales the cool damp air. "Thank you, God for open space," begins his heartfelt prayer. It's time for morning devotions. Today without a Bible.

Instead, he walks the perimeter of the property, gazing at the trees his folks had planted in hopes they'll become shade for their soon to be finished house. Dew diamonds bejewel the grass, peachy pink clouds nuance the sky, and warbling birds welcome him. They too have started the day early.

"Thank you, God, for life." He pauses at the back property line that abuts the Catholic section of the town cemetery. One of the reasons his folks could afford such a large parcel of land on which to build their dream home is because their lot lies next to this graveyard. That assures them privacy for a long time. The cemetery probably is the reason there have been no protests about his parents living so many years in a vacation-size mobile home. Most of the folks who'd bought land when Ken's parents purchased theirs now are in their permanent homes. Talk about permanent homes. The tombs over there in the cemetery. Hmmm. Well, they're permanent alright.

In a leisurely stroll, meandering through the uncut grass on the far side of the lot, around the recently capped basement, under the new trees grown enough to shade him, Ken ambles back to the trailer steps. Perambulating their acre lot is enough to get his mind off himself and onto the challenges for the day.

During his years in the service, Ken had gotten into the habit of reading the Psalms. This morning he reflects on this past week and life in general, wondering about the upcoming day; he's going to need the strength of the Lord to be the kind of Christian witness he feels he's called to be. What with Thia, his parents, and who knows what with Angie, he tries to decide which Psalm to meditate on today.

Psalm number one that he'd learned in junior high school, still speaks to him today. That's why he'd taught it to his young campers. Ken would begin their camp day quoting the first two verses and asking the guys to repeat it. In fact, the passage became their verses for the week.

> Blessed is the man who does not walk in the counsel of the wicked
> or stand in the way of sinners or sit in the seat of mockers.
> But his delight is in the law of the LORD,
> and on his law he meditates day and night.

As expected, during the first few days, the guys snickered and repeated the lines simply as words they heard him spouting to them. But as they did the daily cabin spruce up, Ken would pause, call them to attention, and ask them what they thought the words were saying to them, as young males. Who did they look to for counsel? How often did they find themselves the mocked, and how often did they find themselves the mockers?

It took nearly the entire first week before the boys felt comfortable enough with Ken and with each other to answer the questions honestly. Every morning as they made up their cots and straightened the cabin, Ken would call out the verses and ask them to repeat after him. It became a game to them. But by the end of the week, they all knew the words by heart, and during the second week, Ken would ask different ones to lead it. At first they joked around, but by the close of camp, most of the guys identified with the verses and sensed their seriousness. Some of even started memorizing that Psalm.

KEN RECALLS THE ANTICS of Captain Ike Murphy, a military chaplain who volunteers at youth camp. He's sort of a grizzly brown bear in looks, a gravely polar bear in voice, and a tender teddy bear at heart. Cap'n Ike has eyes like heat seeking radar, sensing when things are getting hot among the guys, and they need outside help to behave right.

He would appear on the scene, growling in the *basso profundo* of the most villainous opera singer, shaking the walls or rumbling the trees. The toughest teens trembled, wondering which one of them would be the target of Cap'n Ike's displeasure. They knew it was displeasure, not dislike that fueled his energy, and the boys tried not to disappoint him by acting like young men with no self-discipline.

162

Boys suspected of misbehaving in the dorm, the cafeteria, or on the athletic field had to deal with The Bear. He'd use his size and voice to get their attention, and then his loving heart to convince them that doing right and living right is the correct way to behave.

He often scared them silly, but he seldom upbraided a troublemaker in public. Instead, he'd encase the miscreant in a one-arm bear hug and walk him out of the view of his peers. With his back to the boys, Cap'n Ike's physique could shield the trembling teen from the startled stares of the new guys and the knowing nods of the regulars. Ken learned that over the years, most campers had had a session with Cap'n Ike, so they knew what it was like to be the target of his laser like eyes.

By the end of the two weeks of camp, the new guys knew that The Bear was not really scary, just serious about their growing up to be men of integrity. Cap'n Ike put up with no bullying in word or deed. He insisted they show respect not only for the senior and junior counselors, but for their fellow campers as well.

KEN BITES HIS APPLE, chews and swallows, and then repeats the Bible verses. Next, he raises before the Lord the names of each of the young men he's had this year at camp. Larry, of course. And his brothers Sam and Ricky; Pete, the teaser; George, the leader. Joey, the clown. "Oh my goodness," Ken gasps. "Joey! His sister's coming this weekend! Not another woman! Lord, I don't have time for this!"

He doesn't like the direction his thoughts are taking. Who knows what Joey's sister will be like? And ice queen, Angie. "She certainly chilled my interest with those frosty looks last night. Dear Lord, why women this week? I'm supposed to be concentrating on getting my education. I don't have the emotional energy to be dealing with any of them now," Ken fusses with God as he finishes his apple and decides to cut short his devotional time.

Well, he needs to get his run in and get back to eat. His mother promised to fix breakfast, and he's agreed to do one more morning up at the garden. They have a bumper crop of green beans, and she wants to get another dozen jars canned before he leaves next week.

Ken drops the core in the trash can next to the storage shed behind the trailer. Then he tightens the laces on his sneakers and starts with stretching warms up for his run. Right finger tips to left toe; left finger tips to right toe. Right, left, right, left. He smiles and thinks of the garden. "The harvest is great, but the laborers are few. That Bible verse really applies to this family," he huffs as he begins his jumping jacks.

He's careful to do this jumping in a flat cleared place in the yard. One time in high school, exercising out here, he'd jumped up and landed on a stone just large enough to throw him off balance. He'd twisted an ankle.

That kept him from basketball for a couple of weeks. Off the courts anyway, but not out of the gym. He still showed up every day he could get away from the house.

EVERY AFTERNOON, when he'd finished whatever chores or was through working with his uncle collecting junk, Ken would head over to the gym and watch the older guys play. That was one of the summers the mill had laid off scores of workers, so lots of the grown men met at the gym to burn off the vexation of not working.

The fathers couldn't face the disappointment in their kids' faces when day after day daddy would shake his head when the ice cream truck went by. Tinkling musical invitations to the kids. Distressing dirge-like accusations to their dads. It was tough earning no income to meet the needs, let alone the wants, of their families.

So the guys went to the gym to quench the fire of frustration with the sweat of killer basketball. Up and down the court. Dribble, pass, shoot. Blocked! Snag the ball, dribble the ball, flick it to a teammate or launch it themselves, aiming to arc it just so to swish the nets. Back and forth. Up and down. They'd run – hot and steamy. Doing something right. Something to show they're capable; something for which they're respected.

For weeks, injured Ken sits – cool and calm. He watches. Closely. He observes the moves guys telegraph just before they fake a pass, lurch around the guard and try a jump ball. He notices some of the guys bounce the ball the same number of times at the foul line, eyeing the basket as though it'll move before they can get off their shot.

164

He recognizes the camaraderie; he detects the enmity of guys from different sides of town. Admires the ones who play fair even when losing and scorns those who resort to cheating. With no referees, the teams play by the honor system. Some of the guys obviously have none. Still, the same guys show up every day. And so does Ken. But he is more than a spectator. He has become a student of the game.

In the gym he watches. At home he stretches, doing any exercises he can without aggravating his ankle. Near the end of the summer, he returns to the court. Since he'd been such a loyal fan, coming to see them play every day, the guys humor him and let him play. They're shocked, in awe, even. Despite his weeks on the sidelines, young Ken has become a formidable opponent, astonishing the older guys with his agility on the court and ability to read their game. Little does Ken know that Coach Mac had been watching, too. That's when he had offered to help Ken get a scholarship for college. The one Ken never mentioned to his family.

===

"AH! THAT SHOULD DO IT." Warmed up and flexed, the now older Ken starts his morning run. Out onto the dirt road, look right. Check for oncoming cars. None. Turn right onto the paved road. Shoulder wiggle to get out a little twinge from the jumping jacks. Pump knees high, swing arms in sync. Jog in place. Wait for fast cars to pass on the main road. Cross the road and run facing the traffic. Pick up the speed. Get into a rhythm. Rhythm. Rhythm. Rhythm. Rhythm. One. Two. Three. Four. One. Two. Three. Four.

Songs from last night's service swell and play in his inner ear. The kids had sung with such passion that song, "A Servant of All". Ken wonders if they have learned more than the words that week. One. Two. Three. Four. One. Two. Three. Four. Jesus taught that being great, means serving, too.

That probably means serving ones parents, too. "O.K. Lord. I'm getting it. I gotta work on my attitude. I do want to be great in Your eyes. And well. I'm not doing so well at home. Apparently. Since You're bringing these thoughts to my mind, I gotta be more servant minded." He runs and muses. Trying to keep his mind on the Lord and off of Angie. "I thought I was immune. What's with this Angie woman?"

10 - Communions

BONG! BONG! BONG! BONG! BONG! "Oh no! Not morning already," Angie gripes, wiping her eyes and trying to shade them from the sun squirming through the calico curtain on their dorm room window. Grammama's back. With her internal clock, she never needs an alarm or the campground bell. She doesn't like to wait in line to use the shared bathroom, so she's probably been up half an hour already. Grampoppa swings his legs over the side of the bed and slips on the well-worn house shoes she can see below the blanket dividing their room.

Angie's grandparents don't have a lot, but what they have, they spend on good leather shoes. Grammama always says, "If your feet not comfortable, nothing else gonna be. You gotta start from the ground up." Their sons usually see to it that both parents are well shod with new leather slippers for holiday gifts and birthday presents.

Grampoppa's broken in house shoes will provide support for the short trip down the hall to the men's bathroom. He collects his kit bag of shaving supplies and other toiletries and pulls his towel and wash cloth from the hook next to the door. Thinking Angie still is asleep, neither grandparent speaks. They just go about their morning routine of getting up, washed, dressed, and out to the morning prayer service.

She is tempted to join them this Friday morning when the Faithfuls will be sharing the Lord's Supper. But she doesn't. Her heart isn't ready to participate in that sacred sacrament. Even after a full night's passing, she's still puzzled by the anger and, yes, the jealousy she feels toward Ken and the Lady in Navy.

Angie lies there, pretending she's still asleep just in case Grammama pulls aside the blanket hanging between her cot and their side of the room. She sensed Angie's mood last night, but said little more than, "Sleep tight, Angie."

No doubt Gramamma noticed the crowd at the ice cream stand after the evening service and assumed Angie was simply pooped. Angie had twisted and turned a good portion of the night trying to get physically comfortable on the cot and emotionally comfortable in her heart. Grammama respects folk's privacy and seldom pokes or pries. She just prays.

Grampoppa returns quickly, not wanting to hold up the other men eager to use the facilities so that they too can join the regulars at the sunrise communion service. Some of the men, though, had gotten up even earlier to work on the grounds. A number of the staff share an eight-bed room at the end of the hall near the back door, the one closest to the kitchen. Since they get up at the crack of dawn anyway, they're not disturbed by the pots banging around below.

Within half an hour, both grandparents are dressed and out the door, having eaten no breakfast before taking communion. Angie lies there, visualizing the communion service she'd attended with them the summer she was twelve. She'd accepted Christ as her Savior during youth camp that year, and her grandparents urged her to take her first communion with the Faithfuls during their Friday sunrise prayer service. Though a little groggy that early in the morning seven years ago, Angie readily joined them, still awed about what they called her new birth.

===

IT IS A MISTY MORNING. Walking down the stairs from the dorm rooms in the still dark of dawn, Angie is surprised to see so many campers-- men and women, teens and tweens, young mothers and dads -- all walking serenely to the tabernacle. Few talk. None laugh. Not sad, just solemn. Pensive and reverent. Expectantly anticipating the time honored ceremony.

Over the years, Angie has seen people take The Lord's Supper, as they call it at her church, but has never taken part. Only those who are saved are invited to "sup at the table," as they say there.

Angie has seen the dressed-in-white deaconesses adorn the communion table with white damask cloths. They arrange the shiny golden plates filled with tiny cups of grape juice in a double tier of trays, covered with lids that have a cross serving as a handle. This container they'd set in the center of the draped table.

Flanking this cross topped tray would be two golden plates stacked with tiny cubes of bread. These plates the ladies cover with matching crisp white linen napkins laid on top so the corners fall just so.

Then two deaconesses stand at either end of the table, and a third tenderly lays a second cloth so that it falls gently, tent-like from the cross topped trays with the juice. The two deaconesses at the ends lovingly unfold this second cloth and arrange it so that it hangs neat and even.

Finally, they all stand solemnly facing the table, pray a silent prayer and walk sedately to the front row. Here they sit until the pastor invites them to assist him serving the elements of Lord's Supper during the communion celebration at her home church.

HERE ON ZION'S HILL, TWELVE YEAR OLD ANGIE is anxious about participating for the first time in this ancient sacramental rite.

This morning, the side doors of the tabernacle are closed, and everyone is heading to the rear, but no one hurries. Once there, each person pauses at the door as though shedding something, then steps up onto the cement slab outside the doorway and enters the silent tabernacle, free of whatever. No piano. No organ this morning. Just silence. Strange, Angie observes. It's silent, but not quiet.

She and her grandparents pause, enter, walk down the center aisle, and take seats in the front section about four rows from the white draped table. Grampoppa stands aside so Grammama can go in first and then, with his hand on Angie's shoulder, guides her to the next seat and then sits at the end. With no one directly in front of her, she can see very well.

Angie's a little uncomfortable. Things are very different – different from regular church service, sure, but also different from the communion services she's seen at her home church. She peeks around furtively to see if anyone else thinks things are strange. No one looks puzzled. Each one seems absorbed and other worldly – walking without seeming to look where they're going, but not bumping into furniture or other people. Rather surreal.

Angie sits between her grandparents and scrutinizes the layout up front. There's the snow white cloth on a long narrow table sitting front and center on the main floor just below the purple bannered lectern on the rostrum above. There are no golden trays with cross topped lids; there are no golden plates topped with white napkins.

Instead, Angie sees what looks like a brown shoe box nearly covered with a large white cloth. A washbasin sits on the table, and a small hand towel lies folded next to it. And there also is a golden goblet. A white hanky looking cloth is draped across the top of this tall wide mouth chalice.

Flanking these objects, on heavy squat brass candle holders, fat white candles glow boldly. They provide the only illumination in the room, other than the dawn light slipping through the narrow windows high up the side walls, just below the ceiling line. It's rather dark, but, oddly, not the least bit gloomy.

The congregants sit calmly with hushed expectancy. Angie can feel it all around her. She shuts her eyes a moment, feeling drawn to prayer. She's not sure why, or what to say, so she just sits prayerfully. Soft singing brings her back.

Let us break bread together or our knees
Let us break bread together on our knees.

Angie opens her eyes to three robed men walking out of the small room at the left side of the pulpit area, and down the steps from the rostrum. They sing a cappella and in harmony. The congregation joins in

When I fall on my knees
with my face to the rising sun
O Lord, have mercy on me.

The second verse says "drink wine together." By the time they get to the third verse, "Let us praise God together" everyone is standing and singing loudly and joyfully.

Angie is a little surprised that they're standing instead of kneeling, but she stands along with the rest of the congregation gathered here this morning. Though there are significantly fewer folks than attend the regular camp meeting services, those in attendance fill the tabernacle with their song of entreaty, "O Lord, have mercy on me."

169

The three robed men now stand side by side in the narrow space between the rostrum and the communion table, still singing in harmony as though they are a trio who has practiced for months.

But Angie recognizes these ministers; they're from different states…still they sing in close heavenly harmony. The shorter man on the left has a pure high tenor that floats above the others, yet fits right in. Strange that thought – floating, but fitting.

The men lead a repeat of the whole song, and by this time Angie has picked up the tune and joins in, feeling very much an integral part of the Faithful gathered in the tabernacle this morning.

Her grandfather's rich baritone rumbles from his chest. Her grandmother's voice is not all that melodious, but she does know all the words and sings with gusto. Angie hears a throaty alto behind her to the left and a lyrical soprano to the right. What joyful sounds, and she's right in the midst of them all.

The song ends, and the minister in the middle leads an opening prayer. The ministers on the left and right go sit in the front row. By this time the sun is a little higher and the room is a little lighter. Still, with no artificial lighting, the room remains shadowy and mysterious.

The minister behind the communion table opens a big blood red leather Bible with those gold edged onion skin pages. Will he read the same verses her pastor reads when they celebrate this sacrament at her church? He doesn't.

Instead, he closes his Bible and declares, "Saints, we just sung a familiar old song about breaking bread together on our knees and praising God on our knees, but all we done is stand up and sit down. Brothers and Sisters, I'm gonna invite you to turn right around at your seat and get down on your knees and thank the Lord for what he's done for you. On the cross and in your life. Let's give him a little time this morning. Let's give him some praise and thanksgiving."

And, then he breaks out into singing and clapping. "Oh, Oh, Oh, Oh what He's done for me. I never will forget what's He's done for me." Most of the congregants know the song and join him as they get up, lay their Bibles and purses in their seats, and kneel down on that concrete floor. Singing ceases.

Settling down, they fold their hands and bow their heads as though kneeling on cushioned pads. Angie copies what her grandparents do and kneels too. And also looks around wondering what she should be doing now.

All at once, folks all around her start praying out loud. Out loud. Everybody talking at the same time.

"Thank ya. Thank ya. Thank ya. Lord," erupts from grateful worshipers.

"You has been a good God and I just wanna thank ya for it," from the right.

"God, you done took care of me good this year. You has brung me back to these hallowed grounds and I just praise yo' name for it," from the left.

"You've taken care of me and my family. You've made a way outta no way," from another lady a couple rows away.

"Lord God Almighty. You're a wonderful friend. I lost my wife and you haven't let me feel too lonesome," comes a deep voice from further right.

Angie kneels there feeling like an eavesdropper. Should she be listening? Should she be praying herself? What should she be saying? She glances over at her grandmother. No clue. Grammama's just kneeling there with tears dripping onto her knuckled hands. She's not even trying to wipe the tears away.

Angie peeks at Grampoppa. His lips are moving, but no words are vocalized. So she just kneels there taking it all in. It feels strange, but somehow right, whatever that means. She's puzzled, but not frightened by the unusual sights and sounds.

Soon, from the front comes the booming voice of the middle minister leading out the Lord's Prayer, "Our Father, Who are in Heaven…" which the congregants join one or two at a time until they all are saying the prayer in unison, while, as though signaled to get up, they pick up their Bibles and purses and return to their seated positions.

171

"... for thine is the Kingdom, and the Power, and the Glory forever and ever. Amen."

What next?

"Don't you feel better, Brothers and Sisters? Don't it feel better spending a little time giving thanks? Giving thanks and praise for all God has been and all He's gonna be to each and everyone one us? Don't you just love this great God of ours? Can somebody say, 'Thank you, Jesus!'"

Thank you Jesuses and praise the Lords reverberate.

"Don't you just love Him? You know He loves you, don't you? And He's been loving you for a long time. You know the Bible says in the fifth chapter of book of Romans, verse eight, that '... God demonstrates His own love toward us, in that while we were yet sinners, Christ died for us.'"

"That's what we're here to celebrate this morning. The love of God. The love of His Son, Jesus Christ. The love that got us up this morning. Thank you, Jesus!" He does a little hop, skip and jump.

"The love that started us on our way." He claps his hands.

"The love that drew us to this hallowed campground O praise His Holy Name!" He shakes his head incredulously.

"The love that says we gotta do what Jesus did. We gotta show His love to others. You all were here last night. You heard our sweet little children singing "Jesus Loves Me This I Know." Do you know it, Saints? Do you know it deep down in your souls that Jesus loves you?" He pauses a second or two.

"No matter how you may have felt this morning getting up and getting washed with cold water because the folks ahead of you had run out all the hot water. No matter how pained you feel 'cause Ole Arthur slowed you down with a crick in your side or a creaking in your knee.

"No matter how sad you feel 'cause you here on Zion's Hill for the first time since a loved one passed away. Jesus loves you. He showed His love on the cross when He stretched out His arms and died for my sins and your sins.

"But, hallelujah! He didn't stay on the cross; He didn't even stay in the tomb. Praise God, Jesus rose again on Easter morning! Praise God, He's coming back to take us home with Him in heaven. He gonna come back and get those who've trusted in His death and resurrection, and we gonna go and live with Him forever. Can somebody say Amen?"

Thoughtful, cogitating silence.

"Can't anybody up in here say 'Amen'" he implores again.

Amens roll across the tabernacle, along with some hand clapping, glories, and hallelujahs.

"You all were here last night when the Sister preached about trust. That's what we gotta do Brothers and Sisters. We gotta trust that the same God who raised Jesus from the dead is gonna raise us up, too. In the meantime we gotta trust that the Holy Spirit that He sent to comfort us, to strengthen us, to teach and guide us is gonna be here when we need Him.

"Praise the Lord! God don't leave us alone. He got Him some sons and daughters, some Saints like them sitting on yo' left and yo' right who gonna be here for you. Who gonna show you the love of God? The love of God we come here to share this morning at this here communion table."

Angie notices that he slips in and out of a dialect…one she's heard lots of times at her home church. Sometimes the minister sounds real intellectual. Sometimes he sounds real conversational. Breaking it down. Sounding comfortable, easy to follow.

"Communion. Do y'all know what communion means? If you look it up in the dictionary, it would say something about being a Christian sacrament with bread and wine eaten and drunk to remember what Christ did for us way back on Calvary. That is true. That's one meaning of "communion." It also means 'intimate fellowship'. Intimate fellowship." He pauses again to let the thought sink in.

"That's what we celebrating here Brothers and Sisters. We all in the old ship of Zion, right here on Zion's Hill, sharing in the joys and sorrows of one another. Why? Because we becoming more and more like Christ. The Christ who loves us tells us if we wanna show we like him, we gotta show love.

173

"Y'all heard the children singing last night about being a servant of all. That's a nice song and all, but the Bible say, if we gonna be like Christ, we gotta serve one another. That's just what we gonna be doing this morning.

"We, my brother ministers here, we gonna be like Christ told us to be. Servants. Just like Christ took the bread and broke it and served it to his disciples, we gonna break the bread this morning and serve it to you. Brother Jefferson and Brother Marshall, y'all come on up here and help me prepare this bread and wine to serve this morning."

The two ministers rise and join the middle minister at the communion table. He goes on…

"To illustrate this is intimate fellowship, we gonna do something a little different. We gonna share the same loaf and share the same cup. But we ain't gonna be drinking out of the same cup," he chuckles. "We got health codes we gotta follow, but we are gonna use one cup.

"This what we gonna do this morning. We gonna ask y'all to come up row by row and take a little piece of bread and then dip the corner of that bread into the cup and eat it. This way we gonna be sharing the cup and the bread a little more intimately than if we was to pass the little hunks of bread and those little bitty cups.

"Yes, we know. This gonna take a little bit longer, but as you wait yo' time to come up, we gonna ask you to be in prayer for those who didn't come join us this morning or couldn't come for one reason or another. Be in prayer for those who made decisions for the Lord this week and those who are being nudged by the Holy Spirit to accept the salvation we celebrating here this morning, by joining in this intimate fellowship, by taking the bread and wine representing the body and blood of Jesus Christ, who loves us every one.

"Brother Smitherman, will you go on up to the organ and play us some quiet music that will keep our minds focused on the love of God and the sacrifice of His Son as we come take the bread and the wine?"

The organist quietly climbs the steps and flicks the switch on the organ. He scoots onto the bench and begins playing softly, in a minor, "Let Us Break Bread Together".

The two robed ministers join the preacher at the communion table, stand at attention as he washes his hands in the basin and dries them on the towel that lay on the table. At the right, Brother Marshall, takes the hankie off the top of the golden goblet. He neatly folds the cloth and lays it there. At the same time, Brother Jefferson, at the other end of the table, ceremonially removes the linen cloth revealing the oblong shape that turns out to be two loaves of uncut bread. He too folds and lays the napkin neatly on the table.

The preacher looks at Brother Jefferson, who picks up the red Bible, and this time the preacher does read from it. It's the same scripture from Corinthians that Angie hears at her church, "…the Lord Jesus the same night in which he was betrayed took bread."

Brother Jefferson holds the Bible for the preacher so his hands stay clean. The preacher picks up the one loaf, holds it up high so everyone can see it and then he breaks it and as he sets one half back down on the plate, he continues with the reading… "Take, eat: this is my body, which is broken for you: this do in remembrance of me." He lays the bread on the plate.

Then he steps over to the golden goblet and gently clasps it with both hands and raises it high so everyone can see it. He finishes reading the passage from Corinthians, "After the same manner also he took the cup, when he had supped, saying, this cup is the new testament in my blood: this do ye, as oft as ye drink it, in remembrance of me."

Brother Jefferson closes the Bible and reverently places it on the rostrum floor behind him and steps back to his end of the table. The preacher prays and then hands the plate of bread to Brother Jefferson and the cup to Brother Marshall. Now, standing with his arms spread wide, he gestures with upturned palms, signaling the ushers to direct the congregants to come to the supper table. They begin from the rear and move forward row by row, orderly, not really needing the ushers this morning.

The organist continues softly playing a medley of songs. Some are familiar; some are not. All make Angie think of Jesus and about the decision she made to trust him with her life. When it's time for her row to go forward, she files out behind her grandfather. They approach the table.

She remembers she's supposed to take a little piece of bread and dip into the goblet and then eat it. Break, dip and eat. Break, dip and eat. Break... She notices that Grampoppa stops a foot or so behind the man in front of him...giving him privacy at the table. Angie decides to do that too.

She's close enough to hear Brother Jefferson say, "This is my body broken for you." as the man breaks off a little piece of bread. He walks over to the other side of the table and stops in front of Brother Marshall. Angie hears him say, "This is my blood, shed for you."

The bread, Angie can see and understand that. There's a real loaf of bread here. But the Bible reading said "Wine," and now the minister is saying "Blood". Her stomach flips and flutters. It was weird enough thinking there would be real wine.

The folks in her church don't believe in drinking wine so they serve grape juice for communion. If it's not grape juice, maybe a teeny dip of wine wouldn't be too bad. But blood. Yuck! By this time Grampoppa's gotten his bread and is walking over to the cup. The usher's gloved hand beckons Angie to move forward to get her bread.

She steps up and stands in front of Brother Jefferson. Listens to "broken for you" and reaches up to get her piece of bread. Wouldn't you know it? The closest part of the loaf is the crust. She tries to break off a teeny, little piece and the bread starts to slide on the plate. She stops. Looks up at Brother Jefferson. He smiles at her and nods his head, encouragingly. She takes a deep breath and reaches up and a little more firmly, easily tears off a little hunk of the crust. She lets out her breath and walks over to the golden goblet.

She stops and stands in front of Brother Marshall. Listens to "shed for you" and reaches up to dip her bread. Brother Marshall holds the cup down a little so she can see inside. It's really dark and red in there. She takes a deep breath. Decides to go for it and dips the corner of her bread in the cup with shaking hands.

She dips too deep, and the whole piece seeps red. Even her fingers go into the liquid. "Oops," she gasps. She looks up and Brother Marshall simply smiles and nods. Whew! Angie puts the soggy bread into her mouth. Hmmm.

176

It's a little sour. Not sweet like grape juice at all. Angie smiles back at Brother Marshall and returns to her seat. Maybe, she postulates, it really is wine. She's taken communion. She's had the bread and the wine. She's doing just what Jesus told them to do – in remembrance of Him.

===

"IN REMEMBRANCE OF HIM," older Angie deliberates lying abed after her grandparents leave for the sunrise communion service. "In remembrance of Him." In the seven years since that first communion, Angie's read the Bible regularly and recalls that when Jesus felt out of it, tired and maybe out of sorts, He'd go off someplace by Himself to spend time alone…alone with God. Angie's got to do something to get herself together. The attitude she's been showing is not the least bit like Jesus.

So she rolls out of the cot, slips on her house coat and slippers, gathers her toiletries and heads down to the ladies' bathroom. Thankfully, no one's there and she quickly washes, brushes, and combs, and then scurries back to her room to dress. She drapes a sweater around her shoulders and grabs her Bible. She's got to find a quiet place where she can spend some time alone with God.

It's still dewy outside and Angie's glad she's got on shoes she doesn't mind getting wet. She's put on the clothes she'd worn last Saturday when she helped Stella clean the ice cream stand before opening it to the public. The wrinkled clothes she's donned smell a little rank from the sweat and all, but Angie doesn't plan to be with anyone else this morning, so she's okay looking a little less put together than other times.

She's heading up to a spot higher up the hill to a section of the grounds where little cutting and trimming is done. She'd heard in one of the business meetings that the Zion's Hill management is reserving that acreage of the campgrounds to build a senior citizen retirement village.

They envision an attractive planned community for the church folks to invest in while they're still working and then move up here to live when they retire. The plans call for a community center with a small chapel, dining room, recreation facilities, and a clinic staffed with medical professionals trained in geriatrics who will live on site to assist with health issues of aging residents.

The plans even showed closed-in walkways between the condos surrounding the community center.

On the drive here this year, Angie learned her grandparents have looked at the retirement community prospectus, but haven't made a decision. They'd both prefer living nearer to family when they retire. Angie's all for that. She wants to be able to visit them all year long. The campgrounds would be pretty cut off in the winter.

The trail she follows this morning is rocky and steep, but Angie's in good shape and soon crests the hill. To the left, she can't see it, but hears water rippling and roiling. She imagines it twisting and tumbling over the rocks along the hillside just like her agitated feelings. She searches for a ledge she'd seen before.

She climbs a little further and carefully scans the area, listening intently to make sure she's frightened away any snakes and field mice, but not the birds and butterflies. Angie's a city girl, a little tense out in untamed natural spots, and skittish about seeing wild animals, even little ones like chipmunks.

She doesn't really recognize which little animals are dangerous and is more in danger of hurting herself trying to get away when startled by one. That's how she felt her first year at youth camp. Their counselor, Sister Barkely, had brought them somewhere near here the last evening for a special time together before saying goodbye the next afternoon.

===

"NOW GIRLS," Sister Barkley begins when they finally reach the flatter area at the top of the hill. "Let's look for a spot where we can sit in a circle." They've brought folded tarps to sit on and their flashlights to scatter the darkness. That's about it. Something to sit on and something to see by.

Once they're all seated, Sister Barkley tells them to shut off the flashlights. Angie, a little nervous, shrinks from the shadows that lurk in the night, but she's with friends, so she complies, trying to remain calm.

"All right, girls. Now just relax. Get yourself as comfortable as you can, sitting on the ground with little stones poking your behinds."

They giggle, of course. They're twelve and thirteen years old. That's what tweeny girls do in peer groups like this. They're in awe of their leader and want to impress her, but don't want to lose the respect of their friends. Each wants to appear cool, but all are just a little uncomfortable out here in the open. In the dark.

Up to now, their evening activities have been held just a few feet from other groups. Tonight, they're all alone. It's a little creepy. Angie's just a little uneasy. Yes, and also a little scared.

Sister Barkley shushes and chides them. "You can do this, ladies. You can sit without squirming and talking for three or four minutes, can't you? I know you can handle a little bit of quiet. Come on now. Sit in a circle, back to back so you won't be distracted by one another." They settle, backs touching.

"It's like we're in a museum or a library where you gotta be quiet," Angie hears from behind her. A couple nervous sniggles. Soon, though, they all are mum; they mentally turn and listen. Just before they become unsettled in the silence, Sister Barkley continues in a hushed voice.

"Now, my dears. Look up."

They do.

"Just absorb the silence of the night and glory in the splendor of the sky."

They tilt back their heads and look up. They revel in the clear, cool night and gaze at the dark sky sparkling like a diamond-encrusted evening shawl draped over the transparent walls of the world.

A black silk shawl like the one Angie used when she and her sisters made tents to play in the dining room. Their mother had a hissy when she came home from shopping to see her heirloom stole flung so carelessly over her Duncan Phyfe chairs. The sky tonight looks like that scarf. Real dark, and shimmering with stars.

The night sky. So fragile looking. So breathtaking, enticing. Light years away these nebula of contracting gasses look so tiny from way down here on earth. What an awesome thought that the shimmering stars don't fall right out of the sky.

179

After a couple minutes Sister Barkley begins reciting Psalms 19,

> The heavens declare the glory of God;
> and the firmament sheweth his handiwork.
> Day unto day uttereth speech, and night
> unto night sheweth knowledge.
> There is no speech nor language, where their voice is not heard.

The girls shiver, considering the God of the Universe and the work of His hands.

Sister Barkley is silent for a couple more minutes. The girls tilt again, leaning their heads to the side to keep from bumping into their back to back partner. They watch. Sister Barkley's deep voice begins, "O Lord, our Lord, how excellent is thy name in all the earth! Who hast set thy glory above the heavens..," from Psalms 8. They contemplate the answer.

Angie tries to imagine what it looks like above the heavens. It's so gorgeous right here. How much more glorious would things look, from God's perspective, observing them from above the heavens?

She remembers sermons about the time when Jesus is to come back to take the saints to heaven. The pearly gates and the streets of gold. At home, in church, it's hard to imagine such a place. Out here, up on this hill in the dark, hearing Sister Barkley quote from Psalms, Angie can believe that such a splendiferous heavenly home could be a real place.

> When I consider thy heavens, the work of thy fingers,
> the moon and the stars, which thou hast ordained;
> What is man, that thou art mindful of him?
> and the son of man, that thou visitest him?

Sister Barkley's contralto voice makes the verses sound like a song. A song to the Creator. She begins to hum, "He's got the whole world in His hands, He's got the whole world in His hands." The girls join in softly, singing the chorus several times, a little louder each time, reverently, but not as boisterously as they sing other camp songs. It just doesn't seem right to be too noisy out here. They stop singing, but don't begin chattering. They wait. Patiently. No talking; no wiggling.

"Ladies, tomorrow is our last day of camp. We've had a wonderful time these two weeks getting to know one another and getting to know the God of the Bible a little bit better. Tomorrow we head back home, and I know from past experience that once you get back home, lots of the excitement and enthusiasm of camp will simply evaporate. You'll be back in situations where you'll be challenged to live out the faith some of you have just recognized you have."

The girls nod, faintly.

"Your parents will make demands of you that you feel are unfair. Your brothers and sisters will be their regular obnoxious selves, pushing your buttons and making you wish you were back here, away from it all. Well, it'll be another year before we'll be having camp here again, but in the meantime, you'll not be alone."

Eyebrows rise, but the girls say nothing.

"This God we've been studying about, this God we've been talking and singing about. This God we've been experiencing together here on Zion's Hill, He'll be with you in the form of His Holy Spirit. You just have to remember that and allow Him to bolster you with the strength and the courage to do what is right."

The girls sit up and look at her with uncertain expressions.

"Yes, my dears, it's going to take courage to live the Christian life. Some of you already have seen that here at camp. Back home, you'll be teased. You'll be ostracized. You'll think you've made a bad decision to accept Christ as your Savior. You'll wonder if it's worth being left off invitation lists for some of the popular parties. You'll question yourself, doubting you can hold up being talked about when you champion the weak, when you volunteer your weekends working on some service projects when you could be hanging out with your friends at the park or playground."

Shaking heads suggest the youngsters believe they will remain faithful once they leave camp.

"I know, I know. I really do know. Once you leave, all that we've experienced here will seem like a dream. You'll wonder if you've had an out of this world experience. You haven't. This is real. And, I assure you, you can withstand the fiery darts of the Devil that'll come at you when you return home.

"Fiery darts," someone repeats.

"Yes, fiery darts. Remember that lesson about the whole armor of God? You're going to need it. One thing about that armor, young ladies, is that it has to be maintained. In order for the Breastplate of Righteousness to resist rust and the Shield of Faith to stay shiny, they'll have to be oiled. That's where prayer and Bible study come in. Keep the helmet of salvation firmly on your heads and carry the sword of the Spirit with you at all times."

Angie raises her hand ever so timidly and asks, "Sister Barkely, what kind of sword are we supposed to be carrying? This ain't a real sword, right?"

"No sweetie. We're talking about the Word of God, the Bible. Girls, this Armor of God is figurative language. That means the writer uses familiar language to talk about something unfamiliar. In his letters to early Christians, the writer, Apostle Paul, uses the imagery of a soldier when writing about the hostility these early saints would face."

The girls nod, but really don't understand. Sister Barkley senses this and breaks it down a little more.

"This apostle looks at the Christian life as a battle against the Devil who doesn't want you to live your lives as Christians. In this case, the Sword is the Word of God. That's why we encourage you to memorize Scripture verses so they'll be with you all the time. You know the story of Jesus being tempted by Satan?"

The girls nod soberly.

"As a young man, Jesus studied Scripture, and knowing what the Word of God says helped Jesus to resist the temptation of the Devil, Satan. If Jesus needed that kind of sword, you can be sure as shooting that you will need it, too. He thwarted the darts of the Devil with Scripture. You, too, can survive the darts of the Devil with Scripture."

182

Another girl raises her hand, a little more boldly now that she sees Sister Barkely is open to questions of clarification.

"Um. Sister Barkely. What do you mean by 'darts of the Devil'? Will we be able to see him shootin' at us?"

"No, Honey. You're not likely to be faced with a fork-tailed little guy in a red suit with horns growing out of his forehead." The girls look at one another and giggle, thinking, That's what I was thinkin', too.

"That's a cartoon Devil. No, my young darlings, the Devil you will encounter may have the face of your best friend tempting you to betray your calling to follow Christ. The Devil you sense may be within you, tempting you to skip your Bible reading, tempting you to cut short your prayer time, taunting you to say something mean to hurt someone who hurt your feelings.

"You will be enticed to do all manner of ungodly things. Actions or inactions that will cause you to doubt your faith, doubt the strength you have to withstand and to stand firm. To stand for right regardless of the situation…in a group or all alone.

The girls groan. This is getting close to home.

"Knowing God's Word is the best way to protect yourself and to prepare yourself for what you'll be facing every day until Jesus comes back again. Until that time, trust in the Lord. That's what the Scripture means about having a sword. That's God's Word that you wield during temptation and you can win.

"Trust in the Lord with all thine heart; and lean not unto thine own understanding." Sister Barkley has moved now to the book of Proverbs. How impressive that she can quote all the verses without looking them up in her Bible. This is one of the verses their counselor has had the girls memorize, and now she invites them to quote it with her.

Softly and tentatively, one voice after another joins the spoken chorus when she begins the verse again. Sister Barkely always makes them cite where to find the verses in the Bible or what she calls the "address of the verse", so they begin with the name of the book, the chapter and the verses.

Proverbs three, five and six.

> Trust in the Lord with all thine heart;
> and lean not unto thine own understanding.
> In all thy ways acknowledge him,
> and he shall direct thy paths.

NOW, SEVEN YEARS LATER, near the same location, Angie sits with her legs dangling from the ledge on a promontory overlooking Zion's Hill and the more distant Shenango Valley, reciting those same words, words that have stayed with her all this time. Words she needs to apply to this current emotional situation. "Trust in the Lord ... submit to Him...O.K. Lord. I know what the verses say. How do they fit today? Ken, men, or the lady in navy?

"Back home, most of my high school classmates either are engaged or married already. They keep asking me if I'm going out with anyone yet. Who I'm attracted to and wanting to date? That's not for me   I don't have time for that now. I don't feel like that's what You want for me either. I'm supposed to be finishing my college education. I know that. And anyway, I've only known Ken for a few days. Why should I feel jealousy?

"I don't know why I feel like I'm tempted to abandon my dreams and consider a future with Ken. He lives here in Pennsylvania; I live three hundred miles away in Michigan. I don't see a future in such a long distance romance. It's impossible. So, why do I care that he brought another woman with him last night? He's a free agent. He's made no promises to me.

"Anyway. We talked about that the other day, and we agree. Keep our eyes on the prize. A college degree in education for me and in engineering for him.

"Yeah. Well, he did seem mighty comfortable with that woman. His hands were all over her. Well, not all, all over. But he and she were sharing a lot of personal space. That usually is a sign that a pair is a couple. And she was dressed so nice, too. Even if I catch everything on sale, I could never afford an outfit like that." Angie's enjoying her pity party.

"And even if I could, I probably wouldn't look that put together in it. I don't have that kind of fashion sense. I wonder if that's what Ken's looking for in the woman he'll marry. Marriage. What am I doing thinking about Ken and marriage? This is ridiculous!

"Lord, OK. So, I guess I am a little jealous. I don't know if it's simple jealousy of the situation or envy of a woman who is so good-looking and well-dressed. Maybe it's not jealousy. I've never been all that interested in clothes.

"This is different. I really don't like to think of Ken being with someone so unlike me. She's slimmer, lighter complexioned, has longer hair, lovely legs, and she wears a hat on a Thursday night! If that's what he likes, I don't have a chance! This stinks, Lord." She's about had enough.

Angie gazes out over the treetops. "I'm not getting anywhere with this one way conversation. Just going around in circles." Angie flips open her Bible to distract herself from these swirling thoughts and accompanying emotions.

What should she read? Nothing comes to mind. She shuts the Bible and holds it shut with her right hand caressing the leather cover with her left. "I'm too frustrated now to even make out the words on the pages anyway. I'll just sit and absorb the ambiance."

It's still early and relatively quiet. Few people are out and about down on the main section of the campground. The Faithful are still at the communion service, and just a couple groundskeepers are setting out extra trash receptacles for the weekend influx.

Angie sits still and stiff, hard-backed and square-shouldered, willing peace to enfold her. Of course, that doesn't work. She decides to do a deep breathing exercise. Maybe it will help her relax and allow the Spirit of God to infuse her heart, help her refocus onto Christ-like thoughts and Christ-like behavior.

Breathe in eight counts. Breathe out seven counts. In for eight. Out in seven. In. Out. Soon her shoulders loosen; her shadow's a softer silhouette.

Senses now open. Sweet floral tones. No spicy, or maybe minty notes. Crushed weeds beneath the shoe leather. Dew dampened socks. Itches from saw-toothed grasses brushing her calves. Wiggles. Oomph, pokey bumps in the rock seat. Dimples in the leather covered Bible sensed in her stroking fingertips.

In for eight. Out in seven. Cool morning air. A little sneezy. Gently breezy. Ah, birds. There on the tip of the tree branch. Bobbing in the air, but not falling off. What's that Emily Dickinson poem, 'Faith is a thing with feathers...'? No, I think it's

> Hope is the thing with feathers
> That perches in the soul,
> And sings the tune—without the words,
> And never stops at all...

"Well, I'm going to substitute "faith". That's what my faith is. Like that bird sitting, just wobbling on the limb and warbling its heart out. God, You know my heart. I trust You with my life, but I'm wobbling now. Not sure whether I should be waiting or working on this relationship."

Angie looks out over the vista in the valley spread before her--a panoramic view she's nearly missed--so inward-looking she's been.

Here on Zion's Hill, high up above the expanse of the Shenango Valley. From here, full-leafed tree-tops look like the tips of broad-spreading bushes. So many shades of the same color, side by side they look distinctly different. Kelly greens. Jades with a hint of grey. Lime green. Chartreuse with nuances of yellow. Deep shadows of British racing green. Dusky army green.

"Wow. There's bluish grey green. Hey, those frothy celadon colored ferns over there look like green foam in the sunlight. Yeah, I've seen that on Korean pottery. Pines. Of course, Christmas tree green. But shamrock, and moss and camouflage green over there where the sun's peeking through. God, You're some kind of artist! So many greens on Your palette when You painted this valley."

The wind shifts and Angie hears strains of the organ in the tabernacle. She closes her eyes and imagines music, cartoon notes riding the breezes, floating on undulating music staffs.

"What's the song?" She cocks her head downhill. "Can't tell yet..." She listens and sways to the rhythm, trying to tune in enough to figure out which hymn she hears. Angie senses the words before she recognizes the tune and begins to hum along. It's the third verse that she hears in her head,

Just as I am, though tossed about
with many a conflict, many a doubt,
fightings within and fears within, without,...

"What am I really fighting, Lord? What is it that I fear? That You won't keep your promises to me if I do put my trust in You? I say with my mouth that I believe You want to me finish college and that You'll work out my relationships in the order that is right for me. But Ken feels right. Well, he did. Until last night. Last night when he showed up with the Lady in Navy!"

The strains of the song flow around her; the words nudge her to delve more deeply. The fifth verse insinuates itself,

Just as I am, Thou wilt receive,
wilt welcome, pardon, cleanse, relieve;
because Thy promise I believe,
O Lamb of God, I come, I come.

Surrounded by His beauty, suffused in His majesty, reminded of His Love and welcome, Angie releases her anxiety to the Lord, acknowledging, "Yes, Lord, I've been anxious. Worried about much that is frivolous. I'm so glad You know me, love me, and understand that my truest desire is to be welcomed, pardoned, cleansed, and, yes, relieved.

"I've got to really trust You with all my heart and stop leaning on my own understanding. 'Cause I obviously don't understand what's going on right now. I guess, I'll just have to be on the lookout for Your leading and directing my path, accept and follow that." She breathes deeply, and exhales slowly, releasing a little more anxiety with each exhalation.

"Thank you, Lord, for meeting me here on this hallowed hill. Hallowed, not just because the Brothers and Sisters of Love so many years ago prayed that all who come to this camp meeting will be blessed. But hallowed today because You're here. You're here with me, and I thank you for it. Thank you, dear Lord. I just thank you so very much."

Cleansing tears peek from her eyes and leak down her cheeks. Angie sings along with the organ notes that float through the air.

Just as I am, Thy love unknown
broken every barrier down;
now, to be Thine, yea Thine alone,
O Lamb of God, I come, I come.

Angie stands and stretches. Her Bible still clutched in one hand, she raises her hands above her head in a gesture of both openness and acceptance.

No need to read from the printed page this time. Verses she'd memorized as a child have ministered to her heart. The manuscript inscribed as trees and flowers have spoken God's Word into her mind. The music hovering around her and the lyrics inside articulate for her, as surely as reading from a text, that she is a beloved child of God and that she can trust that all will be well with her today. All will be well.

STRIDING DOWN THE HILL, glancing at her watch and recognizing that although she has less than half an hour to change clothes and grab something to eat, Angie still slows down a bit, to savor this time with the Lord.

She'll get to the playground in time to help set up snacks for this last day of Children's Church before heading over to help Stella at the stand. Today they'll have a colorful tablecloth and small favors to remind the little ones of the lessons they've been learning this week.

Fred and Sharinda always pick just the right trinket – nothing expensive, but something to symbolize the message of the week. What a blessing to work with them. Angie prays that when these young ones get into a situation similar to hers today that the Bible verses and songs they've been taught in Children's Church will arise in their consciousness to strengthen them for their journeys.

11 - Friday Morning - In the Garden

ACROSS TOWN, Ken returns from his run totally fatigued instead of fully recharged as he usually is after such a workout. Perhaps spending time up at the garden will do it for him. Get that woman off his mind. It's dragging him down and raising doubts about what he had heard from the Lord. He knows what he is feeling in his head, but his heart doesn't agree.

He sheds his shoes, shucks his smelly shirt, and rinses off at the outdoor water spigot. There's no reason to take a full garden hose shower since he'll be getting all sweaty again in just a little while. Still, his mother won't like his coming to breakfast stinking up that end of the trailer. So, maybe a spray with the garden hose is in order.

"Good morning everybody," he says reaching back to keep the screen door from slamming behind him. "What's for breakfast?"

His mother points to the rooster on the cereal box.

"Not corn flakes and bananas...again." That's about all they've had this hot and humid summer. His mother claims she'll melt and ooze out the door if she has to prepare hot meals...especially on days she is going to can.

Well, today is canning day, so today's breakfast is corn flakes and bananas, again. Ken reaches over his mother's shoulder to get a bigger bowl from the cabinet behind her. She leans to the right, while pointing that she'd already put his bowl out. Ken frowns at that little soup bowl. It didn't hold enough to even waste time sitting down to eat from it.

"Mom, you know I eat my cereal out of this white bowl. I have been since high school," he reminds her as he sets the large vegetable serving dish at his place and begins pouring the orangy brown flakes into his bowl. The flakes only fill half the bowl. Ken shakes harder...only crumbs left. "Mom, can I have a peanut butter and jelly sandwich to round out my breakfast?"

"Ken, do you still have hollow legs? I thought you'd fill them in while you were in the service or at least at that school you're going to now. I didn't imagine you'd still be eating so much now that you're a grown man."

"Ah, Mom. I'm hungry. You know I got out and ran this morning, and I'm getting ready to go up and finish picking the green beans for you. I gotta eat something to keep up my strength. You don't want me fainting out there in the field all by myself, now do you?"

"Of course, not Ken. But you eat as much as the three of us put together! We can hardly keep up with grocery shopping since you came home this summer."

"Oh, Mom. I'll be gone in a week, and you guys'll be able to get back on your budget. I get my last check from camp this week, and I'll go shopping before I leave next weekend."

She bows her head, ashamed she's mentioned the matter. Ken apologizes.

"I didn't mean to be a burden to you all this summer. I'll be gone soon, okay?" By this time, Ken has finished slicing his banana and poured the last of the milk on his half bowl of corn flakes.

DURING HIS FIRST COUPLE OF MONTHS HOME, when he was working long hours at the plant, he'd been getting his meals at the little diner next door to the plant. He'd spent more than he intended, but getting back so late, he hadn't wanted to be messing up the kitchen fixing himself something after the family already had eaten. They'd gotten so used to his not being around that they hadn't shopped with him in mind.

During the weeks at camp, his meals had been included, so he could understand Mom not knowing how much he ate daily. Still…he didn't realize he was such a burden to the family. "After all, I am family," he silently grouses as he hurries to finish the cereal. Corn flakes certainly aren't very filling. Even with a banana!

Noticing his silence, his mom apologizes. "Ah, Ken. I didn't mean to make you feel bad. But you do eat a lot! Of course, I'm glad you're healthy and helping out since you've been home, and all. Don't get me wrong. We're glad you've got a job this summer and are going to college. We're really proud of you."

Ken stops scarfing in the cornflakes and smiles. Mother continues,

"Yes, and I know you've got to stay in shape for basketball, but, like I said. You're virtually eating us out of a house and a home. We thought we'd have more saved to get the basement outfitted so we can move in there before winter. Oh well. It's been this long. God's taken care of us so far, and we'll have to keep trusting Him, now won't we?"

Ken's nearly finished the cereal and is tilting the bowl to get the last of the milk and wilted flakes before grabbing the peanut butter and jelly sandwich his mother has made for him while she talked and he ate.

"Yeah, Mom. You and Dad really have disciplined yourselves not to take shortcuts on that house. Do you really think you'll have the basement wired and the utilities in so you can move in this winter?"

"Your dad believes we will. Some of his buddies from church, you know the Coopers and his crew, are coming next week to give us a couple of days. They're all going up to the campgrounds for meetings this weekend. By the way, how's it been for you this week? Do you find the camp meetings much different?"

"Yes, ma'am. It's really different after being away all this time. Before graduating and going to the Air Force, I wasn't a Christian, and so I didn't really spend much time in the worship services up there. Back then, me and the guys just hung around and gawked at girls when we weren't playing basketball.

"This year, I've gone to service every day, except Wednesday, and, yeah, it's different." Yeah, in more ways than one. Angie. "The sermons have been pretty good. It's great, too, to be singing the old songs." He chomps on the sandwich, slowing to flick glucky bits from the roof of his mouth. Too bad there isn't any more milk.

"I went to Christian services on the base sometimes and attended some Sundays on campus when the team wasn't traveling or hosting a game. But the music was different there. I didn't realize how much I missed the songs I grew up with."

His mother starts clearing the table as Ken finishes the sandwich, wishing he had milk to wash it down. Instead, he reaches down to get some ice water out of the little refrigerator below the counter Just a couple of glasses of tasteless water, then off to the garden.

"Will Dad be back soon? He said I can take the car up to the field since I'll be bringing back the green beans. I can't carry much stuff on that old Schwinn mutt bike I been riding all summer."

"Yeah, Ken. He said he'd be back soon. He's going to stop and pick up some milk and bread on his way back. He should be here by eight or so."

Ken glanced up at the clock on the stove. Just a few more minutes. Also an hour since he'd thought about Angie. Good.

"I hope so, 'cause I want to finish up there before noon. There's no shade up there you know. I wanna get back so I can get some studying done this afternoon before I get cleaned up for services tonight." So he can see Angie.

Ken gets up, aching to stretch, but there's no room. He tries to decide whether or not to put on a fresh shirt to go work in the garden or to just wear the sweaty one he'd had on this morning.

He hears the car in the gravelly yard, steps outside, and grabs the same shirt and pulls it over his head. The garden tools are stored in the lean-to up at the field, but the baskets to bring back the beans are in the shed next to the trailer, so he says goodbye to his mother and goes over to get the baskets.

"Morning, Dad. Glad you're back so I can get up there before the sun gets scorching hot. Thanks for letting me use the car, too. It's still okay for me to use it this evening, too. Isn't it?" So he can see Angie.

"Yeah, I promised I'd be back, and here I am. I said you could use the car this week if you remembered not to drive too fast over that horrid road up to the campgrounds and get dings all in my car. I checked this morning. Didn't see any, so I guess you been driving all right. So, yeah, you can use it today."

"Thanks, Dad," Ken replies, choking the urge to say, "I'm not a kid!"

"I shouldn't need it this afternoon, so you can have it earlier. Don't forget you gotta fill up the tank, too." He reaches in to pull the bag of groceries from the back seat.

"Okay, Dad, and thanks. Thanks a lot!" Ken grimaces at his ungrateful thoughts earlier. He takes the keys his stepfather tosses, shoves the baskets into the trunk, crams a baseball cap down on his head, and gets into the car.

No point risking sun stroke on this final Friday morning before he heads back to State College. "If you need the car this afternoon, I can take the lawn chair out to the shade tree back here and do my studying till you're finished. Okay?"

"That's fine, Ken. See ya." Dad switches the grocery bag into his left arm, opens the trailer door with his right hand, and leaves Ken to go about his work for the day.

"Well, that's done," Ken says to the steering wheel as he backs out of the driveway, turns, and heads out towards the field garden. "I really didn't think my coming home would be such a burden. I thought they'd be gladder to have me around this summer. It's tough to be a grown man and a burden on my family.

"Well, just one more week here and three more years at school, and I'll be out of their hair for good. Maybe, I can find a job in another town or something next summer." He settles into the seat, drapes his wrist across the top of the steering wheel, and drives listlessly up the highway.

SOON, KEN REACHES THE TURN-OFF to the unpaved road leading up the hill to his uncle's farm. To help his favorite sister, he had let Ken's parents plant a garden when they moved into the projects. They had kept it up when they moved. So far they'd not had time to clear away enough rocks to till their own property for gardening. No big deal.

Uncle has seen how hard his brother-in-law has been working to save for that house and truly admires him for taking time to go back to school to get a better job. Uncle said that the least he could do was to share what little he has. He's never had much cash, but he does have land.

Ken gripes to his mother sometimes about having to work up here this summer, but really he has rather enjoyed it. It gives him something physical to do, and it does help put food on the table. They've had fresh vegetables all summer, and it looks like his mother is doing a pretty good job of canning extras so that during the winter they'll have good food to supplement store-bought groceries. Ken gets out of the car, strides over to the lean-to, and pulls out the garden hoe. He gets right to work. So he can finish and go see Angie.

He chops weeds from the row of cabbage and three rows of collard plants. He stops, wipes the sweat from his eyes and wishes he'd remembered to bring the knit headband he wears when playing basketball, even though it's probably rather crusty after the games yesterday. A cap blocks the sun but doesn't absorb the water streaming down his face or keep salty drippings from stinging his eyes. He chortles when he remembers his mother and sister teasing one another about sweat.

"Ladies don't sweat; we perspire!" Mom would say looking up from the bread dough she was kneading.

"Ladies don't sweat; we glow!" Joann would interject as she pushed the vacuum down the hallway.

"Ladies don't sweat; we glisten!" styled Thia, standing with her hand on her hip watching them both.

Right. Perspiring, glowing or glistening, the liquid saline secretions burn his eyes, and he wishes he had a sweatband!

He turns at the end of the row and peers from under the bill of his cap at the long rows left to be weeded and decides he doesn't have to do the beans since he is going to be stripping those plants today. He stoops to pull a couple of carrots, shakes off the loose dirt, and puts them in his pocket. He'll rinse them off up at the well before he leaves. They'll be his lunch. Mom won't mind his eating a few carrots…especially if he doesn't mention it. Just another week and he'll be back on campus. Team meals are provided during the season. No need to worry about meals again till spring term.

Images of slaves working in the cotton fields come to mind as Ken begins the next row. He even smiles when he remembers Gram's expression, "You've got a long row to hoe." It's more than a figurative expression today. Of course he only has a couple dozen rows, not acres of field to be bothered with. Still, he does have a long row to hoe and had better get on with it.

Soon, he is into a rhythm. Chop, pull, turn. Chop, pull, turn. Chopping the weeds, pulling them away from the plants, turning over the weeds so they'll dry up and die. Chop, pull, turn. He hums as he works. Melodies from old Negro spirituals come to mind…nothing particular that he can identify, but he can almost hear the singing and sense how those songs soothed the souls of his ancestors forced to labor long and late through all the heat of the day.

A COUPLE HOURS LATER, an exhausted Ken takes the time to re-stake the tomatoes and check the vines for tomatoes ripe enough for salad. A few are. He checks the cucumbers and zucchini. A few are ready to eat, so he adds them to his basket. On the way over to the shed, Ken will inspect the squash and pumpkins for the glossy green worms and those ghostly white ones. Of course, his mother expects him to peel back the mini umbrella leaves to see if there are worms hiding down there, too. She had planted marigolds nearby in hopes they'd repel the worms, but that didn't seem to be helping much. Nothing seems to keep all the pests away. So here he is flicking worms.

All in all, the weather has been pretty good this summer. Ken has only had to hand water the garden a couple of times in mid-July using water from Uncle's well. His uncle has inside plumbing now, but his well still is the place they go for water when they're working outside.

That well water is pretty good, too. Cold, rather crisp and always refreshing. Not like the reddish irony water they get down on their new property. They have to boil water before drinking it. Ken's dad said they'll have to install a Culligan water filter when they move into the house. Now, they have to put up with cleaning those rusty rings from the sinks and toilet!

Ken guzzles a drink, rinses and eats the carrots, and then goes back to chopping weeds for another half hour or so. He needs another psalm to keep his mood from souring. Which one? What'll do it for him this time? "This is the day that the Lord has made; let us rejoice and be glad in it." He repeats it a couple of times, like a mantra hoping that the words will wash over his soul and assuage the resentment he feels when he thinks about breakfast time this morning.

Strange how the Enemy is bringing David's imprecatory psalms to mind when Ken should be thinking more pleasant thoughts. "No, Satan, I'm not giving in to ingratitude and temptation to wish anyone harm. I will praise the Lord in Psalms.

"This is the day, this is the day that the Lord has made. I will rejoice, I will rejoice and be glad in it!" he chants and de-worms the remaining pumpkin plants. "I WILL rejoice!"

195

It's nearly eleven thirty. Ken had better be picking green beans. He tramps back over to the car and hauls out another of the peck baskets he's brought. He stands by the car, breathing a sigh of relief. He's gone most of the morning without thinking about Angie!

It's getting so hot out here, and he grins. "I sure could use that glacier glare she was shooting my way last night." With a smile, he grabs the edge of his tee-shirt, pulls it up to wipe his forehead and decides he'd better get busy if he is to have the car back by one as he promised his dad. Just in case he's changed his mind.

Ken certainly hopes Thia is over her snit by the time he gets back. Mom will want her to help with the beans and definitely will have no patience with Thia's moodiness.

Of course, it will be better if Melvin has called…with a good reason for why he hadn't come last night. Ken doesn't want to be around if Melvin does call or his explanation doesn't satisfy Thia. That will just send her into a deeper funk!

Ken wonders if Angie sulks when she's upset. Not that it would matter for at least three years anyway. He shakes his head as if to shake thoughts of her out of his head, stacks the baskets, closes the car trunk, and tromps back over to the last row of beans.

Ken is in good physical shape for basketball. He's used to reaching up to block passes and to shoot baskets, not bending down to pull recalcitrant legumes off rows of low growing bean bushes. Standing up and rubbing his back, he estimates how much longer he'll be here and goes back to work. Another fifteen minutes or so should do it.

Whew! Finished at last. He hauls the baskets of beans to the car and arranges them in the trunk before taking one more hike up to the well. There he sloshes water over his head and arms to clean up and cool down. He grabs the towel he'd left in the shed from his last trip up here and dries off before getting into the now steaming car. Pee-yew! Truly odoriferous!

"Ouch! I should have at least left the window down! It's hot enough to cook the beans. I should put those beans in a bucket and add some well water. They'll be done enough to eat by the time I get home. Mom will love that."

Ken checks the clock in the car…. Twelve noon! That's nearly three and a half hours of not thinking about Angie…except for a nanosecond when he was getting a drink. Not bad. Really good. He has other things to do than spend all his energy on what probably will never happen, and if it does, it shouldn't happen for at least three years. So, it's a good thing he hasn't been thinking about her…much.

AFTER HE PARKS THE CAR in the yard, Ken walks around to the trunk, wondering what he'll have to eat. Angie would be having a full dinner with her grandparents, but he's eaten only carrots since breakfast.

He hauls the baskets of green beans to the picnic table next to the trailer. "Hey, Mom," he calls through the screen door. "Think this'll work a little better for you? It's not bad. Still warm out here, but not stifling like it probably is in there." He fills the large metal tubs with water so Mother can clean and string the green beans out here and catch a few breezes.

He sees through the screen door that his mother has the kitchen all ready to begin washing the vegetables in preparation for canning. The jars in the wire racks in the blue-speckled canning kettle are set on the stove gently boiling.

"What?" she asks dripping to the screen door, peering out to see what he's said. "What? I couldn't hear you. Oh, that looks refreshing. There is a little breeze out here, isn't there."

"Yes, ma'am. It's not bad. Why don't you work out here awhile?"

"Thanks, son. I'll string the beans out there. Let me get my transistor radio. You know Evangelist Kathryn Kuhlman's program's about to begin. I just love hearing that Dino playing hymns on that Steinway piano. I'm gonna order me a couple of his cassettes."

While she walks back to their bedroom to get her little radio, Ken rinses the surface dirt and sweat from his face and arms using the garden hose. It'll take less time in the teeny toilet if he only has to soap and rinse with the hot water inside. He and his mother exchange places: she outside; he inside.

His step-dad comes from around back of the trailer and sits at the picnic table with his mother. Ken can hear them talking and smiles when he learns his Dad's going to be working on something in the basement. That means the car may be available after all, and he can head up to the grounds earlier than he'd planned. Dad usually squeezes in small tasks whenever he has a couple hours free. Little by little he's nearing their goal to move down there before winter sets in.

Refreshed from his quick sluice, Ken stands in front of the closet trying to figure out which of his three shirts he'll wear this afternoon. Before this week, what to wear had never been an issue for him.

In high school, it had been jeans and a tee shirt around the house, slacks and Ban Lon polos for school, his one brownish suit for church and whatever dress shirt still fit. In the Air Force, he'd had uniforms. Now that he's met Angie, he's thinking about what he'll look like in what he wears.

Well, he'd worn the blue one yesterday and the silvery grey one the previous day. That means, it's the orange shirt today. It's not a color he'd have picked for himself, but Thia had gotten it on sale. She called the color "salmon". She gave it to him as a late birthday present when he got back from college in June. Yep, he'd wear the salmon-colored shirt tonight. Or should he wear his white dress shirt?

This is Men's Night, and they'd asked the men to wear white shirts. But that was for the choir. Though he misses singing with male groups like he'd done in high school and the Air Force, Ken's not singing tonight. He's been away from Zion's Hill for years and doesn't know the guys, and he hasn't really kept up with contemporary church music. They rehearsed this morning, and he was up working like a field hand. Anyway, he'd better save the white shirt to wear on Sunday with his one and only dark blue sports coat and the charcoal grey slacks he'd worn last Sunday. So, yes, by process of elimination, it'll have to be the salmony orange shirt tonight.

Ken pulls it out, gives it a snappy shake to relax the inevitable wrinkling in a cramped closet, and tugs the shirt over his head, still a little damp from where he had gotten his hair wet using the garden hose. He picks up the brush and pulls it through his curly reddish brown hair, glad that his *quo vadis* hairline still is relatively neat.

He'd been extending time between haircuts to save a little more for school. Tuition would be due right away, and though his scholarship covers that, he has a cash deposit to pay for the room he'll be sharing with a fellow engineering student this school year. Of course, there also will be textbooks to buy.

He doesn't like asking his parents for help. After all, he's a grown man and going to college is his choice, his dream, and definitely his expense to meet. His folks need their savings to get that basement wired and ready to move into before snow fall. They probably can't endure another year in the trailer. Too many adults in that small space is taking its toll on family harmony. But his parents already have agreed to drive him back to campus, so he won't have to put out any money for the Greyhound until he returns for Christmas at the end of the term.

Thankfully, the Penn State coach arranged on-campus jobs for the team members to earn a little pocket cash to supplement their scholarships. Last year, Ken sold programs at the football games. He did pretty well and was able to end the year with no outstanding school debts.

Ken wrings the washcloth as dry as he can. Anything to reduce the humidity inside the trailer. With the canning kettle boiling for the next three hours, it'll be a sauna in there again. Then he decides to take both the wet cloth and damp towel outside and hang them on the clothes line. Every little bit helps. Satisfied the little toilet is as clean and neat as he found it, Ken leaves, reaches back to slide the closet door closed, and exits the trailer.

Ah, a breeze. Maybe this portends a cooler evening. It will take several hours before the heat dissipates enough for comfortable sleeping…especially when one sleeps in the kitchen.

199

"Ken, your dad says you can use the car this afternoon. It may need a little gas, though."

"Thanks, Dad. Sure, Mom. I'll put in some gas. I think I'll just get lunch while I'm out, too. Melvin's aunt Liz has that hamburger stand up on the grounds. You know she still uses that special seasoning and then charbroils them out back on that 55 gallon drum grill. Remember?"

"Yeah, Ken," his dad agrees, "I do remember her burgers. Makes me want to ride up with you and get a couple myself."

"No you don't," his mother scolds. "You're not leaving me down here with all this work to do. I know you're not going to help me with the canning, but you got a lot to do down in that basement. You know it might rain tomorrow, and you gotta get all those boxes of tile off the pallet they delivered yesterday. You don't want my special tiles to get all moldy, now do you?"

"You're right, Honey," Dad replies. "See, Ken. A man's work is never done, and his wife won't let him forget it. So you go ahead, and you better get on out of here before she finds another job for you."

He gives his wife a pat on the shoulder as he heads over to the boxes on the pallets. He glances back, lifting the first box, "Ken, you got just another week home, and you'll be back into the thick of things. Basketball practice starts right away doesn't it?"

"Yeah, we start conditioning in the weight room the first week of school. Speaking of school, the profs call it the winnowing year."

"Winnowing? They trying to get rid the student? That sounds strange."

"I know, but you remember, we have to declare our majors after sophomore year, and if we don't have the grades, we won't be allowed to continue in the program. So it's going to be nose to the grindstone this year. I can't let my grades fall and lose my spot in the school of engineering." Ken pulls out the keys and calls across the yard, "Thanks, Dad for letting me use the car." Ken leaves, and his step-dad gets to on with his work.

12 - Mr. Conley's Coming

ADMITTEDLY A LITTLE TIRED from working with the kids at Children's Church, Angie is satisfied with the results of their craft making. Some of the projects turned out really cute. Now, hustling across the grounds, she's on to her paying job. Part of Angie's responsibility is to sweep the floor, wash all the surfaces, and wipe down the fronts of the freezer compartments once her work shift ends. That's every day. Today they're doing a deep clean for the weekend.

To assure that they have hot water on hand throughout the day, Stella brings a ten gallon insulated jug of boiled water. It remains pretty warm all day, and when enough is left, they dump it into buckets, add a few drops of bleach, and clean the place thoroughly. Stella has errands to run today, so Angie is alone in the ice cream stand.

In addition to ice cream, Stella also gets her other supplies from Mr. Conley because he'll deliver them at no extra charge. In fact, a delivery is scheduled this afternoon, and Angie's watching the clock. The place had better be up to snuff if Stella is to have that contract renewed for another year. Angie needs the job. A payment on school fees for the fall term is due the last week in August. That's next week!

Angie tips the Thermos jug to drain the last of the warm water before sliding the jug back on the table so she won't knock it over as she sweeps, and then mops the floor. She does get a kick out of their using the spigot on the side of the metal Thermos as a faucet. That makes it easy to dampen cloths and keep up with the splashes and spills of dipping ice cream hour after hour. Whenever the traffic of customers slows, Stella expects Angie to return the place to spic and span order. She's to refill the cups and cones dispensers, neaten the napkin holder, and clear any accumulated trash. It would be nice if this job were as much fun as it is necessary.

She grimaces and then grins as she lifts the Thermos to wipe the little corner table, then sets the container down, fingering the raised Thermos label on the jug. It's the same brand of metal insulated jug her family carried on road trips when her parents were still married.

Angie's dad liked fishing for perch and pike in Michigan's fresh water lakes. Every once in a while, he allowed the family to go along when he went to state parks to fish. Since the divorce, though, Angie and her sisters seldom see their dad. Her brother, Isaac still went fishing with him sometimes. It must be a guy thing.

RECOLLECTIONS OF SUCH FAMILY OUTINGS evoke a mosaic of memories for Angie. Dad preferred getting up before dawn to be on the river at sun-up. So Mom, not an early riser, had to fix everything the night before so everyone could get up and out in a timely manner.

They'd have just a glass of juice before leaving and later cook breakfast on one of the charcoal grills at the state park. Cooking eggs over an open fire meant carrying the cast iron skillet and cushioning Dad's eggs to prevent their cracking during the trip. He liked his over easy, so having the eggs already cracked and stored in a Mason jar wasn't an option. And then there was the toast. Angie never learned to hold her bread over the flames without scorching the edges. Probably because she preferred buttering the bread before toasting. It dripped and smoked. Not good. Not fun at all.

On the other hand, she thoroughly enjoyed sitting on the river banks in the cool of the morning, reading her chosen book of the week. Later in the day, when reasonable people arrived with their families, gaggles of kids would gather at the swing sets, climb the monkey bars, and compete in pick-up softball games. That was good. Lots of fun.

Dad generally fished until the sun reached its zenith and then returned to the campsite for lunch. Tension again. He liked hamburgers made with only lean meat. Mom preferred a little fat in her burgers. According to her, a little fat gives them more flavor. The kids had hotdogs.

No problem with those. Stick 'em on a stick, rotate them across the flames until they get crispy but not burnt, and eat 'em. Of course, searching for just the right balance of heat and flame, she and her siblings would swat one another's dogs aside. Invariably, someone's dog would fall off the stick into the fire. Not good. Not fun at all.

Mom's potato salad and relish tray of celery, carrots, and pickles complemented the meats, and the frosty, tart lemonade from the green metal Thermos jug provided just the right balance of textures and flavors. Full from the tasty meal, everyone usually was in better spirits and ready for homemade cookies or pound cake. Mom saved fresh fruit for snacks in the car on the drive home later that afternoon. Fruit is neat to eat. Neat was important when in the car and at the campsite.

Angie and her sisters had to tidy up after the meal, and afterwards her brother would bag up the garbage of used paper products and food leftovers and haul it over to the trash barrel near the parking lot, obeying Dad's yelling to make sure he closed the lid tightly. There were wild animals in the woods, and the campers were responsible to leave no stuff out for the animals to strew all over the place. Good lessons. But, not much fun at all.

Then, once home, it was scaling and gutting the fish. Definitely not fun.

===

IN THE ICE CREAM STAND, Angie finishes cleaning and lugs the bucket of dirty water outside and over to the sewer drain behind Stella's mobile home conveniently set up to the right of the ice cream stand. Returning to store the bucket under the table where the Thermos of hot water sits, Angie sees the Conley delivery truck coming up the hill.

Relieved! She's finished before Mr. Conley arrives. Just as he sets the air brakes, Angie's there to greet him. Patting hair back from her sweaty brow, she greets him with the trite, "Hot enough for you, Mr. Conley?"

"Sure is, Angie," he replies, climbing down from the cab and fanning curly blond hair out of his face with a crumpled Pittsburgh Pirates' cap. "Yinz want alla dese flavors in here," he calls out in the Pennsylvania dialect she always has to re-tune her ears to understand.

"Or you want I should carry some back over to da big freezer in the hamburger stand?"

She shrugs.

"It's the same difference to me. Gotta go over dere anyway." As he hefts a tub of vanilla and huffs over to the freezer, Mr. Conley visually scans the stand.

His sharp blue eyes miss nothing. The Conley Ice Cream sign hanging perfectly parallel to the floor, the sparkling clean containers for the dipping scoops, the completely filled dispensers for cones, cups, and napkins, and the freshly washed aprons hanging on the wall.

Stella's right. Mr. Conley is persnickety. At least once a visit, especially close to contract time, he reminds them that the ice cream stand must reflect the Conley Family standard of service and setting. His sharp eyes sweep over the freshly mopped floor, and he nods. Angie releases her held breath. So far, so good.

Although they only sell eight different flavors, the freezer unit can hold twelve of the bulk five gallon cardboard tubs. Stella usually has two each of the most popular flavors. But it's the weekend, and lots more young folks come on Saturday and Sunday. So they'll probably be selling more of that new bubble gum, too.

"Let me see." Angie checks the note left on the corkboard. "Looks like Stella wants an extra maricopa in addition to her regular order. Got one on the truck?"

"Yeah. Sure. Dat's been pretty popular for yinz up here this year? Same for us down to the store. Our customers sure miss da black walnut though. Folks up here been asking for it?"

"Yes, they have. Just the other night one lady held up the line fussing at me 'cause we don't have it this year. She finally settled for the maple walnut," Angie relates as she trails Mr. Conley back out by the truck.

It's still morning, but blazing hot already. The freezer door whooshes open, emitting gusts of trapped air tempting her to shove Mr. Conley aside and stick her head inside to cool off a bit. She's melting from cleaning inside and now from the scorching sun outdoors. She resists, though. Not good for the business. She pays attention as Mr. Conley chats away,

"We got some regulars who don't wanna buy nothing else. D'er complaining don't cut no ice with us, though. Anyway dey know we only use da best ingredients in our creams and da local black walnuts been bad dis year"

"Yeah, Stella mentioned that."

"We can't afford to buy dem foreign black walnuts, so we just not making dat flavor now. Customers gonna have to wait a whole nother year. Dey be glad though. We make da best creams around!" he brags as he checks the inventory in the truck's freezer compartment.

"So, yinz want two each vanilla, chocolate and strawberry, one bubble gum, and three maricopa? How dat black cherry going for yinz? Selling much of dat?

"The black cherry's been selling pretty steady, but we got enough for today and tomorrow. Stella doesn't have that flavor on this list here. If we need more for Sunday, she'll call you. Okay?"

"Okay. What other flavors you want here, and what you want over in da big freezer?'

"Ummm," Angie considers as she scans the freezer again to confirm which flavors are low. "Let me have one maricopa, one chocolate, and one bubble gum. The rest can go out back."

"No problem. I got some milk and cheese to deliver over to da Wilkins' hamburger stand. Gotta go round der anyway. Here you are," he grunts, shouldering Angie aside and dropping the giant tubs into the freezer. He knows the order in which Stella arranges their flavors, and he settles them in the right places.

"And... Uh. Mr. Conley. You and the family want to come up to the grounds tomorrow night? Saturday is Youth Night. There's gonna be some great gospel choirs coming from three states to put on a special concert after the evening service," Angie gushes the invitation as he leaves.

He nods, but says nothing. She goes on.

"I hear they even got a band coming. The concert usually starts about nine o'clock and ends by ten-thirty. The old folks get pretty upset if it goes past eleven. You know how they are, don't you?"

"Yeah, I know how we are," he chuckles. "I'm one a da old folks now, so I probably won't be coming out that late. Saturday's pretty busy for us down to da store. But I'll tell da kids. You know dey all in high school now. Da oldest is driving and it's not far from our house to come up here. Sure. Yeah. Thanks, I'll let'em know. Nine o'clock you say?"

"Yes, but they better come a little after eight if they want to find a place to park. You know how crowded it gets up here on the weekend. Those who live in town but are not staying for the concert probably will be leaving after the evening service. It usually gets out about eight-thirty on Saturdays so the concert can start on time."

"Sounds good. Thanks. I'll tell da kids. Gotta get going. See ya Sunday morning. Yinz take care, you hear?" He hands Angie the invoice for the ice cream, leaves, careful to see that the screen door shuts tightly, climbs back up in the truck, and drives round back of the hamburger stand where Stella's friend, Liz Wilkins, lets them use space in the corner of one of her big freezers.

Angie notes the time and sees there's not much left to finish here. She's in a hurry to get back to the dorm to freshen up and change clothes. Ken just may stop by this afternoon. But after last night and the Lady in Navy, Angie wonders if he actually will come. She makes one more swipe across the lip of the freezer smudged when Mr. Conley jostled the jumbo ice cream tubs into place.

She swishes the rag in the cooling rinse water and wrings it out, regretting the absence of rubber gloves. Her hands are crinkly and smell like Clorox. Not that it really matters. Ken probably won't look her up this afternoon, and it's too late to connect with anybody else. This week is just not working out as she had planned.

Stella's back now, doing her own visual survey of the place. Using the corner of the apron, Angie wipes her forehead again and dries her hands

206

before taking off the apron and chucking it in the basket with the dirty towels and cleaning clothes. Stella will take the dirty things to the laundromat and return them for Saturday.

"Ange. Will you take this dish pan back over to Liz in the hamburger stand? I borrowed it and promised to get it right back. I'm gonna carry these dirty things on out and put them in the trunk. Yeah, I know they'll probably get sour in this heat, but I don't have time to drive home now. I promised to meet my husband in the campground business office in half an hour to see if they've approved our vendor's license for next year."

With the basket in one hand and car keys in the other, Stella shoves open the screen door and backs out saying, " I better run over to our trailer and rinse off a bit. I'm past perspiring! I'm gone start sweating for sure!"

Angie asks as she takes the basin, "What time do you want me back?"

"I'm thinking five today. And Angie, can we count on you next year?

"Yeah. Sure. And thanks. I've come to depend on this job myself," Angie replies as Stella hands Angie the key to lock up.

"Thank you. Angie. We'll be glad to have you back."

"But," she murmurs to herself," it's cramping my style! What'll I wear this afternoon? It's gotta be something nice, and something that will look nice just in case Ken comes back. I may not have time to change later. Hmmm. It's Friday, Men's Day today. Wonder who's preaching," she ponders as she locks the door and leaves.

She knocks on Stella's side door. In fact, both doors are on the side. It's a mobile home with a front side door and a back side door. Stella's family has a special permit to set up their trailer close to the ice-cream stand so they can have access to water and a stove to heat the water for cleaning. They have one of those experimental gas-generators. Still, it takes about an hour to boil the water in one of those blue-speckled canning kettles that Stella leaves warming on their two-burner hot plate. They use a couple of pots full just for the ice cream stand.

"Well?" Stella asks as she swings open the trailer door to let Angie come in with the Thermos. "I forgot to ask. How'd it go? Did Mr. Conley have all the flavors we need?"

"Yeah, he did. He brought some in and took the others over to Liz' freezer. You should have seen him scrutinizing the place. Inside and outside."

"Everything okay?"

"He didn't say anything. I guess he's satisfied."

"Good. Anything else?" she asks, swinging the door a little wider."

"No," Angie replies, one foot on the cinder block step and holding the dish pan on her hip. "Oh, yeah. I invited him to the concert tomorrow night. He said he and his wife probably won't come, but his kids may. Do you think they will? Not too many white townies usually come up here for the services, do they?"

Stella closes the screen door, but stays inside. "Some years, lots come. Other years, not so many. It depends on who's speaking. You did your job, Angie. You invited him. I do know that he and his wife are Christians, active in their own church."

"Yeah, I thought they might be. Mr. Conley is nice, even with his laser-like x-ray eyes checking out the place whenever he comes. You see the Conleys much around in town?"

"We see them sometimes at community service meetings. When the high school team made state finals last year, the Conleys had a fundraiser in their store to help the guys with travel expenses. Yeah, my husband and I find them to be good partners here on the grounds and in town.

"Oh, and he mentioned his regulars down at the town parlor miss the black walnut ice cream too. Anything else?" Angie asks, backing away from the door, eager to get going.

"Nothing more to do, but there is something else. You know it's going to be real busy this weekend, especially with the youth concert tomorrow night. So, I've ask Randy to come us help."

"Randy? Your son? Randy?" Angie's stomach lurches. "I haven't seen him around much this summer."

"He hasn't been home. The college offered him a job on campus so he decided to take a couple summer classes since he was going to be there anyway. He wasn't here last weekend 'cause he had a paper due. Anyway, he'll be here this afternoon." she says with a proud smile.

"But, but. Um. Won't Randy just be in the way?"

"What do you mean?"

"You and me, Stella. We got a system, a routine that works. There's not all that much room in there, you know." Angie flinches and wrinkles her nose. As much a stickler as she is for cleanliness, Stella didn't seem to notice how funky Randy smelled coming to work, sweaty from shooting hoops. He was a royal pain, with BO to boot.

Randy, tall and broad shouldered and handsome, played football in high school is a braggart always talking about how many admiring girls he had stringing along. She cannot imagine working in the tight space without brushing against him … by accident on her part; on purpose on his part. Just thinking about Stella's son makes Angie cringe. Actually, she has been relieved he hasn't been around this year.

Angie doesn't feel free to say what she really thinks about Handy Randy who thought he was hot stuff just 'cause he was already in college. Ugh! He gave her the willies. Always coming on to her like she ought to be flattered he gives her the time of day; honored he deigns to bestow his attention on her. But worse than that were his wandering hands, brushing against her, bumping into her bottom… by accident, of course.

She would be just a little uncomfortable about working in such a tight space with any twenty year old man. Now if it were Ken. That'd be another story. Another story indeed.

"Well, if you think it will work," Angie concedes. "I gotta get going, Stella. I need to get cleaned. I'm having lunch with my grandparents, but may have some time afterward. Ken may be coming by, too." Or he may not. He may be having lunch with the Lady in Navy.

The stand usually isn't too busy when Stella opens after lunch, so she hasn't scheduled Angie to return until about five o'clock. It's the fish sandwich and burger stands that are busy earlier. Folks sometimes amble over for ice cream afterward. Resigned to put up with Stella's son, Angie hands over the Thermos and heads around to return the dish pan, and leaves for a much needed break.

JUST TWO MORE DAYS AND CAMP MEETING WILL BE OVER. Angie had had a good time early this morning up on the hill, meditating and reflecting on God the Creator and God the Way Maker. But those feelings are fading fast. Apparently she hasn't given this "thing" between her and Ken to the Lord. It keeps poking its way into the worry section of her brain and the wonder section of her heart.

Until Thursday, it looked like she and Ken would be more than the typical one week stand...meet, spend time together, share a meal, exchange addresses, write twice...maybe three times...and get on with their lives. There seemed to be more. Well, appearances obviously can't be trusted, even though Stella has said Angie should trust them.

===

THE TWO OF THEM HAD BEEN DOING INVENTORY, getting ready for the expected weekend onslaught. They'd only been restocking, washing scoops and wiping things down and not taken time for deep cleaning until this morning. Yesterday, they chatted like friends, just from different generations.

"You know Ken? How?"

"Oh, Angie. Ken goes to our church. Or at least he did when he was growing up. He's been away for nearly five years now. First off to the Air Force and now he's in college."

"Yeah, I know that. He told me all about that."

"Well, you must know the young ladies at our church have set their cap for him."

"Set their cap?"

"Yeah, you know. They primp and preen when he's around."

210

"Primp and preen? What's that?"

"Oh, you don't know that expression either? Will you hand me that bottle of bleach? Gotta keep it clean around here or the Board of Health will shut us down."

"Primp and preen," she continues, "Oh, well, you know. Whenever the girls heard from Joann or Thia that Ken is due home for furlough or, now on break from college, they dress in their best clothes and flit and flirt around hoping he'll notice them. Primp and preen."

"Has he dated any of them? Seriously, I mean." Angie doesn't want to seem too, too interested since this is just another camp encounter "Is Ken seeing anyone this summer?" Angie isn't sure she wants to hear all this. Still, truth be told, she is more than curious, quivering in anticipation, eager to hear, but fearful to learn.

"I don't think so. Haven't seen him sitting with any of them in church. You know, when I think about it, he didn't do much of that even when he was in high school."

"He didn't? What's the matter with him?"

"Believe it or not, he's always been sort of shy."

"Ken, shy? That's hard to believe. I thought he was in a singing group."

"Not anymore. I don't think so anyway. All the guys in the group have left the Valley now. Yeah, in high school he and the Cooper boys sang in an *a capella* quartet."

"Really? Where'd they sing?"

"Oh, they used to sing at school dances and such. They were pretty good, too. I heard them once when the guys entertained at a party our ladies group gave a party at the old folks' home."

"What kind of music?"

"Mostly close harmony songs of the forties. Not too much of the Elvis Presley rock and roll stuff. They did pretty good with new Motown and Philly sounds, too. My favorite, though, was 'In the Still of the Night'."

211

"That's some range of music."

"They really were rather versatile for an informal high school group. Ken also won awards competing with an Air Force quartet. He's quite talented."

"Hmmm. It's hard to imagine someone singing all in public and still be shy. But...he played basketball too, didn't he?"

"He still does. He's a Nittany Lion for Penn State now. When Ken lived here, he was named the Most Valuable Player the year his high school team won the Valley Championship...and beat Coach Mac's team in his own tournament!"

"Coach Mac?"

"Yeah, Coach Mac. Here in the Valley, Coach Mac is a legend. Until that year, he'd taken basketball teams to state championships for years. It was Hillside High, Ken's team that broke that record."

"Really? Did you ever see him play?"

"Sure, I was at that game with my family. We couldn't decide whether to cheer for our high school or Ken, our friend from church. Ken shot the winning basket for the tie breaker! Nobody in the Valley's ever gonna forget that game. I betcha Coach Mac hasn't!" Stella did not stop scrubbing even as she related stories about Ken.

"Our Ken and Hillside High broke Mac's ten year winning streak! Everybody was sure Ken would get a full ride at a college. You know...to pay all his expenses."

"Full ride! That's really something."

"You're right about that. I heard Coach was so impressed with Ken that he offered to get him a couple of interviews with his personal coaching friends. Word was a couple of small schools did try to recruit Ken, but they didn't offer enough money. That's why he went to the Air Force."

"How come? Some money is better than no money." Angie scorns, putting the clean scoops in jars of fresh water and setting them just so to be in easy reach when they opened the stand later in the afternoon.

More folks than usual are on the grounds for Women's Day. Must be Missionary Albert and Christine Taylor drawing them up here. Stella is planning for ladies to stop by after the mid-day service to extend their conversations with friends they've not seen and to share the specialty Conley ice cream they've not had since last year.

"Well, my husband said Ken has always wanted to go to Penn State to study some kind of engineering. He's like his folks, I guess. They don't take second best if they believe waiting will get'em what they want. You know they've been living in a trailer for nearly ten years waiting to build the house of their dreams"

Angie nods and she pulls the apron over her head and hangs it on the hood near the door.

"You finished with those scoops?" Stella asks as she dumps the dirty water in a bucket and heads out the door to go for a nap in her trailer.

===

THAT WAS WEDNESDAY. Today's Friday. "Maybe that's what God wanted me to get out of that conversation with Stella. Ken only wants the best and is willing to wait for it. Maybe he was only playing around with that Lady in Navy because he waiting for me to finish college. He's probably not serious about her at all.

"Tuesday, we both agreed that neither of us has time for a serious relationship right now. We have to dedicate ourselves to achieving our goals. Well…my goal this week was to meet a nice guy, spend time with him and to be seen walking around the camp grounds on the weekend when everyone comes. I almost made it. Almost.

"But, what if he brings that woman back? If she dresses that sharp on Thursday, what will she be wearing tonight? I don't stand a chance. God, why did you let me meet him and then let this happen? Why should I care, anyway?

"Now, I probably won't get off till a couple hours after service tonight! Even if Ken comes up tonight, he probably won't want to wait around that long. Anyway, I'll be too worn out to be good company anyway. Who cares?

I'm having lunch with my Grammama and Grampoppa. They want to spend time with me and help me reach my goals".

In her mind's ears, she hears her grandmother. "Angie, sweetheart. We're so proud of you. You're going be the first girl in our family to go to college. And you're going to be a teacher.

"Not many of our people even have the chance at college. Maybe you'll be like Mary McCloud Bethune or Booker T. Washington. You remember me reading them books to you? They done a lot for our people, you know." Then Grammama gives her a hug and hands her a crumpled five dollar bill.

"Here, baby. A little something to help you 'long the way. Grammama know it's not much, but God can bless it and make it help you when you need it."

Angie had underestimated the cost of supplies for her sociology project. That week, Grammama's five dollars was just enough for a bus pass. Without it Angie would have had to walk to work or hope to catch a ride until she got her next paycheck. Why is it so hard to trust a God who faithfully provides for her needs? Where is He now? I need some help with Ken or at least with my feelings about him!"

===

NOW BACK UP IN HER ROOM, Angie realizes she has an hour before the morning ministers' meeting ends and she has to meet her grandparents for lunch. She decides to shower later. Right now, a quickie nap. Lying with her hands clasped behind her head, hoping to catch up on the sleep she missed last night, Angie reluctantly admits to herself, "God has been good to me." So many times in just this first year, Angie has received just what she needed to bridge the gap between not enough and just enough.

A better than average student, Angie did not earn grades outstanding enough to get a full academic scholarship. She'd played field hockey in high school, but didn't know anyone who offered full athletic scholarships for that sport, so that was out. But, as Grammama always said, "God'll make a way out of no way".

===

IN HER SOPHOMORE YEAR OF HIGH SCHOOL, Angie was having a rough time with Latin. In just so happened a neighbor taught Latin and English at the high school across town. It just so happened that this teacher, Miss Wicks, was looking for someone to help her with the inherent English teachers' paper overload. Now, it also just happens that someone had told her about Angie needing a job and Miss Wicks sent word asking Angie to come see her. Who but God could arrange all those elements to come together at just the right time?

Miss Wicks invited Angie to come to talk about becoming a grader. She was willing to exchange Latin tutoring fees for grading service. What a bargain.

Miss Velma Wicks is a kindly, no-nonsense, no excuses kind of person. From the very beginning she not only hired Angie, but also insisted that she knuckle down and learn how to translate Latin literally. She also encourages her to switch to a French modern, spoken language that Miss Wick also knows. Once Angie began studying French Miss Wicks insists that she speak that language with her Angie to help develop the ease of speaking like a native. No more guessing and hoping. During the next three years, Miss Wicks becomes Angie's tutor, advisor and then mentor. *Très bien*!

In exchange for those tutorials, Miss Wicks assigned Angie to correcting grammar worksheets and reading first drafts of sloppily-written student essays. Surprising to them both, Angie proved to be an effective and efficient teacher's aide. Her wide reading trained Angie's ear for good writing. She had a good sense for what works and what doesn't and often included useful recommendations for students to consider as they began the revision steps in their writing.

Looking at essays from the teacher's perspective, Angie gained insight about herself. Paper after paper, Angie observed ways that careless writing clouds communication. She began to take more time not only with her French homework, but also on English assignments as well. Over time, under the tutelage of Miss Wicks, Angie's grades rose slightly and leveled off across the content areas, and she began to see herself as a competent high school student who possibly could become a teacher.

That meant going to college. No one else in her family had finished college and it wasn't expected of her. The guys in her family got government jobs right out of high school and the girls got married. Period.

After working with Miss Wicks for about a year, that period became a semi-colon. Miss Wicks had attended college in town and stayed at home with her family until she graduated and got her first teaching job. She encouraged Angie to explore similar options and assured her that having four years of foreign language would help round out Angie's college application. Knowing Latin is fine, she said, but Angie also should take a modern language, *ergo* French.

One of the memorable stories about speaking French that Miss Wicks shared occurred in Charleston, South Carolina when she had gone to a convention for foreign language teachers.

THAT FIRST EVENING, SEVERAL OF THE LADIES MET for dinner at an offsite restaurant, but the maître de wouldn't seat Miss Wicks, the only Negro in the dinner party. Her friends, embarrassed for her and for themselves for not remembering where they were, agreed to get take out and return and eat at the convention hotel so Miss Wicks wouldn't be alone.

The next evening, she had worn African attire and the group went back to the same restaurant. This time they only spoke French! The same maître de nearly fell over his feet, scraping and bowing and leading them to the *meilleure table à la place,* right by the front window.

Years later, Miss Wicks smiled telling the story, but both she and Angie grimaced, sad to think how awful it must be for others who live in towns and work in restaurants, but cannot eat there – not even seated back by the kitchen, far away from the window. While the two of them would sometimes chuckle about this incident, Miss Wicks wanted Angie to get the message that confidence in oneself and just a little *chutzpah* can go a long way.

Angie needed to keep that in mind when she saw her friends applying to several out of town or out of state college. Most of their parents either could afford to pay their college expenses or the classmates had earned an academic or athletic scholarship. Angie had neither.

True, Angie had a decent record in high school, had taken all college prep courses, played on one of the less competitive sports teams, even became field hockey captain, and to embellish her college application, joined a wide range of school clubs and even volunteered as a library aide.

Instead of a second study hall, twice a week she worked in the school library, reading the shelves, making sure the books remained in Dewey Decimal order, or typing out late notices for students who failed to return books on time. Being around books was a pleasure, even if she seldom had time or interest in reading more than assigned books and her middle school preference for thumb-thick historical novels written as series.

OVER THE YEARS, MISS WICKS proved to be an invaluable mentor, challenging Angie to think about all sorts of things.

"Making any progress on your college applications, Ange?"

"Yes, Ma'am. But, Miss Wicks I really want to go to Michigan State."

"You get an acceptance letter?"

"I got accepted and all and have been saving for tuition. But I'm never gonna have enough to pay for room and board, too."

"So, Angie, why don't you wait and work full time for a while?"

"Aw, Miss Wicks. I don't really want to put off starting college if there is something else I can do. My mother isn't in a position to sign for me to get a loan. She's maxed out already. I've applied for scholarships, but my grades aren't quite good enough."

"So, Angie. Why don't you go to school here in town?"

"Here in town? You gotta be kidding. That would mean I'd have to stay at home. I wanna GO to college. Staying here in town would be like going to high school. I've had it with high school. I wanna go away."

"What's more important to you? Going away or going to college?"

"I want both."

"What if you can't have both?"

217

"I've been praying about this and I believe God's gonna make it happen."

"What if He doesn't?"

"What do you mean, what if He doesn't? He promised if two or three pray and agree, He'd do it. Carol at church and Lily from camp meeting are praying with me. That's three. That means I should get what I want, right?"

"That's not the way it works, Angie. I'm not all that religious, but I know that God doesn't always give us what we want just because we and our friends pray for it."

"Well, why bother? Why bother asking somebody to pray with you or for you if God's not gonna answer your prayers and give you what you want?"

"I'm not sure, Angie, how all that works. But my advice is to be prepared for the answer of 'No.'"

"No? Not me! I'm praying and believing. Carol and Lily are praying and believing with me. So there! Can we just talk about something else, *s'il vous plaît*?"

"Sure, Angie." Wise Miss Wicks knew when to drop a subject. "Let's study those irregular French verbs. You're not going to find French that hard after studying Latin, but there are just enough differences to trick you into making silly errors. Remember, you've got to pay attention to the patterns in families of verbs. So again, how do you conjugate the verb, *devoir*?"

===

GOD DID NOT ANSWER ANGIE'S PRAYER to go to her first choice college. She did not get to go to Michigan State and she did have to live at home her freshman year. Her grades were good, so she applied for a scholarship; but didn't get it. However, she did get accepted into the work-study program and her mother agreed to let her move onto campus in September, if she could pay her own expenses.

That's why she was working so hard this summer. Not buying all new clothes for camp meeting, but saving for school fees! And that's what was keeping her from Ken. This job on the grounds and no nice clothes. "God, why'd you let me meet such a nice guy and then put this bill for college in my way? Why can't I have both? I've been good."

218

She's says she's been good, but she certainly hasn't been napping. It's eleven forty-five already. Better get up and at 'em. Gathering her toiletry bag, wash cloth and towel, she heads down the hall, thankful the communal bathroom is unoccupied.

"Oh. Oooo – weee!" The shower water suddenly turns cold. Angie shivers, turns off the faucet, jumps out, grabs her towel and dries quickly. She puts on fresh underwear and applies a generous application of Yodora cream deodorant.

She doesn't want to be the one in the stand whose antiperspirant breaks down in the heat of the day. She doesn't want to be like funky Handy-Randy. Angie shrugs into her housecoat and scampers back to her dorm room, noting by the clock that more time has passed than she thought. She scuttles back to the room. She's arranged to meet her grandparents for lunch before their afternoon nap.

Quickly slipping into her skirt and shirt, Angie slides into her dark green flats. They'd been one of her few impulsive purchases. On sale, of course. From Reyers Shoe Store. And they do complement the flowers in her skirt so well; she didn't even try to resist the urge when she saw them.

Now she's glad she hadn't. She may not be a fashion princess like Ken's Lady in Navy, but Angie is satisfied with the way she's dressed today. She grabs the suitcase handle and drags it out, crams her stuff inside, shoves it back under her cot, looks around to see that all is in order and leaves, locking the door behind her.

When she reaches to the top step of the stairway, she catches sight of her grandparents walking together out of the side door of the tabernacle; they glance around as though looking for her. She'd promised to be waiting just outside the dining room so they could go in together where she will treat them to one of their favorite meals. It's meatloaf day and that home-style meal always draws a crowd, but fewer at lunch than at dinner.

Thankfully, this year, her uncle had given her cash for her birthday with which she'd planned to buy the text for her summer class. But, she'd been able to get a used one; she saved the remaining money just for this occasion.

Her grandparents are dear to Angie. She and her siblings had lived with them off and on over the years when Angie's mother had been ill. Even after her mother's recovery, Angie continues to spend at least a week with her grandparents each summer, usually right here on Zion's Hill. Such a nice break to be an only child for a week.

Her grandmother spots Angie and nods to acknowledge they're on their way. But, someone taps Grampoppa on the elbow and he turns to talk with him. Grampoppa is well known on the grounds and loves chatting with Saints he only sees here once a year. Grammama is used to waiting for him, even if it means they'll be a little late for lunch. They usually take a nap afterwards, so they're not in a hurry.

But Angie is. Ken just may come up this afternoon and she has to eat and then get back over to the stand by five o'clock. Why does she cares? What about the Lady in Navy?

WHILE SHE OBSERVES HER GRANDPARENTS TALKING WITH FRIENDS, Angie recalls a poem she wrote about them in her freshman English class. The assignment was to use vivid vocabulary, appealing to the five senses to create mental images and to recreate a memory of someone special to you. She chose Grampoppa.

Observing her classmates' response to Angie performing it, the professor had asked if he could include her poem in the college literary magazine he edited. Angie consented with pride that her grandparents would be memorialized in that way.

Today, she sits on the top step of the dorm porch and to pass the time until lunch, Angie quietly quotes it, to herself this time.

Grandfather, or Grampoppa, we called him
Working at odd jobs
Living out his faith.
God called him to pastor
To shepherd his flock,
To care for his family.

Amidst the dusty-pew odor
And sour, mildewy hymnals,
Intermingled with colognes
and after shave
Energine and perspiration,
I see him sitting on the platform
In a small rented church,
His skin glistening like warm maple syrup,
His bald, billiard bare head
Thrown back or cocked to one side,
Inspired, but unmusical hymns
Stirring him to respond.

Sometimes Grampoppa would
raise his arm
To beat the time
Like a mime
Restricted to precise,
but invisible boundaries
Like a Marine
Guarding the tomb
of the Unknown Soldier.

Sometimes the emotions
burst from his glowing face
In an arousing "Glory!" or "Hallelujah!"
These eruptions startle and amuse us,
We, who sit in the pews, observing like peeping Toms,
Our grandfather's response to
Songs of praise
Songs of adoration
To the God who called him to be a pastor.

Pastoring his family —
Providing food, clothing and shelter.

Fond memories of love and devotion
For each of us and his wife for life.
His wife of fifty-five years – loving to the end.

I can see the two of them
She in a small-print cotton dress
Covered with a full-checkered apron,
Hair neatly combed
Feet neatly shod,
Carrying him a tray of food
Throwing him kisses before returning to the kitchen.

I see them – my first house guests my first year of marriage.
Me – married fewer than fifty-two weeks;
Them – married more than fifty-two years!
What a model! What a challenge!

"Oh!!" Angie yelps. "Me married a year!" Startled at the thought, she stands and stomps down the stairway from the dorm. "Was I really thinking about my own marriage when writing that poem? Was the Lord speaking to me in anticipation of my meeting Ken here on Zion's Hill?"

She'd heard authors admit that their characters sometimes speak for themselves. Here, as she recited the poem, she realizes she'd included incidents that had never happened, and may never happen, at least not with Ken. What she'd seen last night, Ken with the Lady in Navy, didn't look like he was interested in Angie any longer. Oh well. So much for recreating past events in a poem. Or was she really writing prophecy?

Puzzled by the thoughts, Angie has already descended the stairway when she sees her grandmother looking at her watch and tapping her grandfather's elbow. He nods, gives his friend a hearty handshake, adjusts his preacher-sized Bible under his left elbow and reaches for his wife's hand.

It's nearly twelve twenty before her grandparents join Angie in the line waiting to enter the dining room. Lily waves them through saying, "No charge today!" and one of the teenagers, like Angie had done years ago, escorts the senior citizens to a quiet section of dining room. Another trio of grey heads have just left, so there is room for the three new diners. When her grandparents question the no charge, Angie just says it's all been taken care of. Thankfully, they accept and sit down to enjoy the meal.

How proud she feels, being able to treat the ones who have cared for her so long. Angie pulls out the chair for her grandmother as the young lady does the same for her grandfather.

This new group of assistants is being trained the way she had been...to treat the elderly with care and respect. That's probably why so many older folks return to Zion's Hill year after year. For some of them, it is special on many levels. Eating the lovingly prepared home-style dinners in the dining hall where they were treated so well makes the meager furnishings in the dorm rooms and sparse cabins tolerable.

Since there is only one entrée choice each meal there is no need for menus. Today, waiting diners are served a generous plate of meatloaf, just a little crispy on the top, but succulently moist inside. The cooks don't extend the loaves with loads of breadcrumbs, but blend three kinds of ground meat with their secret blend of spices, just a touch of chopped onions and green peppers, then baste the firm loaves with a tasty tomato sauce with a hint of brown sugar to give them an appetizing glaze.

Angie had observed the cooks lots of times when she was younger and had been assigned kitchen duty. That meant sweating downstairs, cleaning up as the prepping was done, and washing pots and pans after the cooking was done. She soon graduated to dining hall duty. That was cleaner and cooler work with less contact with the cooks and more interaction with the diners. But, Angie has never forgotten the conscientious cooks who believe preparing food for the Saints on Zion's Hill is their offering to the Lord. It is a talent they are investing; they really take seriously the Bible verse admonishing them to do everything as unto the Lord.

After a groaning full lunch, Angie bids her grandparents goodbye, kissing Grammama on her cheek and Grampoppa on his shiny head. They thank her again, push from the table and head up to their room for a nap. She leaves the dining hall to seek out a cool spot to sit outdoors for a while, strolling across the grounds, nodding at some of her customers, but not stopping to chat. She appears purposeful, but really is walking aimlessly, trying to figure out whether to head up the hill to the spot she'd sat to meditate earlier or to go down and browse in the bookstore.

But, if she goes to either place, she might miss Ken. He may decide to come back early. The only phones on the grounds are in the office. Staff there frown on folks using the phone for personal calls, so Angie didn't even consider asking Ken to leave her a message telling her if or what time he'd be back. Anyway, why would be calling her anyway?

So, what should she do for the couple hours or so before returning to relieve Stella in the ice cream stand? What can she do to keep her mind off working in the stand with Randy of the roaming hands?

She wanders down towards to playground. Only the wind gently sways the swings. The little kids must be napping or having quiet time after lunch, so Angie foregoes a seat on the bench and chooses one of the swings. Grasping the chains, she toes herself back and basks in a nostalgic return to this childhood pastime. Words from the Grampoppa poem return to mind and she quotes more lines from that summer's writing.

After dinner, Grampoppa tells humorous anecdotes
Of his first years as a pastor.
She listens as though each detail is new to her.
But even I know the story of that dinner invitation.

After church one Sunday, one member said,

"Rev'n Wi'yums, yawl gotta come and hab suppa wif us.
Suppa is ready. Yawl won't haf ta wait."

Dinner really was ready; already on the table.

"Come on in," she invited.

"Sit right down," she cajoled,

Grabbing a soup spoon, flicking the flies
From the fat, floating atop the now congealing soup.

Gramamma smiles at the punch line; my husband laughs on schedule.

"Husband!" Angie gulps. She drags her shoe. Stops the swing. Planting her feet in the dirt, she spurts, "There it is again! A husband in my poem. Not once, but twice! Like getting married is uppermost in my mind. One would think I'm not really committed to finishing college before getting married."

True, most of the girls her age at Angie's church are engaged or already married and seem happy about it. But she doesn't want to get entangled in a man that will distract her from reaching her goal. BA before MRS. "God, have you been trying to tell me something? Am I not to graduate first? Or am I simply writing fantasy fiction or prophetic poetry? Talking about stuff that might happen years from now?"

Freaked out to be upset about the possibility of hearing from God through her writing, a notion antithetical to what she'd planned, agitated Angie cogitates. Would she really resist if God told her to quit college and get married? Angie drags her feet, flinging up a spray of dust, impetuously pushes up, abandons the swing, and tromps away.

DEEP IN THOUGHT, Angie suddenly finds herself on the slightly trodden narrow path leading away from the playground. It's a little used trail the teens take when they want to sneak down to town and can't get a ride.

Head hanging, ignoring the sweeping dry grass snagging her stockings, she does not see the small car slowly cresting the hill and about to turn onto the road leading through the gates to the campground parking lot. So deep is she in thought that the driver honks twice before Angie even notices it has stopped. She looks up and blinks, doubting her vision.

It's Ken! He's come early. He must have skipped his library time. Or whatever chores he'd been doing. Wow! His dad lent him the car. In a nanosecond, all these thoughts shoot through Angie's mind. Ken grins and pulls the car closer to her. He points to the opposite door. She nods, grins back, scrambles around to the passenger side and gets. It's hot inside, but cool that she's riding with Ken.

"Hey, Ken! What're you doing up here so early? I thought you had to work in the garden today. Didn't you say your dad was using the car until this evening? It sure it hot out, isn't it? I'm really pooped."

"What?"

"Spent all morning cleaning the stand. She likes it spotless in there. Stella, you know. And Mr. Conley came by, too. He checks the place like a health inspector. Makes me nervous. Huh?"

"Slow down, Angie. What's going on? You look flustered. And you're chirping like a magpie. Yes, I finished early. Yes, it's hot. Yes, I obviously have the car. Want to go for a ride? I can turn around in the parking lot and we can head down to town. Have you had lunch?"

"A ride? Sure. I ate already. I ate with my grandparents. Have you ever been up here on meatloaf day? It's really good. I used to watch them cook."

"Sure, I've had their meatloaf. The same cooks are here for youth camp." Ken replies softly in hopes that it will slow down Angie's chatter.

"The cooks really believe cooking is their spiritual gift. You ever seen anything about cooking in the list of spiritual gifts? I know I never have. Huh?" Angie pauses when she notices Ken's questioning look.

"Angie, what's up with you today? You're still rattling on. You're not giving me time to think about your questions let alone time to answer them.

"Oh, really?"

"I'm glad you had lunch with your grandparents".

"Yeah, that was fun. We don't have much time together up here with me working and all."

"Think I'll get to meet them? You've told me so much about them, I bet I'd recognize them walking across the grounds. You lived with them a long time, didn't you?"

"Yes, I did. I lived with them when my Dad was in the service and again when my Mom was in the hospital. I tell you about that?"

"No, I didn't know that. And, Angie-girl slow down. You're still talking a mile a minute and unloading lots on me."

"Oh. Really?" She tries to slow down. She looks around. "Hey. Where we going, Ken?"

"We're nearly there."

"There? Where?"

"To the Veteran's Park. We can get out and walk in the shade a while and maybe you'll unwind enough to tell me what's really got you all wound up. Okay?"

"Sure, Ken, that'll be fine. I've been wanting to get away from the grounds for a little while. You know there's not much shade and privacy up there. What?"

"Angieeeee."

"Huh?" She turns and realizes she's babbling, again. "Well I guess you know all that 'cause you stay up here during youth camp, don't you?"

Ken shakes his head and concentrates on finding a parking place in the shade.

"Oh, this is really nice, Ken. A beautiful spot in the middle of a mill town. You know I never knew what a mill town was till you told me your family works there. I can't believe how hot it must have been where your grandfather works."

"Yeah, he works at one of those open-hearth steel furnaces, really close to flaring flames."

"Wow! He must really be a strong man to put up with that. I know you say the pay is better, but that sounds really dangerous as well as hot. I can hardly stand to cook food in the oven in the summer."

"We're here. Let's get out a walk down that path." He sits there for a moment. Now that the car has stopped moving, maybe Angie will stop talking. She doesn't. So he offers, her a drink.

"I have some cold water in this thermos. You want a little?" He reaches into the back and pulls out a slender silver Thermos bottle, sitting on top of a crumpled McDonald's bag. He decided he couldn't really afford Liz's burgers after all.

Angie looks out and around at the lovely grove of full-leafed trees. Even though she is a city girl, she does know these are old growth oak trees. She sits, just gazing, and then blinks when she realizes Ken is asking her if she'd like a drink.

"Sure, a drink of water would be great. Thanks." He hands her a squat orange Thermos cap of cool water. Angie sips. "Is this the Thermos you take up to the garden when you're working up there? Did you stop at that spring and fill it before coming up here?"

"No I stopped at one of those road-side springs."

"That's funny. I can't imagine a spring that runs clear, clean and cool in this kind of weather. It's one of those miracles of nature, isn't it? Um, Ken, can I have a little more?" He pours a little more.

Finishing her drink, she hands the cap back to Ken. He wipes it with a handkerchief and screws the cap back on the Thermos before exiting his side of the car and walking around to open her door.

"What a gentleman you are, Ken. Thanks." Angie emerges decorously and accepts his outstretched hand. He doesn't let go as he guides her aside to close and lock the car door. He keeps her hand in his and leads her to the shade of the wide gravel trail. They walk slowly not talking, just letting the natural serenity soothe their spirits.

Ken suddenly realizes he is still holding Angie's hand, wonders why he hadn't let go of her hand when she was safely out of the car, but decides not to do so now. Somehow it seems right to be holding hands with Angie.

They walk in silence for ten minutes or so. Ken is calming down, too, releasing the tension from the morning. He'd been nearly as tight as Angie when he stopped and picked her up. Her verbacious spate hadn't helped him relax one bit. And she still hasn't told him why she appeared so angry with him yesterday evening.

Angie seems glad to see him. He can't imagine what could have morphed her into the campground snow queen. Nothing to do with him. Well, it looks like they'll be able to enjoy these final two days of the meetings. She's okay today.

Just around the bend, they reach one of the benches the members of the local VFW post installed along the footpath. Local World War I veterans take after dinner walks along this tree-lined trail and few of the older ex-soldiers can still make the whole two mile stroll without short breaks.

A few years ago, after lightening felled one of the larger oaks, the guys harvested the wood and made these special benches. One, apparently quite a, spent an entire winter shaping the seats to have curved slat backs and spindle arm rests. Then, he and his drinking buddies sanded the benches until they were silky smooth. They still are. No catching your clothes in splinters on these finely crafted VFW benches.

Angie and Ken are tranquil, not talking, comfortably seated, content to be together. Birds chirp on a low branch to their left and a pair of barely camouflaged white-throated sparrows scratch around the ground at the base of the oak nearby.

Through the air, off to the right comes the somber whoo-whooing of a distant dove. Its high pitch coo belies the mourning dove's name. Below, to the left, a bronze-striped chipmunk skitters through the grass and into some taller weeds. From above, slants a lemony yellow beam, spotlighting the small patch of red flowers straining toward the sun for the short time it shines through the narrow slit in the branches overhead.

Ken turns, still holding her hand and gently queries, "Angie. Didn't you rest well last night? You're really wound up today."

Surprised and pleased that Ken is so attuned to her, Angie shakes her head, but doesn't reply.

"I could see you were busy last night and you say you cleaned the stand this morning. Did Stella keep the stand open extra late?"

"Yeah, it really was late. The line seemed to go on for a marathon mile. Thankfully, we only ran out of one flavor so most everybody got their first choice."

"That's good. I'm sure Stella was glad to have your help and company."

"She was, but I was worried about being out that late. My grandparents don't sleep till I come in. But I couldn't leave Stella there by herself."

"They probably understood. They saw the crowds, too."

Angie nods. "Yeah, I guess so. Anyway, by the time I got in, I was too tired to be quiet. They didn't say anything, but I could hear them tossing a bit. They finally settled down once I got into bed myself."

"But you say you didn't get much rest."

"Yeah. It took me a while to get to sleep. What about you? It must be awfully hot in that tight trailer. From what you said about the size, I can't imagine you get much circulation in there?"

"Well, luckily for me, there is a small window in the kitchen where I sleep and my step-dad situated the trailer so it gets a nice cross breeze…when there is one. I slept all right, all things considered. I was up pretty late, too, trying to get Thia settled."

"Thia? What was the matter with her? She anxious about starting at the new secretarial school? Shorthand's pretty scary. I took a shorthand course in high school to help with note taking in college. Doesn't help much, though. What's with Thia?

"Well, she was really upset when her boyfriend, Melvin, didn't meet us outside the tabernacle for service last night. It was that and the fact that she twisted her ankle in those high-heeled shoes she insisted on wearing.

"She's the youngest and when she gets upset, she still gets clingy. You probably saw her hanging on my shoulder when we were sitting on the bench after service last night. I was hoping you'd get a break so I could introduce you to her."

"Your sister? That's who was with you last night?" *The Lady in Navy is Thia, his sister?*

"Yeah, Thia, my baby sister. She was supposed to come up with Melvin. That's why she got all dressed up. He was going to pick her up early so they could get to the grounds and find a good parking spot. She likes to wear high heels even though there are no paved sidewalks on Zion's Hill. But when he didn't get there by the time I left, so as not to waste her outfit and all the time it took her to get all gussied up, she rode up with me."

His sister! Angie mentally smacks herself for being so quick to jump to conclusions. She thought the Lady is Navy was his girlfriend. Why shouldn't she? She'd never met Thia. And, she and Ken certainly spent a lot of time in each other's personal space. What else was she to think?

"Thia thought for sure Melvin would meet us there. He never showed, so Thia was really ticked. After the service, she stomped out of the back door. Stepping off one of those little cement pads, she twisted her ankle."

Angie wasn't really listening. In order to rationalize her jealousy, Angie had applied what she'd learned in her psych class about personal space. She'd seen how close Ken and Thia stood outside the tabernacle waiting for the usher to seat them. And then, during service, they shared a Bible and everything. That proved they were familiar with one another and maybe even a couple! Oh so she thought based on her Psych class last year.

Angie'd left early in a huff, and because the customer lines had been so long, she'd never gotten a chance to meet Thia. Once she spotted them, Angie just kept her eyes on the two of them sitting close together on the bench. People have to be pretty close to be that intimate in public. A couple, right?

So, it was a twisted ankle. That's why he had his arm around her waist when they left. He must have been helping her balance as they walked back down to the car. She wasn't "the other woman"! Just his sister. Ha!

231

"Thia's your sister. I thought…." Angie can't say it. She doesn't want Ken to think she is jealous or anything. Well, she isn't really jealous. There's nothing to be jealous about. They are not a couple, going steady or anything. They've only known each other for a few days.

"You thought what?" Ken probes. Last night, he'd had time to think of little more than getting Princess Thia home. He shivers remembering Angie's glacier stares, cold enough to freeze steam into ice cubes! Now, slow on the uptake, it finally dawns on Ken that Angie thought Thia was his girlfriend. It makes sense, now.

He recalls the way they'd sat on the bench, almost cuddling while Thia complained about sitting there so long just to meet some girl Ken had only known for a couple of days. Since Melvin hadn't come and she'd twisted her ankle, she couldn't understand why big brother Ken wouldn't take her home, at once.

She had tried tears and leaning on his shoulder. That used to work. But not anymore. Fed up with her whining, the lateness of the hour and eventually the cold stares from Angie convinced Ken to take Thia home right then and there.

Today, working up in the garden, Ken did not realize how such actions may have suggested to Angie that Thia was his girlfriend and not his baby sister. Ah. Now he gets it. That's why Angie was all aflutter when he picked her up just now. What a relief!

Ken looks at his watch. He had promised Angie he would try to get up to the grounds as early as possible so they could have a little time before she had to be back to work. It's nearly four o'clock.

"What time do you have to be back to work, Angie?"

"I don't have to be back till five today. I'm not in a hurry. He's going to be working at the stand with us this weekend, so he'll take the early shift."

"He? Who?"

"Stella's son"

"Which one?"

"Oh, it's Randy. He's home this week and told his mom he'd help."

"Randy!" Ken exclaims, vexed.

"It'll be awfully crowded in there though. You know how big he is. He'll be bumping into me all day," she grouses.

"Yes, I remember Randy. I saw him town yesterday. I wondered if he'd be working up on the Hill this week."

"Well, you know, he used to help out. He does know the business. Stella likes it because he's good with the customers, too. Especially the young tweenie girls," Angie interjects, sarcastically.

"Don't I know it," Ken remarks, but Angie keeps talking as though she hasn't heard.

"A couple years ago, when Randy worked the weekend, the gigglers became our most steady customers. Of course, they didn't spend much at a time. But, sometimes they did come back twice a day, always during the hours he was working. It'll be so tight in there with him and Stella during rush hours. I'm not looking forward to it."

"Well, at least his mom will be in there with you. Randy won't get too much in your case if she's there, right?" Ken feels bile rising and envisions the green tinge of jealousy oozing through the air.

Why should he be jealous of Randy and Angie? She is just a woman he's only known for a few days. But it's been a special few days. Just then, Ken rewinds to what he heard the first time he saw her in the tabernacle.

JUST FOUR DAYS AGO, Angie sat in the row in front of him, wearing the creamy colored outfit. The top was lemony yellow with white stripes, he remembers. With a mother and two fashionista sisters, Ken notices details about clothes. Yes, it was Sunday evening. He's sure he heard, "She's the one for you." Not out loud in his physical ear, but in his spirit. And, though this is the first time this has occurred, Ken is convinced he has heard a message from the Lord.

Well, if Angie's the one for Ken, the woman who's to become his wife, he certainly is not going to stand by and see her man-handled by Randy!

"Do you have to work the same hours that he's in there?"

"Yeah. It'll be okay. We used to have a system. It won't really be a problem. He's left handed, like you are, Ken." She looks down and squeezes the hand that still holds hers.

"So, he works on the right side of the stand, and I on the left. Stella usually takes the orders, collects the money and makes change. It may really work out okay. We might not bump into one another too much." She smiles a little, picking up the vibes that Ken may be a little jealous…just as she had been last night. That's nice. He's worried about her being in such close proximity of another man.

Well, Ken shouldn't be. Angie's neither interested in Randy now nor will be interested in Ken after Sunday, or so she tells herself. As in previous years, he's the guy of the week. What's the likelihood they'll exchange addresses and even exchange more than a couple of letters?

Not many guys are all that good about writing. She and Ken won't have phones in their rooms at college and the pay phones in the hall require a stack of coins to pay by the minute. He probably wouldn't call.

And she'd better not. Her Mother always says nice girls don't call guys. But it is nice to think Ken's just a little protective of her. Just the way he was protective of Thia. Ha! Thia, the Lady in Navy, is his sister! What a waste of emotional energy and loss of sleep!

Ken looks at his watch again, surprised that it's nearly four-fifteen, and a little uncomfortable with the thought that he's taking Angie back to a place where she'll be in such cramped quarters space with another guy. He does remember Randy.

He and Ken are about the same age. They grew up going to the same church, but had gone to different high schools. Both left town right after high school and had only seen one another a few times in the interim.

Ken hadn't gotten back to the Valley much when he was in the Air Force. When he did return, he wasn't often in town on weekends and seldom got to see folks from church. But, he does remember that Randy used to be quite a ladies' man, with a reputation as a flirt. Maybe he's more mature now. Maybe he's already married. Lots of guy their age are. But, maybe not. Though he'd heard some rumors, Ken hasn't heard anyone talking about Randy being engaged or anything.

"Come on Angie; let's start walking back to the car. We've got to get you up the hill and back to work. Do you have to change clothes?"

"No, I'm going to wear what I have on. You've seen those big all-over aprons. I don't get too messy when I work the stand. Just warm and a little sweaty. Oh!" She slaps her hand over her mouth.

"Ladies aren't supposed to sweat are they? You have sisters. You've probably heard them saying that pigs sweat, men perspire and women glow. Well, after a busy day dipping ice cream, my glow drips!" she chuckles, walking and talking comfortably with Ken about such bodily secretions.

With a half hour before having to leave, they finish the trail, walking briskly. They soon are back in the car, again him perspiring and her glowing from the heat and both knowing that open windows will not likely be enough to cool them off before they reach the grounds again. Still, Angie is less tense. The Lady is Navy is his sister. Ken, however, is a little tenser. This weekend, Angie will be working with Randy, the Handy Man.

13 – The Tweenies

THE TWEENIES QUEUE UP WHEN THE WORD GETS OUT that Randy is working the stand. He already has a big head when it comes to the ladies and, in the spotlight of adoring fans, it swells even bigger. In his tiny mind, he acts like BMOC means Big Man on Campground! The space in the stand shrinks and stifles.

Showboat Randy starts showing off right away. Disregarding the others in the stand, in a flash, he speeds up his dipping and filling the cones with the varied requests for ice cream flavors. Earlier, he and Angie had alternated taking orders. Now with the teeny-boppers watching, Randy tries to fill all the orders.

It's tough to work in an orderly fashion. The narrow freezer, stocked with the five gallon tubs just two deep and nine across requires Randy to reach over into shared space to get to some of the flavors. Stella, trying to maximize efficiency, stocks two tubs each of the most popular flavors, one each of chocolate, vanilla and strawberry on the left and right ends of the freezer, but the five other flavors are arranged in the middle.

The eighteenth slot is for an extra maricopa, which has been a favorite this year, now that there is no black walnut. So Randy and Angie each have space in front of them for four tubs they don't have to share, but often find themselves reaching across the other's arms to get to the flavors in the middle.

The outdoor temperature has ratcheted up and is hanging on to eighty-five degrees. The line lengthens, and the three workers in the stand are getting really busy.

"You know what?" Stella informs them. "I'm going down to our house in town and bring back a bar stool to use this evening and tomorrow. The weatherman's saying it's gonna be just as hot tomorrow. And we know that with increased pre-registration, it's probably gonna be just as busy. It's just too tight in here. I'm gonna set the bar stool outside. I can still set my change box on the window ledge and work from there."

"Sounds good to me, Stella." Maybe it'll be a little less tense in this box tomorrow. When Stella leaves to rest in their trailer, Randy wants to talk, to catch up since he'd last seen Angie. Angie isn't particularly curious about his life, but it wouldn't be polite to appear impolite.

She's glad when Stella returns to help with the after dinner trade. Now Angie can stop listening to Randy and mentally recreate the afternoon she'd spent with Ken.

How surprised she was to have jumped into the car with him when she was supposed to be angry with him. Then, what a relief to learn that the Lady in Navy was not a *femme fatale*. She was, in fact, Ken's sister. And what a lovely young lady! If the rest of his family is attractive as she and Ken, it bodes well for handsome children. Children! All right, Angie. First, "husband" in your poems and now "children".

"What?" Angie asks, startled that someone may have heard her thoughts. "What were you saying?"

"I was just asking what classes you took last term. Still planning to be a high school English teacher?"

"Yes, Randy. I'm still planning on getting my teaching license along with my Bachelor of Arts degree. I have a friend who's been helping me map out a way to do both in four years."

"Get your teaching credentials and BA at the same time? You've got to be kidding. When are you going to have time for any fun?"

"Fun? Who's got time for fun in college?"

"College is a time to have a good time before you have to get a real job, get married, and get all bogged down with being a responsible grown-up!"

Between customers, the conversation goes back and forth, primarily between the two young workers. Stella focuses on taking orders, making change, and seeing that the cones and cup dispensers remain stocked. She'd had to refill them both twice this afternoon. She left for a few moments, hiking up to the office to call in an order for more supplies.

"Hey, why aren't you singing tonight?" Angie asks. "I thought all the men are supposed to sing. It's Men's Day, you know."

"Yeah, I know. Friday's always Men's Day!" He winks.

"Don't you sing in your church choir?" She ignores.

"Nah, I'm not doing any of that anymore. In fact, I hardly even go to church anymore. I'm just up here this year to help out Moms. She called me the other day and whined that even with your experienced assistance, she'd need extra help this weekend."

"Yeah, right."

"You know her cousin is the camp registrar. She told Moms the numbers really are up this year, especially for the weekend. Moms didn't want to train somebody new for just a couple of days, so she begged me to come. That wasn't enough, though. She threw in how cute and grown up you'd gotten since I saw you last. Now, that was a big draw."

"Yeah, right," Angie throws back. Just a little pleased that someone else is attracted to her. Too bad it's this guy.

"Of course, I can't let my Moms down after all she and Pops did for me last year."

"What's so special about last year?"

"Well, I got into a little trouble, and they had to bail me out."

Angie's eyebrows fly up with curiosity.

"Nope. Don't want to talk about it. It's all over now. I'm off parental parole, but I still have to pay them back somehow. They're letting me finish college. Still, I owe Moms, so, like the really great son that I am, I'm here." He sticks out his chest, a strutting rooster in the one foot of space between them, then hearing his mother's return, reaches to scoop out some vanilla for the customer waiting in line.

Angie, too, double tasks. She is topping a triple-dip sugar cone with a perfectly round ball of that blue bubble-gum ice cream. She hands the cone to the teenage boy who scarfs down the ice cream on his way to the rear of the tabernacle where she'd seen other teens gathering.

Customers gone, Angie responds, "No problem, Randy." Sanctimoniously, she continues, "But, you know you ought to stay connected with your church family. They'll be able to help you get back on the right track. Who's the pastor in the church where you live now? You know the most important thing is to get back on track with God. How're you doing with that relationship?"

"Like I said, Angie. I don't want to talk about it. I get enough of that from my parents." Randy stiffens, stops his skinning and grinning and focuses his attention on dipping and serving the pair who've just walked to the window.

Angie's okay with that. But, when there's a lull in the traffic, Randy becomes more aggressively attentive in what seems to be an even smaller space than before. Too often he bumps her arm reaching across to scoop ice cream in the tubs on her side, but he also brushes against her when it has nothing to do with their work.

Yes, Randy still is handsome. Yes, he still is a big talker, until you touch on a subject too close to home. But neither his looks nor his conversation attract Angie. She keeps comparing her times with Ken, and Randy just doesn't measure up. She'd known him longer, but that doesn't matter. Ken is the man she would rather be dipping and talking with in these close quarters.

AN HOUR AND A HALF IS NEARLY PASSED. Angie glances around the shoulders of her customers at the male choir members strolling across the grounds to the tabernacle. They come from trailers up behind that cavernous building, from cottages along the road to the right, and from cars in the parking lot down the hill to the left.

The singers are dressed in dark pants and long-sleeve white shirts. Many are tugging at the red bow ties their director has asked them to wear this year. They look like clip-ons, but the guys keep twisting and turning them as if that will make the clip-ons sit as straight and snug under the collars as hand-tied bows.

The streams of dapperly-dressed men converge at the rear of the tabernacle, and the assemblage flows around the corner and settles into two lines at the door. Through the speakers on the tabernacle eaves, piano and organ music signals the service is about to begin. Ah, it's "We Are Soldiers," just like last year.

The male choir sings a rousing version with the passion of the renowned gospel singer, James Cleveland. The men in line sway with the music. They'll process in, stepping in time, backs ramrod straight, like ushers in a wedding. Right foot forward. Left foot joining. A beat with feet together. Left foot forward; right foot joining. Feet together. Right, together; Left, together. Rocking, swaying, and singing. Oh! That's Men's Day on Zion's Hill.

Stella's back. Why doesn't she just put up the "Closed" sign? If she'd just stop taking orders, they could clean up and leave a little earlier tonight. But that is not to be. Even after the sign is up, people still hang around, hoping they'll get a cone and finish it before the choir has reached the front and the ushers allow latecomers to enter. Stella says she'll just take one more order, but won't close the window in the faces of the customers. Those in line get the message and reluctantly turn away.

Angie shrugs in resignation and wrings out the cloth sitting in the Clorox water. It's her job to wipe the little shelf where customers lean elbows, grasp with grimy hands, and thump purses that have been set who knows where. Awaiting their ice cream or searching for coins in their purses or wallets, customers leave an amazing mess. And those sticky drips from consumers too slow to lick ice cream dripping from their cones and cups. Yuck!

The organ and piano have begun the introduction to the first congregational hymn before Stella nods for the two helpers to leave. She's satisfied that all is clean, stocked, and ready to open for business immediately following tonight's benediction.

Angie grabs her purse under the counter and pulls out her compact. Yes, she's glowing a bit from both the work and the tension, but doesn't want to run back up to the dorm room. Instead, she just pulls out her red sponge, wipes her face, then dabs on a light dusting of powder in hopes it will mute the shine and create a satisfactory matte finish on the currently splotchy one.

240

The men's voices join the musicians. Angie clamps the compact closed, stuffs it into her purse, and, ignoring Randy's imploring eyes, steps out the back door of the stand. Randy stays close. Angie tries to shake him off without being impolite and looks around, trying to spot Ken through the crowd of latecomers standing restlessly at the rear of the tabernacle.

She rises up on her tiptoes, but that doesn't help. Randy's neither taking the hint that she's looking for someone else, nor is Angie able to see Ken. She decides to just be assertive, say nothing more, and step away more briskly. She and Randy will be working together after service, and she'll just deal with him then. Ken is waiting for her somewhere.

===

YES, KEN IS WAITING. It will be awhile before the ushers seat late arrivals like him and Angie. That'll be alright. He'd noticed how busy it was at the ice cream stand and that Stella will have them clean up and set up before she lets Angie leave. He's decided not to worry about Randy, the Handy Man. At least, not much.

Oh, great. There's Angie, and Randy's right behind her. The first congregational song ends, the organ is playing the introduction to the second, and the ushers begin seating the late comers. Randy, unaware that Angie's proximity to Ken is significant, reaches out to pull her closer to him so they can be seated together. When Ken takes her hand, Angie shakes Randy off with a shoulder wiggle, and allows Ken to gently pull her along as he follows the usher to the two seats on the end of a row near the middle of the sanctuary. No room for Randy. He is directed across the aisle.

Angie glances over at Randy's frustrated face, shrugs her shoulder again, ignores his questioning look and stands nearer to Ken. He's begun singing the chorus of the new song. Speculating about Ken and Randy, Angie thinks the lyrics "We Are Soldiers," mentioning soldiers fighting until they die, could be figurative about Christians enduring problems and also literal about these two guys vying for a girl. Like her. She's worth the battle, right?

A medley of masculine praise hymns has ended with "Rise Up, Oh Men of God!" The larger than normal bass section lends macho force and authority to this traditional men's choir song, and the congregation sways and claps with the choir.

Soon, it's offering time, and the organist is playing "Saved, Saved," a familiar song the congregation begins singing without the leading of the choir director.

> I've found a Friend, who is all to me,
> His love is ever true;
> I love to tell how He lifted me
> And what His grace can do for you.
>
> Saved by His pow'r divine,
> Saved to new life sublime!
> Life now is sweet and my joy is complete,
> For I'm saved, saved, saved!

Angie is carried along by the beat and lyrical declarations. Ken too. Randy, maybe. For just a few moments they all are taken up by the joyful Spirit in their presence, and none is puzzling over the angst of this past afternoon. Randy, too.

The syncopated back beat inspires the Saints to follow the enthusiasm of the Men's Choir that marches down and around to put their offering in plates on the front table, in much the same way as the Children's Choir did last night. The ushers pass the normal white baskets to the congregation, and by the time they reach the mid-tabernacle rows, many are over two-thirds full.

Offering over, rustling stops, and hushed curiosity drifts across the tabernacle. And by the time it reaches the rear, all eyes are looking forward to see who's bringing the special music selection tonight.

With a firm hand on his elbow, the usher guides a man wearing sunglasses up the stairway and across the platform. The congregation shuffles nervously as they watch his slow gait. He stumbles and then settles behind the podium, gripping the lectern to secure his stance.

Eyes follow the usher's brisk departure, and attention returns to the soloist. He tilts his head upwards, and the ceiling light sparkles off his dark glasses and bronze skin. Head tilted in a Ray Charles angle, the blind singer swivels towards the piano, nods, and the introduction begins to "Peace in the Valley".

Some of the Saints may think it's an inappropriate song choice now, not because of the lyrics, but because Elvis Presley and Johnny Cash have both recorded this Thomas Dorsey gospel favorite. The song, however, is just right for Angie this evening. She's in the valley of decision and would welcome the peace. Ken too. Randy too.

In the vocal style of famed social activist, Paul Robeson, in a deep belly bass and dramatic phrasing, the soloist sustains the whole notes with just a little extra pulse. On the promise of the closing line, "There will be peace in the valley for me," his rich vibrato evokes quiet, reflective tears and soft verbalized "Amens". He stands there as the sense of the song sinks in and the usher comes for him.

Rather than taking him back to a seat on the main floor, the thoughtful usher escorts the soloist to a seat with the choir. Reverend Morris rises to introduce Reverend Clarkson, the speaker for the evening, who really needs no introduction.

"...and to present to those who don't know him, our very own Reverend Peter Clarkson, long time pastor of First Church in...."

Angie doesn't hear the rest; her mind keeps flitting back to this afternoon at work. Angie groans. It's unsettling to have to spend another shift with Stella's son in that cramped ice-cream stand. After shaking him off and seeing the questioning look when she moved in to sit with Ken, Angie isn't sure how collegial they'll be later, even with his mom here.

Randy has a temper. She'd seen it flare up when they'd worked together in years past, and based on his behavior this afternoon, he's not outgrown his tendency to take advantage of a situation in ways that meet his own agenda. If he's upset with her sitting with Ken instead of him, she'll pay.

Angie jerks her attention back to refocus on the preaching that is to come and hears, "Please welcome, our own Reverend Peter Clarkson!" It's a sacred service and not a secular convention, so instead of a welcoming burst of applause, Reverend Clarkson gets a resounding round of Amens!

Focus, Angie. Focus. Listen for the Word. But she doesn't until several minutes into the sermon when she senses the tempo change. She gazes up and forward.

Reverend Clarkson paces from wing to wing of the rostrum, sweating and wiping his forehead with one of his many large, bright white handkerchiefs. At the start of his sermons, he is known to stack five or six on the lectern next to his Bible, and, as he preaches, he lets three or four flutter to the floor in a heap next to the pedestal of the podium.

SEEING THE MOUND OF HANKIES, Angie mentally drifts to another time, but the same place. She remembers men and women snagging those used handkerchiefs like groupies at a rock concert. Apparently they believed Reverend Clarkson's sweat would have the power of the Apostle Paul's.

The New Testament describes early Christians clutching Paul's handkerchiefs and aprons and praying for healing. And, according to the book of Acts, many were healed and freed from demons. Angie is a little dubious about the same being true in the case with Reverend Clarkson. But you never know. God's the same, yesterday, today and tomorrow. Still, who'd want a sweaty hankie, even from a celebrated religious leader?

AS USUAL, BEFORE THE ALTAR CALL, Angie excuses herself and tips down the aisle, out the rear door and over to duty in the ice cream stand. Maybe the weather will stay clear and not rain as predicted with the high temperatures Stella mentioned earlier. Angie'd heard rain in the weather report on the radio when Ken was driving her back up the hill. She had described to him what happened in years past when rainstorms had nearly wreaked havoc on the grounds.

Even though the Saints have been coming to Zion's Hill for nearly fifty years, the Zion's Hill Association has never been able to put aside all that much money. Though it is in their plans, they've not yet accumulated funds to bring in the heavy equipment to grade and re-sculpt the hills and then install sufficient drainage to accommodate heavy downpours.

After all, they rationalize, the grounds are only in use for two weeks for youth camp and one week for services when grown-ups arrive. It has taken most of the registration fees and collected offerings to install and keep the electricity, plumbing, and food services up to code. The Zion's Hill campground has to pass inspection every year, and every year something has had to be repaired or upgraded.

Angie has seen some of the drawings of boulders creating retaining walls behind the cottages lining the road winding around the tabernacle. One rendering includes pictures of paved lanes, landscaped postage stamp yards with small shrubs, pots of blossoming plants, and even a memory garden to honor the Brothers and Sisters of Love. Word is some wealthier members have promised to name the Association as primary, or at least secondary beneficiary of their life insurance policies. Apparently not enough have done so. The re-grading hasn't yet begun. That is the future. This is now.

So now, whenever it rains hard for more than fifteen minutes, Zion's Hill becomes a sluice. Without fail, paid groundskeepers and male volunteers who've been coming for years bring their high top galoshes and work pants, ready to pitch in to help. Without fail, some careless drivers slip on the rain-slicked, tar-topped road, skid, and slide in the ditches. When the men hear the call over the tabernacle's loud speakers, a squadron of the galoshed men scrambles to the rescue. Few drivers have had to call down to town for a tow truck.

Maybe tomorrow will be both factually and metaphorically sunshiny, and all will be well. But she has to get through tonight.

THE COOLNES BETWEEN KEN AND RANDY CHILLED THE AIR in the service and trails along when Angie leaves and returns to the stand. She and Stella are alone. Angie mutters, "I'm not surprised. Randy isn't here yet. So typically thoughtless." Busy, Stella doesn't hear or doesn't comment. The two of them stand aproned and waiting with scoops in hand for nearly fifteen minutes before anyone even approaches the booth.

On the weekend, the ushers usually direct the crowds unable to get into the filled-to-the-brim tabernacle to the overflow auditorium. There they experience the service through speakers set up for that purpose. Others unable to get into either place usually sit on the outdoor benches and listen to the exterior speakers broadcasting across the grounds. These extra folks ordinarily head over to the concession stands as soon as the preacher finishes the sermon. But not tonight.

Reverend Clarkson has that appeal. When he's the preacher, few want to miss a word he utters, even if they can't see him. Most curiously await the congregation's response to his passionate delivery. He may put on quite a show, but compelled by the Holy Spirit, hundreds respond, enthralled and blessed by the power of the spoken Word. That apparently is the case tonight.

THIS EXTRA TIME GIVES ANGIE A LITTLE TIME TO TALK with Stella on a touchy subject, her son. Angie approaches the subject indirectly.

"Stella, you want me to sit outside to take orders and make change tonight? Randy and I can alternate working inside and outside when it gets busy."

"Why you wanna do that, Angie. You and Randy are young and strong. I'm the old lady who needs to sit down."

"Not you, Stella!"

"And anyway, you two are good with the customers. I've never seen it busier than when the two of you are on duty. I don't mind sitting out there and letting you two work in here."

"It's not that, Stella."

"Then what is it? You both college students and have lots you can talk about when it slows down in here." Stella notices the grimace on Angie's face. "What's the matter, Angie? Don't you feel well? I know I've had you working long hours this week. But you've seen how it's been. We've been real busy."

"No, that's not it, Stella. I feel okay."

"Well, why do you think you and Randy can't keep working inside together? I know he's my son and can be distracting with his good looks and chatter, but you gotta admit, he's smart and going places."

Angie says nothing.

"I thought this would be a perfect time for you two to get to know each other better. He didn't come up here last year at all. And this summer, he's been working down there at the college, you know."

246

"Stella, you know I'm not interested in men right now. Even your son, Randy," she says, but thinks, especially your son, Randy.

"Yeah, I know that, but he'll be graduating next year. He may be ready to settle down once he gets himself a job. You're a nice girl, and I like you."

Angie says nothing.

"What's the big deal? Girls your age don't usually finish college anyway. Most of you all are married by the time you're nineteen or twenty. How old are you now?"

"I'm nineteen. Right now, all I want to do is focus on finishing college! Anyway, Randy may not be interested in me. No offense, Stella, but I don't...."

"Hold on, Angie. Looks like we've got a customer." Stella steps closer to the window and leans down to greet the chubby boy at the window. "Hello, young man. What can we get for you?" And so it begins.

Angie is never able to explain to Stella why she doesn't want to be inside with Randy anymore, nor is she sure she should even bring it up again. After all, he is her son.

Looks like the stand will really be busy tonight. She'll probably be so bushed that all she'll want to do is head up to the dorm and crash on her cot. In the meantime, she only has to put up with Randy today and tomorrow. She guesses she can handle that. She hopes.

NEARLY THIRTY MINUTES LATER, RANDY SAUNTERS in and pulls an apron from the nail next to the door. By the time he's finally made his way through the crowd, the customers already have queued all the way back up to the tabernacle. As he turns around, tying the strings and greeting his mother, he notices the look in her eye.

"What's up, Moms? I came straight over just as soon as service let out. You see the crowds. It took me a little longer to get over here. I saw Sylvia and Claudine back there. They stopped to say hello. Did you know Sylvia's getting married next month?"

"Randy. You know we needed you back here to help open up and be ready before service ended! I don't have time for this now. Get to work."

"Chill, Moms. I'm here now. Get your stool and get outside so Angie and I can take care of the customers. Right, Angie? We got this covered, don't we?" He winks at Angie.

Stella doesn't want to make a scene, and letting her eyes do the chastising, she takes the cash box with extra rolls of quarters and exits the stand. True to his word, her son gets right to work. Despite her distaste for her co-worker, Angie and he soon are in rhythm, pulling cones, dipping called out flavors, rounding scoops into perfect spheres and settling them firmly on their customers' choice of cone or cup.

Teens and tweens stroll across the grounds in hordes of guys and bevies of girls, each pretending to be oblivious to the other. Angie recalls her pre-teen years when it wasn't cool to show interest in the opposite sex. Instead, gangs of guys just followed as gaggles of girls led them around the campgrounds weaving in undulating lines like the dragon in a Chinese New Year parade.

No one was fooled then, and Angie is not now. She'd waited on gender clusters all afternoon. Tonight, she sees the girls torn between their craving for double scoops of Conley's black cherry ice cream and their desire to appear to be dieting. They pretend not to notice the attention they secretly crave from the guys standing in line just in front or just behind them. Angie listens to their chattering and recalls when she was their age, just a couple years ago, and spent so much time talking about the preachers and their preaching.

"Did you see Reverend Clarkson in there?" one of the guys asks his pal. "Man, he was dynamite. All before I come up here this year, I was wondering was he gonna put on a show."

"That watn't no show, man. Who told you he gonna put on a show?"

"Yeah, it was. I never seen no preachers jump all around like he do when they preaching. 'Course we got people in our church that dance when they shouting during a rockin' song. But what he done in there tonight was different."

"But that watn't no show. Don't you know the Holy Spirit make some ministers act like that when they preach? And didn't you see all those people going up to the altar."

"Yeah I did. I ain't never seen nothin' like that in my church. A couple of them people up front was even slain in the Spirit. Ain't that what you call it when somebody fall out like that when the preacher be praying for them?"

"Yeah. They so full of Holy Ghost fire they just can't keep still. Some of them can't stand up neither. But, man, I'm telling you. That watn't no show."

"How you know? Sometimes at our church when the altar call is going on too long, one of us just go on up there so the pastor'll think some of us been listening."

"Y'all do? Why y'all do that?"

"We know as soon as at least one somebody go up there, he gonna stop the call and start praying. Then he signal for the benediction song, and we outta there."

"Y'all do that? That ain't giving much respect to y'all's pastor."

"Yeah, but…"

"Don't you believe the Holy Spirit make people feel something after the preaching?"

"I guess so. Like in there tonight. I almost went up there myself."

"Why didn't you?"

"I didn't want nobody thinking I been doing something sinful, so I just stayed in my seat. But I almost went up there, too."

"There was 'bout a hundred people up there already. Nobody woulda thought nothing 'bout you being up there with them."

"I know now. But I'm just sayin'. It look like a show, and I didn't wanna be in it."

"Man, I done tole you. That watn't no show. Reverend Clarkson, he just let the Holy Spirit move him like He want to. He just that kinda preacher. Now, the Reverend Doctor Jamieson. He different."

By this time the boys have their ice cream and move on, trying to look cool while gobbling their confection.

WAS RANDY ONE OF THE HUNDRED at the altar tonight? He certainly returned in an altered state. He didn't get all uptight and react when Stella gave him the mom-stare for coming back late. And, he didn't use every opportunity to touch Angie nearly as much as he had during the afternoon.

At first, Angie put it down to their having established a rhythm that worked. During the earlier shift on, whenever she'd hear a request for one of the special flavors stored in the middle of the freezer, she'd step aside to avoid him. She'd done that all afternoon, but it hadn't really made much different. He found some reason to keep touching her, accidentally of course. This evening, Randy is more somber and detached. Less pushy and less brushy, too. It's strange and Angie feels little of the tension between them she'd experienced all afternoon before the service.

It's nearly eleven o'clock before the last customer leaves and Stella closes the window. She sends Angie off to bed saying she and Randy will stay and clean up. Angie doesn't argue. With heavy feet, she trudges across the lawn to the dorm passing groundskeepers already clearing the trash with those pokey-end poles and emptying the trash cans into the back of an old pick-up truck. Zion's Hill is not yet on the route for town refuse pick-up. They'll drive up to the dump where they'll burn as much trash as can be consumed by flames. What's left is buried.

Conscientious, aware that most residents are in bed and may even be asleep, Angie closes the outside door so it won't slam, and walks down the hall to her room. As quietly as possible, she opens the dorm room door and tiptoes past her grandparents, even though her grandmother doesn't really sleep until Angie is tucked into her own cot.

She slides her nightgown from under the pillow, pulls the suitcase from under the cot to get to her toiletry bag, and tip-toes out and down the hall to the bathroom. Thankfully, there is no one there and Angie heads directly to the toilet and plops down. Ah…at last. She sits there, in peace, staying longer than necessary, just to rest a bit. She finally pulls the handle to start the flush, stands up, steps over and rests her hands on the rim of the sink and looks up into the narrow mirror.

"Ugh! I look a mess! No wonder Randy didn't come on to me tonight! Not that I mind. I was actually dreading this evening, but it actually worked out okay. I'm glad Ken didn't hang around till I got off tonight. I'd scare him away with this flying hairdo!

"It's a wonder Stella didn't make me put on one of those hair nets Brother Patmington used to make us wear in the dining hall. And, I've been trying to keep my hair neat looking all week. Good grief! The combs are even hanging loose. Oh well. Just one and a half more days."

Angie's not sure if it's a good thing or not, but Ken will not be back for Saturday evening service. As a going away treat, his step-dad bought a pair of tickets to a pre-season Cleveland Browns football game. But Ken assured her he'd arrive early on Sunday to get in and save her a good seat in what is sure to be a packed sanctuary to hear Reverend Reeves.

Saturday

14 - SATURDAY with Angie

SHE WRINGS OUT THE SOFT CLEANING CLOTH and wrinkles her nose at the acrid odor of bleach. She'd dumped rather than measured the Clorox into the bucket. She sniffs her fingers. Oh, they are going to stink all afternoon! Angie's been tapped to be on hand for the emergency delivery called in after they nearly sold out of ice cream Friday night. Was it Randy's presence or just the increased number of folks for service for Men's Day? Even more arrivals are expected today, in time for Youth Day and the concert to follow the evening service.

To keep from signaling that the stand is opened for business, Angie has kept the serving window closed. But needing fresh air, she's propped open the back door and can hear chartered buses grinding up the hill and a continuous cavalcade of cars with tails dragging, loaded with luggage. She shakes her head judgmentally at the thought of weekenders who bring as much stuff as those folks who come for the whole week.

Cars coming for the weekend are larger, newer, and cleaner. It's as though the drivers stop by the car wash in town before heading up the hill. Angie can't imagine why. The overflow parking lots still are gravel, and the sparkly clean Lincolns and Cadillacs will be dull and dusty within an hour.

Swishing the cloth, wringing it nearly dry, Angie carefully wipes the edges of the freezer they'd missed when clearing up last night. It's monotonous work, and her mind meanders back to an afternoon in college. Following Miss Wicks' advice, Angie had used the summer session to begin taking classes leading to her teaching credentials.

===

EDUCATION 101 HAS NO PREREQUISITES and is an exploratory course designed to help new students decide if they'd really like to follow education a career path. Some of the students only enrolled because they thought it would be an easy "A". It wasn't. And it certainly gave many of them pause.

For one assignment, the professor had them visit schools and observe classes. He'd made arrangements with teachers in private, public, parochial, inner city, and suburban schools that the college students could reach by carpooling or taking the city bus. They were to visit at least three different school settings.

Most of the students admitted to being somewhat dismayed after viewing various schools from the perspective of a teacher rather than that of a student. While some of her classmates questioned their choice and decided to pursue other professions, the summer experience confirmed Angie's commitment to follow in Miss Wicks' footsteps and become an English teacher who also teaches French.

One class day the professor asked them to talk about experiences that influenced them to prepare to become teachers of English. Angie had volunteered and told her story of winning the contest in fifth grade for reading the most books. Her teacher, Mrs. Wheeler, had taken her downtown, bought her a chocolate sundae and *Myths and Enchanted Tales,* the first book Angie had ever owned. She had been enchanted with reading and writing ever since. She was not sure whether the book or the chocolate sundae was more influential, but that this particular literary experience made her want to be like Mrs. Wheeler…a lover of books and buyer of chocolate sundaes. Now here Angie is dipping ice cream to earn money to become a teacher and having almost no time for recreational reading. Go figure.

===

THOUGHTS RETURNING TO THE TASK AT HAND, Angie contemplates her wardrobe. Now what will she wear to work this afternoon? Just in case one of those fancy dancy cars is bringing up a new guy for her…just in case Ken doesn't come back Sunday. They hadn't had much time to talk yesterday after service. And he said he was going to Cleveland for a pre-season football game with his dad tonight.

Locking up the stand and walking back to her room, Angie takes one last look down the hill. What's with those continental kits? Maybe having those external mounted spare tires gives them room for more clothes in their car trunks. Who are these weekend folks trying to impress anyway? Angie is resistant to their displays of wealth. Or so she tells herself as she reaches the top step and opens the door into the dorm hallway.

Back in the room, having grabbed a hamburger from Liz's stand, Angie quickly eats and continues to consider her limited clothing options. Eventually, she pulls out her perma-pressed A-line skirt. This Madras print will show fewer stains if she happens to dribble ice cream on it or if Randy splats her in his haste to serve the teeny-boppers.

She pulls out a creamy green top with cap sleeves that complements the darker green of one of the broad crisscrossing plaids. Angie's trying to plan ahead. With the short sleeves, she'll be cooler and can just wipe ice cream off her arms before leaving work. Even though the front of her clothes will be covered with freshly laundered aprons, she wants to look good now and later. Those comfortable green Reyers' sale flats will work with this outfit, too. Good planning.

Before leaving the room to go get washed, she decides to take advantage of the nail holding up the window curtain and hangs up her dress for tomorrow. No hanger, but the creases may fall out anyway. She wants to look good for Sunday service, and fewer wrinkles certainly will help.

CUSTOMERS HAD COME. In swarms. She had endured another day with Randy. Now, she's pooped and hauls her tired self back up to her dorm room. Gathering her things, Angie heads down to the bathroom to go through her evening wash-up. Her mind keeps jetting back to this afternoon. "It was weird!"

Angie looks around. She's a little embarrassed to be talking to herself in the mirror, but thankfully, no one has come in. She washes her face, moisturizes with a little Jergens Lotion, and then brushes her teeth. Almost out of Ipana toothpaste, she just squeezes on half as much as usual. She dons her gown. Then, she meticulously parts her hair and oils her scalp with Dixie Peach pomade and rolls up her hair with the pink sponge rollers. Angie ties these awkward looking curlers with the head scarf to keep them from working loose as she sleeps.

She grabs the clothes she'd just stepped out of and left on the floor. She'll just lay them across the foot of her bed till morning. No point in being noisier than she has to be. It's late, and she's sleepy, and she's puzzled. Once in bed, she just lies there; sleep eludes her as she tries to process recent events. The past twenty-four hours have been strange.

Yesterday evening Randy hadn't bumped into her even once or sloshed much when rinsing the scoops. Clean scoops, Stella taught them, make neat balls of ice cream and help keep them from mixing flavors. Keeping them clean can be messy. Yesterday, when they closed, it probably only took ten or fifteen minutes to clean up. Then there was this afternoon.

===

THIS AFTERNOON, SHE HAD WORKED ALONE and overheard lots of teen talk. Angie also wondered what she'd missed when she'd scooted out of the service early last evening. This gaggle of girls at the window is neither giggling nor gossiping.

"You goin' to service tonight? You think Sara n'ose be coming tonight?" one queries casually.

"I don't know. You know her and her brother was in them sit-ins in Birmingham. They had to pay some pretty stiff fines to get her brother out of jail. I haven't seen her and n'em this weekend. So, I don't think they coming this year.

"Really? I guess that's why my cousin's not coming either. She go to Tougaloo College. You know where students did them sit-ins at the Woolworth's down there in Jackson. They family been helping raise money to pay bail bonds to get her brother n'em outta jail. My mama getting scared all that gonna come to our town. What you still frowning about?"

"I guess 'cause I can't feel sorry for them right now. It's they choice. I don't have one. I don't want to be going in there to service," she whines, selfishly.

"What you mean? It's Youth Night! You always go."

"I know. But I don't want to tonight."

"Why, not? The choir's gonna be good."

258

"Yeah, I know. But I'm too bummed."

"What you upset about? You in the choir aren't you?"

"No, not this year."

"Why not?"

"We was late getting here. Daddy nearly blew a gasket when Mama made him go back and check the lock on the back door. She get so uptight every time we go somewhere overnight. You know she always telling us not to sweat it 'til she forget something."

"So...what that got to do with you not singing this year?"

"Daddy so ticked he threatened to hang his Christian suit on the fence and give her what for! He didn't though. Daddy just a lot of lip."

"So? Your dad ain't mad at you, is he?"

"No. It's just we didn't get up here in time for me to go to rehearsal this morning. So I'm not singing in the choir this year. Last year we nearly blew off the roof we was so into it!"

"Really, girl? What y'all sing that did that?"

"Last year we sang 'It's a Highway to Heaven' Them ole sisters walked the aisle almost the whole song! The men was running around like they was at a track meet. And then we sang 'I Got a Telephone in My Bosom'".

"You sing the solo?"

"Nah. They didn't give me the solo like they do at home."

"So that why you don't wanna go to service tonight?"

"I'm going. I gotta, but I don't really wanna. Daddy, he don't give me no choice. He so suspicious. Thinking I'm up to some kinda hanky-panky now I'm sixteen."

"Really?"

"Yeah. He so lame. You know he almost didn't let me have no boys to my Sweet Sixteen party! Can you imagine that?'"

"No, girl!"

"Yeah, but what Daddy have to worry about? Mama just last month bought me a pity bra."

"A pity bra? You mean a training bra?"

"Yeah, you could call it that, but I don't have nothing to train."

"But, you had a party! Did you bring Polaroids? I wanna see the pictures of who was at your party."

Dipping their ice cream for a cone and a cup and overhearing their talk about sweet sixteen parties takes Angie back to her own, but she only has a moment for memories before the next group, how guys, is at the window.

They're preening like peacocks! They think they're so hip! Angie usually avoids speaking slang on the job. But her jive talking sometimes loosens the grip on their money. Why not get as much out of them while they're here instead of hoping they'll come after the concert tonight to impress the girls.

"What can I get for you studs?" Angie asks with her Handy-Randy grin.

"Gimme a double chocolate on a sugar cone," one stud croons, posturing for his peers. "I shore like me some brown sugar sweetness, especially from a foxy lady like you," the boy crows, more to his buddies than to Angie.

"Sure thing," she acknowledges, catching a whiff of his Murray's pomade slicked back hair and noting the stocking cap crease above his eyebrows. He's going to be on the prowl tonight. Angie grins as though flattered, and dips.

"Say, man," he asks turning to his peers, "You staying for the sermon tonight? I hear Doctor. Jamieson is speaking."

"Yeah, I heard. I might just leave after the singing. You know Doctor. Jamieson just reads his sermons straight from a manuscript."

"He does. That gonna bother you?"

"Well, I heard he so intellectual. They say he hardly even moves one step from the podium during the whole time he up there."

"I bet it hard to get into him sometimes," a third teen interjects.

"Yeah," another adds. "He don't hop around hardly at all."

"That don't mean nothing."

"Yeah," a fourth interjects, "I heard them guys down at the hoops say Reverend Peter Clarkson, he a rocker, but Reverend Doctor Matthew Jamieson, he a crooner."

"A intellectual crooner. That sound kind'a funny. Man. I don't know if I'm up to paying attention to all that high-falutin' talk from some college professor."

"Me neither, man. How come they didn't save Reverend Clarkson for Youth Day? I heard he was cooking last night."

"I know 'bout last night. But Mama say I gotta go tonight, too. She got such a headache, she not even coming outta the cabin tonight."

"So that mean you gotta stay?"

"Yeah. She say I gotta bring her back the lowdown. So, yeah Man, I gotta go."

"Me, too," the third admits. "My Dad's ushering tonight. Up in the balcony, too. He got eagle eyes. If I ain't there, he gonna know. If he think I cut outta there to go play cards in Tim's cottage, Dad'll ground me a whole week when we get home."

"Yeah, I'm bummed too. But Mama, she say I gotta be her eyes and ears. She really like Doctor. Jamieson, though. She say he a real meat and potatoes preacher. No fluff about him."

"Fluff is okay. Leastwise you can see it moving."

"Man, I wish I had me one of them cassette recorders. I'd just set it up in the back of the tabernacle and slip out with one of them skirts I seen up the hill last night." The four snicker at the thought, take their cones, and move on.

Though the teens don't really appreciate that the Reverend Jamieson will be the speaker for Youth Night, they all stream into the tabernacle in time to hear the opening songs. Their curiosity is stronger than their reluctance to listen to the gentle speaking college professor present the Word.

Stella dismisses Randy and Angie at the same time, and he offers to walk with her to the service. She's tempted. Ken won't be there tonight. But even though Randy had been more considerate, Angie feels she'd be cheating on Ken if she sits with Randy. So she declines, saying she's got to run up to the dorm to get her Bible.

To make that claim the truth, Angie does take a detour back up there to tidy up a bit and get the Bible. Even though Stella has let them out a little earlier, they'll still have to wait in back until after the opening prayer. Tonight the wait will just be shorter.

On her back to the room, Angie puzzled about what her young co-worker had revealed during one of the few breathers they had had during the afternoon when Stella had gone to take a break in their nearby trailer.

===

"ANGIE. YOU SAVED, AREN'T YOU?"

Startled at the Randy's off-the-wall question, Angie retorts in a condescending, un-Christian-like manner, "Of course. Why do you ask?"

"Well, you know it's sometimes hard to tell up here on Zion's Hill. Most everybody been coming to camp meeting so long they know how they're supposed to act. It's hard to tell if they're looking the life or living it! You a Christian, right?"

A little embarrassed that he has to ask, Angie eases off her high horse, and answers with calm assurance and humble honesty. "Yes, Randy. I accepted Christ as Lord of my life at youth camp a few years ago. It's been a tough go since then. Once I left the rarefied air of Zion's Hill, I found it a challenge to keep my commitment to Jesus Christ. I've had my ups and down."

"Yeah, I know what you mean. I made that commitment at camp when I was thirteen. Cap'n Ike convinced me it might save my life if I gave my heart to the Lord. I was kinda wild back then," admits with a grin.

"I can just imagine you back then. I know about Captain Ike. He was at camp this year, and Ken told me about him. You know Ken, don't you?"

"Yeah, I know him. We pretty much grew up in the same congregation. Well, anyway the summer I was thirteen, Mom made me go to camp. I'd been giving her a lot of grief. She was hoping I would get my head on straight. She was right. Some of Cap'n Ike's stories scared me straight. I did okay in high school, 'cause our church had a pretty happening youth group. But even then, I wasn't all that consistent. And I certainly didn't stay on the straight and narrow once I got to college."

Sensing a different tone in his speaking, Angie decides to let the conversation flow and confesses, "College can be a difficult place to live holy, can't it? It's been more trying than I thought it would be. I hope I can hold on in the fall when I move on to campus."

"You know, Angie, I'm wondering if I even made a real commitment to the Lord. It was easy to say so at camp. While I was at home, it was easy to follow the Christian rules. I just pretty much did what Moms and Pops expected of me when I was in their presence. Out of the house, though, I was something else. I doubt any of my classmates even knew I was supposed to be a Christian."

"Yeah, I got hung up on the rules too, at first. But, at home, our new pastor's a teaching preacher. He's always telling us it's not rules; it's relationship. We have to believe we are children of God and be patient as we grow. It takes time to grow and mature."

"Really. How much time?"

"Well. He says, 'Though accepting Christ as Savior is an act of the moment, becoming Christ-like is the work of a lifetime.' And then, our pastor pauses and adds dramatically, 'It takes longer to develop than a Polaroid picture.' Relationships take time."

"Really? Relationship, not rules? That's a new one. I thought getting saved was it. You know, like fire insurance against going to hell. I got so bummed when I didn't measure up to the rules that I just stopped trying."

"Randy, don't be so hard on yourself. God understands. Remember He is both merciful and forgiving."

"Yeah, but He probably won't forgive me for the mess I been into since I been in college. I been doing some dumb things." He glances up to see if Angie's condemning him with her eyes.

"Dumb things? Like what?"

Not sure, he's ready to trust her, he clams up. "I don't really want to talk about it. Moms and Pops been talking enough."

"Well, you brought it up. Sounds like you want to tell somebody else. I'm all ears. And I can keep a confidence," she invites and then is silent. She notices a customer approaching and gives Randy a nod.

Randy looks up; seeing it's a lady, he steps up with his smiley face, dips her two scoops of strawberry ice cream, and hands her a cup and a spoon. He steps aside for Angie to hand the lady a napkin. No other customers are at the window. Randy turns back toward Angie, drops his shoulders, and erases his smile. Angie's warm eyes invite his confidence.

"What mess you been into, Randy, that's got you all wound up this afternoon? You've been awfully quiet...almost nice," Angie teases to ease the tension a bit.

"Just almost?" he questions, hoping to redirect the conversation to his charms.

"Yes, just almost," Angie goes along. To keep from watching him, she wrings out a cloth to wipe up the few spills around the edges of the freezer of ice cream tubs. Dropping the cloth back into the pail and swishing it around so it'll be fresh next time, she gently probes, "What happened?"

"Well, last night Reverend Clarkson's sermon got to me. I know I haven't been living right, but I thought I was impervious to sermons. I been hearing them all my life. I know how to front like the best of hypocrites."

"Randy you may be a show-off, but you're no hypocrite. I've never even heard you claim to be a Christian. Since I've seen you in action, I didn't believe you were. But not everyone up here on Zion's Hill is. Folks pretty much act the same in public. We've all been taught to respect our elders and all that. But when I think about it, you've always had a sharp edge like you're ready to slice out of the box."

"Yeah, well pretending takes a lot of energy. But I was a gentleman with you, Angie. I wasn't making moves on you."

"Right, Randy! What do you call all that brushing, bumping, and watching me like I am a hooker and you wanted to be my next customer? Really, Randy, you undressed me with your eyes," she grimaced and shuddered.

"Really?"

"Really. I even asked your mom to let me work outside."

"You're kidding?

"No, I'm serious. You were making me real uncomfortable in here. If I didn't need the money for school next week, I probably wouldn't have come to work today."

Almost back to his old self, Randy quips, "You're joshing me, right? I wasn't that bad, was I? I know you're a hot mama, and I've been drawn to the flame."

Angie smiles shyly, feeling good that someone thinks she's hot. She nods. "Yes, you were."

"I didn't know I was coming on that strong. I like to let sexy ladies know I notice. That's just me. Well……" he quietly confesses…….. "It was me until last night,"

"What happened last night?"

"It was something Reverend Clarkson said. You know, about respecting women and treating them like we want guys to treat our mothers or sisters." Randy stops, stands straight, reaches towards his pocket, clenches his fist, then asserts, "I'dda had my switchblade out in a New York minute if I seen a guy treatin' my sister the way I been....been treatin' girls ...this year." Randy ends softly, retreating like a turtle into its shell.

"What do mean?" Angie says equally softly, to draw him back out.

He turns aside so Angie can no longer see his face. "I made some really bad moves this past year."

"And…"

"Then some stupid decisions afterwards."

"Yeah, and…"

"And I had to crawl back to my parents for help."

"And…"

"And, thankfully they came through for me. Angie…

"Yes?"

"I got a girl pregnant!" Randy spurts.

"Randy!"

"And then tried to force her to get an abortion."

He takes a deep breath and exhales slowly as though by verbalizing his sin, he is cleansed.

"And…"

"And, what? They talked me out of it. Said it was her decision to sleep with me, and getting pregnant was the result. She has to live with her decision."

"They did what? That is so cold. Making the girl carry the burden for something you probably forced her into doing," Angie retorts judgmentally.

"Yeah, but that isn't all."

"I should hope not. Not from Christian parents anyway. It takes two to tangle."

"That's two to tango, Angie," he chuckles, relieved that he's unloaded and can now challenge her vocabulary choice.

"No, Randy. I did mean tangle. You have a responsibility in all this, you know."

"That's what I'm trying to tell you, Angie. My parents made me commit to taking care of the baby. They sent me a check for the doctor. My parents say, "'You gotta be there for her even if you don't want to marry her. It's your child'."

"That is so right. Your parents reminding you like Christians ought."

"Yeah, they did. They give me the money, and I went with Linda, that's her name. I went with Linda to the doctor, like my dad told me to do. But…" He clams up again.

"But what? Did she decide on the abortion instead?"

"No, Angie. That's not it.

"Well?"

"Linda lost the baby."

"Oh, Randy. I'm sorry."

"Just two weeks after that appointment confirming the pregnancy."

"That must have been hard on you all."

"Not really. I was glad."

"Randy! Shame on you!"

"I stopped seeing Linda, and she dropped out of college. She lives in Missouri, so I'll probably never see her again."

"Randy!"

"When she went home, I thought I was saved for real. Saved from life as a too young father."

"Oh, how could you?"

"We hadn't told anyone at school about her being pregnant, so I was home free. Until last night."

"What happened last night?"

"When Reverend Clarkson was preaching, I thought I was just caught up in his gallivanting across the rostrum. You know, getting off on his show, not realizing the Word was slicing into me, like a two-edged sword."

"Uh, huh."

"It slowly shaved off the shell I'd let grow around my heart. The Word made me see that the baby may be gone, but not my sin. Not till I confess it and begin to live the way I know I ought to be living as a Christian."

Angie nods, looks up to see if they've missed seeing a customer, sees none, and signals Randy to continue.

"The thing is, Angie. I don't know if that means I'm supposed to look up Linda and apologize, you know, and try to make it up to her somehow."

Angie shrugs, not sure what to say, but feeling inclined to keep that to herself.

"Yes," Randy declares. "I was one of the hundreds at the altar last night. That's why I was so late getting back here. I been thinking about it all night."

"And…"

"What you think, Angie? You believe I ought to call Linda? You a girl. Would you take a call from a guy who got you pregnant and then cut you off after you lost his baby?"

"Randy, I don't know. I've been thinking about that since I heard about the baby. I was wondering if you'd mention it."

"What?" he exclaims sharply, spinning around, looking to see if anyone else had heard his confession. "How you know? Do everybody here know about the baby?" He stomps in indignation.

Randy rants, "That's what I'm talking about. Moms probably asked somebody at church to be praying for me. And one of her bigmouth friends told everybody! You know, Angie. It scurrilous! Finally can use that vocab word! It's awful how the so-called Saints gossip!"

"That may be the case. You know there's a grapevine up here on Zion's Hill. When I heard that about you, I didn't want to work in here with you. That's one of the reasons I've been shying away from you. I didn't want to be the next."

"Hmmmm. That may be why I been getting the cold shoulder from some of the other girls."

"I'm not all that surprised, you know. None of the other girls want to be the next, either."

"The guys haven't even been all that welcoming this time either. I know a lot of guys up here, and nobody said nothing to me other than, 'Hey, man. How you doing?'

"Are you really surprised?"

"Maybe that explains why they didn't stay around for an answer. None of them asked me to play ball or nothing. I just thought maybe they're grown up now and not playing up here no more. You do see more of the young guys down there on the courts," Randy rationalizes.

"What you expect, Randy? The guys probably are both jealous and afraid. They certainly don't want you coming on to their sisters, either." Angie tilts her head, lifts her shoulders and raises upturned palms. "See, Reverend Clarkson is right. Your sins will find you out."

"Yeah, but what about forgiveness?" Randy huffs in exasperation. "Nobody asked me if the gossip is true. And even it is, I didn't do nothing to none of them. It's Linda I got to talk to."

"Randy. I think you've answered your own question. It is Linda you have to talk to. You know, if you've confessed your sin to God, He already has forgiven you. Some place in the Bible says if we know we've hurt somebody, we're to go to that person and ask forgiveness before coming to God in prayer. I don't think that means He won't answer your prayers for courage to do what you know must be done."

269

"You think Linda will talk to me after what I done to her?" Randy asks with remorse.

"I don't know. But you've got to make the effort to reconcile with her."

Randy shakes his head.

"You could wait until Monday to give her a call. Attend the services tonight. There may be a Word for you. Something in the sermon may help you follow through on what seems to be the leading of the Lord."

Randy nods his head, glad for a short reprieve.

"In the meantime, you can depend on me to be praying for you. I know your parents are doing the same. That may be why they forced you to come up there this year. To hear the Word and to be in a setting where you can consider your actions and gain the confidence to do something about it."

"Yeah, that sounds like my parents all right. I do owe them, too. I didn't have money for the doctor. And I was feeling pretty bad about getting Linda pregnant. I was thinking I just shoulda been more careful. You know me, get away with what I can." Randy says, sheepishly.

Angie shakes her head. "You're pitiful, Randy:"

"That's the old me, Angie. I'm really going to try to do the right thing." Then, he stands up straighter. "Yeah, I'll call Linda on Monday. I hope she still got the same phone number. Maybe I can just send her a letter and ask her to call me."

"Randy, you pray about this and do what the Lord tells you to do. And, don't expect her to be as merciful as God is. Even if she's a Christian, she may not be ready to forgive you."

Randy crumples. "Really?"

"Don't let that you stop you, though. Apologizing is your part. Granting forgiveness is up to her."

"You think she still gonna be mad at me? We just got carried away at a party. That's all it was. The weakness of an instant. I was there for her when she was pregnant. We weren't really going steady or anything."

"Steady or not steady. You two had sex and she got pregnant. She lost the baby and went home. According to you, you haven't apologized or anything. You've got work to do, Brother Randy."

"Okay, Sister Angie." He smiles. "I mean it, Sister."

She returns the smile.

"Okay. I'm feeling a little better now. I'll admit, I also feel a little nervous. You know, I'm not the kind of guy to go crawling back to no girl about anything. I got my pride, you know."

"Yes, I know. And, you know that pride goes before destruction and a haughty spirit before a fall. If you don't get down off your high horse and accept that you are a new creature in Christ Jesus who has the courage to do the right thing, you're not going to be growing much in the Lord. You'll find yourself falling back into the same temptation and sin that got you into this mess in the first place."

"Okay, Reverend Angie. I got the message. Here comes another group of gigglers. Let's get back to work. And yes, I'll try to make things right with Linda."

===

SENDING UP A PRAYER FOR RANDY, Angie grabs her Bible and gets back over to the tabernacle in time. She's curious. Will the Reverend Doctor Matthew Jamieson live up to his reputation and deliver a well-crafted sermon that feeds the hearts and souls of young and old? Once inside, she disciplines herself to stay attentive. Tonight, the message may be for her.

Following a jubilant time of praise and worship led by the Youth Choir and reinforced by the soul-stirring music of a youth quartet from Columbus, their pastor, Reverend Dickerson walks to the podium and introduces the speaker of the evening.

"We just so thankful that we have talent like yours with us here on Zion's Hill. We just know the Brothers and Sisters of Love that started this camp meeting are rejoicing in heaven. Hallelujah! Jesus, we are truly thankful." With one hand waving in the air, Reverend Dickerson does a little skip and shout, then pivots back to the podium, ready to proceed.

"Brothers and Sisters, did not our hearts burn within us as our young folks sang this evening? Please, can you give it up for our choir and quartet? Let's have a round of applause. Young people," he reminds them, "this ain't for you. We giving glory to God."

Most of the congregation stand, cheer and clap. After all, it is Youth Night, and some of the strictures are waived for the evening. They sit quickly when Reverend Dickerson gestures with palms turned down.

"We're so thankful young folks have a place on the program every year. We've dedicated ourselves to the Lord so He can use us to tell the gospel story. We know the seasoned Saints will be praying that we also live the life we sing in them songs. Right choir?" The youth in the choir standing behind him squirm a bit, but acquiesce and nod.

"You young folks in the audience. We not leaving you out. We praying for all y'all. We know it ain't easy to live the life you hear about from the pulpit or read about in the Bible. It ain't easy, but it's possible. With the help of the Lord. Am I right grown-ups? Am I right?"

Thunderous replies of "Amens" and "You right" roll across the tabernacle, and again some folks stand and clap. This time, not for the singing, but in affirmation of the words of this minister.

The young folks are not sure if the old folks are agreeing with the fact that living right is hard or that the Word makes it possible. It doesn't really matter, though. Somehow this Spirit-filled demonstration preceding the sermon gets them in the frame of mind to attend to whatever Doctor Jamieson will have to say.

"Brothers and Sisters. This is the last evening service of our 1963 camp meeting, and it is only fitting that we have our young people leading our worship service. Contrary to what some folks say, the youth are not the future; youth are the present."

"You right, Brother. You right," comes back in the traditional call and response of colored congregations.

"If we don't come to the Lord when we're young and hear some sound teaching and get some loving guidance and support right now, we'll be in no condition to lead in the future."

"Ain't that the honest to God truth!"

"We'll be too weak and malnourished. We won't have strong, muscular faith that only comes from the experience of trusting in the Lord year after year after year. Am I right?"

"You right, Brother. You sho is right!"

"Brothers and Sisters. That's the reason the program committee picked Doctor. Jamieson to be our speaker for Youth Day. You all know him well. You know he was raised in a strong Christian household. He made his decision for the Lord when he was a teenager, and he's been on the battlefield ever since. This man of God is a trained musician, and I know he enjoyed the fine music we heard here tonight."

Reverend Dickerson turns and looks at the speaker for the evening and then back to the microphone when Doctor Jamieson nods in agreement. "He even studied for a while over in Europe. But when he come back, he went to college and then on to seminary. He's now a member of the faculty where he graduated. This summer, he been helping organize with Doctor Martin Luther King, Jr. . Yes, and will be with him in Washington, D.C. at the end of the month. Some of y'all be there, too. Am I right?"

"You sho is right about that, Brother. We going for shore!"

"But it's not his musical ability, his academic credentials, or even his civil rights involvement that convinced us to invite him to speak tonight. No, Brothers and Sisters. We invited Doctor Jamieson because he's a man who tells it like it is. He believes the Bible is the Word of God. It is that Word that leads to life and life more abundantly. That's what we young folk need to hear. That's what we all need to hear. So let's get to it. I give you, the Reverend Doctor Matthew Jamieson, our esteemed speaker for the evening."

Doctor Jamieson rises and remains at the high-backed speaker's chair until Reverend Dickerson returns to his seat. During this dramatic pause, a hush ripples across the tabernacle. Adults sit up in eager anticipation. Children stop squirming. Teens and tweens in the balcony look up to see what they're missing.

The preacher of the hour glides to the podium, lays down his folder, and opens his manuscript to the first page. He looks up, panning the listeners in the lazy eight. He makes eye contacts in the center section of the tabernacle, sweeps up listening eyes on the right, reconnects in the center, sweeps up the eyes on the left, and circles back and forth across the tabernacle until all eyes are gathered into his.

He raises his arms, inviting them to stand. They do. He bows his head. They bow theirs. He closes his eyes. They do not. They don't want to lose the connection he's established so dramatically. Silence reigns as the Holy Spirit quietly infuses Doctor Jamieson and Shekinah glory flows back over the choir stand, rolls onto ministers on the rostrum, out across the waiting congregation, and back to the no longer disconnected teens in the back and up in the balcony. All lean forward, expectant, for what is to come.

His rich mellow voice intones, "God, our Gracious Heavenly Father, Jesus our Beloved Brother and Savior, and Holy Spirit, our Constant Friend and Precious Comforter, we thank You for making Your presence felt in our midst tonight. We thank You for the songs we've sung and the songs we've heard sung. We thank You for the generous offering that has been given in support of the ministry here on Zion's Hill. Now, Precious Trinity, we humbly invite You to work through me as I share the Word You have laid on my heart. Open my mouth to speak and their ears to hear. We ask all this in Jesus' Name. Amen. ......Please be seated." They sit.

Their eyes remain on the minister as though connected by a beam of love. Yes, he reads his sermon from a manuscript. No, he does not prance and prate. He simply delivers the unadorned Word of God. In just a few seconds over thirty minutes, he signals the organist to begin "Just As I Am," and with raised, outstretched arms, he summons waiting souls to the altar.

Like last night, hundreds respond, quietly, pensively, drawn to make a commitment or to recommit themselves to the Lord they heard about in the sermon. By eight-thirty, they're singing the benediction, "Blest Be the Ties that Bind," with such love and awe that few people even realize that the service has ended. They egress with such reverence that Reverend Dickerson hesitates to step up to the mike, reluctant, but required to remind them of the special, long awaited concert. It's to begin in half an hour, so he invites them to remain in the sanctuary if they like.

Few leave. Among those who do are Angie and Randy who forgot to slip out before the altar call. In fact, Angie and Randy were among those who'd gone forward for prayer. Now, joining them in the aisles heading out the back doors are parents of small children who've fallen asleep during the unusually quiet service. By their looks back inside, it's clear that these parents are as reluctant to depart from this hallowed hall as those who remain are eager to stay.

STELLA SENSES BUSINESS WILL BE LIGHT TONIGHT and simply chooses not to open the stand after the service. She, too, has much on her mind and heads back to her trailer. She and Randy need to talk. She's been holding against him the anguish of this past school year, the pregnancy, the doctor bills, and the loss of her grandbaby. The family simply silenced it, zipped it up, and stuffed it in the closets of their minds. It's time to open the bag, release the anger and disappointment, forgive, and move forward.

That's what Doctor Jamieson spoke about this evening. Forgiveness – forgiving ourselves and forgiving others, extending mercy just as God has forgiven and continues to extend us mercy and grace. Gently, powerfully, this doctor's words raked up memories; this verbal physician scraped off scabs, and lanced wounds. His carefully structured sermon created cognitive dissonance and made them uncomfortable with the belief that they could be conscientious Christians and withhold forgiveness.

Doctor Jamieson boldly laid out the problem, describing how and why withholding forgiveness is harmful; next he outlined the single Biblical solution and artistically portrayed the freedom of forgiveness. He even quoted that maxim attributed to numerous speakers. "Withholding forgiveness is like drinking poison and expecting the other person to die."

The wise young minister didn't leave them guilt ridden. Instead, with equal skill and understanding of the human psyche, he soothingly poured on the balm of the Word.

And finally, Doctor Jamieson invited to the altar for prayer all who needed to ask for and to release forgiveness. Since that covered nearly everyone, nearly everyone in his hearing was touched by the sermon, and the majority was moved enough by the Word to make some changes. Most started with responding to the altar call. Details were private, so few spoke to anyone but God. The attending ministers understood and simply laid on hands and prayed inaudibly. What powerful quietness for a Youth Night service!

Few are disappointed that the concert is a little less high powered than one might expect of youth musicians experimenting with the more contemporary sounds of gospel. The presence of the Spirit remains, and those attending admit that the lower energy level of the music is no less moving. Instead, they find themselves departing the tabernacle thinking more seriously about the lyrics of the songs than they might have had they not been so touched by the preaching of Dr. Jamison.

BACK EARLIER THAN MOST EVENINGS, Angie has a few minutes to talk with her grandparents about the service; then they all settle down for the night before the last day of camp meeting. Angie draws the blanket-curtain divider and sits for a few minutes on the side of her cot. The lyrics of "I Got a Telephone in my Bosom" play through her mind as she prays again for Randy that he'll have the courage to act, and for Ken, that all is going well for him.

15 - SATURDAY with Ken

ALL IS GOING WELL AND THEY'RE ON THEIR WAY to a pre-season game of the Cleveland Browns. Ken's step-dad pulls the bench seat closer to the steering wheel to accommodate his shorter height. As usual, this means Ken will be scrunched in the front seat of their little Corvair.

Thinking of small, Ken reminisces about his junior high school days, when his legs were shorter and before he started playing basketball. Back then, it was baseball, baseball, baseball. His real dad had been avid about the game, and every Sunday they'd go cheer for whatever Negro league team came to town. Other weeks, he cheered at the ball games his dad coached games at the project's community center in their small town.

Ken was going to be the next Bill White, and like Bill, hit as a lefty and protect first base. This now major leaguer had been his hero since the time Ken's dad had coached Bill as a teenager. Just last week, grown-up Ken had heard about his hero on a radio broadcast of the St. Louis Cardinals, for whom Bill White was now playing first base. The announcer lauded Bill's catch in the last inning with two men on base; he had gotten the last out and ended the possibility of the other team closing the gap and winning the game.

Little Ken regularly played on Little League teams so he'd be ready when the call came for him. Riding along with his step-dad today, Ken recalls the dusty leather seat smell of the school bus that his Little League team rode to Cleveland the summer he was twelve years old. They'd won their division, and this trip was their reward.

===

"ALRIGHT, YOUNS. SETTLE DOWN!" yells the coach, his freckly cheeks splotching red. The bus starts rolling. "Don't forget we representing the entire Shenango Valley this afternoon. When we get to the stadium in Cleveland, I want youns to act like it. You know, we wouldn't be here without the fine sportsmanship you showed throughout the season. And of course, winning the championship," he adds, his green eyes sparkling with pride.

The Little Leaguers give themselves a rousing cheer and are shushed by the coach who has more to say. "That's enough of that. Now turn and look this way. Okay, youns know how to give a round of applause to the men from the Moose Lodge?" The boys nod.

"Come on, now. You know they paid for these brand-new blue and gold jerseys we're wearing today. And, yes, they also got us tickets to see the game." The boys clap, but stop abruptly when coach announces, "You know Satchel Paige is pitching."

"Satchel Paige!"

"Coach, you think we gonna meet him today?" they call out, standing up and holding the seatbacks in front of them to maintain their balance as the school bus rattles across the railroad tracks.

"Where our seats gonna be?"

"We gonna be close enough to see 'im real good?"

"Guys, guys, guys!" the coach hollers. "Sit down. Remember, we're gentlemen, and gentlemen know how to behave."

"But, Coach. We gonna get to meet the Cleveland Indian players, right?"

"I'm not sure. Let's ask Mr. Corbett." He directs their attention to one of the men sitting in the seat behind the bus driver. "Okay, team, give this member of the Loyal Order of Moose a big hand clap to show our appreciation for their support of our teams."

Of course, the little gentlemen comply. Then ask again,

"We gonna get to meet the players, ain't we Mr. Mooseman?"

Mr. Corbett leans around the high-backed bus seat, acknowledges the applause of the Little Leaguers, and promises, "I'll do what I can. The manager is a Moose, too. He may be watching to see if you guys will behave yourselves in the stadium."

"We'll behave!"

"We'll be good!" they promise, *en masse*.

"Yeah, Mr. Corbett. Ask Coach. We know how to behave."

"Ever thing gonna be hunky dory!"

The team settles down when Coach's wife passes out sandwiches and bottles of Coca-Cola the Women of the Moose packed for the team lunches. Some of the rowdier boys soon fall asleep, smearing the windows with their sweaty cheeks.

===

KEN REMEMBERS little of that pro ball game itself other than he had a good time with his teammates and that they got two hot dogs apiece. Mr. Corbett bought them all seconds. What Ken does remember clearly came after the game.

===

"ALRIGHT GUYS. I GOT GOOD NEWS. Mr. Corbett talked to his Lodge brother. He got us a chance to meet the players. Youns come on now. Line up orderly behind Mr. Corbett. We're gonna follow them other Little League teams out to the third base line. When our team is called, we supposed to walk over to the dugout where we'll get to shake hands with the players. Can I count on youns to act like athletes with some home training?"

"Yes, Sir!" comes their unified response, and the team actually lines up in batting order and follows Mr. Corbett down to the field. Coach brings up the rear. His wife has returned to the bus, exhausted and not really interested in being around one more high octane jock!.

Little Ken neither leads the line-up as one of the team table setters who can be counted on to get on base, nor as a slugger who regularly gets a hit. Instead, Ken trails behind, a player at the bottom of the list. Coach places him in that spot because Ken is left handed, a switch hitter, and a good bunter. Coach likes to surprise the opposing teams based on what's on the scoreboard. Being at the end of the line turns out to be a good thing for Ken, this time.

Satchel Paige is a tall, wiry man in his early forties. He'd been a star in the Negro leagues before Jackie Robinson broke the color barrier in Major League Baseball when the Brooklyn Dodgers drafted him. Now Satchel's been playing for three years in Cleveland, and though older than most of his teammates, he's not lost any of his power as a pitcher. A bonus for the boys today is that Satchel Paige still gets a kick out of meeting with the young ball players.

Ken shuffles from foot to foot waiting for his talkative teammates to move along. He stares up in awe at Mr. Paige.

"Howdy do, son," Mr. Paige says, leaning his limber frame down to look Ken in the eye. His outstretched hand is swamped in the calloused limber fingers of this famous athlete. Ken's right knee wobbles, and his throat clogs. He can hardly believe he's actually shaking hands with Satchel Paige! Satchel Paige, who won 104 of 105 games in 1934. Satchel Paige, the oldest rookie in the major leagues, is shaking his hand!

"Um, I'm fine, Sir. How're you?" Ken asks, trying to be gentlemanly, then spurts. "You know I know all about you, Mr. Paige. My real dad. He's one of your loyalest fans! He taught me all about you."

Mr. Paige nods indulgently, having heard it all before, but still is patient with his young fans.

"You know my Dad's gonna get me one of those Topps baseball cards. I collect baseball cards, you know."

"No, I didn't know, young man. But why you want that Topps card? They didn't even spell my name right."

"Yeah, I know. But the statistics on the back are right. I know, 'cause I checked 'em. My friend's dad got one. Anyway, if your name ain't spelled right, the card could get to be a collector's item. My friend's dad says that's a good thing."

"You're right son. Odd cards are rare. Anyone who's got one could become rich!"

"Yeah, I know. I told you I collect cards, right? I got thirty-seven already. If I get me a Satchel Paige Topps card, I could be famous. I play good ball, too. I could be a famous player like you, Mr. Paige."

Mr. Paige smiles benevolently.

"You think I keep playing ball, I might could get famous? They maybe even could make a baseball card for me and put it in one of them Bazooka

280

Bubble Gum packs. You think so, Mr. Paige?" Ken's jabbering, but he just can't stop himself.

"Well, young man. You just keep up the good work that got you and your teammates to this game. You never can tell. Now that they're letting us Negroes in the Major League, you may very well become one of the best in the MLB."

Of course, Ken grins with pride that Satchel Paige himself says Ken might play in Major League Baseball!

Behind him. "Come on Ken, let's move it." Coach impatiently gives Ken a little push to move him along. Ken steps forward, but looks back. He sees the reverence on Coach's face when Mr. Paige grabs his hand and gives it a hardy shake. Coach is as thrilled as the boys to be shaking hands with this baseball legend.

Walking back to the bus with Coach, both glowing from their encounter with Major League athletes, Ken asks, ""You think Mr. Paige right, Coach? You really think maybe I can play Major League Baseball?"

"Maybe so, Ken. You're pretty good now, and if you keep it up, who knows? You may be following in the footsteps of other men of your race who made it in the big leagues."

===

BUT KEN HADN'T KEPT IT IP. He only played one more year of baseball and then switched to basketball. His big sister, JoAnn, dated a guy on Coach Mac's team. Paul gave her complimentary tickets to the whole series, and she took Ken to three games of the high school basketball tournament. Game after game, Ken watched in wonder at how much more fast-paced and exciting that game could be. It's been basketball, basketball, basketball for him ever since.

Except when he's watching football. The Penn State football coach has been trying to recruit him, but Ken keeps turning him down. Ken has never carried enough weight to play that game safely. He is fast, but not bulky. Anyway, he doesn't have time for all the conditioning, practice and extensive travel schedule of the Nittany Lions football team. Besides, Ken wants to be an engineer, not a running back.

Still, football star Jim Brown of the Cleveland Browns is a player Ken admires as the man on and off the field. Even while in the Air Force, Ken had followed Jim Brown's Syracuse College career. He's playing tonight, and maybe, just maybe after the game, Ken'll have a chance to shake the hand of another famous athlete.

"My man, Jim Brown," Ken unconsciously vocalizes and then asks, "Dad, will we have time to hang around after the game to maybe meet Jim Brown?"

"All depends on how long the game last. You know it may be half an hour or more just getting out of the parking lot. Then in this little putt-putt Corvair, we got a two hour drive home once we get on the highway. Your mama gonna want to get up early and go up to the grounds for the final service in the morning."

"Yeah, you're right. She's eager to hear Reverend Raymond Reeves preach. They say he's a big man with a bigger heart. I guess his wife's going to sing, too. I heard Mom talking to her prayer partners about holding them both up in prayer."

"Well, she and them ladies are true prayer warriors. I hope they're praying just as hard for good weather so we can work on that basement next week. Smiley, you know, Smiley, don't you?"

"Yeah, Dad. I think so. Isn't he the guy helping you line up craftsmen to help with the house?"

"Yep. Smiley. He lets me know when good men are between jobs. That's how we been able to get top workers for a little less money. They can only work for us when they between their big paying jobs. That's also why it taking us so long.

"Anyway, Smiley tell me a couple fellas can help with wiring next week. Once we get the walls and cabinets in, we'll be laying tile. I already got 'em in the shed. The tiles I mean. Your Mama, when she found the kind she wanted, she put 'em on layaway. They got all paid for just this week. Ain't that something? Now we got money to pay Smiley and his crew. Your mama say it's a God thing."

"Yeah, Dad. She's big on giving God credit for everything. Say, isn't that our turn up there? The traffic's slowing down, and they all got their blinkers on."

"Thanks, Son. You can relax. We still gonna be here awhile. They gonna flag us into parking places so folks come in organized. But you keep a watch out, hear?"

"Okay. And Dad, if you want, I can drive Mom up to Zion's Hill tomorrow. Thia wants to go, too. Melvin may not be coming to pick her up. I doubt she's forgiven Melvin for standing her up Thursday. She's going make him suffer a few more days."

"That Thia. I don't know why Melvin put up with her. You know what he did for her?

"No, I bet it cost him some big brass, didn't it?"

"You bet it did. You watching for the guy with the flag? "

"Yeah, Dad. I can watch and listen at the same time. I'm a college student now," Ken teases.

"Okay, just checking. You remember, Thia was working for that clothing store downtown. Well, her boss, she really was impressed with Thia. You know how Thia likes pulling outfits together. Well, she was selling up lots of customers, suggesting accessories and things. She do it so much that Thia's boss, she had a contest for the clerks. Whoever got the best sales for four months got to go with her on a buying trip to New York. All expenses paid."

"That probably stoked Thia. She'd do most anything to get to shop in New York."

"It did and she won the contest, too. They was flying on a plane to New York City! But was she satisfied with coach seats? Not Thia. She kept commenting, in Melvin's hearing, of course, how it sure would be nice to fly first class. He must have done something to upset her and needed to get out of the dog house. For her birthday, he got her a upgrade ticket for first class!"

"I can just see Thia. Ecstatic and rocking the trailer with that news!"

"Yeah. Going first class meant she got to dress up special! Her and your mama had them a time deciding just what outfit to wear to fly to New York first class on that buying trip with her boss."

"That's why Thia's so spoiled, Dad. You and Mom let her get everything she wants. And now Melvin's falling right in line. I never got the stuff she gets."

"Ken, you a man. Men don't need all that folderol. You know we been trying to finish this house ever since you was in high school. We just never had much extra to do stuff for you," he huffs, a little insulted at the lack of appreciation he senses in Ken's comments.

"Anyway, did you ever want for anything you ever needed? Huh? Tell me that. You always had a roof over your head and food to eat. Not always as much space or as much meat as you wanted, but you always had enough."

"Aw, Dad. I'm not complaining about you," Ken replies, pouring oil on the troubled waters. "I'm talking about Thia. She's a spoiled little princess."

From the corner of his eye, Ken notices Dad nodding in agreement. Ken concedes, "I don't mind really. I know she's an earnest worker. I know she earned that trip with hard work. Now she's working on Melvin!" Ken laughs to lighten the mood a bit.

He and his step-dad don't often have time for father and son outings like this. Ken doesn't want to ruin it by verbalizing jealousy about Thia, who seems to get so much of what she wants. His parents are even going to pay for her schooling, but not his.

But, that's another matter for another time. As Dad says, Ken's not missed out on anything he's really needed, just what he's really wanted. Right now it's to get to shake hands with Jim Brown and tomorrow to hold hands with Angie. Tomorrow will be their last day.

"Go on, Dad. What happened with Thia and her trip to New York? You make it sound like there's more to the story."

"You bet there is. Well, your mama and me, we drive Thia to the airport in Pittsburgh and walk her all the way up to the gate. She made me and your mama wear our Sunday clothes. Thia probably flown lots of times in her dreams, but this her first real time on a plane. Your mama, she never flew on a plane but that one time when she came to see me when I was stationed in San Diego"

"No, Dad. I didn't know that. I never think about the fact that most people don't fly as much as I have. Between the Air Force and basketball, I've probably logged 100,000 miles in the air! Go on, what happened with Thia? And yes, I'm watching for the flag man."

"Well, according to Thia, she was the last person to board and the only one sitting in first class!"

"The only one? I can't believe it."

"It's true. The whole flight, the only ones in first class were Thia and the stewardess. Even when the plane stopped in Philly before heading up to La Guardia, all the other passengers just passed her by going back to coach. Thia say she looked back, and they was leaning over in the aisle looking up front at her. When she get off in New York, Thia say the stewardess ast her if she was famous or something. She musta thought Thia's people reserved the whole section for her! Hey, is the flagman signaling us?

"Yeah, I think so. Yep, turn left right here. That Thia. I bet she and Mama talked about that for weeks."

"And I had to hear it all. Looks like the parking people are squeezing us in like sardines."

"Must be a sold out crowd here to see Jim Brown play."

Once they are parked and reaching for their door handles, Ken tries a Thia, "Dad, we may as well plan to stay and see if we can shake Jim Brown's hand. Otherwise we'll just be sitting in traffic anyway."

"You might be right, Ken," his dad concedes. "If the game don't go on too long and it look like we can be home not long after midnight, let's see if we can get down to the field and see your main man, Jim Brown."

Second Sunday

16 - Decisions

WELL, IT'S SUNDAY. THE LAST DAY and Angie's thoughts are racing. Will Ken come? Do I really need to wear a girdle today? I wish I didn't have to work right after service. I hope Ken can wait till I get off this evening. I hope there's still some hot water.

===

KEN WONDERS WHY HE IS SO ANXIOUS to get back to Zion's Hill. Will Angie have time to see me after service? I forgot to press my dress slacks. Will Stella let Angie off in time for us to at least exchange addresses? I hope Angie remembers I'm going to get there early and save her a seat. I do hope that Thia doesn't use all the hot water today.

===

"NO GRAMMAMA. YOU'RE RIGHT," Angie confirms. "Monday's my day off, so it's fine to stay over and get an early start tomorrow morning. That'll give me time this evening to spend with my friends." Her grandparents leave the dorm room early this last morning to be among the first seated for breakfast so they can be among the first admitted to the tabernacle when the ushers open the doors.

Angie's got the room to herself, and she's in no hurry this morning. There's no Children's Church today. The youngsters attend the morning service with their parents this last day of camp meeting, and Stella doesn't open the stand until after morning worship. She'll probably close the stand around five or six since most folks will be heading home following their meal in the dining room. Few will want ice cream after the luscious turkey dinner and splendid peach cobbler Sister Mattie's serving today.

Angie stands holding the outfit she's saved for today, patting herself on the back for remembering to take it out last night. She shakes it out, glad for the forgiving fabric as the remaining wrinkles relax and fall out.

She'd already worn her two new outfits, so Angie decided on this dress that she'd worn for her sixteenth birthday party. It's a soft pink and white uneven plaid with a wide shawl collar and three-quarter length sleeves that button just below the elbow. It's not a baby, girly-girly pink, but a dusty rose that complements her dark complexion. The box pleats of the skirt hang smooth. Not like those drop waist dresses everybody's wearing this year. "The box pleats don't ride my butt and make it look big. I'm going to be looking good and grown-up, even in pink," she says to the mirror on her grandparents' side of the room.

Pulling her suitcase from under the cot, she flips back the top and plows down to the bottom for the firmer Playtex girdle she's put off wearing all week. Today is different. She wants to look especially nice, and this girdle makes her feel like her clothes hang nicer. It'll be hot in nylons, but women do not attend Sunday services bare-legged. So Angie gently removes a new pair of seamless stockings from the cellophane package, balls up the paper, and tosses it into the nearly full trash can.

She adds a clean bra and a full slip that she'll wear for added modesty. She then retrieves the straw hat she'd forgotten to take out last night. It's a little schmushed but bounces back into shape fairly well. A friend at college had shown Angie how to decorate a simple hat with a chiffon scarf that complements the creamy shades in her dress. Of course, she'll be wearing creamy white shoes, gloves, and a matching purse she'd borrowed from her mother.

"I'll be totally put together," she brags to the mirror as she dons the crinkly housecoat she's worn all week and heads down the hall to begin her morning routine of washing, brushing, combing, and dressing.

===

THIA IS IN THE BATHROOM before Ken gets up. That's unusual; she usually waits till everyone's up and out. She hates to be hurried when she's doing her hair and putting on her make-up. She hadn't asked him for a ride, so Melvin must be picking her up for service today.

"Hey, Thia. Save me some hot water," Ken hollers softly.

"Just chill, Ken. I'm almost finished. You were snoring so loud when I got up I thought you'd be sleeping a little longer."

"I wasn't asleep, and I wasn't snoring," Ken retorts as he rolls off his skinny bed. Rubbing his back, he gathers up the bedclothes to fold and store so the bedroom can return to its daytime role as kitchen, living room, and entry hall. He'd not slept much, but he is still eager to get up off the board and get up to the grounds.

Knowing it'll be awhile, Ken settles onto the kitchen banquette, recalling the evening with his step-dad as he waits for Thia to finish splashing around in the bathroom.

===

"YOU'RE SURE DAY? We got time to go down to the field?"

"Sure, Ken. Why not? It's gonna be so crowded in the parking lot, we might as well use the time trying to get down on the field. Maybe Jim Brown will hang around a little while. I heard he likes talking to the fans. Especially young Negro college guys like you."

"Yuck!" Ken exclaims, dropping the mustardy wrappings from the hot dogs they'd scarfed during the game. "Hold up a minute, Dad. Let me dump this in the trash bin over there," he calls, searching for a clean corner on one of the napkins. What a mess.

"Hey, Dad. Wait up." Scrambling down the wide stadium steps and passing his dad, Ken flutters with the same jittery excitement he'd felt when his Little League team had gotten to meet Satchel Paige all those years ago.

Ken and his dad follow the crowd gathering around the ball players. "You look like you're in as big a hurry as me.," Ken teases.

"Well. I sort of am. You got to meet Satchel Paige, didn't you? You know I don't have much time for this kinda stuff. I thought it would be a nice treat for us to see this game. But I didn't think they'd finish so fast so we could maybe possibly have a chance to meet any of the players. Don't they usually head right back to the locker room to shower and get on home?"

"Yeah, I believe they do. Usually. But they're so stoked about winning this game, it looks like they're staying to greet the fans. We're almost there. You coming?"

"Yeah. Right behind you. You see Jim Brown, yet?"

"Yeah, he's right over there. A lot of guys are bunching around him, but he's tall enough. I can see him. Come on." The two join the queue.

===

IMPATIENT FOR THIA TO FINISH, Ken steps over to his little closet space, standing tall and proud for having shaken the hand of his hero, Jim Brown. What a blessing to have done so with the dad with whom he'd had such a strained relationship for so many years. But not last night.

Mr. Smiley has been able to help line up workers to help them get the basement tiled next week. Dad was mellow. Ken was grateful. Maybe the family will really be moving out of the trailer into the basement at long last.

"Thiaaaaa! Come on. People are waiting."

"Take a chill pill, Ken. I told you five minutes ago, I'm almost done."

"Almost's not good enough. Come out now. You can finish primping out here."

"I'm not primping. I'm just putting on a little make-up. You don't have enough light out there, and my hand held mirror is too small. Melvin's coming, and I want to look good!"

"So, you and Melvin have made up."

"Yes," she replies, emerging from the toilet, her nightgown trailing over arms clutched around her model's make-up kit, bag of rollers, comb and brush.

"Well, it's about time!"

"It's all yours! What's the big hurry anyway? You just going up to the campgrounds. You been up there almost every day this week."

"Yes, I'm going. I want to be there early. Dad's pooped after last night. ` He's going to sleep in this morning. One of Mother's prayer partners is gonna pick her up. Don't know which one. I don't really care since I'll have the car and don't have to worry about bringing her right home after service."

"How come you wanna stay up there after service? It's gonna be a zoo up there with everybody packing up and trying to hit the road."

"That's why I wanna be there. I may only have time to spend with Angie in service today. She'll have to go to work right afterwards. This may be last time I'll see her."

"And…" Thia tries to tease more confidence out of Ken. She's noticed a difference in her brother this week. "So you really believe she's the one?" The sister and brother stand in the tight hallway for just a moment longer.

"I don't really know, Thia. She may be. I like her. We get along okay. Thankfully she's not interested in a serious relationship right now, though. That's okay with me. I don't have anything to offer a girl right now anyway."

"How're you gonna stay in touch? You gonna write?"

"Yeah, I'd like to stay in touch. I don't mind writing letters."

"Yeah, I remember all the letters you wrote us when you were stationed in the Philippines. My friends were surprised how often we heard from you. Nobody else's brothers sent home so many letters."

"Well, in a way, it was no big deal. I was excited to go overseas, but it did get lonely. The job I had didn't allow much free time. Even when I got back to the States and was stationed in New England, things were pretty tense with the Cuban missile crisis and all. You know President Kennedy put a hold on discharges. I didn't think I'd get out in time to start classes last fall."

"Really, Ken? You never said."

"No, that was confidential. I worked in Special Services, and we weren't allowed to write home about anything having to do with national security."

"Ken, I thought you were in a hurry. You standing out here talking like you got all day," Thia throws back as she saunters back down the short hall to her sleeping space.

"You're right. I better get going," Ken says, grabbing his kit bag and clean underwear.

"Thiaaaa! The water's cold!"

===

THE DINING ROOM WILL BE CROWDED this morning, so Angie decides to eat in her room. She scrapes the last of the peanut butter onto the five saltines left in the little picnic basket. These and some tea will be breakfast for today. She plugs in the coil and drops it into the cup she filled with water before leaving the bathroom. Impatient for the water to boil, Angie sets the crackers on a napkin, sits on the side of the cot, and pulls out her Bible.

Opening to the Scripture passage Doctor Jamieson preached from last night, she begins reading and ponders the portions of the message on forgiveness that convicted her. She admits, "I should have stayed after the altar call and asked for special prayer." In avoidance mode, Angie justified not doing so because Stella expected her to be on duty as soon as the service was over. Angie'd dashed out, squashing the Holy Spirit's prompting that surely would have had her on her knees sobbing at the altar.

"If I'm a Christian, why can't I forget Carlie for calling me a skank? She's supposed to be my best friend. Why can't I forget the way David came on to me? He's president of our youth group and should know better. Calling me a frigid snow queen just because I told him 'No!' I say I've forgiven them, but every time they come to my mind, I get all uptight."

The message had really gotten to her. Made her rethink her growth as a Christian.

"Why can't I forgive myself for drinking some of that vodka before school just because Gwen dared me? Why have I been so judgmental about Randy and reluctant to believe he's having a change of heart? Why can't I forgive myself for not being a more consistent Christian? Dr. Jamieson says Christians are supposed to forgive and move on, living the Golden Rule."

The water is bubbling, so Angie adds the tea bag and watches. The tea bag oozes stringy streams of bronze and then swirls of darker brown when Angie withdraws the heater coil. Picking up the cup, watching the brown take over as the dominant color, Angie begins to understand last night's sermon.

Doctor Jamieson told them that forgiveness comes from God, through the power of Holy Spirit. According to the Scripture, Christians are to forgive others as they have been forgiven by God. The Holy Spirit is a gift from God and also a gentleman. He does not force Himself on anyone. Each must invite and then allow this *paraclete* and companion to infuse one's thinking and guide one's behavior.

Then, and only then do Christians have the strength to forgive those who mistreat them, who hurt their feelings, who take advantage of what they perceive is weakness, but really is meekness. Angie really likes the image the preacher gave to describe meekness.

Meekness, he had said, is the power to do, but the discipline not to. It's like a race horse that has the power to overwhelm his rider but submits to being guided and controlled by a bridle. The horse does not forget what it can do; it simply chooses not to. It's not a weaker animal because it surrenders control; it's just an obedient one.

Angie gets that part. She's supposed to obey the teaching of the Bible and the prompting of the Holy Spirit. "I do that...sometimes. I just can't seem to forget when others hurt my feelings or really, hurt my pride. Doctor Jamieson says I shouldn't be worrying about forgetting. That's what I forget to remember. Instead, he says we're to forgive and move on, treating others the way we'd like to be treated."

Angie's been resisting that, not wanting to look like a pushover. But during the sermon, she learned that she should be giving others another chance if they seek it. The preacher also cautioned that Christians should be wise as serpents, gentle as doves. One can be forgiving without being a doormat. It's not weak to forgive, he promised. It's Christ-like. It's not wrong to remember; it's human. The key to growing as a Christian, he'd taught, is to act with love.

"Well," Angie thinks as she finishes off the peanut butter crackers and tea, "that's more than a notion. I guess I have to be like this tea. When I get into hot water, I've got to let the Holy Spirit ooze through me until I can infuse the situation with love.

"Sounds a little weird when I think about it that way, but that may be the message for me today. Just as my tea cooled down with time, the color did not change. Maybe when I step back from the situations that upset me so much, I'll cool down. I don't cease being a Christian just because I can't do everything the Bible says right now. I'm just not there yet.

"Okay", she prays before putting away her breakfast fixings, "I guess I have to forgive myself for feeling spiteful and rely more often on the promptings of the Holy Spirit to help me be more forgiving and not worry about forgetting."

Angie shakes the crumbs into the trash can, being careful not to sprinkle them on the floor. She just wipes the cup dry with the corner of the towel and puts the cup and coil back into the picnic basket. She has about fifteen minutes to get dressed and out on the grounds where she can be on the lookout for Ken.

She stoops over to pull on her brand new sheer brown stockings. Then stops. ....Before hooking the first nylon to the garter dangling from her girdle, Angie just lets it fall. "I'd better pray...now." She drops to her knees next to the skimpy low cot and pours out her heart to the Lord. She confesses her confusion, her half-hearted forgiving, and gives thanks for her newfound understandings. She remains a few moments, and then stands. Relieved. Restored. Refreshed. Resolved.

In a twinkling, the weight of guilt lifts from her heart. She rises lighter in spirit and finishes getting dressed, unconsciously humming that old hymn, "I Am a Child of God." The scripture, the reflections, the prayer, and the song energize her, ready her to meet the day. She can hardly wait to see Ken and discover how things went with him and his dad at the Cleveland Browns football game.

Girdled and dressed, combed and powdered, shod and gloved, Angie leaves the dorm room, checks the lock, settles her purse on her arm, and then strides down the hallway feeling pretty good about herself. "I'm so glad I don't have to be in church at a physical altar just to talk to God. God is a Spirit, and I can talk to Him wherever I happen to be."

She opens the door at the end of the hall, steps out into the sunshine, stops and stands on the deck leading to the stairs down to the campground. She looks up into the sun and imagines the Son. "Hallelujah!" Then she looks out over the grounds of Zion's Hill.

It's Second Sunday all right. Streaming from every direction, the Saints are showing up and showing out for the Lord and for one another. From the cottages on the hills, frilly-dressed little girls and bow-tied little boys skip in front of their parents, adorned like Easter morning. Ladies' hats of all shapes, sizes, colors and embellishments flutter in the light breeze. Men's hats tilt jauntily, shading skin colors from ginger to clove. Teenagers trip along in shoes that will be pinching toes before the wearers reach the tabernacle. One pair of T-strap heels barely supports the girth of a woman who turns to lock her trailer door before merging into the stream.

Parading up from the parking lots, townies arrive, swiveling their heads to take in the panorama of sights and sounds. From the tabernacle loudspeakers boom the organ prelude. The throb of "We're Marching to Zion" wafts across the grounds. Angie turns toward the parking lot, hoping to spot Ken so she can be down at the bottom step to meet him when he gets there. No Ken.

"Good morning!" comes from behind her. "Scuse us, please." A dorm mate taps Angie's arm, signaling her to move aside so she and her family can get to the stairs.

"Sure. Good morning!" Angie moves aside and asks, "How're you all doing? Isn't it a lovely morning?"

"It shore is, praise the Lord. We doing just fine, too." A whiff of floral cologne and a wham of spicy aftershave assail Angie as they pass her. Stepping briskly, eager to descend the stairs, they join the undulating throng.

Ken still has not arrived. Angie peers down towards the parking lot trying to decide whether or not to head down that way to meet him, or just go on over to the tabernacle and find a seat. It's going to be crowded in there. Maybe Ken has decided not to come after all. They must have gotten in late last night. Excuses buzz.

Suddenly her eyes behold a vision of loveliness in lilac connected to a stocky, sturdy man in a deep charcoal shark skin suit. A flash of green. Envy. Then Angie remembers what she'd seen earlier. She tips her hat to a little saucier angle. Her mirror had told her she is looking quite fine this morning too. Squinting in the morning sun, she glares down at the couple.

297

Why, it's... it's Thia. It's Thia, dressed like a fashion model. She's holding tight to his elbow. What? He has on a lilac tie! That must be Melvin. They glow together. Angie chuckles, "Thia must have forgiven him."

The man Angie assumes is Melvin gently guides Thia to the firmer surface of the walkway next to the dorm. No matter how carefully she walks, her spike heels will be punching into soft ground in the parking lot and the dewy grass between the lot and the walkway.

The lady in lilac looks up and calls out. "Hey, Angie! You're Angie, aren't you?"

Angie nods and glides carefully down the steps, curious that Thia recognizes her. Thia notices the puzzlement. The lady looks just as lovely in lilac as she had in navy. Green again.

"How'd you know I'm Angie?" she asks holding on the stair rail, turning at the bottom to meet them.

"Aren't you the girl in the ice cream stand? Ken's been talking about you all week. He said to watch out for you."

She wonders what Ken has said about her, but replies, "Really?"

"Yes, I'm Ken's sister, Thia." Looking like she's won first place in a beauty contest and her escort is the Mr. Universe winner, Thia continues, "and this is my boyfriend, Melvin. Isn't he handsome?" Melvin blushes a little, and stands just a little straighter. He's only an inch or so taller than Thia's five feet six or seven inches. It's hard to tell with the high heels she's wearing.

"Why're you standing out here? The ushers are gonna give away our seats."

"Our seats? What're you talking about?"

"Ken said he was coming up early to get in to save you a good seat. You forget?"

Angie breathes a sigh of relief. Ken didn't forget. He's here already. Must have gotten here while Angie was still inside primping. She's glad she took the extra time. Reassured, Angie nods, accepts the firm elbow Melvin extends to her, and joins the two of them walking as quickly as they can in the fancy heels both ladies are wearing. But they soon have to slow down behind the crowd now thickening on the walkways nearer the tabernacle.

Standing in line, still holding Melvin's elbow, Angie looks around him to answer Thia's earlier question. "Yeah, I forgot Ken said he'd save seats. I thought he wasn't coming."

"Aw, girl. You don't have to worry about my brother. You know the expression. Wild horses wouldn't keep him from seeing you today!" Thia rejoinders, and Melvin confirms with another nod.

"Really? You're just saying that," Angie exclaims, wondering if her insecurity is showing.

"No. I'm for real," Thia affirms, as they advance and stall behind a group waiting to be seating by the usher at the side door. "Like I said, he's been talking about you all week."

Now Angie blushes. She also feels a little odd. It's the first time all week she's arrived early enough to enter the tabernacle through the side door during the organ prelude and has not had to wait outside the back door until after opening prayer.

Thia teases, "Yeah, Ken told me that when you saw us together Thursday night, you thought I was his girlfriend, and you were jealous."

Angie feels Melvin's forearm tense. He remembers how ticked Thia was Thursday. Melvin relaxes when Thia acknowledges, "Melvin had to work, but he apologized with flowers." She looks at him with such tenderness and adds, "He's such a sweetheart." Melvin returns an equally tender look. Hmmm, Angie thinks. A mutual admiration society, and I'm not in one. A lime green flash. Envy.

"Right this way," the usher invites with open gloved hand, gesturing for the trio to follow him.

Angie's eyes scan the nearly full tabernacle and lock on to Ken's. They smile "Hello". He stands and points to three seats next to him. Melvin takes over. Silently signaling the usher that they have spotted a place to sit, Melvin leads the two ladies to the seats Ken holds in the center section of the tabernacle about ten rows from the front. Ken remains standing, allowing Melvin to direct Thia to the fourth seat from the aisle. He follows her, taking the third, leaving the other two for Angie and Ken. He nods Angie to the second seat, steps in front of the first seat, and sits.

All settled in, Ken leans around Angie to greet Melvin with a handshake and then reaches for and holds Angie's hand. Oh! He lets their clasped hands rest on the seat in the space between them, his gentle grasp loose enough for her to withdraw it if she wants. She doesn't.

Sitting here with Ken both excites her and eases her mind. The way he's set their hands between them, not pushing or pulling, doesn't feel awkward at all. She could get to like this. She's comfortable, but wondering what's next. Then movement draws her eyes forward.

Up front, from the room on the left side of the platform, a parade of five robed ministers enters and walks regally to assigned seats in front of the choir. Angie notes Thia's nod of approval. The ministers apparently have consulted and decided that purple will be the common accent color for the distinctive black robes they each wear.

A tall, slender, but broad-shouldered young minister leads the way, donned in a narrow robe with tailored sleeves and a white clerical collar contrasting with his mocha chocolate complexion. Purple front panels sparkle in the light as he marches to the seat on the far right side of the platform.

The minister immediately behind him is older, shorter and squatter. He picks up the purple in the three velvet stripes on the flowing sleeves of his flaring robe. The overhead lights reflect in the perspiration on his tawny bald head. Though awfully warm in broad velvet panels on his zippered front winter weight gown, he endures. The second Sunday morning of camp meeting is more pomp and circumstancy than the first, and this is his fanciest liturgical attire.

Three or four steps behind this second minister is Reverend Raymond Reeves, the speaker for the morning. He's a big, big man, six feet-five or six weighing nearly three hundred fifty pounds. The impressively statuesque Reverend Reeves is the only minister of the five wearing a solid purple robe. It shimmers in the stage lights. Silvery embossed crosses grace the ends of the dark grey stole he wears. His short kinky haircut is trimmed neatly above his long Buddha-like ears. This third minister stops, lays down his Bible, and stands dwarfing the high-back chair in the center, reserved for the preacher of the hour.

Reverend Doctor Rose, the only woman among the five, enters with the statuesque grace of the Queen of Sheba. Adorning her feminine cut black robe is a broad purple Kente cloth scarf; it hangs over her left shoulder and flutters as she walks; modest gold hoop earrings pick up the gold threads in the zig-zag African design. Her high anthracite cheekbones glisten, as black as the ink on this page, and are softened by the loose chignon resting at the nape of her neck. And below her flowing tea length robe, black patent sling-back heels click across the wooden rostrum floor until she reaches the first seat left of Reverend Reeves.

Bringing up the rear, one of the senior ministers walks more slowly, leaning heavily on a carved ebony cane, pleased he is only a few steps from the preachers' green room. He too is decked out in a black robe with a splash of purple. His more traditional style robe opens in a V-neckline to a stiffly starched white shirt and royal purple tie. While the other four ministers remain standing, this octogenarian shuffles to the seat on the far left, grunts and sits, setting his spiral cut black cane between his knees. The high polish on this accessory picks up the light when, gasping for breath, he leans forward, clasping his big-knuckled hands atop its bronze ball circle handle.

DOM da, da, da, DA, DA, DA, DA. DOM! Few eyes linger on this elder statesman. They search for an unseen trumpet. Notes reverberate across the tabernacle. The choir director raises her arms high in the palm opened gesture for the congregation to rise. All rise. The piano and organ join the trumpet, and on the director's down beat, the choir bursts into exultant praise, marching two abreast from the rear of the sanctuary down the center aisle.

> God of our fathers, whose almighty hand
> Leads forth in beauty all the starry band
> Of shining worlds in splendor through the skies
> Our grateful songs before Thy throne arise.
>
> Thy love divine hath led us in the past,
> In this free land by Thee our lot is cast,

301

Be Thou our Ruler, Guardian, Guide and Stay,
Thy Word our law, Thy paths our chosen way.

At the cross aisle just behind where Angie and Ken sit, the lines split off to left and right aisles, march forward to ascend the steps on their side of the platform and reassemble in the choir stand behind the black and purple robed ministers.

"God of Our Fathers." This 1876 hymn originally written to celebrate the freedom commemorated in a 4th of July celebration in a small New England town today is sung by Negroes, many migrants from Southern cities and towns across the United States. These same lyrics express their longing for the social and political freedom called for in Reverend Martin Luther King, Jr's. "I Have a Dream" speech given this summer in Detroit and all week here on Zion's Hill in services celebrating the spiritual freedom available to all, following the death and resurrection of Jesus Christ.

Refresh thy people on their toilsome way;
lead us from night to never-ending day;
fill all our lives with love and grace divine,
and glory, laud, and praise be ever thine.

The final verse brings the Saints to tears as they anticipate the final Sunday service of the 1963 Camp Meeting. However, it is on the perennial favorite, "Let Mount Zion Rejoice!" that congregants rise to their feet in euphoric exhortation to the God of their fathers about whom they've just sung.

Great is the Lord! Great is the Lord!
Great is the Lord and greatly to be praised!...
In the city of our God!

The sopranos warble, "Beautiful for situation…"

The men thunder, "We have thought of Thy loving kindness…"

302

All sing "Thy right hand of full righteousness...Let Mount Zion rejoice!"

The tenors croon..."Walk about Mount Zion..."

And the basses rumble, "Mark ye well her bulwarks, consider all her palaces..."

The altos join emphatically, "That ye may tell it to generations following..."

All sing jubilantly, "For this God is Our God, forever.."

.... And in dramatic, *pianissimo*, the choir promises, "He will be our guide even to death."

Ken and Angie sit side by side, no longer holding hands because they too are swept up in the majesty of music, the longing of the lyrics, and the promise of that prophetic psalm. And each is content to wait until after the service to see where God will lead them in the relationship that seems to be blooming so tentatively in them both.

ON THIS SECOND SUNDAY, AS ON THE FIRST, ANGIE WILL have to tip out before the service ends. This time though, it will not be difficult to know when to leave. Reverend Reeve's delivery is a familiar style of Negro preachers across the country. His exposition begins in a slow and deliberate pace, acknowledging the men and women who share the dais with him, thanking the choir for their inspirational singing, and with heartfelt humility, expressing words of appreciation for being asked to speak at the forty-seventh annual Camp Meeting held on Zion's Hill.

Following the expected tribute to the Brothers and Sisters of Love who started the camp meeting, he names some of the current and recently deceased men and women who worked so steadfastly to keep the Association alive and well.

Entreating a prayer in his rich, deep baritone, this Sunday morning preacher beseeches God to open his mouth to speak and to open the hearts of his listeners to receive what "thus saith the Lord". Only then does he invite the congregation to turn in their Bibles to a passage he reads dramatically before announcing his sermon title and its connection to the 1963 theme.

Five or six minutes after standing at the podium, the sermon's rising action unfolds over fifteen or twenty minutes, expounding with general stories that demonstrate the minister's knowledge of hermeneutics and eschatology, embellished with personal references to connect with the daily lives of the congregants. Finally, in the eagerly anticipated climax, Reverend Reeves pulls the chain. In a surge of adrenaline, he gushes forth a stream of rhythmically delivered allusions to well-known Old Testament characters and incidents relating to deliverance and freedom, and in this case, to service to others, linking his message to the 1963 theme.

The sweating Reverend Reeves pounds the lectern with the flat of his massive brown hand, beating the time and reinforcing his key points. Both tempo and temperature increase. Congregants seated in the main floor of the packed tabernacle, the teens in the balcony, even latecomers in the standing room only sections of the overflow auditorium, merge into the fever pitched mass.

In antiphonal style, the wound-up audience joins in the traditional cadence of call and response, affirming the truth of the message with "Preach It!" "Amen!" "Glory!" and "Hallelujah!" Some stand and point, "I know you right, Brother." Others remain sitting, elatedly repeating words and phrases pouring forth in the time-honored pattern. A lady behind Angie shouts, "We havin' church today!"

On cue, Chris Smitherman jumps onto the organ bench. With writhing runs on the Hammond, the momentum intensifies; then…. *diminuendo*, a slower tempo, the preaching pace retards. Melodic music meanders and accompanies the *denouement*, falling action swoops and levels off to the resolution as Reverend Reeves reiterates for the listeners, the three key points of his sermon: "JOY comes from service: emulating Jesus, by serving Others, You will be blessed."

Silence. Then soft, somber sounds simulate the whispering of the Spirit.

Standers sit, the repeaters relax, and the teens on the balcony lean back, all emotionally spent from the exciting, interactive experience. Then, when the minister closes his Bible and slips his notes between the pages, Angie slips out. She too is exhilarated and challenged, having heard a prominent minister who not only exudes passion for the Word, but also delivers with panache a participatory and provocative sermon worthy of Zion's Hill.

SO FOCUSED ON THE DRAMA up front, few notice Angie leaving by the side door or Randy slipping out the back door. The two reach the ice cream stand about the same time, smile a greeting, and chat amicably about the sermon until Stella arrives to unlock the door.

Behind them, across the road, other concession stand owners are lifting the wooden doors and locking them aside or above the windows through which they sell their tasty foods. Fragrant aromas and enticing apple wood and charcoal smoke will lure the crowds from the healthy spiritual food that enriched their souls to the tasty grilled physical food that will nourish their bodies. Today both kinds of sustenance are welcome.

At the far left of this row of stands is the French fry shop where customers purchase paper cone cups of crispy potato strips sprinkled with tart cider vinegar. Next is the fish sandwich concession, the popular stand from which Ken has promised to buy her a sandwich this afternoon. Angie can hardly wait for this crusty delight which she plans to splash with lots of hot sauce for extra flavor.

Next is the grill where customers converge for scrumptious lean burgers served on lightly toasted buns. Hot dogs warm on the new roller grill Liz had introduced last year, tired of selling crinkly hotdogs boiled tasteless in vats of water. From year to year, different concessioners attempted to vary the food options, but year after year, these four lead the way in sales.

"Well, Angie and Randy," Stella greets breathlessly, coming up from her trailer where she'd changed out of her Sunday suit, "our last day. How're you two holding up?" She looks up, noticing Angie's hat. "Here's the key to my trailer, Angie. You can put your hat, gloves and purse down there. They'll be fine." She looks down at Angie's chunky heels. "I see you've worn relatively comfortable shoes."

Angie nods and accepts the offer of keys and the approval of her choice of shoes, hoping they prove to still be comfortable after her shift in the stand. While in the trailer, she uses the toilet and looks in the mirror. Fluffing her hat-smashed hairdo and feeling the nappy edges, she promises herself that before school starts, she'll get a LustraSilk perm so she won't have to worry so much about sweating back her hair.

By the time Angie returns to the stand, her partner has hooked open the wooden door to the serving window. Stella has straightened the sign, lugged out her stool, settled to the right of the window, and set her change box on the window ledge. Angie grabs her apron and visually inventories the tubs of ice cream in the freezer, confirming that they all are lined up in the same order they've used all week.

Within five minutes, campers who've not gotten into the tabernacle, who've left early, or decided to have dessert first, begin lining up for ice cream.

"Three scoops on a sugar cone. That'll be seventy-five cents," Angie tells the first in line.

"Seventy-five cents? It was only twenty cents a scoop last year." Angie nods to this customer as she did to the first one she'd had last Sunday.

"I know, but that's the price this year. Twenty-five cents a scoop on a cone or in a cup. You got three scoops, so that's seventy-five cents." Same as last Sunday.

And just as last Sunday, the frustrated customer turns to the others in the line, "Can you believe that? Gone up five cents a scoop! You'd think Christians wouldn't be trying to make a profit off the Brothers and Sisters coming to camp meeting. They know we can't hardly afford the cost of gas and rooms and food for the week, plus offerings at every service. It just ain't right!" This customer adds, "After that last offering call, I only got a sixty cents left for ice cream."

"Well," the lady behind her advises. "Get yourself two scoops, and you'll have a silver dime to take home." And then, just a little different from last Sunday.

Recognizing she's getting no sympathy, the lady orders, "Alright. Gimme two scoops of black walnut in a cup!

Angie tilts her head up to the sign listing the flavors. "We don't have black walnut this year." Fed up, the lady snatches her money off the ledge and flounces off.

"May I help you?"

"You're awfully patient. I be done tole her where to get off, if I didn't just come out of service! Will you gimme some of that mari- mara- meri — you know that ice cream with the caramel running through it." Randy chortles as Angie waits on the customers in her line and he, the next in his.

"Yes, ma'am.," Angie replies. "Would you like one or two scoops of maricopa in a cup or on a cone? Two scoops in a cup. That'll be fifty cents. You can pay Stella, right there." Stella nods in approval.

NEARLY AN HOUR GOES BY BEFORE THERE'S A LULL in the lines and Angie notices Ken, Thia and Melvin standing in a tight circle a few feet from the stand. They look her way, then talk. Ken's shoulders tense. He's upset about something. Angie can't hear him.

"I didn't know Randy the Handy Man was going to be working in there all weekend," Ken grouses to Thia and Melvin.

"Randy, the Handy Man? You mean Stella's son? He's okay. Yeah, I know he got that girl pregnant last year. But he's okay, now." Melvin endorses. "I saw him in town Saturday, and we had a pop at McDonald's. He was a little glum at first. But he eased up. He was nearly in tears telling me about what happened Friday during the Men's Day service."

"Arrogant Randy, teary in public? That's hard to believe," Thia adds scornfully. "That doesn't sound like the BMOC I know."

"Well," Melvin continues. "I believe you're going to find he's different. A new creature in Christ Jesus."

"I'll believe it when I see it." Thia continues disdainfully. "You know he tried to hit on me the last time he was in town. I told him to get lost."

"That was then," says Melvin. "I believe him. He seemed sincerely sorry for what he's put his family through."

"Humph!"

"Thia, he admits he has not been all that respectful of the women in his life. He even apologized to me when he found out you and I are going steady."

Ken just listens, praying that Angie is safe with the Randy he knows, or thought he knew. It's awhile before his shoulders relax. Hearing Melvin, Ken decides to give the guy the benefit of the doubt. But he's keeping an eye out. His eyes roam back over to the stand. They stop when he sees Angie looking at him quizzically. He wonders if she's been watching him, thinking she's pretty sensitive to him, if she is. If she senses he's upset about something, she'd be right. He smiles, nods to her, and slowly starts walking her way.

Before he arrives though, a slew of kids and teens descends on the stand, wiggling and giggling and waiting to see what their doting grandparents will cough up for them this last day.

Ken intently watches Angie and Randy wait on the group. The two work in tandem. Randy is careful not to brush or bump Angie as they crisscross arms to fill this order of eclectic choices. Some want a scoop in a cup, others two scoops on a flat bottom cone; one wants a scoop of red and one of white on a pointy bottom cone. One tweeny cops an attitude when she learns there are no sprinkles, but stops immediately when her grandmother gives her the look. Otherwise, they are a well-behaved group, and Angie and Randy automatically alternate, filling their requests, as though choreographed.

"Is that it? Have you all got what you want?" Grampa asks. The kids look up and nod, spooning and licking the flavors of their choice.

There's just one more girl, about thirteen years old, who's been preening in line, hoping Randy will notice her. However, before she can tell him what she wants, the four year old who'd been first in line, smashes his ball of chocolate with his tongue and it tumbles off. Surprisingly quick, he catches it in his other hand before the schmushy mound hits the ground.

"Oh! Granmommy," he howls and hops, "it's cold!" Tears well up. His eyes beg for help. Gramma and Grampa are just far enough away to be of little assistance. The cousins are distracted with their own treats. Quick-thinking Angie grabs a cup and holds it out to the little one. He's smart enough to roll the ball of ice cream into the cup, and then holds out his drippy hand, tears plopping into the mess dribbling through his fingers.

Randy reaches over with a napkin. The older cousin awaiting her order takes the napkin and flutters her eyes at Randy; only half smiling, to hide her sparkling braces. With loving attention, she gently wipes the little one's hands, flips the dirty napkin into the trash can sitting to the left of the window, then looks up at Randy for approval. He gives her a big brother smile.

Another potential disaster averted, Angie and Randy finish the order, the grandparents pay, and the happy family leaves. Just a few people remain in line. The crowds on the grounds have thinned as loaded cars groan down the hillside roads surrounding the tabernacle, joining the traffic creeping to the highways taking each family back home. Angie notes numerous passengers looking back longingly, sad to be leaving Zion's Hill.

Just another hour and she'll be finished. She too is a little sad to leave, but not totally. The ice cream stand is closing, but the other concessions across the road will remain open until about eight o'clock or until they're sold out. Here in the stand, they've virtually scraped the bottom of their tubs to fill the final orders, so closing at six is good for her. Stella says her husband will come help her do the final clean-up. "Right on!" Angie jubilates. "I can leave at six on the dot!"

Stella smiles knowingly and hands her a generous check, the hourly rate on which they'd agreed as well as a bonus based on the increased sales they've had this week. Angie doesn't wait a second longer than it takes to get her things out of Stella's trailer. Ken is waiting.

He's been sitting alone on a bench a few feet from the stand, just watching the grounds empty of campers. Melvin, keeping his promise to treat Thia to dinner, has escorted her up to the campground dining hall. She may be shapely as a model, but Thia loves to eat well and is comfortable enough with Melvin to pig out in his presence. Ken has promised to wait and have something with Angie when her shift ends. And as he promised, he is here to meet her.

Earlier, as promised, Ken had met his young camper's sister. True to his word, Joey had located Ken, run back to the tree with the knot in it, returned with his older sister in tow, and rushed back up to introduce her.

===

"HEY BROTHER KEN, THIS IS MY SISTER, CELESTE. Remember, I tole you she was coming up this weekend. Where was you last night? We didn't see you. Well?" he queries, grabbing her hand and pulling her forward. "Here she is. She good looking like I told you. Right?"

Celeste is as handsome as Joey had claimed. She's a stately woman, conservatively dressed in a pale green shirtwaist accessorized with a wide black patent leather belt, mid-heel shoes, and a modest sized handbag. Gloves that match her pillbox hat peek out of the side pocket of her purse. She extends her hand toward Ken. He meets hers and gives it a cordial shake.

"Glad to meet you, Celeste." He releases her hand, and then stands with both his clasped behind his back. "Joey's real proud of your new job with the Urban League. Even bragged all week about being in the March for Freedom and hearing Reverend King."

"Really? I can just imagine. The whole family participated. My parents have been members of the Urban League for years and were thrilled when I accepted the job as a legal secretary in the League's office. We've been real busy this summer."

"I can imagine. It must have been exciting, too." Ken replies, trying to express interest in her when he really has none. "Is your office chartering buses for the March on Washington?"

"Yes, as a matter of fact, we've got a waiting list of folks who want to join the march and hear Reverend King again on the Washington Mall. He's one of the speakers lined up to present in front of the Lincoln Memorial."

"Are you going?"

"Yes, our whole staff gets to go. With the thousands of marchers expected, it's going to be tough to get a place close enough to hear him. I'm going to get an early start that day," she beams.

"Didn't I tell you she is smart?" Joey rattles on, and then sees his mother beckoning them. "Aw, Mom's calling us, Celeste." He calls across to his mother, "We gotta leave now? I just introduced them. I want you to meet him, too."

"Okay Joey," she says, and she and her husband join the three, meet and greet and then repeat, "You know we have to leave now."

"I know. I know. Celeste gotta be at work early Monday." He shrugs with resignation, turns to leave, and then eager to extend the conversation asks, "Ken, you going to work tomorrow, too?"

"No, Joey. I'm heading down to State College. Pre-season training starts at the end of the week. I have to get moved into my apartment, pick up my schedule, and buy books before things get hectic on campus."

"Really, Brother Ken? I'm gonna to go to college and play basketball like you. I was really good at camp wasn't I?" Joey asks, looking at his parents, not Ken.

"You're quite an athlete, Joey. I'm sure you're going far. I'll be watching for you on TV." Joey's parents have been introduced, exchanged handshakes, and now all four turn to leave with Joey glowing from praise.

"Bye, Brother Ken. See you next year!" Joey waves. Looking back, he nearly trips off the curb, catches himself with an embarrassed laugh, then gets in step with his family, walking purposefully down the hill.

Ken is grateful. He has been kind to Joey and polite to his family, but he really is not ready to get involved with another woman, even one who is as striking and smart as Celeste.

=＝＝

HE SPENDS THE REST OF THE AFTERNOON in similar fashion. Greeting families of his counselees and waiting. Between encounters, like body guard, he checks out the stand to see if Randy is taking advantage of the tight working quarters to act like a man on the prowl with Angie.

Ken admits that he's begun to care about such things. Though he's not in a hurry to become embroiled in a serious relationship, he does not want Angie getting into one with someone else, even a reformed Randy, as Melvin claims. Reformation takes time, and Ken has no evidence that Randy has really changed. Anyway, God has virtually promised Ken that Angie is the one for him. So Ken waits and watches, then strides over to the stand when Stella carries her stool and change box around back, signaling that business is over for the year.

"You ready?" he asks when Angie joins him outside the trailer where she'd gone to retrieve her things. Angie nods, adjusting the hat she's decided to put back on rather than return it to the dorm. "Still want some of that fish?" Angie, hungry, blushes and nods. "Well, come on. The line is shorter now. We should have only a couple minutes to wait."

"Great. I'm starved. Other than the peanut butter and crackers I had for breakfast and a few licks of ice cream off my hands, this will be my first real meal today. How about you get the fish sandwiches and I get the fries? I'm not rolling in dough, but I did get paid today. Stella even added a little bonus. That be okay with you?"

"Sure, that should work," Ken says with relief. He wants to be generous, but he's a little cash strapped. He's holding back a little because he wants to invite Angie to go bowling with him, Thia and Melvin this evening.

Among the folks he talked to after service this afternoon are some of the camp counselors who live nearby or who aren't leaving for home until tomorrow. Most are going bowling at eight this evening. As his belated thank you for their work during camp, Brother Ralph, their camp director, has rented out the place for all who want to attend. It's just the kind of date Ken can afford. Three free games and shoe rental thrown in.

Ken and Angie get their food and stroll down to the picnic table next to the playground. The area has been abandoned by kids on swings and even teens playing basketball. Most families are packing or have left, and things are quieting down all over the campground.

Angie is relieved that Ken settles for cups of water they got from the hamburger stand. He's delighted that she is as sensitive about money as he. On the walk down the hill, Ken asks, but she doesn't respond to his invitation to go bowling.

When Ken explains that Lily and other counselors she'd met will be there, as well as Thia and Melvin, she accepts, no longer reticent about going off the grounds in the evening with a man she'd just met a week ago. Now seated, Ken asks the blessing, and they eat companionably and chat about the morning service.

In Angie's eyes, this is another plus for Ken. Here's a man comfortable talking about money and also comfortable praying out loud in public. That's two plusses.

"I really liked the song Reverend Reeves' wife sang before the sermon." Angie opens. "I know I'm still a teenager, but I really do like some of the old hymns. "He Hideth My Soul" is one of my favorites."

"I'm with you. Those oldies but goodies are nostalgic for me. When I was in the Air Force, hearing the old songs on the radio comforted me, and also made me lonesome for home. As eager as I was to leave the valley, to get out on my own and on with my life, I missed the music at our church. Music is emotive for me, evoking memories of special people and special times."

"Really? Me too. What are your favorites?"

"Favorite whats? Songs, people, or incidents?"

"Well, all three. Is there one song that brings back all three?"

"Um," Ken takes another bite of his sandwich as a delay tactic, trying to organize his thoughts on a song, a person and an incident. "As a matter of fact, there is. Melvin's father has a deep bass voice. He loves the hymn "We Reap As We Sow," a song that has a bass repeat on the chorus. In my mind's eye, I can see him throw back his head as he sings. In my mind's ear…"

Angie laughs at the image of a mind's ear. "In my mind's ear," Ken continues in spite of her laughing at his imagery, "his rumbling bass repeats a message I'd sometimes like to forget." Ken sings the refrain.

> Soon you shall gather what you now scatter,
> Unto your life give diligent heed;
> What we are sowing surely is growing,
> That which we reap shall be as the seed.

She recognizes the song and joins him on the second go round. He sings the answering bass line. They look at each other and smile when they realize they've sung the final phrase in perfect harmony. In thoughtful silence, they finish their fries. Both wondering what this singing together may signify.

"Those lyrics are a challenge." Angie concedes. "They remind me of Doctor Jamieson's sermon last night."

"Yeah?"

"You missed a really good one, Ken. You know his delivery style is so different from Reverend Clarkson's that some people miss the power of his message.

"It's almost like being cut with a scalpel. You hardly realize you're cut till you see the bleeding." Angie stops and looks down at her greasy fingers. Her eyes are revealing her heart, and she's not sure she's ready to share what happened to her in the dorm room this morning, so she tries to re-direct the conversation. "Um, Ken. You gonna need that extra napkin?"

"No, one's enough for me. I can just lick my fingers," he replies handing her the napkin. "Those fries are something else, aren't they? " He licks his fingers.

She takes the napkin, "Thanks"

Ken continues. "You know, this is the only place I eat them with vinegar. Don't know why I don't think of using vinegar at home."

"Me too and me neither," she replies, still trying to redirect the conversation. "It's the same with fish sandwiches. I don't put hot sauce on them at home. I usually just use tartar sauce."

Not fooled, Ken probes, "Angie, what did you mean about Doctor Jamieson's sermon? What about the reaping what we sow and his sermon?"

Turning her head to keep her teary eyes from giving away the depth of her feelings, Angie sits silently, and then continues softly. "Well, Doctor Jamieson preached about forgiving and forgetting."

"And?"

"I have a hard time with both."

"And?"

"He also asked why we should expect God to forgive us if we don't do the same for others. You know, like in The Lord's prayer."

"Yes. The part that goes, 'Forgive us our debts and we forgive others?'"

"Yes. That bothered me. I don't want to block God's forgiving me. I've misunderstood a lot."

"And...? You okay, now?"

"Yeah, I am. Thankfully, Doctor Jamieson is a teaching preacher who helped me understand more about God's grace and mercy. Doctor Jay actually cleared up a lot for me.

"I'm glad for you, Angie." He stands.

"Huh?"

"Excuse me a moment."

Ken excuses himself to go to the men's rest room. Puzzled that he would leave at such a pivotal moment, Angie takes the opportunity to run up to the dorm room to check-in with her grandparents. She hopes Ken is not disappointed in her because she's not a more mature Christian. She's pleased she had the breakthrough this morning, but is not sure she's ready to go into details. Even with Ken.

Now up in the dorm room, Angie is surprised how difficult it is to approach her grandparents about going bowling. So many older Christians in her church disapprove of bowling alleys. They have bars and they sell beer. Alcohol is a no-no. But, Angie assures Grammama that Brother Ralph has reserved the alley just for his group and they'll not be selling beer. Reassured, her grandmother gives her consent. "I want you home by eleven, you hear?"

"Yes, ma'am. I'll be home on time." Angie excitedly replies. Quickly changing to the green outfit she'd worn Saturday, the night Ken didn't come, she scrambles out the door hoping to beat Ken back to the table. And hoping he doesn't return to the topic of forgiving and forgetting.

He's waiting at the bottom of the steps. Skipping down, Angie joins him, and he escorts her to the car. Strange, he says nothing about the conversation they'd been having. And strange, she finds she doesn't mind.

===

"WELL, WHAT SIZE SHOES DO YOU WANT?" Ken asks pointing at the weird-looking green and red shoes sitting in slots like hotel mailboxes behind the desk.

316

"Why can't I wear these?" she asks, pointing at her loafers, pleased that she had changed into flats rather than wearing the high heels she'd worn all day. Angie hates to try on new shoes at the department stores and really is freaking out about wearing old shoes others have worn and gotten all sweaty.

"What you mean? You wouldn't wear loafers when you bowl at home, do you?"

"I wouldn't know. This is my first time in a bowling alley."

"Your first time? Thia!" he asks looking at his sister overhearing and trying to hold in her laughter.

"Did you know Angie's not a bowler?"

"How would I know? We only just met today. When she agreed to come, I assumed she'd been before."

"Okay. Angie, I guess I'd better start at the beginning with you. I used to set pins here when I was in high school. I've heard the bowling coaches give zillions of spiels to the old lady groups who bowl in the daytime."

Angie can tell from the smile and in his voice, he is not belittling her, so she looks up expectantly and listens. He explains about the shoes, shows her how to select the right ball based on weight and finger span, and leads her to the lanes they've been assigned.

"I'll never get the rhythm of the three steps and slide," Angie complains after the first game. She sits re-tying her shoe laces, to hide her embarrassment at being so inept. But soon is back into the game.

It's fun getting to know more of the young adults in the larger than expected group who've accepted Brother Ralph's invitation to bowl. Surprisingly, under Ken's patient tutelage, on most rolls, Angie keeps her ball on the lane.

Several in the group plan to stop by McDonald's for a late snack, but Angie reminds Ken she has to get back. With regret. But she had promised. Ken agrees to leave now. With relief. He only has cash enough for gas. Ken shows her where to return the balls to the rack, and they exchange those weird-colored shoes for the ones they'd worn to the bowling alley.

317

Angie picks up her purse and turns to say her goodbyes. "Well, see you next year, Lily, and gives her a hug. Then joins, Thia. Melvin and Ken. It's been great getting to know the two of you. Oh, Thia, when does your fall class start?"

"We start right after Labor Day. I can hardly wait. Secretarial school's just a two year program. So I'll be finished before Ken graduates Penn State. What about you? When do you start?"

"I have a couple of weeks. Wayne State doesn't open the fall term till a week after Labor Day. I won't know my schedule until I get back. I know what classes I want, but don't know if I'll get them all. What about you, Ken?" They continue talking as the four leave the bowling alley.

"In Chem Eng we don't have much choice the first three years. The classes are all laid out for us."

"Do you have a heavy load this semester?"

"Yeah. A pretty tough schedule this fall. Sure hope the reviewing I've been doing in organic chemistry is going to help. With basketball, I won't have much weekend study time."

"You'll be fine. You sound like a disciplined kind of student. You know I'll be praying for you, right?" Oops! Is she being too forward? "I'll be praying for you, too, Thia," Angie says, leaning over to give Thia a goodbye hug. Melvin looks eager to be going; Thia's got a curfew, too.

"Thanks, Angie. Let's stay in touch. Yeah, I'm ready, Melvin. See you, Ken. You know you better get home soon. Dad'll be worrying about his car. Don't forget to fill the tank, too."

"Okay, Miss Bossy. See you, Melvin. You ready, Angie?"

All wave goodbye to those also exiting the bowling alley, and shake hands with Brother Ralph, thanking him for arranging the social event. Ken reaches for Angie's hand. She allows him to hold it.

Pensively, they walk out to the car. Angie wonders. What now?

Back at the turquoise Corvair, he opens the passenger door and assists her getting into the car. What a gentleman.

Walking around to the driver's side, Ken wonders, *What now? I don't really want to get into anything serious, but I'd like to stay in touch. God says she's the one, but He's also made it possible for me to have finances to attend college. Can't give that up for a woman I don't really know all that well.*

Sitting in the passenger seat, waiting for Ken to get in, Angie sees through the driver's side window that he's just standing there. She whiffs her under arm, murmuring, "I know I was sweating in there a little, but I don't stink. Why's he waiting?" She hears the key scrape in the lock. "I should have unlocked the door. That's the least I could have done. I hope Ken doesn't think I'm thoughtless."

Ken pulls open the door, swings his long legs in, sits, and pushes the key into the ignition. Then he looks over to Angie sitting stiffly in her seat. *How can he prolong their time together and still get her back by eleven?* The engine starts right away, and Ken shifts into reverse.

"Angie, wanna ride with me while I go fill up the gas tank. There's that station right at the turn-off up the campground?"

"Sure, Ken. Just as long I get back in time. You know."

"Yeah, I know. We got a little time. Um…Angie. You got a pen or pencil in that purse?" She nods.

"You want to give me your address? We can write once we get back to school. You can tell if you get the classes you want."

He wants to write! This is not the end. Maybe something will come of this.

"Let me look," Angie says, scrambling through her junky purse. She finds a pen in the bottom corner. *I hope it's got some ink.* "You gonna give me your address, too or should I wait for you write me?"

She wants to write, too. Cool. "Um, you got two pieces of paper in there? I'll give you my address and you can write yours on the other piece. I can put it here in my shirt pocket."

By this time, Ken is turning left on the street with the gas station. He'll be there in a minute. *Should I ask for her phone number, too? It'll be a long distance call from State College. Why not? We don't have to talk a long time if we're going to be writing.* "Angie, why don't you add your phone number?"

"I'd like to Ken, but I don't know the number of the pay phone in the dorm. I can give you my mother's number. She'll know how to get in touch with me, or I can put the number in a letter once I get on to campus."

"Sure, why don't you do that? Do you know the dorm address? Or, are you going to give me your home address and let your mother forward it to you?"

"I know the dorm address, and that's what I put on here. I'm moving in on Labor Day weekend."

"That'll be a couple weeks. That'll give me time to get settled. We start training and conditioning for basketball the first week I get back. Not sure how much time I'll have for writing."

"That's okay. Just write when you can. Isn't this the gas station?"

"Oops! Wasn't paying attention. I can make a U-turn right here." He does, pulls into the station, and stops at the single pump. The sign says thirty-one cents per gallon.

No one comes. The station's supposed to be open another ten minutes. The manager's already inside counting the cash in the till. He glances out the window and shoves the drawer back into the register. He keeps an eye on Ken, trying to decide whether or not to serve him. Apparently he decides money is more important than ignoring a colored customer. So he cautiously approaches the car and asks how much Ken wants.

"Gimme three dollars."

The owner completes the service and reaches for the greenbacks. Ken hands over the last of his extra cash.

Resigned, Ken leans forward and returns his wallet to his back pocket. He starts the engine and swings his arm across the seat, so he can see to back up and turn up the road to the grounds. This is really their first date. Should he ask her for a kiss?

Ken is thoughtful driving the incline back to Zion's Hill. With no street lights, the car beams provide the only illumination on this moonless night. Just as distracted, Angie wonders what she should say if he asks her for a kiss? This is actually their first date. Riding down to the park the other day doesn't really count. Does it?

Once through the gates, the car bounces over a rut into the parking lot. It's nearly empty, so Ken can drive up and park pretty close to the dorm. The lamp posts on the grounds cast little light along the walkway to the dorm stairs.

"Wait there, Angie. I'll come open the door." She waits and wonders. What next?

Ken walks around to her door, opens it, and reaches in for her hand. She takes it, letting him assist her out, even though she doesn't really need it. They stand together next to the car, looking up the hill.

The tabernacle lights are still on where the grounds crew is still working. Ken and Angie can see one man up on a ladder dismantling the sound system to store it until next year's convening on the hill.

As if in tandem, Ken and Angie's eyes follow the line of the tabernacle roof down over to the ice-cream stand and both recall misunderstandings seen from and into that narrow space. They look at one another and shake their heads. Ken looks at his watch. It's a couple minutes to eleven.

"I better get on home."

"Okay."

At the bottom of the stairs up to the dorm, they stop. Ken gently puts both hands on her shoulders, but doesn't pull her into a hug. His warm brown eyes gaze into hers.

"May I kiss you goodnight?

She wants to nod.

"I don't think so, Ken. It would be nice, but I'm not sure it would be right."

He nods.

In unison they chime, "Maybe next time?"

Angie turns and walks up the stairs. Maybe next time.

Ken turns and walks down to the car. Yes. Maybe next time.

SWEETHEARTS OF ZION'S HILL
*Couples who met on Zion's Hill and later married.

Blair	Harold Gregory	♡	Marvine	*Binion*
Cray	William	♡	Jean	*Bell*
Fowler II	Ronald	♡	Kishna	*Davis*
Goode	Richard	♡	Loistine	*Clemons*
Grizzell, Sr.	Martin	♡	Phyllis Jean	*Billingsley*
Hollaway	Jodie	♡	Katie	*Gibbs*
Huntley	Richard	♡	Olamay	*Veasley*
Jenkins	David	♡	Alice	*Hayes*
Lott	Clarence	♡	Esther	*Adair*
Lott	Leonard	♡	Olamay	*Sales*
Lott Sr.	James	♡	Mary	*Suddeth*
Massey, Sr.	George	♡	Elizabeth	*Shelton*
Massey, Jr.	George	♡	Jerelene	*Smith*
Massey	Melvin	♡	Helen	*Jackson*
Pollard	Rodell	♡	Ethyl	*Christman*
Pullen	Henry	♡	Richelyn	*Dobbins*
Roseboro	William	♡	Anna J.	*Small*
Sawyer	Thomas	♡	Sharon	*Jackson*
Shackelford	Dante	♡	Riaka (Rocky)	*Jackson*
Staton	Warren Doyle	♡	Birdie	*Goggins*
Turner	Isaac	♡	Lela Rebecca	*Austin*
Ware	Alan H	♡	Antoinette	*Carter*

*Names included with permission of family member
Stories of some of these couples will be included in collection
The Sweethearts of Zion's Hill due for release in 2016.